PERIPHERAL

P E R I P H E R A L

BY EDWIN STANFIELD

FIRST EDITION 2026

Design & layout by Adam Leviton.

ISBN 979-8-9959913-1-1

*Dedicated to every veteran who has sacrificed for our nation...
and to the friends and family members who supported them while
they were gone, and empowered them after they returned.*

CHAPTER 1

Damn, you know you got it bad when you don't want to leave your girlfriend to go to a bachelor party. Conner stole one more glance back at Joselyd from the airport security line. Her short, wavy, black hair complemented her dark, mischievous eyes as she beamed at him. *God, she's beautiful.* Part Cherokee, part Irish and half Cuban, the unlikely combo had produced the most attractive girl he'd ever seen. Gazing at her filled him with a kind of joy he'd never experienced without her. He had been hooked by her fun, outgoing personality the first time they met, when she approached him at a party the year before.

I got it bad... he thought, remembering that moment, and couldn't help but smile back at her. She blew him a kiss and giggled like a teenager even though she was twenty-four. Over the past year that they'd spent together, all his previous pain and internal battles had seemed to melt away.

Sitting in the cramped economy seating of the aircraft, he looked at her picture on his smartphone. *Maybe next year it'll be my bachelor party.* He chuckled before tucking his phone into his pocket and allowed his thoughts to shift to the long weekend ahead. 'Brackish' McCabe's bachelor party—dinner and drinks this evening in Miami, then two nights at a beach house in the Keys, a trip out to the Dry Tortugas and back to the city for the Fourth of July and a big night out before flying home on Sunday. He smiled thinking about the days to come.

Conner really did miss hanging out with his old crew. He'd had solid friends before—the guys he came up with on his high school soccer team in upstate New York, some of his buddies from basic training and tech school—but this group was different. They shared a tight knit bond that came not only from living and working together, but from an unrelenting barrage of open-ended deployments in the uncertain years following September 11th. Friendships forged through shared stress, common struggle and gaining solid trust in one another. There was no strength, weakness, tic or personality flaw left unturned during their tumultuous years together.

They're probably the best friends I'll ever have.

Despite being the youngest, he had fallen into the group and, over time, earned their respect. Their difference in age was barely noticeable now that he was twenty-six, but years ago, at nineteen, his comrades in their early twenties seemed infinitely wiser in all matters of life. *That was a long time ago. Everything feels different now. And since I met Joselyd things have really changed.*

He allowed his thoughts to drift, and tried to remember the last time they were all together. *It must have been during our Kandahar deployment.* A sudden urge to wipe gritty Afghan dust and crusty dried sweat from the back of his neck hit him as the faintly sweet chemical smell of hydraulic fluid flooded his mind without warning. Conner's heart accelerated in his chest, his hands involuntarily drawing tight into fists—hunkering down—while somewhere deep within, the rational part of his brain fought to steady itself.

We gotta go. A slight vibration manifested in the metal floor panels of the C-130's cargo compartment beneath Conner's steel-toed desert combat boots as the winding drone of the auxiliary power unit spinning to life roared through the open paratroop door. Stretch was there in front of him. His lean, hard face ever contrasted by his friendly, intelligent, light-brown eyes. *We gotta go, we gotta go! Please work. Somebody needs us bad.* There was no way to know if it was one man who'd had an accident, or an entire personnel carrier full of guys who'd been hit by a roadside bomb. Impossible to tell if the injured were in stable condition—already helicoptered to a field hospital at the nearest FOB—or bleeding out alongside some dirt strip in the desert with nothing but an overwhelmed combat medic to aid them. *WE GOTTA GO!*

There was the high-pitched zing of hydraulic pumps and Stretch turned aft, switching on his mini mag light and staring intently as the chrome rods of the rudder actuator extended and retracted from their housing. The aircraft rocked as a gust of hot dry air whipped sand across the empty concrete beyond the tall, wiry Midwestern staff sergeant standing on the aircraft's open ramp. Stone leapt up, pulling himself through the paratroop door and into the cargo compartment. Stretch pivoted toward him, flashing a thumbs up before the two pounded fists—dull red hydraulic fluid stains all over his desert camouflage uniform—then gazed directly at Conner and grinned.

Conner sucked in a deep breath, tilted his head back and forced himself to focus on the small circular air vent above his seat as he ran his fingers through his short, but styled, dirty-blond hair. His mind honed in—hyper focused—remembering that day, a few weeks before they rotated home. He had been tasked to fly on an Aero Med mission and as they taxied toward the runway for takeoff a seal had blown. Dark-red hydraulic oil sprayed out of the rudder pack at three thousand psi. *There were no spares. We were the only plane on the ramp, period. It was us or no one.*

Stretch and Stone worked for hours in the tight confines of the aft ramp—managing to replace the heavy, cumbersome, hydraulic rudder pack—enabling the aircraft to launch. Conner swallowed hard, perhaps in a subconscious effort to combat the tightening sensation he felt in his throat. *Holy hell, I haven't had a moment like this in a while. God, losing Stretch was rough.* Conner took another deep breath and wondered if Stretch showed up in the minds of his family like that without warning. *Don't think about it man, it doesn't help nothin'. It happened, it's over. Now things are good. Think about seeing the guys and all the fun you're about to have. How long's it been? More than two years since we've been together.*

First we lost Stretch. Then within a few months it seemed like everybody's time was up. His whole crew had broken apart, some of his friends got out to start families or use the GI bill, while others were transferred all across the world. *God I was lucky all those deployments were with such solid guys. Why didn't I keep in better touch with everyone?*

Conner's mind circled back to Stone. *When things got rough, that guy really held us together in a way I never could have. Tougher than nails, but always with a positive attitude.* Stone kept everyone joking and working as a team no matter what was happening. He seemed to instinctively single out whoever was having trouble and talk them through it.

I was no exception. Conner remembered his heart pounding after being cut off from the bunker by a C-130 with its engines cranked, waiting to taxi. It was his first rocket attack. He stood there staring as mechanics scurried off the open concrete ramp, his mind racing—debating the merits of sprinting in front of the aircraft for the bunker, versus taking his chances running behind it, through the potential jet blast if the thing throttled up to move. Fortunately, Stone grabbed him and shoved him between two blast walls before he came to a conclusion.

After the plane taxied and the sound of its screaming jet engines dissipated, Stone calmly asked Conner about his post-deployment leave plans. He remembered wondering if his sister would be back from her travels through Peru by the time he made it home. Then—between the roar of explosions—Stone followed up with detailed questions as they crouched amid the Jersey-barrier-shaped concrete wedges on the edge of the flight line. Their nostrils filled with a mix of hot mechanical air, the stench of jet exhaust, the sandy grit of the desert and a hint of concrete dust from a rocket impact a hundred and fifty yards upwind.

Stone loved the Air Force. He hung it up though, said he had to, and got out to be with his girlfriend when he found out he was going to be a dad—convinced he'd wreck being a father if he stayed in.

Conner shook his head and wondered if he'd feel the same way if Joselyd were pregnant. *Hell, might not matter, I'm bummed about leaving her for a long weekend to hang out with my best friends. How am I going to feel when it's time to deploy again?* He exhaled as he thought about it. His enlistment was coming up next year. Pulling his phone back out, he brought up her picture again.

Yeah, Conner chuckled as the engines started and the plane began to taxi, *I might be done regardless.*

CHAPTER 2

Conner powered his phone back on as he made his way through the terminal at the Miami International Airport. A text message from Joselyd popped up.

I miss you already, but remember DON'T
CALL ME! Have a great time with your
friends and I'll be here when you get back.
Love you!!! <3 <3 <3

Ahhh, how does this girl do the simplest things and they make me feel so good? Doesn't even make sense. He shot her back a smiley face and his phone buzzed in his hand before he could shove it back in his pocket.

"Mathews!"

"Where you be at? I've been knocking down mimosas for over an hour waitin' for your trifling ass!"

"Well, I'm here now."

"Meet me outside the baggage claim and we'll grab a cab to the beach while we wait for these other jokers to show up."

Even though he hadn't seen him since his transfer to Yokota, Japan more than two years ago, Conner picked the tall, dark-haired, white kid out of the crowd right away and waved. Mathews, who always had a goofy grin, loped toward him with a loose and fluid stride. His dark navy cargo shorts seemed worn, with little grease smudges, and his lanky arms made the sleeves of his tight gray T-shirt appear comically short. He wrapped Conner up in a big bear hug and lifted him off the ground.

"Get off me, you drunk!" Conner laughed.

"Damn right, been drunk since I got on the plane in Japan and I intend to stay that way until I fly to see my parents on Sunday. I'm going on a straight bender, baby."

Conner shook his head though he was still smiling. "You hardly ever drank, now you're lit before the plane even lands?"

"Damn, bitch, you just don't know because we were always in the desert where there ain't nothin' to choke down but hot bottled Euphrates water!" Mathews chuckled. "Nahh, I'm just playin'. I ain't had a drink in six months, I only drink on leave. But I'm on fuckin' leave now and I'm gonna have a good time! Come on. We're going straight to South Beach, check out some ladies. That way, when McCabe shows up we'll be close to the room."

Thirty minutes later the two strode down the white sand of South Beach, wearing tactical-styled black backpacks and small shoulder slung duffle bags. Mathews carried his shoes as they took in the sun and the clear aquamarine water. There were only a few people on the beach. Eleven a.m. on a Wednesday must have still been a little early, even during the summer.

"McCabe's gotta get here so we can ditch our bags and get in the water," Conner said, gazing out at the ocean as they walked.

"You're not lying," Mathews replied. "Let's duck in somewhere though, I want another drink."

"Pshh… Way too early for me, I need something to eat though."

"Weak *sauce*," Mathews replied before gesturing to a beach-themed bar and grill in the bottom of a high-rise condominium just beyond the sand.

They sat outside with a view of the ocean. Mathews knocked down two beers and started on a third before Conner's food came out.

"You gotta try some of these things man, this shit is good," Conner offered, dipping a chunk of deep-fried gator tail into Cajun sauce.

"Nahh," Mathews replied after taking another swig from his pint glass. "I don't eat predators, bro. Bad juju. Not happening."

Conner looked up in amusement, "Why the hell not?"

"Bro," Mathews stared at him, "What if some crazy shit happens? Like a survival situation, or some end of the world catastrophe and I gotta make my way through the swamps, or live there like the Seminoles, and I come face to face with one of these cold-blooded reptilian monsters. I need to look that motherfucker dead in the eye and say 'if you wanna fight, it's on, but I didn't eat nonna your kind when I had the chance, so we could just go our separate ways—no score to settle here.'"

Conner laughed and shook his head. "Your loss, man. This tastes amazing." He took another bite. "You really think an alligator is going to care what you ate today if you're ever eyeball to eyeball in a swamp?"

"Bro, you never know!" Mathews exhaled. "Plus, predators aren't designed to be eaten."

Conner squinted at him.

"Animals' reproductive rates align with how often they supposed to get eaten. Zebras produce way more offspring than lions, cause zebras gotta get eaten. The lower down the food chain you go, the faster things multiply. Think about rabbits and mice, those mugs are nonstop cranking out copies of themselves."

Conner shook his head. "You're an original, man." He went to work wolfing down the rest of his gator tail while Mathews finished his beer.

"Come on bro, let's get back out to the beach, maybe there'll be some eye candy by now. I ain't seen nothing but little-titty Japanese girls for two years."

Conner chuckled.

"Honestly, I was always a leg man. I never really thought about the tatas at all until there was nothing but Asian A-cups around. That shit's not healthy. I think we're designed to see a little more bass in the boobies than what they got going on over in Japan."

Joselyd's got bass, Conner thought as they trudged through the sand toward the ocean. He visualized her frolicking toward him on the beach in her bikini. *Doesn't even make sense, I see her naked every night and then I fantasize about her in a swimsuit. What a complicated tangle our minds must be... or maybe not. Maybe we're wired exceedingly simple—food, shelter, girls with bass in their bras—and I just want there to be something deeper to it all.*

They turned parallel to the shore line and continued to hike south. The sun was strong now—directly overhead—but a light breeze came off the water, cooling the sweat that formed on Conner's forehead and ran down his sides. The line of high-rise condos to their right appeared unending, until he glanced left at the seemingly infinite ocean.

"There ya go, man," Conner said nodding toward two girls with long, tan legs in bikini bottoms and sun shirts on either side of a plastic cooler, carrying it toward the surf to claim a spot in the sand. "I guess you can drink on the beach here. So there's two of your favorite things all together."

Conner watched them as they moved away. They were mighty fine looking, but he would have still preferred Joselyd. *I should send her a picture of the water... After we are clear of these long-legged ladies.* He glanced side-eyed at Mathews, realizing he hadn't answered.

"I wonder how much that cooler cost?" Mathews asked, as if in response.

Conner tilted his head slightly as he looked at his friend.

"I mean, it can't be that much, a couple of girls on vacation have one."

Conner squinted at him.

Mathews halted. "It's horse shit, bro."

Conner took two more steps before he stopped as well. "What is?"

"Everything! This whole goddamn world is full of so much fucking horse shit I can't hardly stand it!"

Conner took a deep breath, slowly nodding his head, waiting for his friend to meet his gaze, but he never did. Mathews just stood there, staring out at the cooler, or bikini bottoms or perhaps the ocean, it was impossible to tell which.

The sound of the crashing waves traveled up the beach in a rhythmic succession. Gulls drifted down the shoreline squawking out a slow series of rising wails. The girls stopped and set the cooler down before skipping the last fifteen yards to the water. Ankle deep in the foamy caps that rushed up onto the sand, they turned away from the ocean. The taller of the two extended her arm, awkwardly holding her phone backward while attempting to press a button on the key pad to snap photos as the girls posed together, giggling and grinning with waves breaking behind them.

"Now's your chance man! Go ask 'em if they want you to take the picture. Get a conversation going."

Mathews didn't answer. His eyes drifted to the sand before he turned and continued trudging down the beach. "Horse shit," he muttered, "what a bunch of fucking horse shit. I can't hardly stand it."

Conner took a few quick steps to catch up, and they strode along together again.

"You alright, man?"

Mathews shook his head, "I think I need another beer already."

CHAPTER 3

Conner was stretched out in the sand with his head against his backpack, gazing up at the perfect blue sky through his sunglasses. Mathews sat beside him, holding a beverage concealed in a paper bag and staring out to sea with an introspective expression that didn't match any of Conner's memories of him. On occasion he would momentarily return to his old self—notifying Conner of ladies strutting down the shoreline that would be worth sitting up to see.

Strange, Conner pondered as he stared upward, questioning this reserved quiet spell Mathews had slipped into for the last hour. Wondering if his friend could have actually changed this much since he had seen him last, or if what he was witnessing was just the reaction to a combination of alcohol, jet lag and seeing America again for the first time in years. *He was damn near exactly the way he'd always been ninety minutes ago.* He glanced side-eyed at Mathews—confident the observation would be hidden by his tinted lenses—hoping to see a more familiar expression, but his friend still held the same unmoving, pensive look that seemed alien on his face.

There was a pulsing buzz. Mathews reached in his pocket, flipped his phone open and brought it up to his ear. "Bro!"

Mathews sat up straight, his back rigid, his eyes shifting from side to side as he held the phone to his ear.

"Yeah! That joker's right here with me."

He tilted his head back slightly.

"Well text me the directions, mutter fookaaah!" Mathews ended the call and flicked Conner's bicep with the back of his hand. "Yo, get in gear! Check out that unicorn in the black bikini while I chug the rest of this forty. Then we're going to the condo to meet McCabe, change and drop this bullshit off so we can get in the ocean!" Mathews nodded his head slightly toward a woman strolling down the beach before bringing the paper bag to his lips and tipping his head back.

And he's back. Conner sat up with a smirk.

"Shapely redhead with a tan," Mathews observed, bringing the bag back down. "You don't see that shit every day. Come on, let's go!"

They took the elevator up to the fourteenth floor of the high rise and Mathews launched himself into the room, tackling McCabe as he answered the door. Conner shook his head, watching his friends roll around on the floor, laughing as they attempted to outmaneuver each other. Before a minute passed, the laughter shifted to heavy breathing as muscles strained and twitched, while the two desperately struggled to suck in enough air during their intensifying competition. They broke apart for a second—Mathews managed to make it up on his knees while McCabe rolled into a sprinter's stance, found some traction and exploded toward him from the floor. Conner sprang forward, brushing past his entangled friends just in time to yank the glass coffee table back—saving Mathews from crashing through it.

They came down with a thud and McCabe's foot hit the end table by the couch, sending a ceramic lamp to the floor where it cracked into pieces as the bulb shattered. "This is why we can't have nice things!" Mathews called from the ground before being slowly twisted onto his face by McCabe. McCabe—having gained the advantage—worked to force Mathew's curled wrist against the carpet and hold it there while applying pressure to the top of his elbow, causing him to tap out.

"Damn, you've been working out," Mathews gasped, reaching up from the floor for a hand.

"And you're getting sloppy," McCabe answered. The dark-haired Jersey boy was just as tall, but his chest and arms were thicker than Mathews' lanky frame. They locked hands, each having a powerful mechanic's grip—the dark, woven, bands of Celtic tattoos encircling McCabe's bicep flexed as he hoisted Mathews off the floor. When they were both upright, the two fell into a tight hug.

"Alright bro, get off me!" Mathews yelled. "What the hell got into you out at March Air Force Base? This California-girl fiancée you got make you all touchy-feely sentimental or something? I gotta get ready for the beach, son!"

McCabe moved toward Conner, beaming. His muscular chest, arms and legs were barely concealed behind a casual, loose-fitting, beige button down and black board shorts. McCabe's genuine grin filled Conner with a sense of belonging. He smiled back as the two smacked hands and pulled each other in for a back-slapping embrace.

"It's good to see you Conner, I'm glad you're here." Mc-Cabe's dark eyes were uncharacteristically happy and full. "Now, go pick a bunk and change so we can get some beach time in. We only have a couple hours before we have to be back here to meet Stone."

"Ahh, this feels nice," McCabe declared thirty minutes later as he stepped out onto the sand. He pulled his shirt off revealing the Celtic Cross in dull black ink spanning the shoulder blades of his muscular back and held his arms wide open in the sun.

Mathews trotted past him down the beach and into the waves. A minute later Conner and McCabe waded in after him. The water was cool but not cold, and after the initial shock, felt good on Conner's skin. A light set of waves came in and Mathews nosed toward them, diving under the crests.

"Don't go too far, dude," McCabe called when their friend had resurfaced. "I hear you've been drinking for damn near eighteen hours by now."

"Bro," Mathews retorted, staring back at them with an exaggerated head nod. "Don't even worry, water is denser than alcohol. The more I drink, the easier it oughta be to float. I'm gonna be more buoyant than a cork by the time we hit the Keys." Mathews tipped backward into the clear aquamarine-blue and bobbed over a swell on his back with his arms outstretched.

Conner smirked as he turned toward McCabe, "Hey Mathews, I didn't think you were seeing your mom until Sunday?"

Mathews let out a cackle without looking up.

McCabe shook his head. "How did I ever get along without you boys?"

"I didn't cross the Pacific to hear your sarcasm!" Mathews yelled.

"The hell you didn't!" McCabe called back and the two erupted in laughter.

Conner's mind drifted as he watched them. It sparked a memory from years before. *2002 maybe? It was all of us. McCabe, Stone, Mathews, Lewis, Stretch and a couple other guys. Stone had fought with supervision and gotten us an eight hour pass to leave Al Udeid, and we were all swimming in some fancy hotel pool, and then the Persian Gulf.* He remembered it vividly. The guys were wrestling and splashing around in the water. Then, despite the fact there were no girls, a round of chicken fights broke out. Guys hopped on other guys' shoulders and worked to knock each other off balance until only one team remained upright. The air was so hot and the water in the Gulf so warm that it barely cooled them down, but anything was preferable to the scorching concrete of the flight line, where they'd been working thirteen hour shifts for more than forty days straight. The metallic surfaces of the aircraft were so hot they had to wear gloves to keep from burning their hands while attempting to perform maintenance.

"Guys, remember when Stone got us that pass to leave base in Qatar?"

"How could I forget," McCabe answered. "That was back when things were starting to amp up and I wasn't used to working so hard. I needed a break so bad. Then like magic all four of our aircraft were off station and none were scheduled back on our shift."

"Yeah!" Conner let out, "We were all sitting there outside the tent on the flight line staring at each other and Stone said, 'I'm going to take us off base to have some fun.' I don't think anybody believed he was serious, even though he was already a staff sergeant back then. He said something about it to the master sergeant, who promptly told him he'd lost his fucking mind."

McCabe nodded and continued. "Stone got that sharp hard look in his eye—you know the one I'm talking about—it was so sudden and fierce it kinda scared me at the time. He followed the master sergeant into the tent, and the door slammed shut and when he came out, he said 'I can take half of you off base.'"

"Bro! I saw it," Mathews interjected, popping back upright in the water. "I'm not trying to say they were yelling, but it was certainly an animated conversation. I was like—damn, my boy Stone's got stones for real. I thought he might lose his staff stripe before they were done talkin', but he raised hell and we filled out a bunch of paperwork, signed for a vehicle and rolled. Only time I saw anything in Qatar other than concrete and sand the whole trip."

"That was the first time I got angry," McCabe admitted. "I bought it all before that. World's greatest Air Force, and patriotism and freedom and this is what has to happen because Al Qaeda hit us on September 11th. Then I see, just a couple miles away from our sand-bottomed tents, porta johns and chow tent that served *chicken* and rice, *chicken* and beans or *chicken* and noodles for every meal is one of the most modern cities in the whole goddamn world! We were swimmin' in a fucking 'cooled' swimming pool outside a five star luxury hotel shaped like an Aztec Pyramid! Literally a half an hour drive from the desert squalor we were living in. I know we had it good compared to the Army guys living in field conditions down range, but there was no option there. It didn't have to be that way for us. Yet there we were, telling ourselves we're the best there is, while the locals laughed at us."

"What was the name of that hotel?" Conner asked.

"Sheraton," Mathews responded. "That was so much fun. We all dove in the Gulf right there just to say we did it. We wrestled around for a little bit, but it was too hot so we went back to the pool."

"Cooled swimming pool," McCabe sneered. "We couldn't even get something cold to drink on base."

"Ol' Brackish McCabe," Mathews scoffed, "You're still a little salty, aren't you? I guess some things never do change. You really gotta learn to let shit go."

McCabe stood motionless with his arms crossed, the reflective lenses of his sunglasses seemed to stare daggers at Mathews.

"Stone really hooked us up on that one, huh? The first of many times. Was that the same deployment he took that random forklift and drove two miles away to the chow tent in the middle of the night and came back with a whole pallet of Gatorade?"

"Yeah it was!" Mathews answered. "He was wheeling back to the flight line and the master sergeant saw him, started shaking his head and literally covered his eyes. Then when the forklift stopped he yelled 'not here! Somewhere no one can see it, particularly me, like in the conex' without ever moving his hand away."

"The damn chow tent didn't have Gatorade for a couple days, but we were set until we rotated home," Conner grinned remembering it all. "I can't wait to see him, he's gotta be one of the most solid people I've met in my life."

The light swells lapped on their upper bodies as they stood together, just beyond the surf. Conner's gaze shifted between his two friends, attempting to discern why neither had responded. Mathews' light blue eyes stared down at the water. Despite McCabe's shades it was easy to tell he wasn't looking back either.

What did I miss?

"Yeah," McCabe finally muttered. "I'm pumped to see everyone."

Mathews nodded without speaking or glancing up.

Conner stepped into the common area, his skin still flushed from his shower and fingers working to button his collared shirt for their evening out when he felt McCabe's dark eyes lock onto him. He stopped whistling mid note, instinctively glancing up. Conner found his friend sitting across the room at the glass dinner table. Squinting, he waited for McCabe to speak.

"Hey, come sit down, let me talk to you for a minute."

Conner pulled back a chair and looked at his friend, "What's up, man?"

"Look dude, you need to know, Stone's not the same as he was before."

Conner's eyes narrowed.

"He's had a lot of problems. I don't want you to get caught off guard."

"*Stone?*" Conner questioned, "Get the fuck outta here. Stone is like, the most solid person I've ever met."

"Dude, listen to me. Stone is not the person you knew before. He's lost his edge. I don't know how he's going to act when he gets here."

"What do you mean, he's lost his edge?"

"I mean he's fucking lost it, dude. He's way different now."

"Come on."

"He's got no phone, I think he's living rough, in a van maybe. Gets around with an old road atlas. Traveling from place to place out west, staying in national forest and BLM lands. He stops in at a public library every couple weeks and checks his email. That's it."

"What are you talking about? He got out to go be a dad."

"Yeah, when he gets here don't bring any of that up."

"He's not with Shannon anymore?"

McCabe shook his head slightly, though his eyes remained fixed on Conner.

Conner sat back in his chair, "Well, if that's the case, what happened?"

"I don't know exactly," McCabe exhaled slowly as his eyes drifted down to the table. "It's not for me to say anyway."

Conner tilted his head to one side as he stared at his friend.

"Look," McCabe began, "Some people don't care what they do, or if it means anything at all. Some people have no greater purpose, no deeper meaning, no drive to do good or change the world or challenge themselves. Maybe they're just trying to survive, or are angling for a paycheck. But some guys..." McCabe looked up, locking his eyes with Conner again.

"Some guys need a purpose, a hill to charge up or a mountain to climb. Meaning. To help someone else or do something they feel might make the world better. That could be doing our little piece to give freedom to people who never had it or just holding your guys together until they get to go home. Sometimes it means leaving everything you know to go take care of your girlfriend and be a dad. Stone lost all those chances and now he's adrift. He's not the same as you remember him. I just wanted you to know."

Conner stood up shaking his head and paced across the room.

No fucking way.

He turned, glancing back at McCabe. "When's he supposed to get here?"

McCabe shrugged. "I'm not a hundred percent sure he'll show."

"Well if he's got no phone, how's he supposed to find us?"

"I emailed him the address. He wrote back once, said he'd meet me in front at 4:30 this afternoon. That was weeks ago. I've tried to talk to him since and he never responded." McCabe sighed, "We'll check and see if he's there, but if he isn't, I'm not hanging around all night waiting. I promised myself I was going to enjoy this trip. Not spend the whole time stressed out because I'm worrying about everybody. I always do that shit, but not now. We are here to have fun together. This is our time."

CHAPTER 4

The three of them stood there outside the high-rise condo-minium in silence. Mathews slightly apart from the other two dragging on a cigarette. No one spoke.

Conner fidgeted. He pulled his phone out of his pocket for the second time in five minutes. 4:29. *He'll be here. If he told McCabe he'd be here, he'll be here. Stone is fucking solid.*

Conner glanced at his friend, but McCabe didn't make eye contact, he just continued to scan the parking lot in vain. Conner couldn't help but unlock his phone and look at his favorite picture of Joselyd. Her playful smile and dark, intelligent eyes made him wish she were there. There's something he wanted to ask her, but he couldn't identify what it was. Maybe he just wanted to talk. To tell her about Stone. To say, 'don't worry, he'll be here. He's an amazing guy, you'll love him,' and see her beam back confidently, knowing that he was right. McCabe's dismissive attitude toward Stone's character had been festering in the back of his mind. He flipped back to the home screen. 4:31. His heart rate accelerated. *How long will McCabe wait?*

"Son of a bitch," McCabe whispered.

Conner's eyes flicked first to McCabe then to the parking lot, where Stone, smiling, strode confidently between rows of vehicles toward them.

He had a dark tan, sunglasses and styled clothing unlike

Conner had ever seen him wear—khaki pants and a deep blue Hawaiian shirt with a crimson floral pattern. A plaster cast covered two fingers on his left hand and extended halfway up his forearm. It must have been fresh—it was still a bright white in the Florida sunshine—sharply contrasting his sun touched skin. He was thin, but with compact muscle, the endurance variety that comes from physical activity, not hours in the gym.

"Congratulations, brother!" Stone sprang up on the curb, smacking hands with McCabe before pulling him in for a hug.

"Your watch must be off, bud. You're a minute late," McCabe announced, "Wasn't sure you'd make it."

"You kidding me?" Stone's voice was deep and powerful, "No way I'd leave you hanging. I've missed you fuckers for real."

"I've missed you too, dude," McCabe replied. "Life ain't the same without you."

Stone pulled back and grinned, "Who sends a bachelor party invite but no save the date? When do I get to meet this girl?"

McCabe chuckled as he gazed at his friend and then fell into a full-on laughing fit. "Never!" he finally managed. "She's a *nice* girl! None of you assholes ever get to meet her!"

Mathews tapped his temple—a cigarette burning between his fingers—before pointing at McCabe in agreement. "Smart man." He flicked his cigarette as he moved in bumping fists with Stone.

"Conner!" Stone stepped forward and gripped his hand with intense strength before yanking him in for a hug.

A wide smile forced itself across Conner's face. *Here, and even stylish clothes! I've never seen him in anything more than jeans and a T-shirt when out of uniform.*

"How you been, man?" Conner asked a little too loudly as Stone released him.

"Catch up over beers and steaks, boys," McCabe cut him off, pointing to an approaching taxi.

The cab had dropped them in front of a building that had once been a bar, but seemed to have been closed for some time. Instead of calling for another ride the group had spent the last fifteen minutes trekking up the sun-drenched city sidewalk attempting to find the actual location. "Hold up guys, I don't know if we're going the right way," McCabe stared down at a sweat dampened tourist map of Miami in the humid air.

Conner glanced up the street, "We've definitely wandered out of the tourist district."

Mathews gestured to the 7-Eleven on the corner in front of them. "I'm going to get some smokes while you boys figure it out."

"That shit'll kill ya!" McCabe called after him.

"Nahh. Taliban'll kill ya, Al Qaeda'll kill ya, aircraft mishaps and anthrax vaccinations, Bosnian Serbs, Iranian SA-20s and Colombian FARC will kill ya. But not cigarettes, they'll just calm your nerves a little."

"Fair enough."

"Yeah you should try it, ya high strung Irish fuck."

"Not this guy!" McCabe yelled back. "I've got big plans, I'm getting married and living in sexual bliss. No need to settle my nerves or anything else for that matter."

Mathews chuckled and shook his head as he strode away.

Stone stood by silently as cars hummed past on the busy street beside them. The exhaust seemed to hang in the hot, still air, waiting to affix itself to their sweat dampened skin or clothing the second they moved.

"Conner, help me figure this out. There's supposed to be a brewery with a steak house just a block over from it," McCabe said, staring back down at his map. "I don't even know if we're on the right side of I-95."

"I hope you're better in bed then you are at navigation or you won't be married long," Conner smirked as he pulled out his iPhone 3.

"You wanna know how good I am? Ask your sister! Until then, help me figure out where we need to be!"

Damn, I missed these guys, Conner thought, grinning. Shrugging a shoulder to wipe the sweat from his face, he tried to look at his phone but the bright sunlight coupled with his polarized shades made it difficult to see the screen. He studied it, without much luck.

"This place might not even still be open," McCabe sighed, "let's just pick someplace else."

"YEAH!" Stone's voice boomed over the traffic.

Conner's head snapped up alongside McCabe's, their eyes darted up the sidewalk and then across the street in search of their friend.

Where the hell did he get to so fast? Conner's gaze swept the street again.

"Let's fuck with this kid!" Stone's voice roared.

Conner's eyes locked onto him, thirty yards ahead in the alley alongside the 7-Eleven. *Shit, what's he into?* Instinctively Conner took off at a quick pace toward his friend. McCabe fell into step beside him but he barely noticed.

"You guys are street, huh?" Stone held his casted left hand in front of him and made a fist with his right in a boxer's stance. "I'm street, too! Let's fuck this kid up!"

There were two athletic-looking boys in their late teens—though possibly still high schoolers—in front of him, with the deeply tanned skin of locals. A third boy in a sweat-stained polo shirt—shorter than the other two and a few years younger—stood defensively with his back against the beige brick facade of the 7-Eleven. The dark, mixed tone of his skin contrasted his white shorts as he trembled.

"Yeah!" Stone shouted with enthusiasm. "You guys look like some real badasses! Let's do this!"

McCabe was right, he's lost his damn mind. Conner increased his pace, cutting toward the front of the building to avoid the teenagers' field of view. *I'll try and pull Stone out of there first, but if something happens quick I can blindside the biggest one. No weapons that I can see and they haven't noticed me yet.*

Conner's attention broke as he was yanked backward. Mc-Cabe had caught him by the bicep and spun him around. Conner stared at him wide-eyed.

McCabe shook his head frantically.

"You were right man, he's lost it. Grab Stone and I'll cut these guys off if they try anything."

McCabe shook his head again. "No. Let him be," he uttered in a low, forceful tone, his grip tightened on Conner's arm. Stone yelled again, and Conner swung around to look at him.

"Here we are just a bunch of street badasses, let's do this!" Stone shouted, wielding his casted arm around in the air as if rallying a crowd to join him.

The two teenagers glanced at each other side-eyed. The shorter one's mouth had dropped open while the other seemed to have his jaw clenched.

"Hey mister, we don't want no trouble," the taller boy offered, staring at Stone wide-eyed as he took a half step backward into the alley.

"You don't want any trouble?" Stone tilted his head as if pondering. "You don't want any trouble? I just saw you slamming this kid up against the wall! You were fucking shaking him down like a real gangster!" He brought his hands in front of him, as if clutching an imaginary body and jerking it rapidly. "I can tell you're smart too, picking out someone half as big as you who doesn't look like he can really fight back. Then you double teamed his ass just to make sure you couldn't lose!"

"Look boss, I—"

"You WHAT?" Stone stepped forward, shouting with such ferocity that all three boys flinched. His steel-gray eyes filled with fire. "Hey, I got an idea! There's two of you and ya both look strong. Why don't you come at me?" Stone threw his arms to the sides, leaving himself vulnerable. "I already got a busted hand and everything, no way you street badasses can lose!" Stone walked straight toward them, making no effort to defend himself.

Shit! Conner attempted to yank free from McCabe's ever-tightening iron grip.

"LET'S GO!" Stone roared, quickening his pace.

The second boy's gaping mouth snapped shut as his face flushed with fear. He backed away slowly, looking to his friend as if for help.

"We out, this fucker's crazy," the tall boy called before turning and hustling away. His friend chased after him.

Stone's gaze followed them as they retreated.

Conner let out a long exhale, allowing his muscles to relax. McCabe's grip on his bicep eased then released completely. Conner realized Mathews was standing beside them with an already lit cigarette.

After the two aggressors had disappeared into the alley, Stone stepped forward again and the younger remaining teenager cringed, closing his eyes tight, causing tears to stream down his dark cheeks. Stone squatted down closer to his height and just hovered there in silence. A long moment passed before the kid managed to open his eyes.

"Hey buddy," Stone said in a soft tone.

"Look, I... I don't have any money," the boy whimpered as tears flooded his eyes again.

"I know that might have been a little scary, but I was trying to help you out kid." Stone straightened up again. "Look, you've got to stick up for yourself or those guys'll just keep messing with you." He took a deep breath and let it out slow. "And that's no way to live, man.

"The first time's the hardest, kid. Sure, you'll take a few hits. It's not like the movies where the scrawny kid rises up to knock down the bully, that's all fiction. But you'll learn quick that it feels a whole lot better to take a beating and be a man, than deal with the emotional fallout you're going through right now."

The kid stared up at him hard, perhaps still grappling with the idea that the individual in front of him did not actually mean him harm.

"Then one day, when you're stronger and have more confidence you can stand up anytime you see someone getting a raw deal," Stone paused as if pondering it. "Then you'll never have to feel bad about anything."

The boy blinked up at him, a new set of tears slid down his brown face in the sunshine.

"You have no idea what I'm trying to tell you, huh?"

A light breeze blew, gently stirring the thick humid air as the cars buzzing by on the street behind them slowed to a halt. When the kid exhaled his lower jaw visibly quivered, and he pulled his polo shirt up to wipe the tears out of his eyes.

"Well why don't I get us some drinks. All that yelling made me thirsty. Would you like that?"

The boy nodded in silence.

"What's your favorite color Gatorade?"

The boy shrugged, but his posture was beginning to relax.

"Well come inside with me, and you can pick one out."

Conner watched them as they moved toward the door and disappeared behind the sun-glared glass. He shook his head. *Maybe Stone hasn't lost it after all?* But he wasn't sure. This certainly wasn't the way he remembered him.

Conner turned to McCabe, but his friend's dark eyes were focused on the ground. Mathews brought his cigarette to his lips without saying a word. The smoke hung in the hot, still air as the rumble of idling traffic persisted. Conner's gaze flicked between his two silent comrades.

"Well, that happened," Conner managed, hoping someone would offer a deeper insight into the situation.

"It did," McCabe agreed and took a deep breath.

"We need more drinks soon," Mathews interjected. "I'm almost sober again."

CHAPTER 5

"This is what I'm talking about," Mathews announced, raising his sunglasses as they entered the cool crisp air of the brewery. The building appeared to have been converted from something industrial, and the owners had allowed some of its character to remain as part of the decor. The floor was polished concrete and corrugated roofing material had been affixed to the lower portions of the walls. Mathews stopped near the entrance observing a sign reading 'no bandanas.' A frown crossed his face before following the other guys as they ventured in slowly—allowing their eyes to adjust to the seemingly dim lighting—and pulled up stools at the stainless steel bar.

A short, busty beach-blonde in a low cut tank top and cut-off denim short shorts revealing tan, muscular legs tossed coasters at them as she asked for drink orders.

"Hoppiest IPA you got," McCabe replied without consulting the colorful chalkboards that hung on the wall behind the bar.

"Bro! Why?" Mathews sneered. "IPA sucks, I can't wait for this trendy craze to end, it's gone on way too long already."

"Get the hell outta here, I got class. I know what drinks to order."

"Your last days of freedom and you want to drink that bullshit." Mathews stood there shaking his head. "You know why it tastes so bad? The Brits had to put all those extra hops in it to keep it from skunking while they shipped it from England all the way to India for their soldiers abroad. You drinking that crap here for fun would be like some Tommy walking into a steak house on Downing Street and ordering an MRE for dinner.”

“You should make a beer origins movie, like Marvel just did for Wolverine.”

“I should, and you oughta watch it.”

“Alright,” McCabe nodded, looking at Mathews. “If you’re so sophisticated, what are you getting?”

Mathews turned his attention to the bartender, “Blueberry Wheat, please.”

“What? All that shit you gave me and you’re going to order something with fruit in it!”

“Damn right, it’s a summer beer and it tastes good.”

“Yeah, if you’re a woman!”

“I’m secure with my sexuality, hopster,” Mathews asserted, turning away.

Rolling her eyes, the beach-blonde turned to Conner with a slightly annoyed look of amusement.

“I’ll take a pilsner,” Conner said in an attempt to avoid ridicule. He glanced down the bar to see Mathews with a look of extreme disappointment and McCabe beside him shaking his head.

“Then there’s Conner,” Mathews uttered. “Always playing it safe.”

“No sense of adventure whatsoever,” McCabe agreed.

“He’s like plain-white, store-brand sandwich bread, in a

grocery aisle full of wheat, cinnamon swirl, sourdough, potato rolls and even pumpernickel," Mathews continued.

"For God's sake, Conner, you're on vacation! Live a little!"

Conner smirked and shook his head. *Better to just smile and take it.* Despite his years on the flight line, he'd never been able to keep pace with his friends' quick-witted banter.

"Be bold!" Mathews howled. "Take your shirt off, get a little crazy!"

"I'm sorry ma'am," Conner confided to the bartender. "He's been in Japan the last two years, he don't know how to act anymore."

"Don't go to her for sympathy! Look at this girl! She's got style, she knows better!"

The bartender put a hand on her hip, cocked her head to the side and shot a semi-agitated, yet playful, expression toward Mathews.

"Ma'am, don't give me that look! You know what I'm talking about."

She tilted her head even further but continued to gaze back at Mathews.

"Would you ever travel a thousand miles from home to a nice establishment such as this one and order a pilsner?"

"Never," she blinked and smiled as she turned to the taps, filling a glass.

"Exactly," Mathews clapped, staring at Conner.

Conner smiled and shook his head as the guys chuckled. "Wait, wait," Conner asked. "Ma'am, what would you order?"

She turned and produced a bold grin. "Blueberry Wheat."

"Ohhhhh!" McCabe shouted, pointing at Mathews before slapping the bar.

Mathews' head dropped into his hands, as Conner chuckled and the beach-blonde giggled, unable to contain her amusement any longer.

When she caught her breath she gestured to Stone.

"Ice water," he replied.

The girl behind the bar squinted at him for a moment as if debating whether or not it were a joke before she began filling the glass.

"Come on, Stone," Mathews pleaded, "have a beer with your ol' buddies, I'm buyin'."

"I appreciate it," Stone answered, "But I'm a cheap date. I'm good with water."

"Well, in that case... Coin check, bitches!" Mathews hollered, slamming a Pacific Air Forces challenge coin down on the bar.

Conner fumbled with his wallet to produce the 9th Air Force coin General Moseley had given him after they flew him to a meeting in Kuwait in 2002, and placed it next to Mathews' coin.

"What do you think this is, amateur hour?" McCabe asked, dropping a coin from his unit at March Air Force base beside the other two. The three of them turned to Stone who smiled ever so slightly as he revealed an old and battered airman's coin, the type they had all been presented at their graduation of basic training.

Mathews chuckled and dropped his credit card on the bar. "See? Told ya I was buyin'!"

"Hey, wait a second," Conner let out. "You guys gave me a blast of shit for ordering a pilsner and you're letting Stone slide with a water?"

"That man right there," Mathews pronounced, pointing to Stone, "can do whatever he wants."

McCabe slowly nodded in agreement as the bartender added a pint glass of ice water to the row of beverages on the stainless steel bar.

Conner stared at the line of different colored drinks, each with its own style vessel. The tulip glass of dark IPA, followed by the weizen glass holding an opaque unfiltered liquid with an ever-so-slight blue hue, then his own narrow-based pilsner glass with its transparent contents, and a good ol' American pint glass filled with ice water. It seemed like there was some kind of metaphor there, as he stared at it. *Maybe something about individuality and friendship. Together, but different.* He found himself wondering what Stretch or Lewis' glasses would look like if they were there.

Damn, I haven't talked to Lewis in forever. I guess not since he got out to go to school... Where did he get accepted? Conner's eyes narrowed, his head tilting slightly as he continued to stare at the row of drinks. *Somewhere in North Carolina, I think.*

"Come on boys, let's do this," Mathews suggested and they all reached in and grabbed their respective drinks. "Here's to McCabe's last days of freedom!" They all looked each other in the eyes, touched glasses, then tapped them on the bar together before taking a drink. "May he live happily ever after, even though he's chosen to tap the same piece of ass for the rest of his now variety-lacking life."

"You should try it, you dirty man-whore, ya might like it!" McCabe laughed before taking another drink.

Mathews gave an exaggerated shrug, "Well alright, give me her number."

"Get the hell outta here!" McCabe spouted, sending Mathews back a few feet with a one handed shove as they both roared in laughter.

Conner held his drink and watched them vacantly, as he searched his memories for the last time he'd seen Lewis. *It must have been just a couple months after we lost Stretch.* Then there it was in his mind—Lewis reaching out and shaking his hand. He was standing by his old beat-up black Civic, and it was packed so tight you couldn't see out the back windshield. His lower lip quivered, and he said, "I'm sorry to leave you guys. I just gotta get out, Conner. I can't do this anymore." Then he climbed in his car and drove away and that was it.

"Hey McCabe," Conner began, "I forgot to ask you before man, is Lewis coming?"

The smile washed off McCabe's face. His eyes seemed to fill with some kind of un-verbalized question that Conner couldn't quite pick out. Beside him, Mathews exhaled hard and turned toward his drink on the bar.

"I invited him," McCabe finally answered, "I didn't hear back."

"Huh," Conner replied. "That's strange, maybe he's real maxed with school or something. I guess there could be a summer semester."

McCabe raised his eyebrows as he turned away. "Yeah maybe, I really don't know."

"Conner," Mathews projected in a flat tone, "you really ought to keep in better touch, bro."

Conner glanced toward Stone for support. Stone, however, locked eyes with Mathews as they exchanged a knowing frown.

Again? What the hell have I missed here? Was there some kinda argument? Best to drop it and ask later. Or just give Lewis a call sometime.

The guys ordered two more rounds, discovered the beach-blonde bartender was working Saturday night and promised to return for a real night out. They opened the door and stepped outside into a wall of hot, humid air, then proceeded up the street to the steak house.

CHAPTER 6

"Hey, I got this one," Mathews announced, "Order whatever you boys want."

"I'll split it with you," Conner offered.

"Hell no, you guys don't have to buy me dinner," Stone cut in. "I'm going to get a prime rib, it wouldn't even be fair."

Mathews turned his head slightly and stared at Stone out of the corners of his eyes. He seemed to be debating something in his mind.

Stone glanced up and caught his gaze. "McCabe's the one getting married, we'll buy him dinner together. Not on your own, you just sprung for a plane ticket across the Pacific."

McCabe shook his head. "No need fellas, save your money. I'm marrying a college girl, I'll be just fine."

Mathews continued to stare hard at Stone.

"You worried about me, Mathews?"

"Of course not," Mathews replied without breaking his gaze.

"I've still got money saved up from all the times we were deployed without expenses, and I don't hardly spend anything now."

"I didn't say you were short on cash," Mathews answered. "I was just trying to be nice 'cause I'm super happy we're all hangin' out together."

Stone nodded, and no one talked. A few minutes later the waitress arrived with their drinks and took their orders, breaking the silence.

Conner's gaze flicked between his friends, but no one made eye contact. He took a deep breath searching for anything to prevent a new round of silence. "Hey, Jon Krakauer's got a new book out. It's on Pat Tillman."

"Pshh…" McCabe let out. "I remember when he quit the NFL and joined. I thought it was real inspiring that somebody like that would walk away from all that money and their dream job to be in the military. I remember seeing it on the news in the breakroom and one of the older sergeants saying 'what a dumbass.' It really ticked me off at the time, that someone would say something like that. But now, being engaged, and seeing the way he went down, and knowing how much bullshit we went through, and how fucked the world still is, I think that sergeant was right."

"He joined in the very beginning before anyone knew how bad it would be," Conner replied.

McCabe shook his head. "Nahh dude, don't sell nobody short like that, everyone knew. Even before all the medevacs we flew and bodies we pulled out, I knew. When the towers came down and the Pentagon got hit, we all knew and we all went anyway, and so did he. Now that I'm getting married though, I think maybe it's best to try and avoid bad situations, instead of flying into them."

"Bro, all of life is a gamble," Mathews responded. "You could stay home and do something nice and safe like go to college and still end up game over. Look at all that insanity they had at Virginia Tech. Thirty-some people just trying to go to class. Done."

"It's best just not to be in that situation to begin with," McCabe asserted, "and if you get super unlucky and end up in the middle of something like that, to try and get yourself out. That's why the training says 'run, hide, fight,' in that order. You get out if you can, and if not hunker down and wait for the security forces personnel or law enforcement to come in and neutralize the situation. That's what they get paid for."

"Yeah, so you run away and leave everybody else behind, then what?" Stone asked.

"Then you're out of the situation, doesn't matter after that."

"Bullshit."

"Sure, it's bullshit," McCabe huffed. "But sometimes you just gotta save yourself. Bad shit happens all the time, God knows we've seen plenty of it. Sometimes you just have to get out so you're not on the victims list and hope everyone else can too."

"Then how do you live knowing you bailed and left people hanging?" Stone shot back.

"The best way you can, it'd help knowing I didn't leave my fiancée alone, though."

"Hey," Conner jumped in, "if everybody can get clear then the pros can come in with their negotiators and SWAT teams if that doesn't work."

"No, forget that garbage." Stone's uncasted palm smacked the table just hard enough to make their pint glasses shutter. "If you're ever in a real deal life or death, you don't hold back, you destroy the threat. There ain't no talking somebody down and worrying about their feelings. If someone is threatening your well-being you end them." Stone closed his eyes and shook his head slightly, "why we even talking about this? You guys all know this."

"It's because of Hollywood," McCabe answered. "These guys who have never had a weapon pointed at them or a projectile flying their way are cranking out TV and movies left and right. Damn near all of it is completely unrealistic and people believe it anyway. Like down deep on the subconscious level in their understanding of how the world works. Then something bad happens in real life and people are like 'why didn't they just talk to that poor misunderstood man with the bomb?' or 'Why'd the cops have to kill him when they could have just shot the pistol out of his hand?' Our society's perception is so skewed that people don't have the slightest idea what reality is like. They think you can get punched in the nose and keep right on fighting, or that you can use a firearm without hearing protection and not deafen yourself or that you can sit inside the cargo bay of a military aircraft with engines running and have a conversation."

"Well that's certainly true, man," Conner responded, "but you wouldn't want your fiancée to get smacked in the nose or go to a combat zone just so she understands the reality of it."

McCabe shook his head rapidly. "I'm not saying that at all. I'm saying, TV, movies, literature, it all ought to mimic reality. That way peoples' ideas wouldn't be so far off the truth."

"Sure," Conner nodded. "But I guess it's just not as exciting to have a realistic story. Your hero takes a hit and they're down. People want things more drawn out like a boxing match even though there's no mitts or professional training or rules that would stretch out an actual fist fight."

"Well, that entertainment value is coming at a hell of a price. I mean, I'd say our society is approaching a point of total ignorance."

"Maybe," Conner countered. "But all of us sitting here know better. Four out of four."

The woven bands on McCabe's bicep rippled as he leaned back, crossing his arms. He sat there staring across the table at his friend, then let his eyes drop and shook his head. "Regular people aren't like us, Conner."

McCabe's words hung in the air a moment. When McCabe glanced back up, Conner stared into his dark eyes, considering, before slowly nodding in agreement. Mathews held his beer up and said, "Here's to all of us, not being fucking normal." All four of them, including Stone, tapped glasses and took a drink.

"But seriously, bro," Mathews continued looking across the table at Stone, "you gotta be careful about interjecting your-self into situations in areas you're not from. There's some legit gang shit down here."

"How would you know?" Conner asked. "You're not from here either."

Mathews shook his head. "You need to stop dreamin' about that girl you got and pay attention."

Conner's face flushed as he eyed Mathews suspiciously,

"How you know I got a girl?"

"Bro, I ain't gotta be Sherlock Holmes over here. You got a picture of some sexy dark-haired thang on your phone you look at every ten minutes."

McCabe chuckled.

"Whatever," Conner snapped. "How you know about the gangs?"

"I asked the bartender for basic details while you were zonin' out."

"That sexy-ass bartender with her toned legs and cut-off shorts and the best thing you could think of to talk about was gang activity?"

"Wanted to make sure I know what's up while I'm here, not trying to live through all the conflicts we've visited and then get clipped on vacation for some bullshit I don't know nothin' about."

Conner shook his head, "Why would a girl like that even know?"

"Bro, you need to wake up!" Mathews fired back. "Clearly I figured she knew because of the sign,"

"What sign?"

"No bandanas," Stone answered for him. "Keeps them from showing their colors so easily. Anyway, thank you for your concern," he waved his hand dismissively, "but I'm not worried about it."

"I know those jokers this afternoon were just little shrimpy teenagers but those are the ones that are trouble if they're gunned up," Mathews persisted. "It's not like when we were growing up and you could just knock somebody in the head until they acted right. There's all this toxic masculinity and shit now. They don't work things out like we used to, mugs these days want to shoot everybody up to get even."

Stone waved his hand again. "Nahh, those were just your standard teenaged bullies—"

"That what you thought the last time too?" McCabe asked, gesturing to Stone's broken hand.

"Ahh," Stone shook his head, momentarily lifting his cast. "This was different, I knew I wasn't coming out of this alright before it even started. Lucky a busted hand was all I got." He sucked in a breath and exhaled hard. "But these were just dumbass kids that needed to get slapped down a few pegs. Hopefully they'll think about it a little more next time. Or that other kid will learn to buck up and defend himself."

"They're like little baby rattlers," Mathews continued. "They can't control their venom, don't know when to inject it or how much they're pumping in. I heard on the radio last week some unfortunate kid got smoked for his sneakers."

"Don't worry," Stone replied. "Ain't nobody coming after my shoes, I don't have enough style."

"Rewind dude," McCabe interrupted. "What did you say? Toxic masculinity?"

"Yeah," Mathews asserted. "Toxic masculinity."

"Where the hell did you hear that?"

"Bro, it's this whole sociological theory. I dated this grad school chick for a couple months and she was big into re-searching it. Told me all about it.”

“I can assure you I’ve slept with two grad school girls in my time and I’ve never heard the words toxic and masculinity together in my life.”

“She says it’ll be mainstream one day. Especially because of all the school shootings and shit. Basically it says we all oughta be in touch with our feelings all the time and being a tough guy is toxic. Which is total bullshit. I mean, how the hell would any of us have survived half the shit we been through if we weren’t tough?”

Mathew’s leaned back and threw his gangly arms up in the air. “What would’ve happened all those times we were down range eighteen hours into our duty day, covered in hydro and sand and grit and still turning wrenches ’cause ‘the mission had to go?’ And how would the infantry boys win wars without being tough?”

His arm’s dropped as he leaned forward again. “I mean, these people would think it’s bad the way we nonstop hassle the new guys on the flight line. They don’t get it. They’ll never get it. It’s a hell of a lot better to realize someone can’t handle a little austerity at home, before you send them to a base in Afghanistan or Iraq where they’ll have to deal with some hajji throwing rockets and mortars on the flight line while they’re trying to perform aircraft maintenance.

“Anyway, those college kids got one thing right, this next generation is full of pussies. Instead of doing the shit we did,” he gestured toward Stone, "hiking and biking," then glanced between Conner and McCabe "sports and lifting weights, and hell, we all joined the military—put the work in—became tough guys the right way. This next pansy-ass generation behind us tries to skip all the hard work and use guns to make 'em tough."

"Huh," McCabe exhaled slowly. "Every time I think you're a total dumbass, you say some shit that makes perfect sense." McCabe paused as if contemplating. "I think this shit is already happening. That's why everyone goes and cries to their boss or their lawyer to sue someone instead of being an adult and confronting the individual they have an issue with to work things out. An entire society of emasculated weaklings that can't stand up for themselves or handle getting their feelings hurt is being created."

Conner rubbed his chin as he glanced between his friends and wondered what Joselyd would think of all this. "Hey guys, to fix what you're describing you'd have to build people's confidence up the right way. You'd have to start early with teachers and coaches and whatnot."

"For that to work," McCabe answered, "we'd have to be in a country full of young people who wanted to work hard, and just didn't have direction. I'm not sure that's the issue we're facing."

"There's always good ones out there," Stone cut in, "and there's always pieces of shit. When you see someone who needs help, you gotta help them out, and when you see someone who don't help themselves, you gotta let 'em drown."

"Bro, about that," Mathews attempted again. "Ya done a good thing today. I'm just saying don't be puttin' yourself in a situation where you're running up against some jokers who are packin'. That's all."

"It don't bother me much. In certain situations it could even make things easier," Stone answered.

McCabe's eyes narrowed as he turned his attention to Stone, "How so?"

Stone gazed back, "The belligerent was in possession of a deadly weapon which he brandished in a threatening manner, thus, fearing for my life, I terminated the aggressor with extreme prejudice—protecting myself as well as other defenseless individuals on the scene." Stone turned his head slightly, raising his eyebrows. "Solved. It's the situations where the aggressor is unarmed that people can make up some crazy shit and get you in trouble."

"Where'd you learn to talk like a damn cop?" McCabe asked.

Stone shrugged.

"Yeah bro, unless you get smoked," Mathews argued. "Then none of that cop talk'll matter."

"We only get so many opportunities in life to stand up and help people. I got no intention of passing up any because I'm worried about some dumbass, toxic mascu-bullshit teenager."

Mathews blinked and shook his head.

"As long as you're trying to help someone and not just angling for a fight," McCabe suggested, glancing diagonally across the table at Stone to gauge his reaction.

"McCabe, anybody could see those punks would turn tail quick. I've been far too tired to go out searching for a fight for at least half a decade. I'm not going to walk past some kid that needs help though, and honestly neither would any of you. I just saw the thing first."

"Fair enough," McCabe answered and took a swig from his pint glass.

The waitress returned with their steaks and they all dove into their meals.

Mathews disappeared to smoke a cigarette when he'd finished his food. McCabe eventually asked the waitress for their checks, only then realizing Mathews had already paid for the entire tab.

CHAPTER 7

After dinner they cabbed back to South Beach and wound in and out of the various bars and dance clubs along A1A and Ocean Drive, eventually landing in a packed nightclub with a concrete floor and high ceilings affixed with swirling colored lights. Pulsating house rhythms radiated off the walls as the sweating twenty-something crowd in low-cut designer halter tops and popped-collared pastels partied under the spasmic flashes of primary color. They cheered with their hands in the air at the start of each song, adjusted their movements to the new sound, rocking in sync while grinding against each other to the gyrating beats.

The guys headed to the bar, where McCabe had to shout their order. The four of them stood awkwardly to the side, taking in the scene. "This is where it's at," Mathews began, his eyes scanning the crowd. "There's gotta be a bachelorette party in here somewhere we can link up with."

"Ha! Not even you're that fuckin' lucky!" McCabe called back, passing out bottles of beer. "We can have some fun here though for sure."

A few tracks played before Mathews took the lead, maneuvering into the crowd, angling toward the far end where he'd apparently identified a group of unaccompanied ladies that looked reasonably open to some male attention. McCabe followed, then Conner, though Stone remained on the sideline leaning against the bar, sipping ice water from a clear plastic Solo cup.

When the music broke between songs Mathews immediately leaned in, saying something into the ear of an athletic-looking dirty-blonde. A moment later he was pointing at McCabe and nodding before extending a lanky arm to grab Conner's shoulder and drag him toward a petite brunette who seemed just shy enough that she smiled when he appeared in front of her. Conner blushed a bit, as thoughts of Joselyd filled his mind. He hoped the quick succession of blues, yellows and reds from above would keep the girl in front of him from noticing until his face cooled.

Another song passed and they were dancing together. The tight crowd helped, forcing them against each other in a way that seemed natural. The alcohol had taken just enough of the edge off that Joselyd drifted into the background, though a persistent twinge of guilt remained on the forefront of his emotions. Conner's eyes flicked to McCabe as if for guidance from an older brother in the same situation, but McCabe smiled broadly, his hands resting on the hips of the dirty-blonde in front of him. He leaned forward, whispering something in her ear that made her throw her head back, cackling with laughter.

McCabe caught Conner's gaze, but didn't interpret it as an ask for advice and instead thrust an open palm in his direction. Conner instinctively completed the high five and when he did McCabe looked so happy Conner couldn't help but grin back.

"Wooo!" McCabe let out, loud enough to divert the attention of the people around him.

Mathews glanced up from a spunky, dark-haired girl with a pixie cut he'd connected with and burst into laughter seeing McCabe's uncontrolled release of emotion. As techno sets rolled past, the brunette in front of Conner pressed herself tighter and tighter against him. If he focused on what was happening it seemed crazy—having some sexy stranger he'd barely talked to this close, her ass exerting so much friction in just the right place.

McCabe passed each of them shots, and then double shots. Time began to blur. In one moment he glanced over to see Mathews doing his best to hunch forward, barely making it possible for him to lock lips with the much shorter girl standing on her toes in front of him. Seemingly moments later Mathews was fighting his way back through the crowd with another round of drinks for everyone. *I need to pull a Stone and start drinking water,* Conner thought, though he took the beer that was handed to him.

Speaking of... Conner's eyes slowly meandered to the spot against the bar where Stone had been. Even through the crowd and ever changing wash of colored lights, he knew Stone was no longer there. *How long since I saw him? More than an hour? Two hours?* Conner shook his head, unable to tell.

When the girls huddled up and made a move for the restroom together, Conner attempted to make his way toward the bar. But McCabe wrapped him up with a powerful arm bringing him into an off-balance three-way hug with Mathews. They swayed heavily to one side and then found their way upright again. A ping of annoyance hit Conner until he freed himself enough to glance up at his friends' faces. Seeing their goofy smiles, he couldn't help but laugh.

The girls returned and pulled him back onto the dance floor before he could escape to search for Stone. It felt late when they broke away. The brunette hugged him tight and kissed his cheek, which—despite being way more innocent than any of her dance moves—sent what felt like electricity radiating across his skin. He watched the small group of ladies make their way to the door.

"That's alright," Mathews let out, standing beside him, watching them go. "We'll get more."

Conner shook his head. "I'm not sure I want more. I feel like I just got a two-hour-long lap dance."

Mathews produced a sly smile. "Ain't it great? God, I've missed America."

Conner patted his friend on the shoulder and did a lap around the bar searching for Stone but he didn't see him. There was another room attached to the main space with its own bar but he wasn't in there either. Conner looped around the place again but it was becoming clear Stone was no longer there. He stood against the wall and let his eyes drift through the crowd. *Would he have walked back to the room without saying something? I don't even think he has a key. It's like back in the day before cell phones were a thing. You'd spend half the night looking for your friends when you tried to go out.* Conner let out a long exhale and decided he needed some air.

Outside was still hot and humid, though much cooler than the dance floor. After standing there a moment doing his best to wipe the sweat from his forehead, he moved south on Washington Avenue. *Take a walk. Try to sober up a bit.* Joselyd was back in his head and so was that nagging guilt. *All you did was dance.* His mind shifted to the brunette. *It didn't mean anything to her, she didn't even slip me her number, or hang around giving me a look like she wanted me to ask.* He reached up and ran his fingers through his short hair. *It's over, quit thinking about it.*

Turning left toward the ocean, he strolled past a foul smelling alley lined with dumpsters that ran between two rows of expensive hotels. A dark-skinned man with a nappy beard eyeballed him as they moved toward each other. Watching him closely—unsure why he was receiving extra attention—Conner's fists clenched as they neared. When they passed the man leaned in, "I got weed, dank shit." Conner smirked and shook his head without breaking his stride.

Rounding another corner, he went by a series of closed restaurants, their outdoor tables and chairs still crowding the sidewalk. Ahead of him were the bright pastel lights and blaring Latin dance music of Mango's Tropical Cafe. People had spilled out onto the street smoking and laughing. Inebriated ladies chattered away, wobbling heavily off balance in their stylish heels as their preppy-looking boyfriends conversed in loud drunken woots beside them.

Half a block up, a similar scene unfolded outside a club blasting rap music, lit with blue neon lights. Instead of maneuvering through the debauchery again, Conner cut across Ocean Drive to a stretch of sandy park interspersed with palm trees. The moon was so bright it didn't even seem dark, with the exception of a few paths that led to the beach through foliage covered dunes. It struck him as odd as he continued on—gazing through the empty park and then across the street to the roar of music, colored lights and crowded sidewalks—the way people grouped themselves so tightly together. It reminded him of landscapes he'd seen from the air, especially at night. It didn't matter where you were in the world, there were bright clusters of lights all concentrated together, and then broad swaths of nothing. *This is just a microcosm I guess. Surely there was some psychological explanation for it—the way people behave. Evolutionary maybe, the desire to be close to others and perhaps stay out of danger.*

His mind drifted as he moved on, wondering how much of our actions were really us, and how many are driven by primordial desires we only understood on a basic level. Ahead of him a string of tall hotels jutted upward, breaking the night skyline with their rows of lit floors. *About time to turn back toward the street, catch up with the guys.* His peripheral vision registered something in the shadows of a beach path. As his eyes flicked to the spot his heart rate spiked and the lean silhouette of a man materialized from the darkness. In a world where every other person seemed to be moving, this man stood motionless, watching him approach.

"What's up, Conner?" the silhouette asked.

His pulse steadied as his buzzing mind realized the man was Stone. Conner took a breath and hoped Stone hadn't seen fear on his face in the moonlight. "Ya doing alright, man?"

Stone nodded.

"Hanging out by yourself?"

"It was too loud in there. I've been on the beach watching the ocean. It's been a while since I've seen it."

"Well alright man, that's nice."

"Yeah, it's kinda like when things are quiet, only it's not. It's better because of the sound of the waves coming in and out. It covers up all the ringing in my ears."

"Yeah, that makes sense." *Another reason to quit working on jets.* "I'm glad I don't have that shit any worse than I got it."

"Uhh, drives me crazy... Sorry, I wasn't trying to complain, a bunch of guys get out with injuries a whole lot worse than tinnitus."

"You're not complaining man, just speaking truth."

Stone's eyes drifted away from the rows of lights lining the red walkway of Ocean Drive and back into the darkness, toward the water. "That first winter after I left, I took my van down into Baja, slept on Playa El Coyote for almost a month. It's in a little inlet off the Gulf of California. Fucking beautiful man. I'd just ride my bike in the hills on Route One, or hang out and watch the water. There are little islands right off the coast, and this old guy I met would let me borrow his kayak sometimes. There were whale sharks, thirty feet long. The water was so clear I could look down and see them perfectly. Every detail, every speck of color on their backs in the refracted sunlight. It was incredible. Nobody bothers you down there. Anyway, I think that was the last time I saw the ocean."

The sound of the sea was there, the waves crashing in and then rushing back out, but he had to focus to hear it through the mix of R&B, house, and Latin beats competing on the street behind him. "Well," Conner finally offered, "you wanna come back inside? There's a little bar off the main room that's not so loud."

Stone shrugged, but took a step toward the street when Conner gestured.

They'd made it around the block and almost back to the club when they passed a clean-cut teenager with a smooth Latino face. "Miami's herbs and spices."

Stone stopped mid stride, turned toward him slowly and looked him directly in the eyes.

The boy flashed a smile as he gazed back. "It's good stuff. I can cut you a deal."

Conner stopped too, squinting at his friend. "Come on man, let's go."

Stone made no indication that he had heard him.

The teenager swallowed hard, his eyes flashing briefly to Conner before focusing back on Stone. "Good deal, I promise."

Stone leaned in without breaking eye contact. "You're better than this, kid. I can see it in your eyes. You want more outta life than sitting at home getting high and watching old sitcoms while you eat Froot Loops, that's probably why you're out here slinging. But this ain't the right way to go about it." Stone took a deep breath. "In your heart you probably know it. This will only lead you to trouble."

The kid's eyebrows drew together but his gaze remained locked on Stone.

"I know you think you're smart and quick and you probably are. But at some point you'll just get unlucky. All your stash and cash will end up confiscated or stolen, and then whoever fronted it to you will come looking, and you end up doing something more dangerous to try and catch up. Next thing you know, you're in real trouble." Stone straightened back up. "Get outta this, kid. Go do something that helps people. Make some legit money so you can go all the places you wanna see."

The teenager swallowed hard again and Stone turned away.

Conner shook his head. *I certainly wasn't expecting that.* When his friend was alongside him again, they continued down the sidewalk together.

Stone pivoted on his barstool to glance at Conner. An incessant backdrop of bass vibrated across the room from the opening to the dance club, and though the crowd had thinned, a dull murmur of conversations swirled around them. "I saved a baby once," Stone said.

Conner stared back waiting for some form of punch line, but none came.

"Toddler maybe, I guess. Too young to talk in any case," he took a breath. "Shannon was always good at looking at kids and knowing stuff like that. What they needed or how to make them laugh or how old they were. I never had a clue."

"Yeah? I guess I could see that. I don't know anything about kids either."

"Anyway, I was coming outta Target, and for whatever reason this tractor trailer was making its way super slow across the front parking lot. Moving like two miles per hour. It was strange 'cause normally all that kinda stuff goes straight to the loading area in the back, but there it was.

"I stood there in front of the store watching it because it was blocking my path. From somewhere off to my left, this grocery cart comes flying into the parking lot. There's this little boy on the kid seat with his legs hangin' down. He had dark skin and curly hair that shot up in a wisp that bounced around as he moved. I remember him sittin' there, his big brown eyes staring at his hands, holdin' onto the handle like nothin's wrong at all."

"Really?"

"Yeah, it was too quick for me to do anything by the time I saw it. The whole parking area was on a hill, but by some bit of luck the grocery cart went nose first into the middle set of semi tires. When it hit, the kid's head jerked back with so much force, I couldn't believe he was still just sitting there—

totally content. The cart bounced off and came straight back a few feet in the street, perfectly perpendicular. That truck was moving so slow that when the cart rolled forward again, it hit the back set of semi tires which whipped it around in a three quarter spin and the damn thing went pretty much under the trailer. Only the edge of the basket with the kid in it was sticking out, and the trailer was moving just behind his head. The rear wheels were coming straight at it and when they caught, the cart was doing these violent little sideways shudders as the rubber on the tires kept trying to pull it under.

"I was in a dead sprint at that point. In front of me the baby was still hanging onto the handle with one hand and smacking it with the other, like they do. Then I could hear some lady behind me screaming. Not even words really. Not that I could make out anyway.

"I had to break my stride and take quick little short steps at the end to slow down and not run smack into the trailer. When I grabbed the cart handle, the basket was caught on the rear wheels. I yanked back as hard as I could. It skipped and bounced on the tires for a second as I pulled, they'd kinda gripped the cart. It was like it was sucking it in. I don't know why, but when I yanked back on it the second time the thing broke free. Another second it'd have all gone under and been crushed."

"Damn, man." *We've all been through crazy shit, but Stone always seemed to get a little more than his share.* Conner took a breath, his eyes still locked onto Stone. *Why's he thinking about this now though?*

"Yeah, I still remember it perfect, even though it was almost ten years ago. The lady was screaming and the kid was sitting there staring at his tiny hands. The frame of the cart was bent and it wouldn't roll right. It kept going sideways while I was trying to push it up the hill through the parking lot. The lady was all fat and super upset and I just brought it up and gave it to her. Honestly, I was pissed because she about got her baby killed just 'cause she let her cart roll away, so I didn't say anything. I just waited until she grabbed ahold of the basket then turned and walked away."

"It's a good thing you were there, man. Otherwise there'd be one less kid in the world."

Stone's mouth seemed to force itself into a frown and his slate-gray eyes showed a slight hint of emotion.

Conner's eyes narrowed as he watched his friend, "Stone, you alright?"

"Of course," he replied, turning toward the bar where his water glass stood alone. "You running low, whatcha drinking?"

Conner held his gaze on Stone's face as he flagged the bartender with his casted hand. "Honestly man, I'm good. I've had enough tonight."

"That's not how the world works. You want someone to listen to your dumbass stories, you gotta buy 'em a drink. Unless that someone is a fine-looking lady, then you have to buy 'em a drink and say something interesting. Jack and Coke still your go to?"

"Sure," Conner shrugged.

"Another Jack and Coke for my friend." His lower lip flinched as he stared down at the polished red oak bar in front of him. "I hope I actually saved that kid. I hope he's somewhere now—eleven or twelve—being happy and not in some shit situation. I hope his mom took better care of him after that."

"I'm sure she did man, after a scare like that. She probably took incredible care of him."

Stone ran his fingers through his close cropped sandy-brown hair then turned slowly, his face straight but his gray eyes filled with emotion as he stared up at Conner from the bar stool. "I really hope you're right, Conner."

"Hey, I gotta talk to you," Conner called over the dance music.

"Always brother," McCabe replied, "but I can't hear shit." He gestured toward the door before turning and calling to the group of girls he'd been dancing with. "I'll be back for you ladies!" He bent forward and slinked playfully backward, pointing at them as he went.

"Whoaaa! What a night!" he howled on the street. "Of course I'm getting married now, after I've finally learned to kick ass being single." He held his arms wide open and tilted his head toward the sky, letting out a long slow breath. Dropping his hands to his sides he looked back down at Conner. "What's up, dude? You having fun, brother?"

"Hey man, listen, I think Stone is messed up."

McCabe stared at him, then glanced away, exhaling hard. "Yeah, no shit he's messed up!" McCabe's eyes darted back to Conner. "What was your first clue? That he lives in a goddamn van? Or that he used to be a super-fun charismatic guy and now he's all serious and quiet? I told you he was messed up earlier and you wouldn't believe me!" McCabe turned away and brought his hands up to cover his face.

"Well, what do you want me to say man? I was wrong, you were right?"

McCabe spun around facing him again. "I want you to go back inside and drink drinks and dance with girls and have a great fucking time! It's my bachelor party!"

Conner tilted his head slightly as his eyes narrowed.

"Look, we all went through shit. We all deployed over and over again with damn near no break and flew shit tons of missions. Worked under legit, no-bullshit stress. We all went on aero medevacs and picked up bodies and got covered in cancerous oil while we lost our fucking hearing and got shot at, as our parents were home alone getting older with their medical problems and our girlfriends found better options. This weekend is about forgetting all that shit and being together to have fun on my last hurrah before I'm locked down for life."

"What about Stone?" Conner persisted.

"What about Stone?"

"We need to help him."

"How have you not figured this out yet? You can't help anybody! Neither can I, neither can anybody else!"

Conner stared at him unflinching.

"People gotta save themselves. That's the only fucking way out."

"You don't believe that."

"The hell I don't!" McCabe exhaled and gazed up, his eyes seemed to settle on the moon amid the radiant city lights tinting the night sky. "I tried to help Stretch and now he's gone. I tried to help Lewis and he's disappeared." His eyes drifted back down to Conner's face. "Look at you. I left for California, and you were in a flaming death spiral, and now you're doing great. I don't even gotta ask you, I can just see it in your eyes. Ya saved yourself."

Conner squinted at McCabe, "What do ya mean Lewis' disappeared?"

"I mean he's fucking disappeared! His phone doesn't ring, straight to voicemail. It's still him, but you can't leave a message because it's full. No new pictures on his Facebook in two years."

"Maybe he's maxed with classes and stuff or did a semester abroad or something."

"Mathews drove all the way down to Raleigh—before he transferred to Japan—talked an admin girl into dishing out some info in the name of health and welfare. He never made it through his first semester."

Conner shut his eyes tight. "WHAT?!?"

What the fuck is happening to my friends?

He took a slow methodical breath before opening his eyes.

"Well, Stone is right here. He hasn't disappeared."

"Yes, and if he wants to set his shit aside and have fun with the rest of us, he's more than welcome. I got him here, I can't help it if he wants to sit at the bar by himself, drink water and babble about cryptic shit I don't understand."

"Why'd you invite him if you don't even wanna talk to him?" Conner snapped.

McCabe's eyes locked onto him. The two glared at each other. Conner wasn't sure if he'd ever stared this intently at any of his friends before. Somewhere deep within he wished Joselyd were there. He'd never been in conflict with McCabe in his life and he didn't like it at all.

"Because," McCabe began, "he's my best fucking friend. You all are! Stone and Stretch and Mathews and Lewis and you, Conner. You're my best fucking friends and I wanted everyone to be here and be ok and have fun together just for one fucking weekend, without any of this bad stuff happening. I want us all to be happy together one time.

"Now Stretch is gone and Lewis has disappeared and Stone's messed up and Mathews seems different and I'm really fucking glad you're doing great Conner, I really am. I'm glad that you're doing great and that I met this amazing girl I'm going to marry..." his voice broke, "but I don't know what to tell you right now.

"When somebody is in this you can't help them. It's like they're surrounded by this translucent barrier." He held his hands up in front of him as if pushing on an invisible wall. "You can see all these terrible things happening to your friends but it's impossible to get in and do anything about it. You're locked out and all you can do is watch while it falls apart." McCabe took a deep breath and turned, taking a few steps away. "They can only save themselves."

Conner swallowed hard. "What the fuck am I supposed to say when I can feel it happening and… and, and he's talking to me and I want to help?"

"You say," Mathews' voice came from the side, making Conner flinch as he wheeled around. "Hey bro, I care about you, and I know things are rough, but you're tough, so keep fighting and don't never give up."

Mathews' face illuminated as he dragged on a cigarette. "Then you invite 'em to any fun thing you do and hope they show. If they don't, you don't get mad. You just try again."

McCabe paced on the street. Inhaling and exhaling deeply before rejoining them. He stuck his fist out and Mathews tapped it with his own. McCabe turned to Conner, "you just say something human. Something real. Not some bullshit that you think is funny or you heard in a movie or you don't really believe. Something human. That's all."

The anger in McCabe's eyes had dissipated, but they still felt intense as Conner stared back. There was another emotion there, one he couldn't identify. Conner swallowed hard, somehow afraid to blink or look away. It felt like McCabe's gaze was cutting through him. Asking tough questions: Where have you been for the last couple years while our friends were falling apart? How could you not know Lewis had disappeared? That

Stone was in a van? It felt like McCabe was peering into his soul. Demanding answers.

McCabe exhaled slowly, he blinked and when his eyes opened they appeared softer. He leaned forward and draped an arm around each of his friends' shoulders.

Mathews moved quick to hold his cigarette away and blow the smoke off to one side.

"I'm so glad you guys came," McCabe muttered. "Let's go back inside, have some drinks and dance with more girls before I fucking get sentimental." He grinned as he pushed them toward the entrance.

CHAPTER 8

Conner tried hard to force his eyes open as he recognized the smell of bacon and the sound of eggs frying. The room was already full of light and his eyes blinked back shut trying to adjust as he registered a dull headache and overwhelming urge to down copious amounts of water. When he opened his eyes again he realized that the twin bed across from his was empty, just a tangle of sheets where Mathews had been. With a groan Conner willed himself upright and moved toward the common area.

"About time, you lazy bastard," Stone gibed.

"G'morning," Conner managed.

"Ibuprofen and Gatorades are on the counter, bacon and scrambled eggs are under the paper towel there. Help yourself. If you want over easy, tell me now. You want anything fancier than that then fuck you, you're on your own," Stone said passing him a plate.

"This will be fine, thanks man."

"Hell yes, it's my pleasure. This is nice, I haven't had a stove to cook on in a minute."

"You roll out early and pick all this stuff up?"

"Yeah, you were sleepin', ya bum. I took Mathews to get the rental car and grabbed groceries on the way back."

Conner sucked down half a Gatorade with two pain pills and made himself a plate. "Where's McCabe?"

"Left for a run on the beach a while ago."

"That man is dedicated."

Stone's eyebrows raised, his head tilting to one side as he ran a hand through his short sandy-brown hair.

Conner squinted at him. "What?"

Stone shook his head, "Nothing."

Conner continued to stare at his friend.

"Not my place to say," Stone added, shifting his attention to making his own plate before sitting down at the counter next to Conner. "Eat up!"

They made their way to the parking area after they'd finished. Stone needed Conner to help him tighten up a few bolts on his vehicle. Conner gulped as they approached. The Ford E250 cargo van was a dull white with a hodgepodge of scrapes and dents. Bits of old company decals remained on the faded paint. A plastic luggage carrier was mounted to a roof rack atop the van, likely holding all Stone's possessions that weren't contained below. *McCabe was right. Stone is living rough.*

There were no windows beyond the cab and when Stone opened the side doors Conner didn't really want to gaze inside—afraid he'd be haunted by the conditions his friend had been living in. But when he looked, the interior surprised him. The original floor had been removed and replaced by sheets of steel then covered with painted pieces of plywood—jig-sawed to a near perfect fit around the raised wheel wells on either side of the floor. It was clean. A bunk was hinged laterally to the far side wall and strapped up with retractable legs to allow more space when not in use. Various shelves had been strategically fitted to the van's interior to provide storage space for an assortment of tools. Secured to the near wall across from the bunk was a bicycle. Beside it hung a Camelbak, the exterior covered with customized pouches and sheaths guaranteeing easy access to a variety of essential gear—including a bright red canister of bear spray.

Actually, this don't look so bad. Conner nodded, glancing up at a series of solar powered vent fans pulling hot air out through the metal roof. The idea of traveling around the great American West—hiking or biking all day in some remote and beautiful countryside—flashed through his mind. He pictured himself sitting outside the van in a camp chair reading a book as the sun set in the distance. When the light faded, he would gaze up at a magnificent bowl of stars before climbing inside the van's bunk and drifting to sleep. Then to wake up and do it all again the following day.

Would Joselyd be into something like that? At least for a summer? Maybe after I'm out of the military. That girl works though, she's so dedicated... I might be able to convince her to take a break. He imagined her lying beside him on a blanket, in some far off meadow as the evening sunlight shifted toward the magic hour—taking all the vibrant yet fading colors in together.

"Man, this is alright," Conner said. "I was a little worried when McCabe told me you were living in a van. The image

I had was you wandering around eating out of trash cans or something. I knew you were doing just fine, though.”

“I keep it looking pretty rough on the outside. Trying to deter anyone from breaking into it. I like things to all be tight and functional inside though, I’m not a total bum.” Stone had a tool box open and was snapping an extension onto a socket wrench. “I love McCabe, he’s an amazing friend. But he doesn’t have an imagination. You step off that path and he gets concerned. Even if ya tell him you’re fine.”

Maybe McCabe was just a little off base. Stone seems solid still, even if he has changed a little. Showing up here right on time. Helping that kid out at 7-Eleven. Waking up early and cooking everybody breakfast. Even as he thought it, though, his eyes drifted to a set of tags on the front seat, one for khaki pants and the other for a Hawaiian shirt. Conner shook his head. *No big deal, people buy new clothes all the time. Makes sense he wanted to look good to hang out in Miami. It’s not like he’s in disguise or something.*

Stone lay on a piece of cardboard beneath the van as Conner worked to tighten the bolts anchoring the shelving mount from the top.

“I attempted this on my own a little while back,” Stone explained. “I clamped vice grips to the nut underneath to hold it and tried to work it from the top. They kept popping off. Some things are just way easier with two people.”

“Here to help,” Conner responded before the steadily approaching blare of DMX rap beats made it impossible to hear.

What the hell? Conner thought, glancing up from the bolt he'd been wrenching down, out the cargo van's side door to the source of the sound—a charcoal gray Mustang GT convertible with black trim. Mathews looked at him from the driver's seat with a goofy grin and shades on, his head nodding to the rhythm.

Mathews turned the key and the music died. "What you boys doing working? We're on vacation! And we are doing it in style! We'll be cruising in this baby all the way up and down the Florida Keys, son!"

"Holy shit man, you sprung for this?"

"Hell yes, McCabe's going to love it! I got his driver's info on there too so he can have a good time."

"We even all gonna fit in there?"

"Haha, the front seat is comfy but the back looks a little cramped. I hope you boys packed light though, because all our stuff has got to fit in the trunk!"

"Good times," Stone answered with a smile. "You know I roll light." He leaned forward and bumped fists with Mathews.

"Finish up whatever you jokers are doing and let's pack up, grab McCabe and roll south! This pretty girl wants to move," Mathews grinned, massaging the steering wheel with his thumb.

CHAPTER 9

The summer air whipped over their heads as the convertible roared down Route One. The guys located their beach house on Marathon Key, dropped their bags, threw on swimming trunks and T-shirts and loaded up the provided snorkel gear before hitting the road again. "Gotta go! Gotta go!" McCabe repeated as he mashed on the gas and the Mustang accelerated across the Seven Mile Bridge. "We're cutting into our lobster time! Look how smooth that water is! Gotta catch dinner, boys!"

At the designated location on Big Pine Key, a burnt-out-looking beach bum type with a blond beard and hippy ponytail led them across a small network of interconnecting docks toward their boat. They passed a variety of other charter boats, high-end power boats, and further out, there were a few commercial fishing boats. The water around the dock was crystal clear and shallow, not more than waist deep.

"Whoa! Look at those monsters!" Mathews exclaimed, pointing into the water just below the planking at a pair of nurse sharks—each over eight feet long—resting on the sandy bottom.

"They're the peaceful kind," McCabe said, "They won't bother us."

"Fair enough bro, but I'm keeping an eye on any wildlife bigger than me, especially the kinds with teeth and fins."

The captain—a pudgy man in his thirties with a black beard, wearing shades, a sun shirt and a baseball cap—greeted them from the boat moored alongside the dock. "Make sure you fellas coat yourselves really good with sunscreen, it's brutal out here."

"Yeah, good call," McCabe agreed, stripping his shirt off and digging in his backpack for sunblock. He squeezed the white cream out into his hand before tossing the bottle to Mathews. "Your pale ass definitely needs some!"

"Whatever, Whitey McWhitester! Your Irish ancestry definitely didn't prepare you for the tropics!"

McCabe stood on the dock methodically rubbing the sunblock in before turning and facing away from Mathews. "Dude, you tryin' to get my back?"

"Bro! You shoulda gotten the spray bottle if you wanted me to do all that!"

"Come on dude, that's the important part!" McCabe spun back around. "We're gonna be floating around looking for these things with our backs toward the sun."

"Shit bro," Mathews chuckled, "you shoulda gotten your fiancée to rub you down before you left."

"And what, not showered for two days?"

Mathews shrugged, "I don't know bro, but I ain't rubbing no lotion into your back."

"Well how you going to get your back then?" McCabe demanded.

Mathews looked at him quizzically before shaking his

head, "Hell, I'd rather get torched than have your filthy, callused mechanic-hands all over me!"

"That's it!" McCabe announced, "Next bachelor party we are bringing at least one honorary woman, just to make sure we don't get wrecked by the sun."

The two stared at each other as the intense mid-day rays streamed down, McCabe frowned.

"I got it," Mathews asserted, nodding confidently. "Turn around."

McCabe turned his back to him and Mathews squirted a thick stream of sunblock in a zigzag pattern along his shoulders and lats. "Ahh its cold!" McCabe giggled. "Hey, aren't you gonna rub it in?"

"Nahh, hell no. Bro, brace yourself."

"What?" McCabe let out in a panicked squeak before laughing as Mathews' shoulders brushed against his own.

"Yeah, yeah, work that lotion in!" Mathews leaned back as far as he could rhythmically shifting his body side to side as his back and shoulders rubbed against McCabe. McCabe leaned forward as Mathews bent over backward against him. Then without a word, as if the entire maneuver had been a choreographed dance move, the two reversed their rolls, McCabe laughing hysterically as he straightened out and then began to bend backward against Mathews. "Yeah, work it, work it!" Mathews continued.

The boat captain shook his head watching them. "Oh, we're going to have a real fun time this afternoon, I can tell already."

"Come on Conner, get in on this so you don't get burned," Mathews chuckled, holding the bottle of sunscreen.

Conner raised his eyebrows and tilted his head slightly to the side before he shrugged, turned and pulled his shirt off.

"Work it, Work it!" Mathews repeated. "Oh yeah, oh yeah, gotta protect you from the sun. Work that lotion in!"

Conner couldn't help but laugh as he felt Mathews' back and shoulders rubbing against his own. "Alright, get off me!" he howled, "I'm protected enough!"

Mathews chuckled, stepping away, before glancing back toward Stone. "You need some sunblock?"

"The sun ain't hurting this skin, man," Stone replied, lifting a corner of his tattered gray Under Armour shirt to reveal that his deep tan didn't stop at his sleeve line.

"Fair enough, bro," Mathews answered before turning his attention to the boat.

They all climbed aboard as the captain cranked the dual Yamaha 200 outboard motors and the ponytailed man threw off the dock lines before stepping on after them. The captain idled the engines through the no wake zones before turning north—toward the Seven Mile Bridge—kicking up the throttle and putting the boat on plane.

Conner gazed back as they rumbled away. Two long arcs curved outward from their path, disrupting the clean blue reflection of the clear sky, as the boat cut a rift in the mirror surface of the water. Big Pine Key receded in the distance until it became a dark organic strip of green that hugged the ocean horizon.

"We'll try this spot here," the captain said, cutting the engines and gesturing for his assistant to drop the anchor. "If this don't work, don't worry, I know some easy spots over by the bridge pylons, I'll make sure y'all catch enough for dinner."

The ponytailed assistant passed out nets with corded loops to attach to your wrist on their metal handles, and four-foot long aluminum rods with a distinct forty-five degree bend near the end. "These are your tickle sticks, fellas."

"Damn, this is a couple inches longer than the one I'm equipped with," Mathews answered.

McCabe smirked as he shook his head, "Would ya shut up and listen to the man, he's going to show us how to catch these critters."

"I'll jump in and make sure we're in a good spot," the assistant said pulling his mask down, "Then I'll show you fellas how ta do it and point some holes out."

The ponytailed man went overboard with a splash, bobbed up for a deep breath and then dove down. McCabe, Mathews, Conner and Stone all stood there in the bright sun staring at the water where the man had disappeared. Almost a minute went by before he broke the surface again. He gasped for air before holding the net out of the water to reveal a dark gangly-looking rock lobster. "Good spot!" he called up, before swimming to the boat and exchanging nets with the captain who dumped the lobster in a livewell built into the fiberglass hull.

"Alright," the assistant called, lifting his snorkel mask up to rest on top his head, "These rock lobsters ain't got no claws or nothing, they don't fight, they'll turn ta face ya then they try ta get away. They swim backward like a crawdad." He held his net out of the water, "Ya just find their hole, and cover it with the net, then ya slide the tickle stick back through it with the bent end facing out," he demonstrated as he spoke. "After that ya just twist it like this, and slowly pull it back. When the bent part touches them, they think the threat is coming from within and freak. Be ready with the net, they'll whip straight outta their hole in a hurry. Jump in when ya fellas are ready and I'll point out some spots for ya."

"Trouble from within is the most dangerous kind," Stone muttered. "Ya have to fight, there's no way to escape."

Mathews turned squinting at Stone. "Bro! I'm trying to get my tickle stick in a hole here and you saying a bunch of semi-poetic metaphoric bullshit like that is wrecking the mood."

"Apologies," Stone responded before pulling off his shirt. A jagged pink curve streaked across his abdomen and onto his right side, contrasting his dark sun tanned skin. The discolored scar was ever so slightly sunken, breaking the natural contour of his skin where there must have been a small amount of tissue loss. Stone bent forward stuffing his shirt into his backpack and producing a roll of waterproof duct tape and a narrow sheath made of thick 8 mil plastic. "Somebody help me out," he asked, nodding toward his casted hand.

The three of them gaped, Conner's mouth actually dropping open.

"Bro, what the fuck happened to you?!" Mathews let out.

Stone squinted back at him, "I can't get the cast wet. I gotta keep it on a few weeks yet. I don't want a bunch of ocean water in there."

"No dude," McCabe cut in, "That ten inch hooked gash you've got mended up on your side."

"Oh," Stone glanced down at his abs, "yeah, that ain't anything. It looks way worse than it was because I didn't get it stitched up by a doctor or nothin'. I just used a shit ton of butterfly bandages and put a couple knots in it myself with some regular thread. You know how scars always look way worse when you patch 'em up yourself and let 'em heal on their own."

"What the fuck happened?" Mathews repeated.

Stone shook his head, "Man, I just tried to help somebody who was in trouble," he took a deep breath and let it out slow. "What they say is true I guess, no good deed goes unpunished." His eyes drifted down as he shifted the duct tape and strip of plastic to the exposed fingers of his broken hand. Seemingly subconsciously Stone palmed his abdomen, his index finger settling on the long divot where the mark lay before tracing it across his side. "Yeah, I spent eighty bucks at CVS buying bandages and antibiotic cream trying to fix myself back up. It took this thing damn near a week to stop bleeding and it hurt like crazy every time I moved. The thing that really sucked though, was I was so scared it would get infected, that every twelve hours I'd clean everything out and dump peroxide on it all. I've never cussed so much in my life." He paused, shaking his head. "Here, help me out," Stone held his casted arm out toward Mathews.

Conner stood on the gently rocking boat, holding his net and aluminum rod, watching Stone slide his arm into the plastic as Mathews held it open. Conner took a slow deep breath and forced himself to look away from Stone. His eyes caught McCabe, whose muscular arms were crossed and face held a steady expressionless pose behind the reflective lenses of his sunglasses, as if he were calculating pot odds in a poker game before making a call. Then just for a moment his lower lip trembled, and a tear appeared on his cheek bone beneath his shades. With a quick shrug McCabe brought a shoulder up to wipe it away as he turned toward the water.

Conner allowed himself to bob there on the surface in the warm water. His body felt the ever so gentle rise and fall of the ocean as he tried to regulate his breathing and become accustomed to sucking air through the snorkel. *What a crazy world.* He stared down—eight feet below—at blocks of colorful coral which began abruptly, jutting up from a bottom of turtlegrass. A school of bright yellow fish—each around the size of his hand, with two black streaks across their heads and squiggling neon blue lines running the horizontal length of their bodies—weaved in and out of the coral as a group. In the middle distance a sea turtle glided effortlessly through the water faster than he'd ever imagined they could move. Tiny halos of refracted light danced across its shell as it slid through his field of view. *This whole other world hidden just beneath the surface. All these colorful fish darting in and out. A full-on underwater National Geographic episode. No doubt complete with thousands of daily rhythms and micro dramas for survival, all acted out in secret from the outside world.* He began to relax, his breathing became almost normal. Somewhere in the back of his mind he wondered if there were other worlds he moved through every day yet could not see. *I guess there is no way to ever really know what's happening just below the surface.*

Conner jerked as larger forms appeared below him, ripping him from his train of thought. His heart rate quickened before his mind identified them as humans in this alien underwater seascape. He could see the ponytailed man pointing out a cleft in the coral block, then Mathews covering it with his net and inserting the aluminum rod. But before he could complete the task he began frantically shaking his head and kicked his way back to the surface. The assistant followed a few moments later. Stone arrived and seemed to be working hard to keep his casted arm down, with the net in place. It appeared incredibly buoyant and after fighting it for half a minute he too returned to the surface. McCabe showed up next, kicking every few seconds to hold himself down as he positioned the net and delicately inserted the rod. A moment later a dark mass shot out of the hole, long legs and antennae thrashed—entangling themselves in his net—as McCabe turned upright and headed topside.

Conner pulled his head above water and side kicked toward his friends. A round of cheers went up when McCabe held the net above water, revealing his catch. Mathews attempted to give him a high five, but they didn't make a solid connection. It seemed to be a difficult maneuver while treading water with a piece of lobster catching apparatus dangling from each wrist.

"It's legal," the captain called from their boat after measuring the spiny creature's back shell and placing it in the livewell.

"I'm getting the next one!" Mathews called in excitement.

"The hell you will! I bet you I pull in three before you snag one!" McCabe answered with a smile.

Mathews and McCabe each took deep breaths and dove down together, the assistant chasing after them to point out more holes. A minute later they surfaced and dove right back down. When they reappeared, Conner made his own attempt. He was surprised at how quickly the pressure mounted in his ears. Staring into a dark crevice, he tried to maneuver the net and rod into position, but felt as if he'd run out of air almost immediately, before he ever had a real chance to catch something.

Treading water and trying to catch his breath, Conner saw the guys surface, and a few minutes later dive again, this time McCabe returning with another lobster. Conner watched through his snorkel mask as Mathews—more motivated than ever—dove down again, determined to bring something back up with him. He finally succeeded, holding his net up high as he gasped for air, then, grinning, he slowly kicked toward the boat.

"Doesn't count until it's on board!" McCabe called, swimming past him with a third lobster in his net.

Mathews sprang to life, grabbing McCabe's ankle and pulling him backward to take the lead. The two tussled in a fit of splashing before Mathews freed a lanky arm, extending his net the last few feet to the captain in the boat. Mathews exhaled in triumph, leaning back to float chest up in the calm aquamarine water.

"I almost had you, you cheating bastard!" McCabe yelled, passing his own net onto the boat.

"Nobody laid out any rules, Brackish," Mathews answered in exhaustion.

"Florida Fish and Game did," the captain called. "Sorry buddy, yours is too small." He held the lobster up against the metal device used for measuring to show them, then tossed the fortunate creature back into the water.

"HA!" McCabe crowed, "too small!"

"Yeah, yeah," Mathews retorted. "I can assure you that's the first time I've ever heard that in my life!"

"Since you've been in Japan maybe!" Conner laughed. "Those girls have little hands!"

"Yeah, yack it up, it ain't like you two have bagged anything for dinner yet."

"I got something," Stone responded. "Not sure if we can keep it or not. Is flounder in season?"

Stone's three friends squinted at him from the water as the captain chuckled on the boat.

"It's definitely big enough," Stone continued, as he slowly kicked his way toward them, his casted hand under the water presumably holding the net closed.

The captain shook his head, "Let me see what you've got. I'm sure it's not a flounder, I've never seen one in the Keys and I've been fishing here since I was fourteen."

Stone peered up at him confidently, "Unless there's some other fish that lays on its side and buries itself in the sand, I do."

The captain tilted his head skeptically as Stone approached, but his eyes went wide when the net was lifted from the water to reveal the speckled brown fish. "How the hell did you catch a sixteen inch flounder in a lobster net?"

"I saw him lying there on the edge of the coral hiding in the sand so I netted that thing. Prodded him in with this," he said holding up the aluminum rod.

"I can't believe it, that's some serious luck. I've never seen any in the Keys at all."

"Seriously?" Stone asked.

"Absolutely. I know one old guy who claims to have caught two back in the seventies off the bay side of Long Key. I always thought he was full of shit."

"Well, let him go then," Stone suggested.

"Aw, you don't wanna do that," the captain replied, "these things are good eatin'. You ever had one?"

Stone shook his head, "Nahh but, if they're not normally here, I don't want to take one. Maybe if I let him go something good will happen."

"Something good did happen!" McCabe blurted out. "You caught a damn flounder while you were diving for lobsters!"

"No, I mean, maybe it's the last one in the area, or maybe I let him go and they make some kinda comeback or spread back down here or something. Then lots of people can catch them."

"You're crazy if ya have him throw that thing back," McCabe insisted.

"Yeah, turn him loose, I don't feel right about it. I'll catch some lobsters instead."

The captain shrugged and shook his head, then pulled a digital camera out of the boat's console and snapped a picture before dumping the fish back in the water.

"You certainly have an interesting moral code," McCabe commented.

"If it doesn't feel right it doesn't feel right," Stone replied.

McCabe shrugged.

"Come on y'all, pile back in. I'll take ya to an easy spot before we run outta time."

There was a buildup of coral and barnacles around the thick concrete pillars of the bridge, and the lobster holes were only a few feet underwater, making them much easier to reach. Together they pulled up more than a dozen over the next hour. Mathews claimed he was officially worn out and that he'd bagged more than he could eat and climbed back onto the boat.

Conner, who had caught two, but mainly floated and watched, followed him a few minutes later.

The livewell was full and the captain had pulled an Igloo cooler out from under one of the bench seats to store the overflow of lobsters. Conner found his shades in his bag and leaned back on one of the bench seats gazing up at the open blue sky. As the boat gently rocked, he wished Joselyd could be there with him. He pictured her lying beside him with a big, fun smile, giving him that look the way she did with her dark playful eyes. He could almost see the way her bright white bikini contrasted her tan skin. *I hope the guys all get to meet her one day. We'd have such a blast. She'd fit right in. I'm sure she could hold her own with these guys better than I can. Maybe one day when everyone is paired off, we could all get together as couples, rent out a place at the beach for a whole week together.* Conner smiled as he imagined it. The heat of the bright Florida sun felt good on Conner's skin as his body began to dry.

"Yo, Mathews, maybe we should plan something like this every year? Or at least every other year. Maybe McCabe could bring his wife one time, and if we all had girlfriends we could bring them too."

Conner continued staring up into the clear blue space, even smiling as he thought about it. *I could lie here like this all day.* The methodical sway of the boat in the warm sun coupled with the sound of waves lightly lapping against its side as he began to drift off. *It feels like that train ride years ago in Germany, only it's completely different.*

"Hey Mathews," Conner tried again, wanting to share his idea before he passed out. When no answer came, Conner forced his eyes open, glancing back to see his friend. Mathews stood in a corner of the power boat's stern, leaning back slightly against the fiberglass transom with his hands at his sides. His face seemed completely void, as if he weren't really there. Conner sat up and turned toward him, quickly realizing despite his blank exterior, there was something distraught deep within his friend's light blue eyes. Mathews didn't meet his gaze, he appeared to be fixated on the cooler in front of him.

"Mathews," Conner called.

His friend's eyes shifted to meet his.

"You alright, man?"

"Bro, I don't know how everything can just be ok, and then end up so fucked up."

"What are you talking about, man? What's fucked up?"

"I should have said something. I mean, I did, but I should have done more. And our goddamn government bro, those mugs set me up for failure."

Conner stood up. "Hey, help me out here, I'm not sure what we're talking about."

"I'm sorry, I'm sorry," Mathews whimpered. He crashed down on the bench seat nearest to him and brought his forearm across his face as if to wipe away tears, but there were no tears. He exhaled hard, unzipped the backpack laying near him and pulled out a forty. He took a slow deep breath and let it back out before glancing up toward Conner again. "Did you want a beer, bro?" he asked, extending it toward him.

Conner shook his head.

Mathews pulled the tab, cracking it open, then tilted the can back and took a long pull. Locking eyes on Conner again he swallowed hard and said, "Hey, good day huh? Nice sunny weather, and I caught more spiny lobsters than I can eat so ol' Brackish can't give me shit," he exhaled and gulped again. "Out here with all the guys, it doesn't get any better than this."

"Absolutely," Conner agreed, "great day." *What the hell am I missing?* His mind churned as he stared down at his friend, and again wished Joselyd were with him. *She'd know for sure, she's so perceptive.* He turned and glanced at the water, hoping his other friends were on their way in, but McCabe and the assistant were still diving. Stone floated alone nearby but didn't seem to be making an effort to pull in more lobsters.

Conner sat back down on the bench across from Mathews but couldn't think of anything intelligent to say. Mathews was nearly motionless, just holding his beer and staring at the cooler on the deck. Conner shook his head and shifted his gaze out to the horizon. *I guess he's ok.*

It was another twenty minutes before the captain called the remaining guys out of the water, started the engines and pointed the boat back toward Big Pine Key.

At the dock their haul of lobsters was placed on one of the built-in fish cleaning tables. Conner watched with a kind of sick fascination as the captain donned a protective glove and proceeded to pick up the bucking creatures one at a time. In a fluid, twisting motion accompanied by a sickly, ripping crackle, he removed their tails. The remainder he tossed into five gallon buckets. They stacked atop each other attempting to climb away—long antennae flicking about—as their cold, unfeeling eyes betrayed no emotion whatsoever.

"Bad day to be a spiny lobster," Conner observed, as McCabe stepped up beside him.

"Yeah and look at them," McCabe nodded toward the pile of tailless lobsters attempting unsuccessfully to scurry backward, trapped by the bucket and entangled in one another's gangling limbs and extensive antennae. "They're dead and they don't even know it. Still trying to escape."

"Yeah," Conner answered, still staring.

"I can understand fighting until the end," McCabe continued, "But if it's clear I'm done I hope I just accept it and don't try to keep on running."

The captain finished his work and handed McCabe an aluminum tin where the lobster tails appeared completely civilized—all lined up in a row as if they were on ice beneath the glass of a seafood counter at the grocery store. *Perhaps it was easier for regular people that way. Not seeing the gruesome details demanded to facilitate the lives they lived. Lobster tails conveniently arranged on a tray ready for purchase, no visual on the trauma their former owners endured. Only the flag draped coffins rolling out the back of a C-17's cargo bay, never the horrific events that brought them there...* Conner shook his head, *where the fuck did that come from? Out of the clear blue on a nice sunny day like today.*

The saga didn't last much longer. Grabbing the two five-gallon buckets, the captain dumped them off the dock into the shallow water. In a swirl of fins and sand the two large nurse sharks which were still lounging motionless on the bottom a short distance away thrashed to life. The once-clear water churned into a cloud of disturbed sand as the sharks crunched through the spiny heads and shells of the rock lobsters.

And that's that, Conner thought, raising his eyebrows as he gazed down into the hazy storm, slightly disconcerted that there were two eight-foot monsters less than a yard away—just beneath the surface—that he could no longer see. *Though I guess anyone who understood what they were looking at would know they were there.* Conner made a mental note never to venture into a turbulent cloud of sand in an otherwise peaceful inlet.

Shaking his head, Conner turned to make his way across the network of interconnected docks toward the parking lot. McCabe was a few paces in front of him, striding tall, his broad shoulders and solid frame holding a steady posture though he seemed to be distracted. His head was turned slightly, tracking the guys as they traversed the perpendicular platform ahead of him. Mathews paused for a moment, offloading two dead forties and a few empty mini bottles into a rusty fifty-five gallon trash drum where the heavy wood planking met the asphalt. Further down Stone walked alone, his worn-thin, gray Under Armor shirt slung over his shoulder, hanging just above the discolored hooked scar stretching around his right side. His deeply tanned back contrasted the bright white cast on his left hand swinging beside him.

CHAPTER 10

"Beer in the grocery store!" Mathews chuckled, placing a case of New Belgium and a case of Blue Moon in the cart. "We must be south of the Bible Belt."

The cart was already half full as the guys meandered up the aisle of Winn-Dixie. Mathews darted off seemingly at random, returning each time with armfuls of groceries. "Gatorade for recovery," he announced, "a couple dozen eggs for breakfast, with cheese to go on top, and of course bacon!" He disappeared again and returned with nearly two dozen ears of corn. "Nothing goes with broiled lobster tail like some good ol' seasoned corn on the cob!"

"Hey man," Conner began, "You know we're only spending two nights at the beach house, and all day tomorrow we're going to be down in Key West and at Fort Jefferson right? I don't think we need all this stuff."

"Bro, live it up! We're on vacation!"

"Well sure," Conner responded. "But I'm not trying to drop my whole paycheck on food we can't even eat 'cause we got way too much."

"Who gives a shit, bro? I'll pay for it. We could be fucking dead next week. Let's have a good time! Drink beer and get fat while we can! When are we all even gonna see each other again?"

"Dude, when did you become such a hedonist?" McCabe asked.

"What the fuck did you just say to me?"

"Eat, drink and be merry, sure, but we're in Florida not ancient Greece."

"I got no idea what any of those toga-wearing, orgy-hopping jokers were doing back then and I don't care." Mathews held his lanky arms out to his sides spanning the width of the grocery aisle. "Also I don't know why you waste so much of your life reading about shit that happened forever ago and doesn't mean a damn thing anymore. You think anybody a thousand years in the future is going to give a flying fuck what we're doin' now? Not a chance."

"You know why we study history?" McCabe shot back.

Mathews stood there staring at him with his arms outstretched and said nothing.

"To learn what ordinary people did in extraordinary situations. It helps you, gives you a little perspective and ideas for the way you might want to respond to events in your own life. It'll make you think about what kind of person you want to be, and what kinda person you don't."

"I know what kinda person I am," Mathews barked, dropping his arms and taking an aggressive step toward McCabe—drawing the attention of several elderly patrons at the far end of the aisle who stood watching with uncomfortable expressions. "I'm the kinda guy," Mathews quickly closed the remaining distance, thrusting his index finger into McCabe's muscular chest, causing him to tense, "who wants Old Bay on his lobster tail. Where the hell you think the spice section is in this place? I ain't had any Old Bay since I left the East Coast." Mathews flashed a grin before spinning around and strolling down the aisle, his eyes flicking between the shelves and the overhead informational sign, then turning the corner and disappearing.

Conner glanced side-eyed at McCabe, who smirked, shook his head, exhaled and turned his attention to Stone.

"He's got a point," Stone remarked, "Old Bay might be pretty good on lobster tail." His eyes shifted down to the cart, "And now we'll have something to season the five ears of corn apiece we have to eat."

Mathews bent forward, staring through the oven window. "Oh yeah, oh yeah, oh yeah!"

"Are they done?" McCabe asked from behind him.

"Fuck yeah! Toss me those oven mitts!"

Mathews took the baking sheet of steaming lobster tails out from under the broiler and slid it on top the stove. "Come load up, boys! It's on!"

The guys stacked their plates up with lobster tails, corn on the cob, baked potatoes and green beans. They took up positions at the dinner table and tapped the necks of their beer bottles together. "This looks great," McCabe smiled.

"I'm straight up excited," Mathews answered. "Let's just stop for a second and not take this for granted. What an amazing time we live in. Here we all are after an incredible afternoon swimming in the tropics, and literally a few days ago I was in Japan, McCabe was in California, Conner was on the East Coast and Stone was somewhere in the Rockies. At no time before in human history have normal people been able to not only travel across the world to see each other, but communicate so easily to ensure it happens. We live in a golden age!"

McCabe nodded, rubbing a pat of butter across his corn as it melted. "It's really great of you guys to use your leave and money to come down here and hang out. Means a lot to me."

"Of course," Stone responded.

Mathews slogged down some more of his beer. "A golden age!" he called again. "I mean, think of it, we were so far apart! Now we're here together! And even the military... I know the first time I realized how lucky we are to come up when we did. Remember when we were doing those troop rotations so the Army guys in Iraq could get a three day R & R in Qatar? Imagine the resources our country has to be able to make that happen and get people a few days off. I'm sure they needed it, the fighting in Iraq was for real then, like it is now, but the infrastructure wasn't built up at that point. Half those guys were sleeping in the dirt and fighting off sand fleas. It was like a hundred and thirty thousand troops they rotated. Never before in history could a government have made that happen. We're in a golden age I'm telling you."

Conner swallowed hard as his mind instantly leaped back six years to the fall of 2003. They'd been hustling for weeks, continuously turning the aircraft in an effort to facilitate their normal cargo mission in addition to the Pentagon's decision to give every service member in Iraq three days off—out of country.

That was all well and good. None of us minded working extra to help those guys catch a break. They certainly deserved it. But anytime that rotation came up, it was the news of the Chinook helicopter getting shot down that flashed through Conner's mind. *Maybe I wouldn't even remember it at all if it weren't for that. I mean it's a war, we heard about guys getting hurt and killed all the time. And often we'd hear about it and then half an hour later be launching an aircraft to go medivac the injured or pick up the bodies. We knew it could have been people that we'd actually flown in there to begin with. Drop 'em off in a war zone then come back and get them when they get fucked up... or make it to the end of their tour—whichever happened first. That's just part of it.*

But that Chinook was different. I used to think about it all the time. Maybe because the military was trying to do something nice for its people for a change. Getting all those guys out of the country even if it was only for three days. Then that helicopter was shot down and those sixteen guys died and a bunch more got hurt. They'll probably never be the same. And then the Iraqis, I mean, it's easy to get mad and think we should bomb that place back to the Stone Age—here we are trying to help them out and they're killing our fucking people. But that's not the whole truth either, that chopper was rotating guys out somewhere near Fallujah, as hostile of a place as you can find.

Of course it was going to get shot at. And even still, locals ran from the nearest village to try and help the guys who survived after the Chinook came down. That's complex enough.

But it all happened because the military was trying to do something nice. I think that's why it really sticks with me. Guys fucking taken out because they were on their way to take a break. Maybe I just never knew how to feel about it. It was so unnecessary, they could have just stayed in place and they'd all have been fine... but then, the government was trying to do something good and give them time off. I guess it still bothers me 'cause I still don't know how I feel about it. Maybe 'cause there's no one to get mad at, since the leadership was making an effort to do something decent and a bunch of Iraqis tried to help when things went bad...

"You alright Conner?" Mathews asked through a mouthful of green beans. "You ain't even touched your food yet."

"Yeah sure," Conner nodded.

McCabe's dark eyes focused on him.

Conner gazed back, concentrating hard on not revealing his emotions and wrecking everybody's good time. *One more thing I've never been good at.* He swallowed hard again, picked up his fork and looked down at his plate, hoping their attention would pass.

"What's wrong, bro?" Mathews persisted, fragments of corn kernels flying from his mouth. "You need another beer?"

Conner shook his head as he attempted to load his fork up with baked potato.

"Ahh come on Conner, I bought cheese and sour cream and

butter and everything for the potatoes. You deserve a little more flavor in your life, bro! Load it up!"

Conner reached for the sour cream without making eye contact, though he registered a frown forcing its way onto Stone's face in his peripheral.

McCabe looked at Mathews out of the corners of his eyes. "Hey, let's just not talk about any more Iraq or Afghanistan shit for a little bit."

Mathews stopped chewing and locked onto McCabe for a moment before shifting his gaze around the table. "Yeah, absolutely, let's not ruin all this good food thinking about the damn desert." Mathews jumped up, stepped into the kitchen and returned, placing three cold bottles of beer down in the center of the table and another water in front of Stone. "I'm sorry guys. Let's have some more drinks and enjoy these lobsters we caught with our own hands!"

"These are good," McCabe agreed, "but they have a real distinct flavor. I'm not sure how many I can eat tonight. They're not like Maine lobsters at all."

"I've never had a Maine lobster," Stone admitted. "They taste different?"

"Way different," McCabe answered.

Mathews nodded in agreement, licking his fingers and then plowing into a new ear of corn.

"Basically they cost a lot, they're juicy and have a real good texture," McCabe continued, "but they're not super flavorful like crabs. They really only taste like the butter you dip them in."

"Why's everybody so into them then?" Stone asked.

"'Cause they're a thing," McCabe laughed.

"Yeah," Mathews agreed with his mouth full of corn. "Guys like lobsters for the same reason that girls like flowers. Because they cost a lot and fresh ones are hard to get!"

CHAPTER 11

The guys dealt some serious damage to the feast in front of them but when they'd finished there were still more than a half dozen lobster tails and a plate stacked high with corn on the cob. Dishes clattered in the adjoining kitchen where Mathews had the water running.

Conner grunted and waved off McCabe when he tried to pass him another beer.

"If you can't run with the big dogs you gotta stay on the porch."

"Shit man, I drink another beer and I'll be asleep. All that sun today wiped me out, and now I'm trying to fight off a food coma on top of it." Conner rose slowly and made his way to the couch.

McCabe shook his head, "You ain't even on the porch, you're still yipping at the screen door."

Conner leaned back and shrugged. "I might pass out anyway."

The sound of water running in the kitchen stopped and Mathews appeared in the doorway.

"We've got the yin and the yang here," McCabe gibed. "Between being on Pacific Time and partying it up, I'm not sure Mathews has slept since he got off the plane."

"I'll sleep when I'm dead," Mathews retorted.

"That's no way to live, man," Conner responded as he leaned back on the couch cushion and closed his eyes.

"You don't concern yourself with how I live," Mathews answered, twisting the cap off another Blue Moon. "That's between me and God."

McCabe groaned.

"What?" Mathews' eyes shot toward him, "Something wrong with the way I'm living my life?"

"Who am I to judge?"

"Then why'd you make that obnoxious little noise?"

"How you live your life is up to you, brother. I was more reacting to the fact that you alluded to some supreme being having involvement in it all."

"What? You don't believe in God?" Mathews asked with a little smirk.

McCabe shook his head. "There ain't no god to believe in."

"Of course there's a God," Mathews responded. "Don't be fucking ridiculous."

McCabe shook his head again.

"You're just angry Brackish, and it's about to get a whole lot worse now that you've limited yourself to the same slice of booty for the rest of your life."

"I'm not angry," McCabe answered.

"Sure you are, you've been angry for years. I thought this woman you're marrying might brighten you up a bit, but you've still got all kinds of darkness hidden down deep. You need to stop worrying about everybody all the time and take it easy."

McCabe shook his head again, "who says I'm worried?"

"Me!" Mathews countered. "And anybody else who actually knows you."

"No."

Mathews exhaled, "All that worrying and no beliefs, huh? You're full of shit."

"We were born, we are here on Earth for a very short period of time and then we're gone. After death I suspect you'll experience something very similar to what you did before you were born."

"You don't believe that."

"I do."

"When I met you, you didn't think that way." Mathew's eyes narrowed, "You've got a Celtic cross tattooed between your shoulder blades!"

"I was nineteen! I grew up Catholic, it took me a while to realize it was all bullshit. What do you want from me?"

Mathews' eyes drifted to the floor. "That's the easy way out, bro. Pretend like nothin' matters."

"Oh yeah, it's easier for me! I'm sure it's much harder to believe all your friends and loved ones that have passed are waiting for us in some great afterlife than to believe they're just gone." McCabe shook his head, "Don't you think it's a little suspect, that whatever religion you pick, they all end in some type of reward? Either the kingdom of heaven or eighty-eight virgins or your own planet that you're the king of?"

"I didn't say nothin about religion," Mathews snapped back. "I said there's a God."

"What's the difference?" McCabe scoffed.

"I got religion, sure, but I ain't one to tell somebody mine is right and theirs is wrong. That defeats the whole purpose of being in America where people are free to do what they want."

"Well you certainly drink a lot for someone who believes there's a greater purpose to everything. What's the purpose in all those beers you've emptied?"

A smirk crossed Mathews' face, "Benjamin Franklin said 'Beer is proof that God loves us and wants us to be happy.'"

McCabe shook his head, "Conner, will you talk some sense into this dude?"

"Man, you guys are on your own. I used to think about this stuff all the time when I was young. I'd wonder about everything, heaven and hell and whatever else is in between. At some point though, I realized I can't get to any answers, so what's the benefit in sitting here questioning everything. I decided to just be the best person I know how to be and I'll find out what's next when my ticket gets punched."

"Way to commit to something, Conner," McCabe responded.

"You planning on riding the fence on every issue in your entire life and into the afterlife?" Mathews asked. "Go drink another pilsner."

The three of them stood there in silence, before McCabe turned to Stone. The other two seemed to involuntarily follow McCabe's gaze to Stone's sharp, intelligent gray eyes.

"Are you asking me?" Stone questioned, looking back at the three of them.

McCabe nodded.

Stone sucked in a deep breath and allowed his eyes to flick between his companions. "Religion is man's invention. It uses stories and fables to encourage faith and try to sculpt society a little for the better. It attempts to imply an order, a set of rules that most likely only exist in our minds. It institutes this 'lord works in mysterious ways,' 'everything happens for a reason' philosophy to try and help people make sense of the chaos. People crave it. They're starving for it. So desperate that people who don't have religion come up with their own shit to believe in—reiki stones or mediums or hidden meanings in their zodiac signs, or even messages from their gut microbiome.

"Now I'll never believe anything in this world is happening for any kinda reason. That's shit people come up with after to make themselves feel better. I've seen way too many horrible things that don't have any kinda purpose to them at all. But the rest of it? Who am I to tell anyone any different? I can say that it's almost certainly there to fill a very specific void in peoples' lives involving meaning."

"There ya go," McCabe scoffed. "At least somebody else around here has some sense."

"He didn't say he didn't believe in God," Mathews barked.

McCabe glared at him before turning back to Stone.

"God?" Stone asked, "I can assure you, with almost complete certainty, there is a God."

"How's that?" McCabe mocked.

"Because I've felt it. The presence I mean, like way down deep in my core and all around me at the same time."

"Well I haven't, so I guess we'll have to agree to disagree."

Stone nodded in silence.

"Wait," Conner said, leaning forward on the couch. "What do you mean you felt it?"

"There's no way to describe it," Stone answered. "You'll know if you ever experience it. It's not an easy thing to do, for me at least."

"What do you mean?" Conner persisted.

"Well, it's only happened to me under some pretty specific circumstances. Like, I've always been alone, and out in nature for extended periods. I think that has something to do with it. All this," Stone gestured to the ceiling lights and kitchen appliances, "I don't know if you could ever feel it in an environment like this. It's too big of a distraction. You're not in tune with anything. If you're out in nature though, without all this—where it matters what time the sun sets, because you won't be able to see afterward, which way the wind is blowing or if it's going to storm and you don't have civilization and technology to protect you—you get real dialed into a very different world than we experience here every day."

McCabe tilted his head slightly, "yeah, what else?"

"I've only felt it when I was completely and utterly exhausted. Not from lack of sleep, but from sheer long distance endurance exertion. Like when my bike is loaded down with gear and I've been peddling for eighty or a hundred miles. But even still, it's only when it's been days on end like that, and normally only when I still have a long way to go."

"What's it feel like?" Mathews asked, his eyes intently locked onto Stone.

"Like I say, it's hard to describe, but it's a real comforting feeling. It's like, I'm pressing really hard with so far yet to go, my body is exhausted, and my mind is in tune with everything around me, and then there's this comforting sensation that I'm not out there alone."

McCabe nodded slowly but said nothing.

"It's easy to forget," Stone continued, "later, when I'm back in all this," he swirled the index finger of his casted hand around toward the ceiling lights. "Easy to talk myself out of it, and pretend it didn't happen. But I know what I've felt, and it's happened more than once.

"I figure, the farther back in time you go—the less technology there was and the harder people had to work out in nature—more people experienced it and religion was popular because they wanted answers."

"Hey," Conner asked, "why'd you say 'almost complete certainty?' Sounds to me like you believe."

"Oh I believe," Stone continued. "But I can't rule out the possibility that somewhere in my DNA there's some bit of code that gives me this sensation when I'm pressing hard like that and I need to keep going. It could be some kind of survival trait to give me just a little push to make it, and be more likely to pass my genetics onto the next generation." Stone took a deep breath and exhaled, "That's something that only occurs to me in the air conditioning, under the electric lights. I don't think it's true, but I can't disprove it."

"Well, I certainly can't argue with any of that… Cheers," McCabe stepped forward and tapped his beer bottle against Stone's water glass.

It seemed like a long time passed before Mathews broke the silence. "Sit down fellas, let's lighten things up for a bit." He shuffled a deck and began dealing the cards out into four piles on the table.

"What are we playing?" Conner asked.

"Is that a for real question?" Mathews scoffed.

"Hearts," McCabe answered. "Just like old times."

"Lewis or Stretch was normally our fourth, but I'm sure you can handle it, Conner. I know you filled in a few times back in the day," Mathews continued, his hands working quick as cards flicked around the table.

Stone pulled up a chair with a sly smile. "It's been a minute, guys."

"Like you forgot," Mathews muttered. "You're the only joker I knew who could non-stop jabber to everyone around you and be counting cards the whole time."

"Can't do it anymore, I forgot how."

"How to count cards?" Conner asked.

"No how to jabber," Stone answered.

McCabe chuckled, "Well that I believe, you ain't said a lighthearted thing since we met up yesterday."

"Yeah bro, what the hell?" Mathews huffed. "It's like I don't even know you anymore! You and McCabe both need to take it easy. Conner and I are the only chill ones here!"

"Philosophy and cards don't go together," McCabe continued, "so you'll have to reconnect with your mindless banter or come up with some other way to divert attention from your attempts to shoot the moon."

Stone grinned as he picked up his cards. "I don't know what you mean."

The cards went around, and then around again. Conner's mind drifted to Joselyd. *Why don't we play more games? I can't complain, that girl works a lot, she always stays fit, and she's educated, she likes to read. Plus we go on walks together, but we never play games.*

"Pay attention Conner, you just bit it again!" McCabe let out as Mathews dumped the queen of spades on him. "We're going to have to start loading somebody else up with points. We can't let Conner bust a hundred before we get Stone out of the lead."

"You're certainly welcome to try," Stone answered.

They went through a few more hands before McCabe began playing Linkin Park on a portable speaker from his iPod. "It's too quiet in here. I never thought I'd say that with Mathews present."

Mathews shrugged and tipped his beer back again.

Conner dropped another card and Stone laid his whole hand down, shooting the moon.

"Damn! You're the devil!" McCabe yelled, throwing his remaining cards in the center. "I even know what you're doing and I still can't stop you."

Stone shrugged, shuffled the cards and dealt them out again.

"The only times I could ever even get close to beating you were when Stretch was playing. You'd be jabbering nonstop about all kinds of funny bullshit, and that dude would be sitting there all quiet, not saying a damn word the whole time. Then sometimes about halfway through a hand I'd see your demeanor change ever so slightly, and you'd start dumping big cards and usually get stuck with some points. And ol' Stretch, he'd just sit there, and I'd see him make eye contact with you and do his little Midwestern half grin. It was like you guys were playing your own secret game against each other and the rest of us were there but not really in on it all."

Stone nodded slowly, "Yeah, Stretch was smart. He didn't miss a thing. I couldn't pull anything crazy unless I really got dealt a barn burner. Though I'd still try."

Conner's mind continued to drift as the cards played out again. *Perspective was interesting really. If I were seeing this when I was in middle school. I'd think it was the coolest thing in the world. A few Air Force guys, drinking beer and playing cards, no parents in sight. And now I'm here and it's fun and everything, but part of me is wondering what my girlfriend is doing, and another part of me just wants to go to sleep.*

His mind moved on, thinking about all the guys who must be deployed right now, playing cards in the tents or dorms in between shifts, cause they're stuck out there waiting to go back to work and they don't have anything better to do. *How many times has that been me? How many times have guys throughout history been far from home sitting around a card table? It's odd to think of it and then realize you come back home and do the same thing because that's what you got used to when you were gone. Maybe it's like those IPAs Mathews was talking about, they put all the extra hops in there to preserve it so the British soldiers could drink it in India, and then they got so used to it they wanted it after they left. 'It became a thing.'*

McCabe eyeballed him from across the table, "Pay attention Conner I took a lot of bullets last hand trying to keep you alive."

Conner nodded, "I got it this time man. I'm focused."

The first few tricks played out. McCabe regarded Stone before glancing toward Mathews.

"I can't stop him this time," Mathews answered the unasked question. "There's nothing I can do, I don't have the cards."

McCabe exhaled hard. "It's you and me Conner. He hits this one he wins. I have to break hearts."

McCabe tossed the six of hearts onto the clubs' trick. Stone pulled the cards in and then came back leading the ten of hearts.

"Ballsy move!" Mathews let out.

"Get him, Conner!" McCabe urged.

"I'm gonna make him eat it." Conner said, following suit with a lower card.

"Dude, you better know what you're doing," McCabe uttered.

"Don't worry," Conner answered. "I got a fist full of heat."

Another trick passed and then another, until only two cards remained in each of their hands, and Stone was still in the lead. McCabe stared at Conner out of the corners of his eyes.

"Don't worry man, I got this," Conner professed.

"I do believe you're all out of clubs." Stone dropped the three and five to the table at once, and then raked everyone's remaining cards in shooting the moon again to win the game.

"You lucky bastard!" Conner let out slamming down the ace of diamonds and the ace of hearts.

Mathews shook his head. "That wasn't luck, he's been playing for that since the beginning. You weren't paying attention."

"Bullshit!"

"Believe what you want," Mathews answered. "But it's hard to say it's luck when he's shot the moon three times in the last ten hands, and none of us have gotten close."

"How could it not be?"

"Well, it's not that complex Conner." Stone grinned, "We're playing with a finite set, that's all. It's not like life where you can try your best but there's always unknowns you never even dared to have nightmares about lurking just out of sight. Here there's only fifty-two cards. A set number of possibilities. Even knowing all the cards that are out there, sure, it could still be tough if it were all completely random, but it's not. There's rules, and a certain order to it because I know what everyone else is trying to do. Then I just watch all the cards that come out and at some point I have to make a decision. Either go for it, or start shoveling off high cards so I don't get slammed."

"How's it even fun if you gotta pay that much attention?"

Stone shrugged. "I don't know, but I'm having a good time."

"Alright boys," McCabe said, shuffling the cards again, "One more game? Then I'm passing out. Early wake up for Key West and the Tortugas tomorrow."

The guys nodded and McCabe began flicking the cards around the table again.

CHAPTER 12

Conner paused, stared at himself in the mirror. He blinked and finished scrubbing his face and brushing his teeth. It was late, but something seemed to pull him toward the ocean instead of his bed. When he stepped outside his eyes landed on Stone, standing there alone in the dim light, gazing up at the night sky. Conner watched him a minute before disappearing inside, returning with two cold bottles of water and standing beside him. Stone never spoke. "How's it going, man?" Conner asked after another minute had passed and handed him a water.

"Just thinking," Stone replied, "I like that it's dark here. You can really see the sky. It won't last long. Soon the moon will rise and all these bright stars will appear dim."

"Thinking about what?"

"It's stupid," Stone opened the water bottle and took a drink. "Stupid and complicated."

"Try me."

Stone let out a long exhale. "Alright, so ya see all these stars out there?"

"Sure," Conner nodded.

"Well, all that light is coming at us, from millions of miles away. It all takes so long to get here that those stars might not be there anymore."

"Right, we all learn that in middle school science, mind blowing in the moment but just sort of a fact now."

"Exactly," Stone answered, "but think about what that means. All that light keeps going after it passes us by. It'll go forever, an endless monument to a star that at some point will have been dead for millions of years."

Stone's gray eyes shifted about, as if honing in on distant points in the starlit sky. "Now, think about all the light from the sun, the moon, from the stars, from anything that's ever happened out there in the universe, it all hits the earth and some of it reflects off, sending all these millions of different light projections of earth into space. An infinite number of them really. All different intensities, all different directions, every imaginable angle, all flying out into oblivion. And they won't stop. They'll continue on forever."

Conner sipped his water and waited.

"It's a record, an unimaginable number of records actually, streaming out for all of eternity. A record of every fucked up thing anybody ever did to anybody else."

"Hey now, people do a lot of good stuff too, if you're saying that human history is out there flying through space, it'll have plenty of mothers cradling their babies, fathers taking their sons fishing, big brothers protecting their younger siblings, and friends like you and I standing here together lookin' up at the stars."

"Yeah," Stone replied. "But ain't nobody'll pay attention to any of that. People will just focus on all the horrible things."

"Well, it doesn't matter. If it's all bouncing off us and rolling out into space at the speed of light, nobody is ever going to see it. It's gone."

"Nothing is ever really gone," Stone responded. "It's going on forever, out there, just like it hangs indefinitely inside our minds. That's what I was just thinking about. All those stars and black holes with light bending gravity, all the nebulas of reflective gases that could act like mirrors. Even with the earth doing laps around the sun, the sun traveling through the galaxy, and the galaxy hurtling through space, one day one of those millions of projections is going to find its way back here. Maybe it already has. I hope nobody ever builds a machine powerful enough to interpret all those scrambled light waves and allow them to see the terrible things we've done to each other."

Conner swallowed hard and searched for something to say, but nothing occurred to him. *Perhaps because there is nothing to say? That's not true, there's always something that can be done—I just don't know what it is.* His eyes flicked to the side of Stone's face, then back up to the sky as his mind continued to search.

"It's..." Stone began again, "haunting."

The rhythmic crashing of the surf in the distance suddenly reminded Conner of that whole other world of coral, bright colored fish and marine life he'd seen that afternoon, all hidden beneath the waves. Even though on some level he always knew it was there—from the National Geographic documentaries his father watched on PBS when he was growing up, or pictures of scuba divers in magazines—it had remained just far enough out of sight that he never paid attention to it. Somewhere deep in his mind he wondered if there was another hidden world above—or remnants of one anyway—coming at them in the form of light from millions of years ago.

"I went to college once, for a semester," Stone offered. "I don't know if you knew that. But anyway, I took this philosophy class. The professor, he said that in the western world, we see things linearly. A, B, C, one, two, three, and so on. Series of events, cause and effect. It's in our culture, it's taught to us, it's how we perceive things. It's wild just thinking that that whole concept was driven into us by our society."

Conner took a breath. "Well sure, that's the way it is. How else would it be?"

"So we see life like we are floating down a river. It starts real slow, a narrow stream of water and we can't really remember it. But as we travel through, we're growing and we experience the rocks and rapids and turbulent sections, and we also go through the calm, slow, steady pools and pleasant enjoyable parts.

"It's so ingrained in our society that it's even reflected in our art. Thomas Cole did a series of paintings back in the eighteen hundreds called the *Voyage of Life*, depicting the different stages on a river. It's interesting, because art is supposed to be outside the analytical, broadening our minds to new points of view. That couldn't have been a new concept though, even back then. But anyway, that's not the point. What I'm trying to say is, that's how we see it, us traveling through a series of fixed points in time from beginning to end until we're done.

"There's an eastern religion, I can't remember exactly

which one now, but they don't envision it that way." Still gazing up, Stone took another drink. "They think of it like your life *is* the river. The whole thing, all at once. It's on a path but it's not linear like. For instance, we see it as hitting a rapid and things are rocky and turbulent for a bit until we get through it. They see it as all of your life up to that point is affected by what is going to happen. Because all those molecules of water from the droplets that roll out of the mountain snow melt into the beginning of the stream and continue down on the long journey to the ocean—their movements are affected by a rapid that may be weeks or months or a thousand miles away. From the beginning it affects everything about how they move, and it continues to affect them after they pass it, on their entire journey to the ocean.

"In other words, everything you already experienced is still dictating your movements now, and all the things you are yet to do, well they're affecting you now too." Stone continued to gaze up at the sky, his eyes slowly shifting from one point of distant light to another. "And all of it, all of it is radiating out there into space. A permanent record of everything we've ever done. All the good, all the bad, blasting into the universe at the speed of light, where it will go on forever."

The abstracts rolled through Conner's mind later as he stared up at the dimly lit void of the ceiling above his bed. *It had to actually be true right? Sure it is, light wouldn't disappear just because it passed Earth. So what would it look like once it ended? A long stream with every bit of light an object ever reflected, and then it just stops. It wouldn't be a flash, it would be years and decades and millennia long. Or it could be a flash... the brief moment that I pointed a flashlight to the sky on a camping trip with my dad long ago in the Adirondacks.*

It was strange to think that there were millions of reflections of Stretch out there, though they were far beyond the reach of anyone to ever see. *Maybe that vision I had of him pounding fist with Stone and grinning at me in the cargo compartment of the C-130. Or maybe an image of Stretch shooting Stone that little half smile as they played hearts together.*

He blinked and shook his head. *Best not to think about it.* His mind moved to the time—just a few weeks after he met Joselyd—that they huddled in the small park pavilion with strangers during a thunderstorm. She had joked with the family's terrified little kids, even getting the youngest boy to stop crying as the storm unleashed a rapid succession of instantaneous flash-booms in every direction. Later that night when the rain was gone, she cuddled up next to him, and they watched the sunset on the lake. How she tilted her head back and beamed as her dark eyes had focused on him. The way her fun smile melted. When he stared back wondering why she had said 'I want to put this moment in a bottle and keep it forever.'

He considered a reflection of her radiating out into the universe, bits of it finding its way to alien worlds or helping melt the ice of a distant comet. Conner closed his eyes and wished she were next to him as he drifted to sleep.

CHAPTER 13

"Come on Conner, get up! Let's go!" Mathews yelled, flipping the lights on—throwing the room into a blinding glare.

"Shit, I thought this was a vacation."

"Wake your goofy ass up, we're rolling out in ten minutes at 0500. I've been up all night waiting for you jokers, and I'm driving so I had to stop drinking at midnight."

"Shit man, it ain't my fault you're on Japan time."

"I don't want to hear it, McCabe got up and went for a run already."

"Seriously?" Conner yawned.

"Boats don't wait, let's go! Stone's got snacks on the table and don't forget your snorkel or your sub in the refrigerator."

Conner slumped lazily, tilting his head toward the sky in the back seat of the Mustang as it surged forward, pointing South on Highway 1. The open convertible top allowed him to gaze up at the stars, though they appeared dim and relatively scarce—the night was bright with moonlight. Cool predawn air whipped just over his head as they roared toward Key West.

It felt good, cruising down the road on a summer morning with his best friends in the world and the sky open above him. *I could sit here and look at this all night.* But as he thought, he felt that persistent grip of sleep closing around him. Somewhere deep in his mind a memory surfaced. He was on an over-night train crossing Germany to return to Ramstein in time for work after three days off in Berlin. The comfortable seat was reclined with a massive window beside him that wrapped onto the ceiling. Sitting there, he watched the snow-covered German countryside go by in the moonlight with that same peaceful thought—*I could sit here watching this all night*—and within minutes he was asleep.

When Conner nodded awake he leaned forward rubbing the sleep out of his eyes. Mathews in front of him drove in silence, right hand on top of the steering wheel and left elbow propped on the door frame. McCabe slumped forward in the shotgun seat asleep, his head bobbing with the minute dips and rises of the road. Stone sat to his right—staring past him, out to sea—with a far off look in his clear granite-colored eyes. Conner couldn't help but turn and follow his gaze to an erup-tion of color on the ocean horizon. The deep blues of the sky met the dark water at some distant point where a hemorrhage of faded pinks flooded the atmosphere before slowly trans-forming into light shades of red and eventually bright ribbons of orange as the earth spun to bring the sun into view for an-other day. *I wish Joselyd could see this.* He smiled, imagining her snuggled next to him under his arm. *I'm so lucky... I hope she gets to meet these guys one day. Have that group vacation I was thinking about.*

They boarded the Yankee Freedom for their ferry ride to the Dry Tortugas at 7:30. *Joselyd should be up getting ready for work by now.* Conner whipped out his phone and tapped out a quick text message.

> Hey babe, wishing you a great end of the week. On our way out to the Dry Tortugas, should be pretty awesome. You decide on any plans for the weekend?

The ship departed shortly after for the two-hour trip to Fort Jefferson. Once they were underway, a bubbly tour guide with a microphone began to explain the history of the Fort and its thirty year construction which began in 1846. She described its significance during the Civil and Spanish American wars, its use as a prison, coaling station and its eventual abandonment by the military in 1906. "If any of you have ever heard of the famous author Ernest Hemingway, he and his friends were marooned on Fort Jefferson for seventeen days in the 1930s after being caught in a tropical storm during a deep sea fishing trip." She went into the details before crediting FDR with designating the Fort as a National Monument in 1935.

Conner leaned back in his plastic chair thinking about what she had said. *A ten hour boat ride for Hemingway to make the Tortugas from Key West in the 1930s. Now nearly eighty years later it's just two hours... and really there's a ferry that'll bring you here. Ya don't even need to know how to sail. How different the world is now.* He pondered it as he gazed across the water—it seemed a lighter shade in this morning light—a translucent wash of turquoise and sea-green. *Maybe the world hasn't changed quite as much as it seems. If we wanted to go to some other little uninhabited island in the Caribbean or Gulf, there'd be no ferry to take us there. It could still be a real challenge that required a ship and the skills to pilot her.*

Seems wild thinking about it now, but it must have been normal at the time. I wonder if my grandkids will ever look back and think about all the times I crossed the ocean in the cargo bay of a turboprop aircraft. By then they'll probably never be able to imagine it.

Can't get from the East Coast to Europe in one shot, gotta stop for fuel in St. Johns, Canada. Then back in the air again—reclining against the red nylon webbing of the troop seats—everything cold and vibrating for thirteen hours straight. Can't talk to anybody 'cause you're wearing muffs and earplugs trying to keep from going deaf. Hopefully ya get some sleep 'cause when ya do finally land, it's straight to work on the aircraft. He shook his head as he thought. *Nahh... nobody that far down the line will ever understand. I doubt the people I went to high school with would even get it if I explained it to them now. People in commercial jet liners don't know what kinda luxury they got. Neither do I, I guess, cruising through the Gulf Stream on this modern ferry.*

Even a hundred years after its closure, the sheer mass of Fort Jefferson instantly impressed Conner. Its outer walls stood forty-five feet high, perfect rows of arched embrasures began two thirds of the way up, allowing sunlight to penetrate its eight-foot-thick brick exterior. A moat of sea water over twenty yards across surrounded the structure, which was only accessible via a plank bridge leading to the main gate. The hexagonal fortress encompassed the vast majority of the key, leaving only a few strips of sandy beach and small dune-grass covered rises along the island's southern and eastern edges.

"Holy hell," Mathews mumbled. "Those boys didn't mess around when they built a fort back then."

"No, they did not," Stone agreed.

"And they built this before anybody was even using electricity. We could learn something from them." Mathews gazed up, his eyes tracing the fortification's high ramparts. "All our guys do now is bulldoze a bunch of sand into berms around a perimeter, then set up some tents, blast walls, haul in a few shitter trailers and call it a day. If they put this kinda effort in now... with today's technology... we'd be living in luxury when we deploy."

"That'll never happen," McCabe sighed. "No place we've deployed will ever be in danger of becoming a national park either."

"Bro, you got that right," Mathews' face contorted into a grimace. "They'll be lucky if all the UXO's and landmines are gone in the next fifty years. Outside Kandahar people keep getting hit by anti-personnel mines from the eighties—shit the Russians laid trying to kill mujahideen—and I heard mugs are still getting wasted in Laos, and Vietnam has been over for damn near four decades."

Conner turned toward Mathews shaking his head. "That's fucked up."

"You're damn right. Anyway, enough of this depressing shit. You guys want to explore this bad-ass fort first? Then grab the snorkel gear and check out the beach?"

"Let's do it," McCabe waved them forward and they moved toward the bridge together.

Entering the gate they stepped out of the brilliant sunlight and crossed into a dark wall of cool shadow. The interior extended about fifty feet, before opening up onto a broad green parade field dotted with old growth hardwood trees. While the outside of the fort was a solid brick wall—its only openings the regularly spaced rectangular gun ports a half dozen feet above the moat's surface, and the high arched embrasures aligned directly above them, where a second weapon was once positioned—the interior structure consisted of hundreds of open archways. Each supported by a symmetrical network of thick brick columns.

"Those floors up top are masonry also," Mathews commented. "And I can't even imagine how heavy those huge steel cannons they supported were. What did that lady say? They could throw a three hundred pound shell five miles?"

"I think she said some of the guns weighed fifty thousand pounds," Stone answered.

Mathews stood there staring up at the interior of the fortress shaking his head. "Amazing some joker was able to design this place in such a way that all the weight from the guns, the shells, the powder and all the millions of bricks could get transferred down to these pillars and be effectively supported."

"Doesn't seem possible does it?" Conner agreed. "I know she said it was cracking in some spots, but it seems to me like those bricks on the bottom would have been straight crushed into dust a long time ago. Imagine the pressure."

"Yet here it is," Mathews continued. "Wild what they were able to do," he sighed. "Come on, looks like McCabe is heading to the second floor without us."

They stood on the midlevel of the fort under an impressive brick archway that had once housed a massive gun emplacement. Conner gazed down the wide corridor, illuminated only by natural light, which made its way in through the large embrasures that had once allowed rifled cannons to fire out to sea. The symmetry was remarkable—dozens of now vacant casemates lay in a perfect row under their own vaulted brick ceilings. The narrow world within the fort descended into a single vanishing point. It was almost like staring into a reflection while another mirror was positioned behind you.

"Absolutely incredible," Conner gasped, "What did that ranger lady say? Sixteen million bricks and thirty years to construct?"

"Yeah, and cracking under its own weight since the beginning," McCabe scoffed. "Kind of a metaphor for our government, if ya ask me. We're probably still paying interest on the construction cost of this place in our taxes every paycheck."

"Ahh come on, Brackish!" Mathews gibed. "You know better than to say that shit, a big history buff like you. You're lookin' at it all wrong. She said the vessels anchored on this shoal here—protected by the fort—guarded the shipping lanes for everything coming out of the Mississippi during the Civil War! That's how that works, you produce something, you gotta pay extra to keep that shit safe until you get it where it needs to be. Not to mention protecting the entire Gulf Coast from Confederate attack."

McCabe crossed his arms and stood there shaking his head. "You're such an idealist, dude. Don't you realize history was written by the winners? They tell whatever story they need to afterwards to justify their actions, and spending."

"Whatever bro, this place is fuckin' cool," Mathews shot back. "It's also amazing, I mean think of the logistics of it all—mid-eighteen hundreds, piss poor communication, and all the construction being done by hand—every bit of material delivered by ship. Not to mention keeping the seventeen hundred men stationed on this little island fed and supplied. It's a testament to what our country can do.

"I mean, think of the magnitude of it all. And the vision the mugs who created this place must have had. At some point this thing was just a sixteen acre spit of sand with nothing on it. Someone identified the vulnerabilities of the Gulf, envisioned this massive fort as a solution and then actually made it happen. Saved people from attack decades later in a war they didn't even know was coming."

"Yeah dude, and they never even finished it or fully armed the place. It was obsolete before it ever came to fruition."

"Bro, I can't even deal with you sometimes," Mathews barked. "You're so fuckin' negative. Look at the positive side of something for once."

"I've based my outlook off my life experiences."

Mathews grunted, shaking his head.

"Why's your ass so full of rainbows and unicorns anyway?" McCabe persisted. "All the shit we've been through."

"Bro, it's the same kinda situation. Think of it, honestly. You heard what she said, this place was plagued by disease, yellow fever and malaria. All those jokers out here, day after day for thirty years mixing mortar and laying bricks in the heat. You think that shit was fun? You think this was a vacation spot then? Fuck no, but they did it because it was important and now there ain't no threats to the gulf like there were then. They did their time and it was for something. They made everything better for us now."

"Dude, you just wanna believe that because you're trying to attach some kinda meaning to all the work we've done, all the time we spent away and the havoc it wreaked on our lives. I'll tell you right now, it's all going to add up to a big fat nothing."

"You don't know that. There's plenty of good things happening, even though the news only hones in on the bad shit. I mean, there's girls going to school in Kabul for the first time in decades. Before the US rolled in, the Taliban were executing people in soccer stadiums for fun. Sure, there's people dying now, but at least it's not a government sanctioned event."

"Give it time, those goat-fuckers over there have no problem strapping themselves up with explosives and taking out families in the town market or whole groups of guys waiting in recruitment lines for a job. It won't be long before everything is back to the way it was."

Mathews shook his head. "Have a little bit of faith, bro."

"I'm sure people said that during Vietnam, too."

"How can you be so negative all the time? You're dragging me down. First I'm not allowed to bring beer into the National Park and now I have to listen to your pessimistic ass spewing negativity all over the place! Whatever you're upset about, you need to get over it!"

"I'm not upset, I'm happy. I'm hanging out with my good friends on a beautiful island and soon I'll be getting married to an incredible woman. I just see the world for what it is, that's all. Only thing I do at work that matters is keeping the planes mechanically sound so hopefully nobody gets hurt flying on them. That and pulling a paycheck so I can build my life. The rest is all bullshit."

"You're wrong," Mathews stated shaking his head again. "I mean, look at Japan, I've been there a while now and of course they've got some problems, but really most things are fine. Sure the culture is different than ours, but it's a country full of mainly good people, just tryin' to go to work and pull a paycheck so their kids can grow up and go to college. Think of it. Their grandparents were worshiping the emperor as a god and committing atrocities all over the Pacific. The rape of Nanking, the Bataan Death March, then when they started losing the war they flew explosive laden aircraft into our ships. You can't tell me that shit was any less crazy than the suicide bombers now. If anything it was worse because the education level of the Japanese population in the 1930's and 40's was light years ahead of these clowns in present day Afghanistan. Fuck don't get me started on Germany, you know all the horrible shit they did, and a bunch of it to their own people. It's a great country now, too. A few generations from now Afghanistan will be completely different. It'll be a good place."

"Never going to happen," McCabe answered gazing out the embrasure to the horizon where the pale-blue sky met clear turquoise patches of sandy bottomed water. "We been there damn near eight years already, and the last time I was in Bagram, the airfield was taking mortar and rocket fire. Eight years and we haven't pushed them out of mortar range of our largest base? If you think anything is going to change you're dreaming." A light breeze came in off the sea through the arched brick opening in the wall. "Stone, tell him."

"Well hell, why you asking me?" Stone responded without turning toward them. "I'm not the end all be all, or even an authority on the subject."

"Because I don't want to talk about this anymore and Mathews won't argue with you like he does with me."

Stone took a deep breath and flexed his shoulders back as the breeze continued past them. "The truth is you're both right. There is nothing fundamentally wrong with the people of Afghanistan or Iraq that won't dissipate if they're put in a stable environment for twenty-five or thirty years. The problem is, the clock hasn't even started ticking yet. Outside Mazar e Sharif, most of Kabul and maybe a few parts of Kandahar, nothing in that country is stable. Iraq has all but been in open civil war for years, with Iran and al Qaeda stoking the flames.

"People need to grow up without fighting. These countries need a whole generation of folks who aren't wrecked with PTSD or blinded by the irrational burning rage that comes from senselessly losing friends and family members. They have to have a solid generation like that come of age and take power for things to get straightened out."

"Yeah? What about Germany and Japan?" Mathews argued. "It didn't take no thirty years there, the war ended, and for the most part people quit fighting and started to rebuild. The US even employed their militaries as a peace keeping force. When we asked them to, the Japanese rounded up their own countrymen who'd been accused of war crimes and turned them in. It was over."

"That's very true," Stone's gray eyes flicked to Mathews. "But that was a different situation. Tokyo along with the rest of Japan had been firebombed down to nothing. Atomic weapons were dropped. I read somewhere that eighty-five percent of Germany's male population between sixteen and sixty had been killed or wounded during the war. More than half of Germany's structures were rubble. The will of those nations had been broken and that's why the fighting stopped.

"That hasn't happened in these wars. Dropping smart bombs on suspected insurgent leadership simply doesn't have the same effect as leveling whole cities. Especially when we miss. It makes them feel emboldened, gives them time to learn from their mistakes and adapt to our tactics." Stone took a deep breath, "I mean, it's been almost seven years and bin Laden is still out there. For our government's approach to work, they're going to have to get a whole lot more effective, and even after that, it's still going to take a very long time."

Mathews' sky-blue eyes narrowed as he stared at Stone. "Bro, you advocating bombing civilians?"

"I'm not advocating anything, I'm just saying this is different, and what we're doing now, it's not working. Americans don't have the stomach for the brutal shit anymore, and even after September 11th and all, I don't think they have the attention span to allow the approach our government is taking now to reach a positive conclusion. The guys on the ground can give it their all, but the longer things keep stretching out, the more of a chance our population has to elect a new round of short-sighted politicians. The more time that passes, the more chances democracy has to wreck it."

Mathews shook his head, "Bro, you certainly fucking know a lot for a guy who lives in his goddamn van."

"Maybe," Stone shrugged, "or maybe I don't know shit. Honestly I hope I'm wrong. I could be, if Iraq and Afghanistan drop out of the news the way Bosnia did, and pulling troops out doesn't become the basis for presidential campaigns. But I doubt it."

McCabe's head shook slightly as he stood with his back to them staring out the embrasure toward the sea. The warm sunlight spilled in around him with the breeze. "Attention span?" he growled without turning his head. "I don't even think most Americans realize we're at war! And technically we're in two of them, not even counting all the shit that's happening in Korea or Colombia or Bosnia. I mean, you know any civilians whose daily lives are being impacted by this shit? You hear people talking about this stuff on the street? Hell no, the majority of our population could give a shit as long as their favorite coffee spot stays open and gas prices don't get too high."

Mathews turned to McCabe, "What the fuck happened to you? You were always a little salty, but you were never this cynical. The world ain't near as bad as you make it out to be. You gotta change your mindset or ain't nobody's gonna wanna be around you and you'll end up miserable."

"My mindset?" McCabe spun around, his sunglasses propped on his head and his dark eyes locked on Mathews. "You need to wake up to the reality we're living in, and ya need to do it sooner than later. Otherwise, when this whole thing falls apart in another election cycle or two, it'll crush you."

"I can't take this shit anymore," Mathews answered, turning away. "Come on Conner, let's go see what the top level of this place looks like."

★　★　★

The top of the fortification had been overtaken by dune grass with sandy paths that wound through its uneven surface. The fact that there was a brick structure beneath the seemingly organic terrain gave Conner a strange feeling that he couldn't quite articulate. *There is something to it. Things always trying to return to their natural state... or perhaps attempting to disguise their complex past in exchange for a simpler existence. Or maybe nothing is working toward anything at all—things, places, people— perhaps they just are. It's our own misconceptions of what we are experiencing that lead to shock when we discover what lies beneath.*

Conner strode along with Mathews until he stopped at one of the massive hexagonal structure's corners. A cool breeze was coming from the ocean and clouds had moved in, providing a break from the intensity of the sun. In the middle distance, sea birds were circling over the water. *Seventy miles off Key West, that seems far even for a bird. I guess they can migrate thousands of miles, from Canada to the South every year, but it seems a little more manageable when they can just land and take a break if they need to. Also, it's not such a big deal if they get off course. Out here they have to be dead on to hit this little island.*

I wonder if they plot it out. If they're aware of what they're doing and how far they have to go. How hard they need to push. Or if they're just reacting, responding to unknown chemicals in their brains, moving on impulses they don't understand. Maybe they're just a force of nature, like the wind with no consciousness at all. Impossible for me to tell, I suppose. It's hard enough to get an idea of what other people are thinking or experiencing, much less a bunch of birds crossing the gulf.

"Imagine stacking BBs in there," Mathews snickered, pointing to a barrel-vaulted masonry arch thirty yards long and twenty yards wide below them on the parade grounds. "At least they had those big earthen blast walls around it so if it went it didn't take out the entire base."

Conner shook his head, gazing down at the old magazine. "It's still here, those guys must of dipped instead of smoked."

"Ha! Bro, seeing that thing makes me think landing on a dirt runway in the Colombian jungle with the cargo compartment filled with wooden crated rockets wasn't actually so bad."

"I guess it's all about perspective," Conner chuckled.

His eyes shifted back atop the wall, settling on the steel shaft of a cannon, laying alongside the path in the sand, no longer mounted. It told the story of universal military truths throughout American history. It would have been cleaned, oiled and meticulously cared for on a regular schedule for decades only to be abandoned with the fort. *Maybe that was success though? Wielding enough military power that it never needed to be used. Standing strong enough no one dares to hit you. Certainly not the case for any of the equipment I've worked on. But I guess it all ends the same. Every aircraft I've ever turned wrenches on will be in the boneyard one day, too.*

Conner reached down and ran his fingertips along the surface of the gun. Its barrel was textured, but still sleek, not etched with rust as he would have expected in the salty air of the gulf.

"Come on," Mathews nodded his head toward the path in front of them. "Let's hike the rest of the way around this thing and then go down and check out the beach."

CHAPTER 14

The clouds cleared and the bright sun felt good on Conner's shoulders as he stood next to Mathews on the light sandy beach staring out at the ocean. The sparkling caps of the minute gulf waves glittered a seafoam-green in the sunlight. Even on this ultra-peaceful water it was difficult to imagine what it must have been like in the past—setting out on a wind-powered wooden ship toward some port beyond the horizon that you couldn't see.

Or maybe things weren't so different. Perhaps sailing toward some invisible point didn't require any more faith than flying into Afghanistan at night. Feeling the g-forces in your gut as you glance between the blackness outside the plane's windshield and the pilot, night vision goggles strapped to his helmet as he manipulated the yoke to guide the aircraft in for a combat landing—a stomach-dropping corkscrew descent into darkness before touching down on the Kandahar airstrip that you couldn't see.

Maybe every generation of service members has their own leaps of faith to endure. By any standard of measurement, we are certainly lucky. The Army Air Corps' losses in World War II seem insane compared to what the Air Force experiences now.

"Look, those jokers are way out there on the moat wall." Mathews pointed toward Stone and McCabe, who were standing on the long stretch of masonry works that extended from the beach around the perimeter of the fort just a few feet above the water line.

There's still something to it though. Conner thought as his eyes settled on his friends in the distance. *We certainly didn't get off for free.*

Conner strode forward with Mathews atop the moat wall, which was about the width of a city sidewalk. To their left lay the wide open peaceful water of the Gulf, while on their right Fort Jefferson's brick walls jutted more than four stories up from the tranquil water of the moat.

"What's up, boys?" McCabe greeted them as they approached.

"We need some brewskis and some fishing poles is what's up," Mathews answered.

Stone nodded slowly. "It was pretty cool to hear about Hemingway and his friends going out deep sea fishing and getting trapped here by that tropical storm. What did the tour guide say? They were stuck here seventeen days? Eating the fish they caught. Sounds pretty fun except that they must have had to go fishing in the rain to stay fed."

"Yeah bro, the world was different then," Mathews replied. "You'd have to go far now to have an adventure like that. Anywhere near civilization and everyone owns everything. No massive abandoned military forts to hang out in for a couple weeks without getting into some kinda trouble."

"Makes you wonder, though," Stone replied. "About the nature of the world I mean. The fort seems so incredibly tough, and the water so calm, but it must get rough. I mean, they built this entire moat—which had to be a tremendous effort—to keep the waves from breaking down walls that were designed to withstand hits from cannon balls. It's just deceiving, the fort's walls look so strong. Maybe they were worried about the accumulation, storm after storm hitting the place until one day things just come apart."

"Yeah bro, or maybe not. They could have been scared of big stuff like Hurricane Katrina, that thing wrecked all kinds of offshore oil rigs and you know those things are built stronger than hell."

Conner's eyes flicked from Stone to Mathews, before scanning the brick embattlements atop the fort's walls. *It'd have to be a hell of a storm to bring this place down.*

"All that and then the thing starts coming apart because the wrought iron reinforcements deep inside the walls began to corrode and expand, popping mortar joints and shearing whole sections of brick off from within. Not cannonballs or waves, just being in this environment for so long," Stone shook his head. "Ironic."

Conner shifted his focus back to Stone.

"This island, too," Stone continued. "I mean, the weather is so nice it feels like it could be a resort or something, but the reality is they used the place as a prison. It's got no source of fresh water, and the workers here were sick all the time. It's odd how different things can look from their actual history."

Conner's gaze moved to Mathews before flicking to McCabe and then easing down onto the water and slowly drifting out into the gulf. The four of them stood shoulder width apart, taking in the pastel-blue hues of the sea and sky as the calls of marine birds floated in around them on the breeze. *This was someone's job once, standing up on that fortification behind me and just looking out, scanning for approaching threats—ships or maybe storms. Some enlisted guy like me from over a century ago.*

"Hey Stone," Mathews began, still staring out across the water. I was gonna ask you something, but I didn't want it to be weird or nothin'."

"Go for it," Stone replied.

"You ever think about looking into the VA? You know, get some assistance. You think maybe it would help?"

Stone turned his head slightly toward his friend, though his eyes never left the water. "Hell no, I don't want nothin' to do with that shit."

"I think about it sometimes. I mean, for after I'm out of the military. Normally I'm fine, but then sometimes I think I'm kinda fucked up. I didn't know if maybe they could actually help. Or maybe it's normal to be messed up sometimes. Maybe everyone has screwed up thoughts, and that's just the way it is. I mean, I don't really have anything to compare it to. I was never a normal adult who wasn't in the military, because I was seventeen when I joined. Still just a kid really. Things were way different then." The small Gulf waves gently lapped against the brick moat wall they stood upon. Mathews tilted his head a little to one side, "You never even thought about it? They say it's set up to help veterans out. That's what it's there for."

"Well, that's great. I'm glad it's there for the people who need it. But, thank God I was lucky I didn't get messed up. I don't need any help."

"You ought to look into it bro, I'm telling you. I went to a briefing on it. It's free medical care, and if they give you a disability rating then they could even send you a check every month."

"I know how it works. But what are they going to do, there's no cure for all the ringing in my ears and I don't want any money I didn't work for. I'm certainly not taking any government handouts, that's step one in becoming a victim. I'm never going to be dependent on anyone and I'm never going to be a fucking victim."

"Well, alright Stone. I ain't accusing you of nothin', I was just thinking about it for myself for whenever I get out and wondered if you had any experience with it, that's all. They call it compensation, they said not to think of it as a hand out. Of course if someone was scamming the system or made up a medical condition or something that'd be different."

"No one owes me shit, and I don't want anything I didn't work for, period."

"Why the hell not?" McCabe cut in. "When I get out I'm going to hire one of those lawyers that specializes in VA claims. I'm getting everything I can get. What you're saying about the government not owing you is bullshit. The shit they put us through, while all their politician-asses are bullshitting in their comfortable offices and letting lobbyists buy them steak dinners every night. I wanna see those bastards fly into a combat zone and take a plane load of war wounded and body bags out. Just one time. That'd be enough that then maybe they'd think about shit a little harder next time there's a vote. Those fuckers could pay me the rest of my life and I still wouldn't get even."

"Well you must have had a different experience than I did," Stone replied without turning to McCabe. "I met great people in the military and saw all kinds of places I never would have gotten to see. I built a lot of confidence and gained all kinds of mechanical skills."

"Sure, dude, but you also went to all the same shit places I did. We flew the same kinda missions and got the same carcinogenic oils all over us. Not to mention all the mental and emotional shit. There ain't no way in hell any of us will live as long as we were supposed to. Sad fact, it's just not gonna happen. I intend to get paid while I'm here."

"Well that's your choice, and there's certainly plenty of people who go that way, but it's not for me."

"Dude, we ain't the same people we were before. Think about it. You really believe it's a coincidence none of us managed to maintain our relationships? All our girlfriends bailed. Other family stuff got stretched until there was almost nothing left at all. We should get compensated for that."

"Girls lose interest and break up, it happens."

Conner swallowed hard, his gaze hovering on Stone's face.

"I take responsibility for my mistakes," Stone continued. "I could have got out after my first enlistment. I knew how much I loved Shannon and that I was gone constantly. It was obvious that shit wasn't healthy. But I stayed in and that's my fault. I'm not putting my decisions and failures on anybody else. Nobody owes me shit. I can make my own way just fine."

"It's just set up to help you get through stuff if you need it," Mathews responded. "I mean, shit's rough sometimes. It ain't about nobody owing you something."

"The hell it's not," McCabe answered. "The shit we went through, you're goddamn right they owe me."

"Bro, why do you keep saying that?" Mathews turned to face McCabe. "'The shit we went through.' Sure, we saw some bad stuff and were on nonstop deployments and missions and what not, but when you say that it makes it sounds like we survived the Bataan Death March or something. Really we just hung out on the edge of combat. Sure, we worked our asses off, but we were never in the thick of it, thank God. When you say that shit you're perpetuating all those stereotypes of veterans being messed up and all angry and alone. Like they can't fuckin' fit into society no more. That ain't us! Look at me!" Mathews held his hands open in front of him. "I still got all my fingers. I'm hanging out in the tropics with my best friends having a great time! There ain't nothing wrong with us, bro! It's not like we watched all our friends freeze to death in the Battle of the Bulge or something. I was just asking Stone because I thought maybe the VA could help a little bit. Not with money really, but other stuff."

"You do you, dude," McCabe scoffed. "I'm getting all I can get, and if you don't, you're stupid."

"Enough!" Mathews exhaled hard. "I wasn't trying to start something. I was just asking a question. How can you argue when we're in such an amazing place? I'm gonna eat my sub, then I'm putting my snorkel mask on and checkin' out what's under these waves."

CHAPTER 15

In the shade, on the narrow stretch of sand between the lightly lapping waves of the gulf and stunted, yet broad limbed trees, Mathews knelt unzipping his black backpack. He tossed Stone a twelve-inch sub wrapped in wax paper before pulling a second one out for himself.

McCabe tilted his head slightly watching them, "Dude, you seriously going to eat that?"

"Yeah man, it ain't no big deal," Stone answered.

"You boys are crazy." McCabe scoffed. "I ate my stuff on the boat, so it wouldn't be sitting in the sun for hours."

"Humans went without refrigerators from the beginning of time until less than a hundred years ago. I think I'll be alright eating a deli meat sandwich that's been out a couple of hours."

"Yeah people also only used to live to be thirty-eight," McCabe shot back.

Stone grinned, "All the near misses we've had and you're worried about unrefrigerated deli meat?"

"Yeah!" McCabe raised his eyebrows as Stone bit into his sub. "Does that have mayo on it?"

"I might be dumb," Stone confessed in-between bites, "but I'm not an idiot. I ordered it with mustard."

"Mine has mayo," Mathews announced, settling down on the sand and pulling his sub from its paper bag. "It's not even

American to get a sub without mayo. I don't trust anyone who says different."

"Dude, do not eat that! You know that stuff goes bad fast when it's warm!"

"Yeah, maybe," Mathews answered, unwrapping his sub, "but I make a lot of bad decisions, so... fuck it, ya know?"

McCabe rolled his eyes as Mathews took a huge bite.

Just like old times, Conner thought, finishing his granola bar. *The guys being themselves and McCabe worrying about them. People get back together and just assume their old roles like no time went by at all.* His eyes flicked between his friends. *Though everyone has changed. I guess it's just the dynamic between us that's the same.* He shook his head and opened his backpack to pull out his snorkel. *Why am I always thinking about this garbage?*

Floating in the warm water of the moat, Conner felt as if he were an intruder in a massive aquarium. Dozens of yellow and blue fish the size of his index finger darted around below him in the chest high water, just out of reach. He kicked slowly forward, making his way along the perimeter of the fort, wondering why all those little fish didn't seem to react to his presence. *Sure, I'm not actually a threat, but shouldn't I appear to be? Shouldn't some massive unworldly creature invading their space elicit some type of response? Maybe this is just how fish act and that's why they get eaten all the time. Or maybe the margins are just smaller, perhaps an arm length away is plenty of response time?* His mind drifted to all the things people do that really wouldn't seem so safe to another intelligent being—walking on a sidewalk next to a street with cars zooming by. Only being separated from electricity by the thin plastic coating of an extension cord. Flying into a war zone on a cargo plane full of pallets stacked high with four foot wooden crates containing seventy millimeter rockets. *Perhaps these little fish are doing just fine.*

Conner moved out of the moat and into the shallow water of the gulf.

"Yo!" Mathews called splashing toward him. "If I drown, don't tell my mom I didn't wait an hour after eating!"

"Not happening," Conner replied. "Tattle tailing on you to Mrs. Mathews will be my top priority."

"I always knew you were a snitch! Come on! Let's head over to the ruins of the coaling station. Maybe we can find an octopus or something cool hiding in the old pilings."

The two slowly made their way around the tip of the key. Popping above the surface the Yankee Freedom was visible, moored two hundred yards in front of them just beyond a series of private yachts and a sailboat secured to a row of small wooden docks running perpendicular to the shore.

"Now that'd be something," Mathews said, nodding toward the ships as he tread water. "Cruising around the Caribbean in your own boat with some friends and a couple honeys. Camping out on random islands at night and drinking beer and fishing during the day."

"By the time we can afford anything like that we'll be too old to use it."

"Pshh, don't be like McCabe and wreck it for me."

"Alright, a couple of years then. We'll save up and buy a yacht, then travel around with our super-hot girlfriends exploring new places and camping on deserted tropical islands."

"That's what I'm talking about! And we'll take breaks to go snorkeling and find octopi! Come on!" Mathews pulled his mask down and fitted the snorkel back in his mouth.

The two swam around the ruins of the coaling station for nearly an hour, taking in the different schools of colorful fish darting in and out of the maze of barnacle encrusted pilings. Sea birds resting atop the old supports held their wings open as they preened themselves, occasionally squawking out their discontent before hopping to more distant columns as one of the guys passed by. "Time's up boys!" McCabe hollered, interrupting the serenity of their underwater ecosystem. "Boat's leavin' in thirty minutes, we're about to pack it in."

The two made their way to the nearest point they could get out of the water, deciding it'd be faster to walk around the campground on the beach to grab their belongings than swim back the way they had come. "Man, this place is really amazing," Conner commented, staring out at the turquoise water lining the brick walls of the old fort. "I wish we could stay here longer."

Mathews slowly nodded beside him.

"We should actually come back one day and camp out like these people are doing," Conner smiled, watching what had to be a father and son eating a late lunch at a picnic table with a cooler beside it, near their tent site on the beach. "That's great. It reminds me of sleeping out in the Adirondacks with my dad when I was a kid."

The calm aquamarine water lapped against the sandy shoreline behind the campers before fading into a deep blue hue on the horizon. Conner turned to look at his friend, but Mathews did not return his gaze.

"Your dad ever take you out when you were a kid?"

Mathews slowly shook his head, but his eyes seemed fixed on something in front of them. *The family at the picnic table perhaps?* Conner squinted at him.

"You alright, man?"

Mathews stopped, exhaling slowly. He opened his mouth as if to speak but instead drew in another breath and then let it out slow too. "I don't know, bro. I wanna be, but sometimes I think I might be fucked up."

"Fucked up how?"

"You remember when we were at Al Udeid? And I was on a trash hauling mission to Djibouti, we were about to go, engines were screamin' and you were there to marshal us out."

Conner's eyebrows scrunched together, "I guess... I mean I marshaled at least a hundred missions out while I was there."

Mathews stared at him before shifting his gaze back to the man with the cooler. "This particular time, the pilot got a radio call, and I had to go out and tell you to take the truck in and pick up a life or death box."

Conner's eyes narrowed, as his mind drifted. "I do remember that... because I couldn't hear exactly what you said, and I thought—what a waste we're burning jet fuel here. Then I picked some guy up at the entry control point and he had a Styrofoam cooler, had 'LIFE OR DEATH' written right on the side in black magic marker. That's when I understood why they held the plane."

"Yeah bro, that was it. Made me happy at the time because I'd been hauling nothing but bullshit around theater and I thought, finally I'm gonna help do something that actually matters," Mathews took a deep breath and let it out slow as he continued to gaze toward the picnic table. "I ever tell you what happened?"

Conner shook his head.

"We landed at the international airport, and the sun was blazin'. I mean *scorching* the fuckin' earth. The air was all thick and hot and smelled like burning shit, and filthy-feeling dust was blowing around. An American contract team and two marines from Camp Lemonnier came out to the jet and helped download the aircraft. Anyway, they pulled off with the last pallet on their forklift and were gone. I guess they didn't know about the life or death box, or maybe someone else was responsible for it. So the aircraft commander, he calls in on the ground frequency and says 'we got this cooler here full of blood and it's important.' They say they're sending somebody out to get it. Well, when the guy gets there it's one of the skinnies, and he's high as shit on khat. I mean all fidgety and still chewing the stuff right there on the ramp.

"I was like we can't give this shit to him. So the pilot called again and we waited a few minutes until he says 'we're going to bust our window, we gotta go.' I knew it was the worst fuckin' idea ever, I thought he'd take the box and just set it in the sun somewhere and it'd all be for nothin'. But the captain said 'get rid of it and let's go,' so I gave him the cooler. His hands were all shaky when I passed it to him. That fuckin' skinny took two steps and tripped over his own feet. He slammed down on the concrete before he even cleared the wingtip. The Styrofoam cooler busted all up in pieces and the bags all broke and blood was everywhere. I ran over to see if there were any that hadn't ruptured, but they were all shot. It was fucking awful.

"The captain stood there shaking his head, and then he said, 'we gotta go' and we cranked engines and took off and left all those liters of blood soaking into the hot concrete. The dry ice from the cooler was boiling off, making a thin sheet of fog hugging the ground like at a Halloween party, and the blood was thick and there were chunks of broken Styrofoam in it, and the ripped plastic bags and a film of that nasty dust that was blowing across the ramp sticking to it all. We came back in and picked up human remains two days later. I can't know for sure that the two trips were related… but there's no way they weren't."

"Damn," Conner said, eyes locked on his friend's face.

"Yeah, I didn't tell nobody. I was pretty upset. Like, why the fuck did I give that high-ass skinny the life or death box? Why didn't I say, 'Fuck no, I'll carry it in myself,' and find the right person to hand it to even if I have to spend the night in Africa?" He never met Conner's gaze, just kept staring out at the cooler, or the family or perhaps the ocean, it was impossible to tell which.

"I was mad at the captain for a minute," Mathews continued. "But then I thought, that man is maxed out tryin' to fly a plane and dealing with command wanting the jet back on time and all manner of other bullshit. I was mainly upset with myself or maybe whatever dipshit was supposed to notify the people on the ground and have someone there..." He exhaled slow and glanced at Conner for the first time since they'd stopped walking. "Now I'm thinking, why the fuck would the Air Force put somethin' someone's life depends on in a damn Styrofoam container? I mean, how much could one of those Igloo coolers really cost? There could have been turbulence or any number of other things besides some skinny droppin' the damn thing and falling on it." Mathews' eyes drifted to the sand before he turned and continued trudging along the beach.

Conner took a few quick steps to catch up, and they strode along together again.

"They really ought to let people bring booze out here," Mathews muttered, shaking his head. "All that fucking blood cookin' in the sun on the hot-ass concrete."

CHAPTER 16

Mathews slumped in his plastic chair, one lanky arm hanging loose, his fingertips almost touching the floor as drool streamed from his open mouth down onto his chest. Conner smiled and snapped a picture of McCabe standing behind him with his tongue out while holding two fingers up behind Mathews head.

"Aww dude, that's great!" McCabe laughed when Conner held his phone out to show him the picture. "You gotta send that to me!"

"He had to crash sometime, I feel like he's been up drinking for days."

"Yeah, he'll be in the States just long enough that he'll be upside down again when he gets back to Japan." McCabe moved forward and slipped into one of the deck chairs on the bow.

Conner took up a seat next to him. "Hey man, I've been thinking."

McCabe turned his head slightly, surely glancing at him from behind his shades. "This sounds dangerous already."

"Naah it's nothing serious." Conner gazed ahead at the pale translucent blue-green of the wide open gulf in front of him, no land in sight. "I was just thinking about us."

"We ain't dating dude, save this convo for your girlfriend!"

"No man listen, I was just thinking about all of us. You, me, Stone, Lewis, Stretch and Mathews. How we went through so much together and got so tight. You think our lives would have been totally different if one of us hadn't joined? Or if we got stationed in a different base or deployed to different spots or joined the Navy or Army instead of the Air Force?"

McCabe exhaled hard. "Why you asking me this?"

"I don't know," Conner shrugged and continued scanning the water. "Maybe because of how everything turned out. You know, how everything is now."

McCabe's expressionless reflective lenses seemed locked on him. "What do you think?"

"I feel like…" Conner drew in a deep breath, "I feel like if just one or two things had gone a little different, everything might have changed."

"Ok, so you know how you feel, why you asking me then?"

"You're a big history guy and everything, I just thought you might have some insights, that's all."

McCabe leaned forward in his seat, "Look dude, the thing about history is—as far as I can tell—individuals rarely matter." His face scrunched into a grimace. "That's not how I mean it, individuals do consequential things that change the course of history all the time, but in most cases they're not important in the way people believe they are."

Conner glanced side-eyed at him. "What do you mean?"

"Take George Washington. Incredibly significant character in the history of our country right? Well say that dude died in childhood of some nasty illness, or caught a random bullet at Fort Necessity, say he was perfectly healthy but born ten years

earlier, or ten years later? Someone else would have command-
ed the Continental Army and the British still would have lost
and the United States still would have become independent.
That's just the way the cards were dealt. It'd just be someone
else's name in the history books.

"So think about it this way, the most critical factor in your
personal success, or contribution to society or whatever element you think really matters, however you define it—the
most important factor in that is the year you were born.

"If you come off the assembly line with a certain amount of
intelligence and curiosity and ability to learn, and you don't go
through some unrecoverable catastrophe when you're young,
you're basically going to be who you are."

"What?"

"I'm sorry, I'm having trouble explaining it. Say you were born
ten years earlier. You'd still be you, would have still graduated
high school, joined the military, met a bunch of guys who on some
level are like minded because you all ended up in the same spot.
You'd have gone overseas and broadened your perspective and
stayed in or got out and your life would have moved on. But you
didn't, you were born when you were and a few years into your
first enlistment Al Qaeda hit the Pentagon and brought the towers down. Then two years after that everyone was still so scared
of another massive attack coming out of left field that another
desert war kicked off. So you are where you are, and I am where
I'm at and Mathews is passed out in a chair and Stretch is gone
and Lewis is disappeared and Stone is living in his goddamn van."

McCabe exhaled again, "If you'd ended up at a different base you'd have made a different bunch of friends and been witness to a different set of triumphs and tragedies. Someone else would have taken your place and we'd still win or lose the wars and life would continue to grind on. For me, that's as complex as it gets."

Conner nodded slowly as he stared out across the water. "I'm glad it was you guys... that I ended up with I mean. I just feel like if a few things had gone a little different everything might have changed."

"See?" McCabe turned toward him and flashed a little half smile. "No point in asking me."

Mathews let out a little chuckle as he dug through his duffle bag in the trunk of the Mustang.

"Hurry up dude," McCabe barked. "It's almost five. I'm hungry. I ate lunch stupid early and I'm not trying to spend all my Key West time in this parking garage!"

"Wait for it, Brackish," Mathews giggled before spinning around with a grin and tossing him a bright orange Hawaiian shirt with golden highlights.

"What the hell is this?"

"Stone's not the only one rollin' in style tonight!" Mathews threw another shirt toward Conner, this one a pastel blue with waves of pink and the dark silhouettes of palm trees imprinted on it. "We're in the tropics, boys! We gotta embrace it!" Mathews pulled his shirt off and replaced it with a third Hawaiian shirt, boasting a vibrant tie dye pattern with a rainbow of colors spiraling out from the center of the chest.

"Well, let's do this shit!" McCabe smiled. He pulled his baseball cap off and donned it backward so that the brim covered his neck.

"What the hell," Conner agreed, shaking his head. "I don't know anybody in this town anyway."

"Seems like I set some kinda trend," Stone commented, buttoning up his own deep blue shirt with its crimson red floral patterns.

They made their way out of the parking deck into a wall of powerful sunlight and onto Caroline Street. "I guess we're in the right spot," Conner said, pointing to a salmon-colored restaurant with white window trim and blue-green lettering reading 'Harpoon Harry's'.

Mathews shook his head. "The line's out the door, bro. We gotta find someplace faster so we can get down to the southernmost point and get some pictures."

Conner glanced at him as they continued on, "The southernmost point? In the US?"

"Yeah, we gotta get down there and get a picture together. They have a marker or something you can stand in front of."

"Well, I mean, we could really get a group picture anywhere." Conner began, "We should've got some at the fort, I didn't think of it."

"Nahh, bro, we gotta get one at the southernmost point, it's a thing."

"Why?"

Mathews turned to Conner as they moved down the sidewalk together. "Because it's a thing! I don't know why, that's just the way it is. You come to Key West and you get a picture with your friends in front of the southernmost point buoy. That's just what you do!"

"A thing," Conner repeated to himself in a low tone.

"Yeah! A thing! It's like seeing a cock fight in San Juan or visiting the arch in St. Louis, or kissing the Blarney Stone in Ireland or putting the moves on a bridesmaid at a wedding. It's just what you do."

"Well I'm sold," McCabe answered. "But first, food. Maybe this place?" Ahead of them was a crude open air structure composed of dilapidated drift wood covered with haphazardly fastened sheets of misaligned metal roofing material. Buoys and thick maritime ropes were strung alongside street signs, license plates, stickers and the names and dates of those who saw fit to carve their designators into the interior planking. A rusty truck from at least six decades before—completely covered in bumper stickers and grown through with vegetation—separated several picnic tables from the sidewalk. Dozens of conversations from within merged with the sounds of the Grateful Dead and tumbled out onto the street.

"B.O.'s Fish Wagon," Mathews read aloud. "They got beer and conch fritters, what more could we want?"

Conner turned to Mathews, "They pretty good?"

"How the hell should I know? I've never even been to Florida before."

Conner shrugged.

Mathews stepped up to a window in the food trailer within the structure and passed his credit card to a tall pale kid of about twenty. "Give me a dozen conch fritters, a swordfish platter with black beans and rice, a Blue Moon and whatever these guys want."

The kid's eyes flicked to Stone, who stood next to Mathews. "What would you like?" he asked in an accent from somewhere east of Germany.

"Mahi Mahi sandwich, and a glass of water," Stone said, holding out a twenty. "Use this to pay for mine, you don't have to put it on his card."

Mathews' head tipped back as he exhaled at the hodgepodge of building materials slapped together to form the ceiling. "I'm trying to help you, bro."

"I know, and I appreciate it," Stone answered. "You're a real friend. But people ought to pay their own way. That's how capable adults should conduct themselves."

"Friends take care of each other, that's how it works. You did more for us than I could ever tell you. You were the most solid person I knew when things were bad—all those deployments. I was just tryin' to buy you a sandwich."

"Man, you and McCabe already paid for the beach house, the hotel and the rental car. If I let you buy me dinner, I'd be nothing more than a common bum. And that's the truth. Whatever I did in the past, it doesn't matter now. It's only what we do today that matters."

"Hey now," McCabe cut in. "No bums here."

"Everything you did matters, man," Conner added. "Come on, you know that."

"I wish," Stone answered. "I swear I wish it did." He reached out and collected his change, placed it on the counter with another couple twenties. "I'll pay for dinner," he offered before leaving the cash behind, moving off by himself and disappearing around the corner of the trailer without looking at any of them.

A frown formed on Conner's face. Turning to McCabe he began to speak, then stopped himself. McCabe stared back and exhaled, scratching his head. Conner glanced toward Mathews, who caught his gaze, but instead of speaking just shook his head.

"No Conner," McCabe preempted, anticipating his question. "We don't have any answers."

"He's so much quieter than he used to be," Conner lamented. "He doesn't joke around like he always did before. Everything he says is so serious."

"Let's just be happy we could all come here and have a good time together," McCabe suggested. "A couple days ago I didn't even know if the man would show up, now he's buying me a fish sandwich. As far as I can tell, we're doing good."

"Both of you, just stop thinking about it," Mathews' eyes shifted back and forth between his two friends. "You're not going to be able to act normal if it's on your minds all the time.

That was my bad, I should have let him buy his own dinner. Nobody wants to be treated different. Focus on the good stuff. Forget the rest. Have a great time, fun is contagious."

McCabe nodded slow, "You know I try my best everyday brother."

Stone returned when the food arrived, but they ate mainly in silence. Mathews kept shaking his head without speaking and ordered several rounds of drinks. McCabe made a few comments about how good the fish was, but conversation never really restarted.

I'm really glad this place has music. Conner glanced at his friends between bites but wasn't sure what to say.

When they were through, they made their way south along the sidewalks past rows of expensive looking historic houses, lines of parallel parked cars and an occasional tall hardwood tree. "That's what I'm talking about!" Mathews shouted, pointing to a gallery window at a large black and white photograph of a mustached man standing on a pier alongside a marlin so massive a crane must have been securing the rope that suspended it in the air by its tail. "Next trip we gotta go deep sea fishing! I've never been, but that shit looks badass!"

"That's Hemingway," Stone responded, nodding toward the photograph.

"What?"

"Ernest Hemingway, the author. That's him in the picture."

"Who the fuck's lookin' at the guy? I'm talking about the fish that's bigger than a damn rowboat! Just look at that thing, it's gotta weigh a thousand pounds!" Mathews shook his head as they continued. "Ahh man, that's wild. Too bad we don't have any more time. I'd find a way to book us a charter right now."

I guess it is pretty wild, those things living out there in the Gulf Stream, the same water we just took the ferry across from Fort Jefferson. Incredible to think creatures like that are just out there in the world, roaming free.

"And that's why," Mathews announced, gesturing toward the black iron gates of a cemetery in front of them. "I'm tryin' to have as many kick-ass experiences as I can before it's over. Maybe leave behind some amazing photographs like that too."

"Hopefully I leave more of a mark on this world than a few pictures," Stone responded.

"Well sure bro, we all want to do some good. I'm just sayin', that ain't mutually exclusive with going on some epic fishing trips."

"Sure," Stone replied.

"And other things too," Mathews continued. "I'm tryin' to do everything I can do."

"Be all you can be?" McCabe chuckled. "Maybe you should've joined the Army."

"You're killing me bro, I'm trying to be serious. We gotta grab life by the tits and not let go!"

"Sounds like something an Army guy would say," Conner laughed.

"Hot damn," Mathews brought his forearm up and wiped the sweat from his forehead. "You boys are drivin' me to drink."

"Oh, now you want us to take you seriously? Here in Key West while you're dressed as a rainbow?" McCabe chided. "Dude, the last time I saw you act serious there was an aircraft that was literally on fire."

"You right, you right!" Mathews answered. "I'm just sayin', we oughta go fishing."

They'd nearly crossed the island and the ocean was in sight when Mathews let out a little whoop and pointed at a colorful pickup truck positioned on the side of the street hitched to a brightly painted trailer serving as a vendor stand.

"Perfect timing," McCabe agreed. "I was getting thirsty." His head tilted as he stared at the montage of fruit painted on the trailer. "You think it's alcoholic?"

"Ha!" Mathews responded. "You ever heard of anybody drinking plain fruit juice? Come on!"

"I'm going to check out the beach while you boys stand in line for your froofy vacation drinks," Stone called after them. "Make sure you ask for the little umbrella."

"Suit yourself," McCabe yelled over his shoulder, already making his way up the block.

Stone shrugged and turned toward the sea. Conner followed him down the sidewalk until the street opened up onto a stretch of sand with a blue and white sign labeled 'Clarence S. Higgs Memorial Beach Park.' Two high-school-aged girls took turns heaving a rock into the air in a failing effort to knock coconuts free from the palm trees lining the beach. Spread out ahead of them were several couples sitting together in the sand or lying in the sun on beach towels. A solitary dark-haired woman in a white bikini with who could have been a Sports Illustrated swimsuit model lay on her stomach facing toward them staring at a book from behind her amber sunglasses.

Conner squinted in an effort to read the cover—as if he were still a teenager, when attractive ladies were elusive creatures and every available opportunity to study them was required to glean even the smallest insights into their psyche. He blinked, unable to see the book's title and allowed his gaze to wash over her body instead. Somewhere deep inside he wondered why he was interested at all. *I've known Joselyd for a year, every book she's read, every movie she's watched, what brand makeup she wears, and still, I never have a clue what she's thinking. Maybe that's just the way it is—though, she always seems to know exactly what I'm feeling.*

Instinctively, Conner retrieved the iPhone from his pocket and opened his text messages, but Joselyd hadn't written back. *That's strange. Maybe she missed my last one.* He began punching out a new message.

> Hey! Just got back to Key West with the guys. Fort Jefferson was really cool. You doing ok? Miss you!

He continued to stare down at his phone, but after a minute passed with no response, he shoved it back in his pocket. His eyes meandered out to the water before drifting in and settling on the woman in front of him. Conner's mind wandered as he took in the girl, enthralled in her book as shallow-ocean swells gently tumbled in behind her. *Would it have changed anything if Stretch or Lewis or Stone had someone who understood how they were feeling? Or maybe if a couple events had gone another way. Everything couldn't have been just destined to work out the way it did.*

He glanced at Stone, still contemplating, "You think that if a few things had gone a different way, our whole lives could have changed?"

"What are you asking me about some butterfly effect shit?"

Conner nodded.

Stone exhaled and stared out at the beach. Perhaps he was focused on the girl with curly dark hair stretched out with her book, or over her to the sun's highlights on the blue-green ocean beyond, or he may have been taking in the whole scene at once, not fixated on anything in particular. "I'm not sure what you're getting at Conner, but most times it's best not to think about this shit at all. You can't do anything about it now and it never leads anywhere good."

"I don't know, I just wanted to ask how you feel about it."

Stone shook his head and let out another breath. "So here's what I think, but it might not be what you want to hear. If you have a pack of wolves, only the alpha breeds.

The others all have their own functions. You can see the different traits in domesticated dogs, though they don't make sense because you're not witnessing the behavior within a naturally occurring unit. Some of them become alarm dogs. They're super vigilant, they'll start barking and throw a fit if they hear anything, but then they just run and hide behind you instead of fighting. There's other dogs that are the protectors, they don't like anything between them and you and they'll fight to the death to protect you. Other dogs go off on long treks and explore, then report back to the pack if they've found something worthwhile. If another alpha matures, he's either going to fight the old leader and drive him out of the pack, or strike off on his own because he's not designed to be a follower.

"These themes repeat themselves with different sets of social animals. But here's the interesting part. If a swarm of bees loses their queen, the workers immediately start treating some of the eggs differently, to grow a new one. If a pride of lions loses its last male, one of the females will literally begin to grow a mane and start assuming the male's role as the protectorate of the group. There's dozens of examples of these types of dynamics in nature."

Conner squinted at his friend, "I'm not sure I understand what you're trying to tell me."

"Groups of people have their own dynamics. I think a lot of times people adjust to fill the roles that are needed in a group. When their traits really don't line up right, they don't become part of the crew, they drift off and fit into some other set of people somewhere else."

"So... you really don't believe any of it matters? We step out for some reason, and someone else just steps up to fill our role?"

"Well, not exactly, I'm saying all that sociological shit is part of it. We fill different roles and it builds our experience and makes us more capable. If it doesn't work, then groups break up and reform into something that's effective. So we all have some impact, but for the most part, when a butterfly flaps its wings in the Sudan, it don't make a shit to anyone at all."

"But if you believe that, then why you sticking your neck out for random kids outside 7-Eleven and telling weed dealers to go make something of their lives?"

"Well, because there are times when what we do really matters. It's just that the vast majority of actions we take will mean nothing. But I don't think we can ever know when those critical moments are until they're over, and by then it's too late."

"So you do feel like if a few little things had changed everything could have worked out different?"

Stone nodded slowly, "I think about it all the time." His steel-gray eyes never wavered, they remained fixed on some point on the beach, or maybe the ocean beyond. "It tears me apart inside."

CHAPTER 17

Twisting away from the water to follow the sound of McCabe's boisterous laugh, Conner glanced toward the street. From his spot in the shade beneath a palm tree, his eyes settled on McCabe and Mathews—their Hawaiian shirts appearing vibrant as they walked side by side down the sun-drenched street. They each had big goofy smiles and carried a pineapple with its crown missing, long straws extending from their hollow interiors and circular wedges of fruit propped around the rugged brim of each husk.

Conner's eyes flicked to Stone who reclined against the trunk of a nearby palm tree—his head angled up slightly, making it impossible to tell if his eyes were still open behind his shades, silently taking in the scene around him or gazing out to some distant vanishing point where the sea and sky met. Perhaps he'd shut his visual on the world for a moment—actually allowed himself to relax, enjoying the sounds of the ocean and cool breeze coming off the water.

Behind him McCabe laughed again, closer this time, "I mean, I'm not gonna lie dude, this thing is pretty good!"

"Yeah! And it probably has like, vitamins and electrolytes and things that will hydrate us in it!" Mathews answered. "It might even be healthy!"

"It's really pretty great!"

"Yeah! It just needs vodka!"

The two let out another round of laughter. They regained control of themselves in time to make eye contact with two passing girls as they departed the beach. Raising their pineapples together and leaning toward the ladies—as if in some dramatic formal tribute—they set the girls into a fit of giggling. The ladies leaned close to one another, glancing back at Mathews and McCabe multiple times between bouts of laughter as they continued up the street.

Maybe feeling good really is contagious. Conner held a hand up and waved toward his friends.

"Ahh you boys found a nice spot!" McCabe acknowledged in between slurps of pineapple juice.

"Hot damn!" Mathews let out, lifting his sunglasses as his eyes focused on the white bikini twenty yards in front of them. "I just got the sudden urge to read a book."

"God, you're ignorant," McCabe cackled.

"I might even be able to write a book if I knew she'd read it."

"You wouldn't get past putting your name on top the first page!"

"I don't know bro, I'm feeling awfully inspired!"

McCabe shook his head as he gazed out at the beach. "Maybe I'll write a book."

"HA!" Mathews responded. "You probably could, and it'd be the most pessimistic and boring thing anybody ever read!"

"Whatever. Come on fellas, let's go find this southernmost point buoy."

"Nahh... I think I'm just gonna live here, build a house out of palm fronds, maybe start a family, Gilligan's Island style."

"You know at some point she'll finish her book and leave…"

"Way to wreck it for me, bro," Mathews sighed. "Might as well go get our tourist pictures then."

McCabe reached down offering Stone a hand, and when he pulled him upright they were on the move again. They made their way up the narrow sidewalks past small, meticulously kept wooden homes with bright white privacy fences defending their heavily manicured lawns. These houses were interspersed with dilapidated structures of the same size, lined with rusting sections of chain link entangled by scrubby weed trees. After a few blocks they turned onto South Street, where the sidewalks widened and various commercial businesses found their way into the mix of buildings. A group of older retired-looking couples rolled slowly past them—conversing loudly on what were likely rented beach cruisers. Another block and they were surrounded by tourist shops, high-end row house vacation rentals and hotels. At the intersection of Duval Street there was a stand touting piña coladas, rum runners, margaritas and frozen strawberry daiquiris. Behind it a tall, high-cheekboned, dirty-blonde in her early twenties leaned against the counter, her eyes flashed to them as they approached.

"Hey now, that's what I'm talking about!" Mathews let out.

Conner glanced side-eyed at him, unsure if he was referring to the frozen drinks or the girl serving them.

"Come on fellas!" Mathews altered his course slightly, making a direct route for the woman working the stand. "Things are getting better all the time."

The slender girl behind the counter straightened up as they crossed the street toward her, her blue eyes seemed to sparkle in the sunlight. "Hallo," she beamed, a Slavic accent punctuating her tone.

"Where'd you pick up that Texas drawl?" Mathews responded.

Her forehead wrinkled as her thin eyebrows scrunched together, "You think I am coming from Texas?"

"No, not at all," Mathews chuckled.

She tilted her head slightly to the side as she regarded him, her eyes narrowing.

"He's just trying to be funny while he asks you where you're from," Stone offered.

"Aye yes, he is making joke," the smile returned to her face, "He knows I no am from Texas!"

"Oh course not!" Mathews gibed. "Texas girls have the boots, and the big hats," he held his hands in a broad circular shape around his head mimicking a wide brimmed Stetson.

"Like real American cowboy, no?" she giggled.

"Sure, you're just a few thousand miles too far east to see any."

"No, I come here to the ocean."

"Well sure," Mathews answered. "Who wants to be a cowgirl anyway? But what are you doing here?"

"Wait," Stone interjected, holding up the index finger on

his good hand. "Taking a break from college, on a J-1 visa... from... Ukraine?"

Her mouth dropped open as her eyes jumped from Mathews to Stone.

"Yes, of course I am on the exchange visitor visa. How you know I conduct my studies in Kyiv?"

"I didn't, it was just a guess."

"No! How you know?"

"Because you sound like you're from Eastern Europe, you don't look Romanian, and girls from Russia never smile like that. You could've been from somewhere else, but Ukraine was the best guess."

Mathews turned and glared at Stone, "What, d'you work at Ellis Island before you were in the military? There's a shit ton of countries in Eastern Europe."

"Well, that's true, but all the girls from EU countries go to London or Germany to work, a lot easier than coming here and they probably make more."

Mathews closed his eyes and shook his head before turning back to the Ukrainian girl.

She looked away from Stone to meet Mathews' eyes, "You say Texas," she giggled, "he say Ukraine. He is good guess. Is crazy no?"

"I may question other aspects of that mug's life," Mathews began, jerking a thumb in Stone's direction, "but I'll never doubt his intelligence."

"Do you like it here?" Conner asked.

"Aye yes, the people, they are very friendly, and the beach, it is very beautiful. However, aye, America so hot. I never have hot like this in Kyiv. Every day it is hot. I no can understand how people tolerate this hot. My colleague and I, we watch The OC on American television before we come here. It is now I understand why the Americans always are wearing swimsuits. It is so hot."

"Why'd you pick here?" Conner persisted.

"My mother she fought me no to go. She say 'You already go to school in capital why is that no enough? America is so dangerous, everyone having guns!' but I no want to stay in one place. The world is so big. There is many places to see and many people to meet. When I get accepted for visa, I feel I have to go. Also," her face flushed as she let out a little giggle, "American boys they listen to the girlfriends and say 'I love you' so many times."

"Where'd you hear that?" McCabe chuckled.

"I see, on all the American television. Is normal for American. The same is not so for Ukraine."

McCabe blinked and shook his head, "Unfortunately, life in the US is quite a bit different than what you may see on TV."

"Speak for yourself," Mathews cut in. "I love everybody."

The girl beamed, a bright untainted joy manifesting in her eyes. "It is good for people to be here in America. Maybe they no understand how good."

Stone nodded, "We are very very fortunate to be here."

A group of middle-aged couples had assembled behind them and were waiting to order.

"I must get your drinks," she said, her blue eyes flashing between them.

Mathews and McCabe smacked their pineapple vessels down side by side on the counter. "Fill this thing up with something good," Mathews began, "and please triple the alcohol!"

A block over, they joined a line of tourists waiting for their turn to snap pictures in front of the southernmost point buoy. A young couple smiled broadly together, then a family on vacation with elementary-school-aged children who were less than enthusiastic, followed by a group of teenaged girls—some probably sisters—who were all grins as they laid themselves out in model poses around the large red, black and white concrete marker, declaring itself the 'Southernmost Point Continental USA'.

Conner's eyes focused on the painted yellow lettering near its top, stating '90 Miles to Cuba', and tried to remember what it felt like before he'd ever traveled to another country. *There was a real mystery to it. Like a nervous energy, an excitement about meeting people for the first time who spoke foreign languages and saw the world in different ways.* He reached up and ran his fingers through his hair. That feeling had been gone for a long time. When he thought about traveling across the world now, it just seemed like a lot of work. *What happened to me?*

Is it exciting for these people here to know they're so close to another country? Or was it that they'd reached the edge of the great

United States? Maybe Mathews was right—it's a thing—people just do it because everyone else does it. Gets them pictures to put on their Facebook pages.

As Conner stood there, he began to wonder if there were any way to regain his lost enthusiasm for traveling the world, meeting new people and seeing new places. Really, he just wanted to spend time with Joselyd, or the friends he was with now. *There has to be some way to get that old feeling back. When everything was new and exciting. That Ukrainian girl had it. Volunteered to cross an ocean and sling margaritas just for the chance to see someplace new. Maybe that's not so different from me signing up for the Air Force.* As he contemplated it, he had to admit, at the time, a year before September 11th, his enlistment had a lot more to do with getting out of his hometown and seeing other parts of the world than it did with patriotism. *Patriotism may have been there, playing some role, but honestly looking back, the majority of my knowledge on the subject at the time came from staying up late on Friday nights watching war movies with my buddies from high school.*

All the real understanding seemed to come later. Knowing how exhausted he was from working months on end and then picking up plane loads full of Army infantry that seemed twice as wrecked as he was. He remembered them passing out the moment they crashed down in their webbed seating. *And the coffins...*

He shook his head and attempted to focus on something else without much success. *All those fucking coffins.* He could see them in his mind. Sometimes five or six of them lined up in the cargo bay, draped with American flags, sometimes just one on its own anchored to the floor with ratchet straps like any other piece of equipment.

He swallowed hard. *So, if Eastern European kids will go to other countries to serve drinks, then American kids probably would too. We just have the military as an option instead.*

Conner turned to Stone who stood beside him straight faced. Any clue to his thoughts or emotions was buried deep within, or hidden behind his sunglasses. "Hey, how'd you know all that about the Ukrainian girl before you even talked to her?"

Stone shrugged.

"Come on."

"I didn't know about her, I could just tell a few surface things. Nothing way down inside."

Conner stared at him.

"Anytime I go somewhere I talk to people. Anyone who's willing to join in conversation really. Some people will explain all kinds of crazy things if you ask them something. I guess people like to talk about how they got to where they are, and what they are trying to do next. The process that goes into it. A lot of people would think that doing something like that is a big waste of time, because it's all people I'll probably never see again. I don't know, maybe I just get lonely sometimes. Who knows, maybe they're lonely too.

"But really, the thing is, the more people I talk to, the more patterns start to emerge. It makes it easier to guess what peoples' situations are. It's all just guesses though. You can tell a lot from looking at someone. Even just the way they walk, do they have confidence in their stride, are they in a hurry, do they stand up tall and proud, or have they been beat down by the world? But there's no way to really know what's going on inside, way down deep I mean. People all feel things differently, and some of them been through crazy shit, things that don't even seem possible. Other people ain't hardly been through anything difficult at all, they live lives so easy guys like you and I couldn't even relate."

"Hey!" Mathews let out, "Quit being so serious and get ready to smile for real! This is gonna be an awesome picture!"

A minute later the guys flanked the sides of the concrete buoy, the highlights of their festive shirts contrasting the deep blue hue of the water behind them. One picture with all their arms crossed, tough straight-lipped expressions on their hardened faces. In the next they were all smiles—holding their arms open—gesturing toward the buoy in what could have been the cover of a tourist brochure.

CHAPTER 18

"Hey, we could go see Hemingway's house. Since we're here anyway," Stone suggested, as they walked up Whitehead Street away from the southernmost point. "I think they give tours."

"Not interested," McCabe snorted.

"Yeah, what you wanna see that shit for?" Mathews asked, slurping more rum out of his pineapple. "He's just another old dead white dude."

"I don't know," Stone answered. "It could be interesting. I like his writing."

"Fuck that," Mathews snapped. "Let's hit the bar! How often you get to party in Key West!"

The group strolled forward up the empty pavement at a quick pace despite having no agreed upon destination.

McCabe shook his head, "Since when do you read anyway?"

"I've read a lot since I got out. If I read the right kinda books it keeps me from getting lonely sometimes."

"I got a *phone*," Mathews jeered. "I start to get lonely, I just call McCabe up and bother him."

"Valid," McCabe replied. "Always in the middle of the damn night. It'll be a lot better for my sleep cycle when your lonely ass gets stationed in a closer time zone."

"Why you like his stuff?" Conner asked.

"I can't immediately tell. In most of his books not a whole lot happens, but they're real easy to read and however he writes them, it keeps me super interested. Most of his stuff that I've read is written from the perspective of someone who's doing alright. Like they're comfortable, and they have a little money and aren't really wanting for anything material. But they have this void, like something is missing and they don't know how to fill it. I guess it doesn't make too much sense for me to be into it, since most my life I've been scrambling. But I can identify with that void a bit."

"Holy shit, don't ask this guy any more questions, Conner. We'll have to start a philosophy class," McCabe scoffed.

Conner tilted his head slightly to one side and glanced at McCabe. "What's your deal? You normally love history stuff. You study it all the time."

"Yeah, well, I don't need to read Hemingway to know I'm not into it."

"You should give it a shot," Stone suggested. "I think you might like some of it. Plus, I don't know if he was technically a veteran, but he was certainly in wars. Red Cross in World War I, war correspondent in the Spanish Civil War and World War II."

"Well hell, even Conner has been to war," Mathews laughed. "That ain't no big deal."

"Conner, look that shit up on your phone and navigate us there," McCabe instructed. "We can stop in front and get some pictures, then anybody who wants to go take a tour or whatever can meet us up later. But I for one am doing something else."

Stone turned slightly as they strode forward, his eyes darting toward McCabe. "Ahh come on man, it could be cool."

McCabe's face twisted in the bright afternoon light beside him.

"Maybe you'll learn some new history facts, make some connections with all the other stuff you've read."

In a rapid jolt, McCabe hurled his pineapple forward. It skipped off the asphalt with a violent spin—flinging bits of its husk in every direction—then skidded across the pavement and rolled in a broad semi-circle before being crushed by a car in the next intersection. The group all stopped together, as if ordered by a hidden command. McCabe spun toward Stone, his fingers forming a knife hand as he pointed at him. "FUCK YOU STONE!"

The shadows of Stone's eyes narrowed behind his tinted lenses as he faced McCabe. Mathews moved forward, his gaze flicking back and forth between his two friends, one hand still clinging to his pineapple, the other slowly opening and closing as if testing his grip.

"I'm not fucking going! Stop asking me! I have zero desire to spend any time in a house memorializing a guy who killed himself!"

Stone's mouth twitched into the slight hint of a frown.

McCabe's eyes closed as he sucked in a breath. "I'm just not into it. Ok?" He turned and started up the street again.

The others exchanged glances before turning to follow him up the sun-filled pavement, silent as their shirts radiated bright splashes of color.

They'd traversed past the fragments of McCabe's froofy pineapple cocktail and through another intersection before Conner reported, "It's literally four or five blocks ahead of us on this street we're on right now. It's not out of the way at all."

"We don't have to go," Stone answered. "Whatever else it is you guys want to do, I'm fine with it."

No one responded as the group trudged forward.

They continued up Whitehead Street. On their right, they passed old two story-houses with spacious front porches, pastel-colored doors and painted lap board siding that matched their bright white picket fences abutting the sidewalk. The small yards were lined with palm trees and native-looking frond plants interrupted occasionally by an old hardwood. To their left, the curved wrought iron fences of the Naval annex were eventually replaced with small yards and houses like those across the street, creating a historic tropical feel broken only by the series of large overhead power lines strung from broad metallic pillars.

"I think this is it," Conner announced, pointing at the two-story colonial structure through a small gap in the surrounding vegetation. The gate was closed, the last tour having concluded half an hour before they arrived. "We can at least get a picture."

The property was surrounded by a wall comprised of rough hand-hewn bricks from another century. Just beyond it stood tall dense tropical trees that obscured any clear view of the place. The group stopped in front of the property on the narrow sidewalk.

"I guess we can get a picture with the sign," Conner concluded and flagged down a passing woman to take the shot on his cell phone.

"Come on, smile y'all," she insisted. "Act like you're friends! You're on vacation!"

Conner glanced at the picture, when she handed him his phone back. Mathews held his pineapple up with a big phony grin as if making a toast. Stone made an attempt, though there was no joy in his eyes, and McCabe stood there straight faced.

Mathews stepped forward shaking his head. "You two are bumming me out!" He pointed at Stone, "You're super serious all the time. You need to stop and lighten up! And you," his eyes shifted to McCabe, "You're supposed to be having a blast! It's your damn party! Instead, you're letting little things take your mind to a bad place, and there's no reason for that shit. It's not what Stretch or Lewis or any other person involved in any shitty thing you've experienced would want! It doesn't help nothin'! I can't even handle being around y'all right now!" Mathews glanced up, exhaling hard. "I'm going to find the Hard Rock, do a couple shots and buy a T-shirt. You two try to get your heads on straight and I'll find ya in a little while."

He stormed up the sidewalk around a slow-moving group of middle-aged ladies and dropped his pineapple in a trash can before spinning around. "Conner, you coming?"

Conner shrugged, his eyes darting first to Stone, who looked as if he were about to speak but didn't, and then to

McCabe, who seemed to be staring at the ground from behind his mirror-like shades.

"Come on Conner, let these guys work their shit out. I'll buy you a shot."

McCabe motioned slightly toward Mathews with his head, and Conner started in his direction. Mathews paused for a moment placing a cigarette between his lips and sparking his lighter. When Conner was alongside him, he took off in a quick stride, blowing smoke over his shoulder and stepping into the street to pass groups of window-shopping tourists on the narrow sidewalk. Conner hustled along behind him, struggling to keep up with his long gangly paces. They'd only made it a few blocks before sweat was forming on Conner's forehead and pouring down the back of his neck.

Holding that quick pace for the next fifteen minutes, the guys missed the turn onto Duval Street and roamed around the block before arriving in front of the building. They made their way through a lively patio—filled with a mixture of families, groups of friends and couples of all ages, lounging in outdoor seating beneath sun umbrellas and colorful streamers. Pearl Jam pumped through the restaurant as they moved into a wall of cool, dry air in what seemed to have been a luxurious historic home prior to its conversion into the iconic tourist bar and grill.

Inside Mathews hesitated for a moment, resting his sunglasses atop his head and waiting for his eyes to adjust to the dim bar lighting. The walls were lined with the guitars of famous musicians and other colorful rock memorabilia. Mathews glanced at Conner for the first time since they'd split from the others, then nodded toward the rich polished hardwood bar. The area above the counter was also cased in trim and adorned with large brightly lit brass letters proclaiming 'Love All Serve All'.

Mathews gestured toward the phrase, "Seems like my kinda place."

Conner followed him as he snaked his way forward through the crowded restaurant and drew the attention of the bartender. "What do you want?"

Conner shrugged.

"Two shots of Patron and a Hard Rock Café T-shirt," Mathews said, thrusting his credit card toward the bartender before turning away and shaking his head as his eyes settled on Conner.

Here it comes, Conner thought, expecting to be berated for not choosing his own brand of liquor.

"They're two of the smartest guys I know," Mathews began before shaking his head again. "But I just don't think they get it."

Conner locked onto Mathews' blue eyes, unsure how to respond.

"I'm glad you're here to keep me sane, bro."

The shots were placed in front of him on the bar and Mathews passed one to Conner. "Here's to making it through all the hard shit, and afterward having the sense to focus on the good things."

Mathews held his shot glass up to Conner, then tapped it on the counter and they both threw them back together. Conner's eyes closed for a moment, his fist coming up to his mouth as he exhaled slowly. When he opened his eyes, Mathews was already ordering them two more.

"They're smooth, right?"

Conner did his best to nod.

The next round arrived and the process repeated itself. Except this time, holding up his glass, Mathews stated, "To absent friends and family." When he'd slapped his shot glass back down on the bar he asked for two piña coladas.

The back of Conner's scalp tingled as they scooped up their frozen drinks and retreated to the corner of the room. Pearl Jam had made way to Aerosmith, then Jane's Addiction and Garage Days Metallica. Conner gazed at his friend, searching for something intelligent to say, but Mathews didn't look back. Instead his eyes flicked around the room, perhaps taking in the faces of the passing patrons, maybe scanning for threats or searching for attractive ladies that didn't seem to be attached.

Realizing Mathews' drink was gone, Conner took a big swallow of his own in an effort to catch up, but only succeeded in adding brain freeze to the first-beer-buzz he was experiencing in addition to his still tingling scalp. He closed his eyes again feeling the sweat dry on the back of his neck as he engaged in a slow and steady effort to finish his beverage over the next few songs.

When both their glasses were empty, Conner began to worry Mathews would order another round. Instead he just continued to observe the room. Conner tried to follow his gaze but it didn't seem he was focusing on anything in particular. "Let's get outta here," Mathews commented without ever turning toward him.

CHAPTER 19

On the street, they moved side by side at a more leisurely pace back in the direction they'd come. Conner periodically glanced side-eyed at his friend. *Perhaps it's not just Joselyd—it's Stone and McCabe and even Mathews, I never know what any of them are thinking.*

Conner's mind drifted as they traveled the next several blocks. He'd abandoned his effort to interpret his friend's thoughts and was wondering where Joselyd would want to go if she were with them. Or what she'd say to keep things fun the way she always did when life got heavy.

"Bro, we only get one shot at life," Mathews let out. "We live everyday once, and then it's gone. These guys gotta get their minds off whatever it is that's dragging them down and just enjoy our time together. We may never get to see each other again. Or at least not all at once. We gotta enjoy it now."

Conner stopped walking and stared hard at him. "Man, why the hell would you say that?"

Mathews turned facing him, "Because it's the truth."

"That's some fucked up shit to say, man."

"No, it's not. I'm sayin' we need to really enjoy our time now because we don't know what's coming."

"You were just talking about not being negative, then you come out and say some shit like that."

"It's true, bro. Mugs just don't want to think about it, so

they walk around pretending we'll all live forever. That the world is somehow different than it is."

"I've been thinking good things, like how we should try to do this every year, or every other year or something, go on a vacation together, and here you are saying we might not ever even see each other again. It's fucked up."

Mathews exhaled as he stared back at him.

"I'm sure McCabe'll send us a wedding invite, for starters, that won't be so far away."

Mathews shook his head slightly. "There ain't gonna be no wedding, bro," the hint of a frown crossed his face. "Not a real one anyway, that joker's getting married at the court house. They're doing it as soon as his girl defends her thesis."

Conner's eyebrows drew together. "Well why the hell wouldn't he just tell us that?"

Mathews lifted his shoulders in a drawn out shrug.

"Whatever, saying shit like 'we may never see each other again' is still fucked up."

"Bro, you remember the last time you saw Lewis?"

An image of Lewis flooded his mind. Standing there shaking his hand by his little beat-up car saying, 'I'm sorry to leave you guys...' Conner swallowed hard, wondering where his friend was now. "Sure," Conner answered as his eyes drifted toward the ground.

"Then—when you saw him—did you think that was gonna be the last time?"

"Of course not!" Conner's eyes shot up to meet Mathews.

"I still hope it's not."

"Well me too, brother. You remember the last time we were all together? Everyone, even Stretch."

"I guess it had to be sometime around the end of our Kandahar deployment."

"No, the last time we were actually all hangin' out together having fun."

Conner shook his head as he searched his mind.

"Yeah me either, that's the point. We gotta treasure the good times. Really have a blast. Treat each other right and not worry about the little things."

Conner's mind was still turning, landing on a memory from long ago—*2002 maybe—all six of us packed into a car in Germany.* His head shook involuntarily as he thought. *Military trips were so much like the nights in high school. You're always stuck somewhere with no transportation, and when someone found wheels, everyone jumped at the chance to get out. We always ended up with a bunch of dudes crammed in a car together trying to find food or beer. Never a single girl in sight.*

In Conner's mind, Stretch was driving, and the normally quiet, mild-mannered kid was singing at the top of his lungs. *We all were. Well, I guess he wasn't a kid, he was older than me at the time—but he seems like one now looking back because he was only maybe twenty-two? Either way, Stretch had the music cranked, "And I need you now tonight! And I need you more than ever!" For some reason the German radio stations always seemed to be about twenty years behind. Those people must really love the eighties. The windows were down, the music blaring out into the world, and we were all singing. "Together we can take it to the end of the line, Your love is like a shadow on me all of the time!"*

Stretch was speeding toward base. When the song came on he'd gotten it in his head that singing Bonnie Tyler to the gate guards would be hilarious. Now he was afraid the song would end before we got there, but it didn't. "Once upon a time I was falling in love, But now I'm only falling apart! There's nothing I can do! Total eclipse of the heart!" Stretch belted out the lyrics and the rest of us sang right along with him. His eyes closing as he shouted out the words—one hand gripping his chest with passion, the other extended through the car window passing our military IDs to the security augmentees. "Once upon a time there was light in my life, But now there's only love in the dark. Nothing I can say! A total eclipse of the heart!" The airmen at the gate doubling over with uncontrollable laughter.

"I do have some good memories of us all, though," Conner grinned. "Singing to the gate guards in Ramstein."

"And if you'll only hold me tight!" Mathews closed his eyes as he dramatically rang out the tune, "We'll be holding on forever!"

Conner laughed as Mathews produced a bold smile.

"That's what I'm talking about! Memories like that, we gotta make more of them!" He took in a deep breath and exhaled hard as he pivoted forward again and continued up the sidewalk. "Ain't nonna us know what's gonna happen."

Conner nodded, falling into step with his friend.

"There's another surge comin' bro, Afghanistan this time. A shit ton of ground personnel and equipment. They're gonna have to use the C-5s and C-17s to get it all over there, then the 130s to shuttle it all around once it's in theater. Just like they did in Iraq. This time next year we're all gonna be scattered to hell and back workin' a million hours a week again just trying to keep up. We gotta enjoy life now while we know we can."

"You serious, man? Where'd you hear that?"

"The writin's on the wall. It's only a matter of time."

Conner swallowed hard again, internally debating the merits of Mathews' ability to predict future US military operations while simultaneously wondering how Joselyd would react if he had to leave for six months or a year. *It might be alright if she knew it was just one time... but what are the odds of that?*

Ahead of them a white guy in his late twenties with aviator glasses, styled hair and a Hawaiian shirt had awkwardly paused on the sidewalk. It felt like he was staring at them though Conner couldn't exactly tell due to the man's shades.

"Hey, y'all down here on vacation?" the man asked, taking a half step toward them as they approached.

"Why you askin', dawg?" Mathews answered. "You already know we are."

"Sure, sure, well, need any help finding anything?"

Conner's eyes narrowed, as he locked onto the man's chubby face. Neither he nor Mathews slowed as they continued past him.

"We're good, boss," Mathews responded.

The man turned and hustled along beside them, struggling to keep pace. Lowering his tone he asked, "You fellas trying to party?"

"Ha!" Mathews let out, "Not in the way you're asking!"

"How about some weed then? I got good stuff, I swear. You'll like it."

A big goofy grin crossed Mathews' face as he erupted into a frantic giggle. Beside him the man stopped walking and stood on the sidewalk, likely glaring from behind his aviators.

Mathews spun around but continued to move away from him, stepping backward on the sidewalk, "You come find me in about ten years when I retire and we'll talk!" he called between sporadic half-giggling bouts.

Mathews pivoted back around and continued alongside Conner, shaking his head. "What a fuckin' jackass! 'Are y'all down here on vacation?' Holy shit, he needs to work on his approach!" He continued chuckling as they walked on, passing a café touting 'world famous key lime pie'. "Let's try some key lime pie! I've never had it, have you?"

Conner shook his head.

"No wait," Mathews produced his phone and flipped it open, "let's go find the guys first. I want to get pie for everybody!"

They altered course onto Petronia Street and found Mc-Cabe a few blocks later, standing on the sidewalk holding an oversized paper shopping bag with hooped handles. Stone stood nearby with his arms crossed, leaning against a pastel-blue store front.

Mathews glanced at McCabe with a big goofy smile. "Keeping the fiancée happy?"

"Dude," McCabe nodded, pumping the bag up and down,

"This is money well spent."

Turning toward Conner, Mathews jerked a thumb in Mc-Cabe's direction, "Smart man. Come on guys, there's a shop up the street, I'm gonna get us all key lime pie."

"I appreciate ya dude, but after all that pineapple and those sweet drinks, my stomach is already upside down. Any more sugar and I'll be miserable."

Conner shook his head, "honestly man, that one piña colada put me in about the same spot."

"Whatever losers," Mathews groaned. "Stone you ain't afraid of a little sugar, are you?"

"I could eat a slice of pie."

"See you jokers in a few," Mathews called over his shoulder as he moved back up the sidewalk toward the café.

"Might as well hang here," McCabe suggested. "There's a bench across the street."

CHAPTER 20

Conner and McCabe sat together on opposite ends of the park bench as various groups passed by—older people, younger people, families, guys, girls, couples, clusters of friends on vacation. No one looked in their direction or seemed to notice them at all. After a while Conner began to feel as if he were invisible. He glanced at people as they walked past, but still no one acknowledged him. *Maybe it's the shirts? Do we just look completely non-threatening? That's good I guess, in a way.* At the same time, it made him remember what McCabe and Stone had said each in their own way. *How the world would just continue on regardless of what they did. The wars would be lost or won without them. Everything was already moving toward whatever was going to happen.*

He turned to McCabe. "Man, I've been thinking about what you said. You know, about how these big trends in history are already in motion. And if some critical player drops off, someone else just steps up to fill their role."

Conner felt a strange sort of relief when McCabe's head turned slightly in response.

"You've already managed to summarize it better than I did when I was trying to explain it to you. Honestly though," McCabe groaned, "I thought you'd have worked this out and be off it by now."

"I don't know, I keep thinking about the big picture like you described with George Washington, only on a smaller scale, like for our lives."

"Ok."

"Yeah, my mind keeps coming back to it. I even asked Stone about it."

McCabe rolled his eyes and shook his head without glancing over at Conner. "I can only imagine what kind of cryptic shit he told you."

"No man, honestly, he kind of said the same thing you did, only in a different way."

"Really?"

"Yeah, he just had one major difference. He said there's these moments in life where you can do something that really matters. He thinks you never know when they're happening, so you have to stand up and do what's best all the time. Any action you take could be the instance that you really change someone's life."

Conner's eyes flicked to his friend to gauge his reaction, but McCabe only sat there with no real expression.

"I was thinking something sort of like that when I asked you. Only not exactly. Anyway," Conner continued, "do you really believe that it doesn't matter? Like nothing we do really has an impact because if we weren't there, someone else would just backfill our role? Maybe I just want people to be more important than they are, but I feel like there has to be more to our lives than just causing inconsequential nuance in the world around us."

A group of fit looking college-age girls in short jean shorts and tube tops crossed a few feet in front of them on the sidewalk. The late day sun glinted off their belly button rings and shiny bracelets as they gossiped loudly about something someone had said, and how another girl had overreacted. None of their eyes shifted toward Conner or McCabe. *It's as if we don't exist at all. Or perhaps they're in some other dimension that we can see, but not interact with. They might as well be... a whole successful trajectory for life, college, careers that didn't require climbing through flap wells, or getting covered with carcinogenic oils, or deploying to combat zones, or your ears ringing anytime things get quiet.*

McCabe turned his head slightly in Conner's direction. "Dude, if you believe what you believe, then why are you asking me about it? What do you want me to say?"

"I don't know man, I just respect your opinion and want to know what you think."

"Conner, there is no answer to what you're asking me. You need to have enough confidence to trust what you believe, even if the people around you feel different."

"Maybe it's like what you said about reading history? How it can help you better understand the way you want to act in your own life if something happens. I just want to hear your perspective, that's all."

McCabe inhaled deep. "Well, I believe, every once in a while someone does do something extraordinary. Something that if they weren't there, whoever took their place might not have done. I don't think it hardly ever happens, not in a meaningful way anyhow. But it does happen. Take ol' GW again. Sure, if he weren't there for whatever reason, someone else would have become the first president. No big deal—the foundation for democracy had been set, the Constitution had been written and ratified, the founding fathers were already well on their way to framing the balance of powers—but... would whoever took Washington's place have turned down the chance to be king? Made no effort to seize power for his family? Deliberately stepped down at the end of his second term to set a precedent for everyone who followed him—doing his best to ensure the US stayed on a path toward democracy? See, that's one little moment where an individual really mattered. Someone else could have gotten greedy and ended our new republic rather rapidly.

"Don't think it would happen? Well there's dozens of examples of countries overthrowing their authoritarian governments in exchange for democracy, only to have their first elected leader become the new dictator. It certainly could have happened here too."

Conner nodded, his mind drifting. "Yeah I get that."

The whole world would be so incredibly different. Hell, our lives certainly would have changed dramatically. None of us would be in the military. Who would volunteer to travel across the world to some distant desert combat zone for a king? The concept of doing something good—bringing freedom to oppressed people—is a whole hell of a lot more appealing. His eyes closed as he exhaled. *But then, for thousands of years people did go to war for kings...*

It's the idea of it, though. The principles that we believe in. If we'd grown up under a different system we wouldn't have fundamentally different values. It's not who we are. It just wouldn't make sense. But even as he thought it, his mind went to the Ukrainian girl who had crossed an ocean just to serve drinks. He shook his head. *Not to serve drinks, she came here to see someplace new and maybe make a little money. No deeper meaning. Maybe none of this is all that complex. Is there just some little urge inside people that makes them want to get out into the world? No matter the method? Or is that just some piece of it, and wanting to help people and make money and be a part of something are all other little elements that get rolled in as well?* Conner opened his eyes again and watched all the people passing by. *Maybe there's no real way to understand what's happening. What a mess life is.*

Conner extended his arm out of the Mustang and the summer air whipped over his hand as they cruised north onto the Seven Mile Bridge. Off to the left, an older bridge ran alongside them. Archaic looking guard rails of heavy gauge steel—etched with a crusted layer of rust—lined its crumbling concrete surface.

Conner's gaze shifted beyond the old bridge into the open expanse of clear turquoise and jade that extended to the pastel-blue horizon where the Gulf touched the sky. His eyes lingered there a moment, taking it in before focusing back on the ruins of the decaying bridge in the foreground. *What a scar on such a beautiful scene.*

"Why don't they tear that old bridge down?" Conner asked over the sound of the air rushing just above their heads.

"It costs money," Stone responded, "And really there's no incentive."

"I mean, they could scrap all that steel, so it could get used for something. And all that concrete, they could use it for fill or jetties or to start reefs or I don't know. I'm not a construction guy but I'm sure there's a lot better uses than to just have it sitting there looking bad as it slowly goes to rubble."

"It's easier just to start from scratch," Stone answered. "There's mines and quarries, production lines all in place to crank out new materials. They can just make phone calls and write checks and it all shows up ready to go. It's a whole lot more complicated to reuse the old, and the systems out there aren't nearly as streamlined."

"Well then they ought to at least turn it into something nice. I don't know what, but anything would be better than what it is."

"That," Stone sighed, "is even more expensive."

To their left, a brush of forest green jutted into the skyline breaking the steady geometric contours of the corroding guardrails. *Amazing*, Conner thought, honing in on a tree that had managed to grow from the center of the crumbling concrete. *Absolutely incredible that life finds a way. How many millions of seeds must have landed on that old bridge for one to even begin to grow? Then to continue to survive, through the wind and storms, with no earth there to hold any moisture or provide any minerals and nutrients, just roots attempting to break their way through the concrete and hold on. And why not? The tree didn't know its odds were a million to one. It could simply believe this is how every tree lives, and its choices were only to try its hardest or lay down and die.*

Conner ran his fingers through his short hair. *Maybe that's the problem with people. We're too smart. We can calculate the odds. Lets us psych ourselves out and give up.* Conner exhaled slowly as his mind continued to churn, finally settling on the sailing ships of old—their crews setting out for ports they could not see, far beyond the horizon. Then to all his own missions into hostile territory, and all the troops they'd flown in. *Individuals who boarded the plane knowing full well they'd be dropped off in a war zone for the next six or twelve months, and they did it anyway. Maybe it's more complex. We can psych ourselves up to get through stuff or even do incredible things, not just talk ourselves into defeat. Or we're just designed to fill certain roles like Stone said, we fall into a group and do what the team expects of us. Or maybe it's not complex at all, perhaps we just have a built-in drive to push for as long as we can. Maybe it's like a limit, and we just go until we run out.*

Conner shook his head as they proceeded past the defiant tree. *Why the fuck do I think about this shit? It's like I can't help it. It's just there. Something in there trying to make sense out of it all.* Attempting to clear his mind, he allowed his hand to ride up and down in the current of air outside as they moved steadily toward their beach house on Marathon Key.

CHAPTER 21

Conner flipped the lights out to go to bed, but when he did the moon shone so brightly through the window that the room was still lit. He stood there for a moment contemplating it, North America with its back to the sun, but the light reflecting with such an intensity that it now illuminated the dark Earth enough to leave sharp moon shadows. He drifted to the door and slid outside. The moonlit beachscape was dreamlike, appearing to have an almost mystical quality. His mind wandered, considering if there was any truth to the old sayings that police and emergency rooms were always busier during the full moon. Or that if women slept outside under the open sky their cycles would align with the moon's phases, thus ensuring their supernatural ability to create new life occurred while the night was darkest, when the men were likely home and not out hunting or causing mischief.

Conner smiled, remembering Joselyd's giggling description of her teenaged self, during nice nights in the summer, donning a bikini and slinking out her window to "moon bathe" on her parents' roof. *Damn, I got it bad...* he grinned, staring up at the celestial satellite, his mind locking onto a concept from some childhood movie, *No matter how far apart we are, we still gaze upon the same moon.*

It was bizarre when he really thought about it, all the places he'd been in the world—terrible and wonderful—it being the same moon every time his eyes had angled toward the night sky. Conner's gaze slid down to the horizon, then to the flashes of moonlight on the crests of approaching waves. It hardly seemed possible that something so quiet, and so far away was dictating the movements of the ocean—the pulling in and out of the tides. *Something we accept as a normal piece of our world, and barely think about, having this massive impact on how we act.*

Conner's eyes followed a swell into the shoreline and then continued, tracing the contours of sand dunes off to one side in the middle distance before settling on a dark silhouette on the beach. He focused on it, wondering why he hadn't noticed it before and searched his mind for anything that had been there in the daylight. It remained perfectly still, though he became certain it was a man sitting in the sand, staring out to sea.

Conner approached slowly at first, plotting a course well to the left of the unknown individual. As he trudged forward in the uneven sand, the figure's features sharpened. "*Stone?*" Conner adjusted to a direct route.

"It's the periphery," Stone nearly whispered as Conner approached.

"What?"

"Sorry... talking to myself," Stone answered, shaking his head before staring back out at the waves crashing on the dark beach.

Conner laughed, clasping his hand on Stone's shoulder and shaking him a bit. "About what?"

The sound of the ocean rushing in and being pulled back out traveled up the shoreline.

"There's some scientific theory that says you can never really study anything because things act different while they're being observed."

"Ok…" Conner chuckled and shook him again.

"You remember Stretch's memorial service?"

Conner swallowed hard. It had been just a couple weeks after they returned from Kandahar, they had been in formation in their blues in the cemetery and held a salute while "Amazing Grace" played on the bagpipes. Conner's hand dropping from Stone's shoulder as a wave of suppressed feelings flooded his mind. "Of course, God, that was horrible."

"Lewis was beside me in formation, we formed up quick and I didn't even know it was him 'til after. He was on the very end of the row. I was next to him holding my salute and the bagpipes started and I could see his chest start convulsing. Like he was crying, but he wasn't, he didn't make a sound. I could just see the shaking in my peripheral vision.

"After, I asked him if he was alright and he nodded. His face looked a little upset, but only because I knew him so well. Mainly he just looked the same as he always did, the same as everyone else."

Conner let out a long exhale and allowed his eyes to shift out to the beach, searching for whatever fixed point Stone seemed to be staring at, but there was nothing there except the dark rhythmic waves.

"You know what he was doing before?"

"Stretch?" Conner turned his head slightly and glanced

side-eyed at his friend, but Stone looked on at the vast dark ocean without meeting his gaze. "Honestly, man the whole thing bothered me so much I didn't ask too many questions or try and find out the details. We'd been stationed together four years at that point."

"He was back in his hometown, on leave, playing basketball. He was on the basketball team in high school, ya know. Just with his high school friends shooting hoops in the park. Even the little hick town in Missouri he was from had cameras on the parking lot. They showed him slap hands with his buddies, wait until their cars left, then he got in his truck, reached under the driver's seat and shot himself in the face. Zero hesitation."

"Jesus."

The waves crashed in the night. The foamy bubbles on top of the caps caught the moonlight as they raced up the beach, and then lay abandoned in the sand as the water was pulled back out, the tiny bubbles popping until there was nothing there at all.

Conner took a breath as if to speak but then said nothing as another set of swells rolled in. Images of Stretch encompassed his thoughts as he made another attempt. "He was always quiet. But he would work his ass off and back us up. You could really rely on him. He was a real friend, ya know? I just could never think what would make him do that to himself."

"There's no real way to know," Stone sighed. "But the way I figure it, basketball was his favorite thing. And he was there with his best friends from home, doing the thing he loved the most and he didn't have any fun at all. Then that was it. Game over. He thought 'I'm doing the most fun thing in the world and I feel horrible. Time to get out.'

"That's what I think anyway. I could be wrong, he could have had the plan from months before, pushed himself through the rest of the deployment 'cause he wanted to get home and play basketball with his buddies one more time before he went. That's possible too, wanting to go out on a high note like that, but I really feel like if he'd had fun with his friends, he would have at least hesitated. Thought, 'maybe I should hang around a couple more days so I can play again.' Or something. Anyway, what the hell do I know? Maybe I'm totally full of shit." He released a long breath into the cool ocean breeze making its way inland atop the waves. His gaze never faltered, as if he were waiting intently for something deep within the dark salty water to reveal itself. "Like I said, it's the periphery. You can't see anything if you look right at it."

Fuck, Conner stared at his friend contemplating as the possibilities manifested in his mind. *I must be overreacting. Stone would never hurt himself. He's just not wired that way, he presses forward no matter what.*

But are you? Would you have thought the same about Stretch a few years ago? After the deployment, before we all went home on leave?

I was too maxed out with my own problems to even question anybody else back then.

But you're not now. So... are you overreacting?

Doesn't matter, can't take the chance. I can't risk rolling the dice just because I don't want to ask an awkward question.

Conner looked at his friend. But Stone continued to stare out at some imaginary point on the dark shoreline.

What did they say in Air Force training? "ACE." Ask the question, act like you Care, then Escort, stay with them until you get them to some type of professional.

Conner shook his head. *That's because there is no fix. If there were a fix it'd be in there. But there's not. The best end result you can hope for is turning them over to a chaplain or counselor. Even then, they can't stay with that person forever. At some point they'll be on their own. What did McCabe say? People gotta save themselves? It's like they're surrounded by an invisible force field. You can see all the bad stuff happening, but you can't break through and help.*

Conner took a deep breath. "Hey Stone," he asked, pausing to see if his friend would turn to face him. "You're not thinking about hurting yourself or anything are you?"

Stone's gaze remained fixed on the crashing waves as the question hung heavy in the ocean air.

Conner felt his face getting hot, he imagined it'd be red if there were more than moonlight and anyone were looking at him. Waves came in sets and crashed on the beach in front of them as Conner hung there in the sand, scrambling inside his mind for something to say that would sound alright. But nothing occurred to him. Beside him Stone remained motionless. *Could he be so deep in thought he doesn't hear me?* Conner sucked in the ocean air and held it before releasing a long slow exhale as his face slowly began to cool.

"Turns out I'm more Eben Flood than Richard Cory," Stone replied.

"What?"

Stone took a deep breath, "I thought about it."

Conner's chest tightened.

"But I'm not going to. I've got some drive and some knowledge from all the places I've been and things I've worked on. I've decided I have an obligation to stick around. Try and help people out when I can. Plus it'd be really hard on my Dad. That wouldn't be fair to him."

Conner exhaled slowly again, though his chest only partially relaxed. "Well hey, there's no need to keep suffering. What would make you feel good? Let's figure it out and work on that."

A cool breeze came in atop another set of ocean swells.

"I've thought about that a lot... I'd be a lot more useful to the world if I was easier to be around and wasn't so upset. But outside some magical chance for a do-over or time machine... the only real thing is if Shannon came back."

Conner took a breath to speak but instead just let it out as his eyes shifted back toward the horizon.

"I know it's not going to happen," Stone responded as if Conner had said as much.

"There's got to be something else."

"There could be one thing..." Stone contemplated in a low

murmur. "I remember when I was in basic—back when it was still hard—before the wars started and recruitment was down and they were just pushing anybody through. My training instructor was a straight fucking psychopath. He'd make a knife hand and jut his middle finger at my eye while I was standing at attention trying to make me flinch. He'd be screaming at me, and I wouldn't even hear what he was saying because inside my mind I'd be doing math. Calculating how many days were left, then hours, then minutes, then the percentage of that time that I would be awake, though I suppose that wasn't fair because the TIs were yelling at me in my dreams as well. Anyway, didn't matter what they were sayin' because I was just running through the numbers.

"I think that if I got fucked up now—I mean really fucking hurt—like crushed orbitals so they'd bandage my eyes closed, broken jaw so I couldn't talk or eat, jacked up fingers, cracked ribs so it hurt if I laughed. You know, put my body in the same place as my mind..." Stone cleared his throat, "I think I'd just be doing math in my head, crunching the numbers on however long the doctors told me it'd take to get well. Maybe months later when I did... maybe my body and mind would come back online together, like some kinda reboot."

Conner gulped, struggling not to look at him, knowing Stone would not return his gaze.

Stone exhaled slowly, "I know that's real selfish though, taking up all that hospital time and shit, occupying all those educated peoples' energy to help me out. So I'd only want it if it happened while I was doing something good. Like saving someone out of a collapsing building or from a mob of attackers or something. Saving someone good, not some other asshole like me."

Conner reached over without looking, clasping a hand on his friend's shoulder. *Life is rough... I've got no instructions or experience for how to deal with this.* McCabe's cryptic advice about saying something human wasn't helping. *Things were easier when it was a clear problem to solve, an aircraft to troubleshoot, a component to replace or even an enemy fight.*

"I'm sorry Conner, I don't know why I said all that. Shit's not fair to put on you. Especially now, out here getting to take some leave and try and have some fun with your old pals at the beach. I didn't mean to let all that slip out."

Conner squeezed his shoulder, searching within for a response that would somehow help. *Shouldn't I have some kind of natural feeling for what to do? Something human? Something that doesn't require training or instructions? Joselyd would know. That girl is so empathetic it seems like she always knows exactly what to do to make people feel better. I'm fucking useless in these situations.*

"Of course, if it was protecting someone from an attacker," Stone continued, "I'd want to put up an epic fight. Fuck the aggressor up a good bit too." Stone chuckled softly between the sounds of the incoming tide. "Smash his nose in good enough that it whistled a little every time he talked for the rest of his life," he laughed. "Give him a little something to remember me by!"

Conner released a slight smile and shook his friend's shoulder a little as the waves rolled. *Perhaps this is the human response.*

CHAPTER 22

There were already voices coming from the common area when Conner stretched awake. He pulled the blinds aside and squinted out into the bright morning light. The sun glared off the sand with such an intensity that he shut his eyes tight and allowed the blinds to swing back into place. It took a few minutes before he managed to open his eyes again. He fumbled beside him for his cell phone, but when he looked, Joselyd still hadn't responded to his text messages. *Maybe her phone is broken or her charger quit working or something. I hope she gets it figured out before she has to pick me up from the airport.* His own charger had been finicky, and he had to position his phone just right to get the thing to take power.

> Good Morning! Just checking on ya. Hope you're doing alright

He forced himself out of bed and pulled his shorts on when his phone buzzed.

Stop worrying about me for once and
go have a good time with your friends.
PLEASE!

Smiling, he glanced down at his phone and tapped out another message.

We're having a great time! Glad your
phone is working again. :)

Conner hit send and made his way to the kitchen.

"I hope you're hungry," Stone called, nodding accusatorily toward Mathews, "Someone bought two pounds of bacon and several dozen eggs."

"You're *welcome!*" Mathews answered. "Better start cookin'!"

Conner tried to speak, but instead let out a yawn as he attempted to rub the sleep out of his eyes.

"There's still a stack of lobster tails in here, too," Stone continued. "We caught 'em, we have to eat 'em."

"Lobster omelets it is!" Mathews let out with a grin. "We can fry them in the bacon grease. It'll be great."

Stone flicked his knife open and sliced into the bacon packages before dumping the contents into a deep rimmed frying pan. Mathews brought a plate of lobster tails to the table and began picking the meat out and placing it into a bowl.

"Is McCabe up yet?" Conner asked, his eyes landing on Mathews.

"You're not real good at picking up on patterns are you?"

Conner tilted his head to one side with a half frown. "Come on man, cut me some slack."

"The thing about people," Mathews continued, "is that a lot of them aren't real smart. But they pick up on patterns really well. That's why the military can take a bunch of guys—some of them real dumbasses—and train them to complete incredibly complex tasks. It's really kinda amazing. Amazing in the same way that a person can teach a border collie to do like a hundred tricks if they work with them long enough."

Conner squinted at him.

"You, my brother, are something else entirely," Mathews continued without looking up. "You're certainly intelligent. You think about things and really can figure stuff out if you put your mind to it. But I'd never recommend you for any kind of trend analysis position. It just doesn't always occur to you to put the pieces together. I don't think that'll ever change, but it'd be great if you concentrated on building the confidence to make a few decisions for yourself every once in a while."

"What the hell are you talking about?"

"McCabe," Mathews' blue eyes shot up to meet Conner's, "is out on a run. He left almost an hour ago."

"Man, you could have just said that. You don't gotta be a dick first thing in the morning."

"We all have our flaws," Mathews continued. "I, for instance, have been told on multiple occasions that I'm lacking in tact. That was my best effort in politely explaining, that you need to fuckin' learn to pay attention and think for yourself."

Conner exhaled hard.

"No bullshit bro, I'm trying to help you out. If I don't tell ya, who will?"

"Whatever," Conner responded. The sound of popping and sizzling gradually came to life through the entrance in the kitchen. "When did McCabe become such a health nut anyway? He always went to the gym, but I don't ever remember him running like this."

Mathews raised his eyebrows and took a deep breath. "He likes being in shape, but I think it's more of a reaction than a desire to be super healthy."

"What do ya mean?"

"I don't know bro. You pay attention and come to your own conclusions. Who am I to say anyway?"

Conner stared at him, his eyes narrowing.

"Don't worry about it. Let's get these omelets going. I want to sit out on the deck in the sun while we eat, so we can look at the water. We gotta soak up this nice weather and these sweet beach vibes while we can."

"Sounds good to me," Conner shrugged.

In the kitchen, Stone had the entire stove top full of various pots and pans. Mathews' eyebrows drew together as he handed him the bowl full of lobster meat.

"Bro, what are you boiling water for?"

"I'm going to hard boil whatever eggs we got left over so they don't go bad so quick."

Mathews exhaled, his eyes flicking to the ears of corn and additional lobster tails lined up in gallon Ziploc bags on the counter top. He blinked and shook his head. "What the hell are you doin'? We're on vacation, there's no time for meal planning! You're supposed to be relaxing! Leave that shit."

"Nahh, it's no trouble. I'm standing here frying bacon and cooking omelets anyway. I might as well."

"It's summer in Florida bro! It's all gonna go bad in no time!"

Stone turned slightly, his eyes shifting away from the stove toward Mathews. "Why you stressing? I got water bottles in the freezer right now to keep it all cold until it gets eaten."

Mathews shook his head again. "If you need food later I'll buy ya more."

"I can buy my own food," Stone answered, turning his attention back to the range and working to flip the bacon. "I just don't want to waste this stuff."

"Come on Conner, let's go chill out on the deck and let this joker do his thing."

"I can hang here and help out," Conner offered.

"No need," Stone replied. "I've got it all under control, and I don't mind making food for you guys."

Conner shrugged before following Mathews outside. The morning air was clear without its typical heavy Florida muggy feel and a fresh breeze brushed past them on its way out to sea. Conner slipped his sunglasses on and gazed across the beach to the water. *Hard to believe this is the same spot where Stone was sitting alone in the dark just a few hours ago. It feels completely different now.*

"Literally the most capable person I know," Mathews began, turning his back to the breeze and flicking his lighter as he held it to the cigarette in his mouth. "Maybe even the most adept person I've ever met, and the man decides to become a fucking hobo."

"I think it's more complicated than that," Conner answered.

"Honestly bro, I thought that mug was more wrecked than he is. Like I must have been stereotyping or something, because when I heard he just dropped off, ditched his phone and disappeared, I figured he'd seriously suffered a mental break of some sort. I mean, it seemed like the most plausible answer, even though I wouldn't have thought it possible before Stretch did what he did and Lewis decided not to be found.

"But Stone, I mean... the guy is still completely rational when you talk to him. He's just not any fun anymore," Mathews took two quick puffs on his cigarette. "Really though, he must not be rational because that mug sleeps in the dirt in the desert beside his van. Honestly, I think the shit might be weighing on me a bit. I need to find a way to refocus and have a good time with everyone while we all get to be together. I don't want to act all negative like ol' Brackish McCabe." Mathews gripped the deck railing, the cigarette burning between his fingers as he blew smoke out through his nose. "I gotta get my shit together."

"Hey man, you're doing just fine," Conner offered. "Nobody can be positive all the time."

The two stood there together against the railing gazing out at the ocean as the slow shallow waves lapped in, making the blue-green water appear chalky where the disrupted sand swirled underneath the surface.

"Yeah," Mathews eventually commented, pulling his shirt off and allowing the sun to hit his light-colored chest. "No more negativity, I'm done with it. I got my mind back in vacation mode. I think I'll get the party started right now, go inside and make myself a refreshing mimosa. Gonna have a bad ass day, and an amazing last night with my friends."

Conner nodded.

"You want one, bro?"

Conner glanced at him side-eyed, "It's eight-thirty in the morning, man."

"Suit yourself," Mathews shrugged. "Oh look, here comes McCabe. Damn that joker was runnin' for a long time."

"Oh yeah, oh yeah!" Mathews let out when Stone announced that breakfast was ready. They made plates at the table and moved outside where Mathews had set up reclining beach chairs from a closet in the common area.

McCabe crashed down in one of the seats and brought his hand to his forehead. "I about wore myself out."

"Yeah, you're out runnin' and I'm drinking a mimosa," Mathews chuckled. "I think one of us knows how to vacation right."

"Saturday night, Fourth of July on South Beach. I'll have plenty of time to party it up this evening," McCabe answered.

"True that!" Mathews nodded. "This place is beautiful, though. I wouldn't even want to leave if there weren't a bunch of Cuban babes waiting for us in Miami."

"I have to agree," Stone said. "I've never been to the Keys before, but it certainly is a nice place."

"Imagine if we lived like ten thousand years ago," Mathews spouted out between huge mouthfuls from his plate, overflowing with a pan-sized omelet and an impressive pile of bacon. "We could just hang out in nature all the time."

"Ha!" Conner laughed. "A couple days ago you said we were living in a golden age. Now you want to go prehistoric!"

"Well sure we are living in a golden age. I mean, normal working-class people like us can buy plane tickets to travel across the world. And think about it, for the equivalent of an hour's wages I can buy a t-shirt or something decent to eat. Working-class people have probably never been able to do that before in history. Hell, our ancestors could have been indentured servants who had to work for seven years to pay for their boat ride over from Europe. I for one know I didn't come from any rich family line—those mugs had to struggle to make it over here. And they must have had it even worse where they came from, or they wouldn't have wanted to leave."

McCabe shook his head, "So you want to leave our 'golden age,'" he asked, holding his hands up shoulder width apart and making air quotes with his fingers, "and return to some past era where you had to worry about malaria and dysentery?"

"Sure, there'd be things that suck about it, but there'd be something to livin' in nature all the time."

"Your froofy ass wouldn't make it a week," McCabe laughed, shaking his head again. "Living off the land is hard, I guarantee it."

"Nahh bro, you think that, because it'd be hard now." Mathews tipped back his mimosa. "It's hard now because people built on all the easy spots. All the valleys with good access to water and food are developed. So when people think of nature they think of mountains and deserts and places that were never any good to live in, that's why they're still empty."

"He's got a point," Stone agreed.

"I don't know man," Conner said, "diving for lobsters made me pretty tired the other day. If you didn't get to eat anytime you had a bad day at work, it'd be pretty rough."

"Wrong again," Mathews answered. "Back in the day things were way different. The world we live in now is depleted. All the animals that were easy to hunt are probably extinct, and the water would have been so clear with so many fish you could get whatever you needed without too much trouble."

"Huh," Conner tried to envision a world before modern civilization, but his mind had trouble settling on anything he could identify with.

"I mean, we all saw those Hemingway pictures in Key West. That joker was bringing in massive trophy fish that weighed more than a thousand pounds, and that was only like seventy years ago. Fish like that aren't out there now, not in any kinda numbers anyway. Imagine what it was like before, way back."

"You might be right," McCabe confessed, "But I think if I had the option to travel back thousands of years, I'd stay right here."

"Bro, I'm telling you it'd be great. Not like now where there's this complicated order to everything. Taxes and bureaucracy, the complex social structures of dating, paperwork, insurance, speeding tickets. You wouldn't have to worry about any of that bullshit."

"Sure, that sounds good, too bad you'd only live to be like thirty-eight," Conner insisted.

"Yeah... that's true, but it might be worth it. I mean, even if you didn't make it to forty, it would all be truly lived. None of your life wasted standing in line, or commuting to work, or studying algebra in high school under a bunch of dim fluorescent lights. Everything you did would be real. Out in nature. Actually living."

"I do just fine here in the modern era," McCabe answered.

"No you don't!"

McCabe's eyes narrowed as he slowly turned his head to face Mathews.

"None of us do!" Mathews met McCabe's gaze without a hint of apprehension. "Why you think you go runnin' all the time? Why you think we all wanted to fly down here and see each other? Or why we like being on the beach near the ocean? Or why we got such a bang out of catching those lobsters on our own instead of just buying food at the store? We need this shit, bro! It's missing in our daily lives and it ain't natural!"

McCabe's dark eyes seemed to soften as he stared back.

"I mean, think of it," Mathews continued. "You'd be with your brothers and the mugs you grew up with out in nature every day. It'd be great."

"Maybe for you, dude. I grew up with a bunch of jackasses that just wanted to smoke weed and play video games all day. That's why I joined the Air Force, so I could get the hell outta there, hang out with some guys that actually had some purpose and some honor."

"Well that sucks for you bro, but I love the guys I came up with. And livin' like that—with your best friends—would be totally badass because you could just hang out and go fishing, hunt deer and fuck cave women all the time."

"I'm not sure it worked quite like that."

"Of course it would! You'd be bringing home the meat! The ladies would actually need us."

"Dude, if that were true then, it'd be true now."

"Naw bro, now is completely different. It's almost two to one, girls going to college. They're the ones getting educated and making the big bucks. I guess there's still a wage gap because that's what they say on the news. But if that shit's true, I'm sure it's cause a lot of guys get stuck doing shit like we are, working outside all winter getting covered in toxic chemicals while we lose our hearing and fly in and out of war zones. I'm sure plenty of guys would take a pay cut for some eight-hour-a-day climate controlled office gig where you didn't have to watch everything you touched for fear of losing a finger. Anyway, what I'm saying is the ladies don't need us now, they're pulling their own paychecks and livin' in a civil society where they don't need protection. That's why we gotta work so hard to get any lovin'."

"Dude would you really want to hook up with some cave girl? Razors and deodorant thousands of years away from being invented. They didn't even have soap back then. I guarantee you those girls were grody."

"Hell yeah I would! Some thick blonde woman with real muscles from doin' legit work, wearing nothing but animal skins!"

McCabe glanced at him and shook his head.

"Think about it, bro!"

"I am thinking about it!"

"No, for real. I'm tired of all these dainty ladies that don't understand me at all. I'm sure there's something to all that school and office work, or they wouldn't pay people mad money to do it. But I'm sick of not being able to talk to a single girl who can relate to me. Like, even if they are working hard in a different way, they don't fuckin' understand me at all. They're not climbing through flap wells to lube grease fittings, or contorting their bodies into some kinda weird ass position to try and reach a bolt that needs tightening in the landing gear.

"Bro, back then, thousands of years ago, living in the wild, you'd have a solid connection with your woman. She'd know exactly what you're about because you'd be working together out in the elements to do the most basic things like find food. You'd actually need each other in some kind of legit primal way. Having a bond like that would be incredible."

Conner glanced at him out of the corners of his eyes, "You don't think people can do that now?"

"Fuck no!" Mathews exhaled. "That's not fair, I'm sure you boys are in great relationships, but that shit's rare now. I mean just look at the divorce rate. In modern society, they just don't need us. We keep going after them because it's in our fuckin' DNA. They're the main drive we have to go forward. There might be more to our existence than just pursuing women, but whatever the rest of it is, it doesn't make sense without them. We can't be happy on our own like they can. At least not for long stretches."

Conner's eyes drifted to Stone, somewhere deep inside wondering what it was really like living out in a van in the wilderness. *I mean, he must have days where he doesn't even talk, maybe even weeks. Just on his own with no one around. How would that be? Not even hearing your own voice for weeks on end. Just lost in thought maybe? I guess I'll never know unless I tried something like that.*

"What do you think, Stone?" Mathews asked. "You ain't hardly said shit since you brought me my lobster and eggs."

Stone lifted his empty plate out of his lap and set it on the deck beside him. "With our luck," he began, "if we were back in ten thousand BC or something, we'd end up in a tribe full of beautiful Amazon warrior women. They'd do all the hunting and fishing and defending from enemy clans and we'd be redundant. They wouldn't need us at all."

Mathews rolled his eyes. "Thanks Stone, way to wreck my dreams."

McCabe shook his head as he stood up. "I don't think the odds of you stumbling across a time machine while you're still in your prime are too great anyway."

"That's not the point," Mathews answered.

McCabe extended a hand to pull him out of the beach chair. "Come on. I don't want to leave this place either, but we should get packed up so we can check out on time."

"It's all going by too fast," Stone commented, almost to himself, lifting his uncasted hand and snapping. "How come all the good times always flash by so quick?"

CHAPTER 23

Stone leaned forward in his seat, his eyes tracking something off to the left. "Pull over, pull over."

"What, you gotta piss already?" McCabe jeered.

"No, just pull over, I wanna see somethin'."

The blinker clicked as the Mustang slowed. McCabe took a right into a beach access and the guys piled out.

"Looks like an alright spot," McCabe admitted, "but it's not too different from our beach house. Just a narrower stretch of sand here."

"Nahh man, over here." Stone turned, striding back toward Route One.

McCabe glanced at Conner, his eyebrows drawing together.

Conner shrugged and moved to follow Stone.

The four of them stood alongside Route One waiting for a break in traffic, then crossed to an asphalt bike path running parallel to the road on the other side. Stone turned left, moving along the path with quick strides, his head turned slightly to the right, shifting in and out in an attempt to see beyond the thick mix of hardwoods and tropical weed trees that filled the drop off between them and the Florida Bay. A couple minutes later they reached a break in the vegetation, a handrail lining the path where the water cut closer to shore.

"That's it right there," Stone said, pointing to a thin rise of foliage covered land less than a quarter mile across the pale turquoise wash of water. He leaned forward onto the handrail gazing out at it. "Veterans Key."

"Typical," McCabe scoffed. "They named some tiny spit of inaccessible land after us that's not even two tenths of a mile long."

"What are we doin' here, Stone?" Mathews hissed.

"I wanted to see it, helps me visualize what I read about. Makes it easier to really get an understanding of what happened here."

McCabe turned toward him, "What do you mean, what happened here?"

"It was going to be a bridge," Stone continued. "It was supposed to extend from Matecumbe Key here, out across the channel and connect through a couple other little islands to Long Key, where we just drove from. The 1935 hurricane came and wiped it out."

"*Ok*," McCabe answered.

"Let's walk down to the pedestrian bridge. It's not too far, we'll really be able to see it better."

"Bro! Fuck the pedestrian bridge," Mathews protested. "Let's get up to Miami and start smashin' beers and hitting on Cuban ladies!"

"Come on man, I might never get to be here again."

Mathews threw his lanky arms out to the sides. "I know! That's what I'm sayin'. It'll take us like ten minutes to get down there, and another ten to get back... Twenty extra minutes of me in Miami spitting game—that could be the difference between some sexy Latina arching her back, screamin' 'aye papi' and some pasty white girl shakin' my hand sayin' 'it was real nice to meet you, here's my number in case you're ever in Long Island.'"

"Pshhhh..." McCabe let out. "At two AM maybe. Not right now before lunch."

Mathews tilted his head to the side scrunching his nose, "You right, you right," he chuckled. "Let's go."

On the pedestrian bridge Stone pointed out again. "Look, you can see some of the pylons they built for the bridge out there in the channel."

"Well what's so special about it?" McCabe asked.

"Depends on your perspective, I guess. It could either be nothing, or a piece of history. In 1932, a couple years into the Great Depression, when people were in real bad shape, tens of thousands of World War I vets made their way to DC. It was a protest really, they stood in front of the Capitol Building trying to get Congress to push a bill through to pay them their military bonuses early. They made all these signs that said 'Bonuses or Jobs.' So they called them the Bonus Army.

"Only it was a little different than protest now, because these guys had no work or anything and nowhere to go, so they just stayed camped in DC in these shanty towns for months. Then Hoover called in the Army, they went in with tanks and tear gas and beat people and burnt their little shacks down."

"I learned about that shit in school," Conner cut in. "Talk about unlawful orders."

McCabe groaned, "Yeah, that was some fucked up shit."

"Anyway, FDR used that shit to make Hoover look bad and win the election. So after he was president, a few thousand vets came back to DC. Built a new shanty town. Now ol' FDR was in a tough spot—he'd politically aligned himself with thousands of veterans who were hanging out on the street outside the Capitol Building and no one knew what to do about it.

"He came up with an idea called the veterans' rehabilitation camps. He sent a bunch of them to South Carolina and paid them to do construction, then they sent the rowdiest ones down here, to build that bridge," Stone gestured to the concrete pylons. "Hardly anybody lived here then so it got them out of the way. They weren't a public nuisance."

"Alright," McCabe replied. "Big deal, they gave 'em jobs when they were starving and hid them away. Kinda makes sense if you ask me."

"Yeah," Stone answered. "Until the fucking hurricane came and killed them all."

"WHAT?" Mathews let out.

"Yeah, one of the engineers, he argued for weeks trying to have a train on standby in case they needed evac'ed for a storm. The government didn't want to pay for it though. Also they thought if they brought all the veterans to Miami, they'd party it up, and make the administration look bad. Then the storm came and it was a bad one. The government finally relented and called the Miami rail yard asking them to pick the guys up. But they'd waited way too long. The railroad hustled once they got the word, but they had nothing ready to go, and it took them a couple hours to prep and assemble the train. The storm showed up and that was it. Direct hit, right here. The train never made it.

"I mean, you gotta imagine it, their camp was just up there on Matecumbe Key only a couple feet above sea level. Then the weather starts coming in. The wind gusts get up to two hundred miles per hour, and the storm surge would eventually hit twenty feet."

Stone exhaled hard and turned to face them. "You know how it is," Stone continued, holding his casted hand and his right hand about a foot apart. "Everybody starts in here somewhere. These guys are a little skittish," he said, shaking his casted hand, "And these guys got some pretty solid nerves," he indicated with his right hand. "Everyone else is somewhere in the middle. Then the crazier the shit you see and the more stuff you go through, the more extreme guys get on either end. That's why you get Vietnam vets flying off the handle because their wives forgot something at the grocery store, while other guys got such nerves of steel they see horrible things and do what needs to be done without much of a reaction at all. They're both bad. You're either covered in raw nerves, throwing blasts of emotion at the people who are tiptoeing around you, or you're *so* steady, and your feelings *so* suppressed that you can't relate to anyone. The world sees you as a cold void of humanity.

"So think of it. These guys were World War I vets, they'd been through the trenches, the barbed wire, the poison gas—

losing friends left and right as they charged straight into no man's land toward the German machine guns at the blow of the whistle. And they were the worst ones, that's why they sent them here. PTSD wasn't a thing back then. So all these guys were either the most jittery or the most incredibly stoic men you could imagine. Fortunately, nothing we see in our lives will ever come close to what they went through. And now there's hundreds of them on this little stretch of sand with the wind picking up and the waves coming in.

"Their camp gets blown to pieces in a matter of minutes. Piles of building materials take to the air, two by fours impaling people like spears. Coconuts being hurled at two hundred miles per hour, literally bashing guys' brains out. At that speed even individual grains of sand became tiny projectiles, blasting into their skin.

"This pedestrian bridge we're standing on now, it's the old rail bridge. They climbed out here because it was higher than the island with less debris swirling around. The authorities estimated that some of them managed to hang on for a real long time, but in the end, the storm surge got them all."

They stood there in silence, gazing down into the channel or with their eyes shifting across the surface of the water, pausing on the pylons or settling on Veteran's Key. The sun, high in the sky, was warm on their skin, with a cool breeze coming in off the ocean.

"And the government never even finished the bridge?" Conner asked.

Stone shook his head. "It was all for nothing."

"Fuck you, Stone," Mathews grunted. "Why the hell would you show us this shit? What did you even want to see it for?" he turned away, moving along the bridge, back toward Matecumbe Key. He made it about ten paces before spinning around with his arms extended wide, calling back. "Only you could take a beautiful day like this, on a sunny spot in the Florida Keys, and turn it into something fucked up."

Mathews pivoted and was striding away again before yelling back over his shoulder. "You guys comin'?"

CHAPTER 24

Holding their small duffle bags and wearing black tactical backpacks, the guys stood in a tight circle, on the white tile floor in the lobby of the South Beach condo they'd stayed in two nights before. They waited as Mathews checked in with the receptionist at the desk across the room.

"Yo, you boys wrecked me for life," McCabe chuckled shaking his head. "After driving around in that Gran Turismo all weekend, how am I supposed to go back to my Accord and be happy?"

Conner leaned back, stretching, "I know that Mustang is a badass machine, and I'm glad you've had fun zipping around in that thing, but those back seats are not designed for full grown adults."

"Valid," Stone answered.

"Next time someone gets married, I'm all about it, I'll be here, but we gotta at least rent something with four doors." Conner insisted.

"Now, what sports car do you know with four doors?"

Conner shrugged.

"Yeah, cause there aren't any." A wide smile crossed McCabe's face. "You're going to screw yourself over dude, you might be the next one getting hitched the way you keep ogling that picture on your phone."

Conner's face flushed as he beamed back at McCabe. "You'll certainly get a call if it happens, man."

"Yeah, and when I do, remember this conversation, because I'm going to rent you a minivan to drive us around in all weekend!"

"Man, if I get to marry this girl, I'll be so happy I won't care what we're riding in!"

Stone nodded, grinning as he glanced between the two of them. "It really makes me happy that you were both able to find girls you like so much." As his eyes locked on Conner they seemed to fill with emotion, though none of it was betrayed in his mannerisms. "It's really great that it's all working out so well. Don't ever lose 'em, guys. Hang on to those ladies tight."

Conner swallowed as he gazed back, unsure how to answer. "Thanks," he finally replied, "I promise I'll do my very best."

They turned toward Mathews together as he approached.

"Get us some room keys, dude?" McCabe asked. "Hey, somebody just kick your puppy? Why do you look like something's wrong?"

"Bro, I fucked up," Mathews responded shaking his head.

McCabe cocked his head to one side. "And?"

"I booked the room for tomorrow night. I'm sorry." Mathews let out a groaning exhale. "I don't know what I did. Maybe because I was in Japan and I was trying to adjust for the International Date Line, but it was probably already adjusted on the website... or maybe I just messed the days up."

"How'd you manage to book the right date on the first night?" Conner asked.

"McCabe booked the first night, we were spreading the

cost out."

"Alright," McCabe said, "Well don't stress, I'm sure they can work something out."

"They're maxed," Mathews answered.

"Dude, did ya try laying on the charm?"

"Bro, she got an engagement ring on, but I flirted with her anyway. Told her if she had any sisters that had trouble getting dates I'd take 'em out for a great time, if she just hooked us up with a room."

"And?"

"She says all her sisters are sexy like her, and there's guys lined up waitin' for a chance just to talk to 'em."

McCabe frowned, "Nothing?"

"I even asked if she had any ugly cousins, she just laughed and said 'sorry!'" Mathews let out a long exhale. "I got her to call around. There ain't shit. Saturday night, Fourth of July. Everything is booked solid. I really fucked us over guys."

"Alright, no point standing around here. Let's head up the strip and see what we can find," McCabe suggested. "It's still early enough in the afternoon somebody's got to have some-thing open."

"I'll follow you in the van," Stone announced, "If I'm ever in the back seat of a Mustang again I hope to hell it's with somebody better lookin' than Conner."

"Hey!" Conner shot back as they shuffled toward the door, "What's wrong, you don't like my haircut? 'Cause the rest of me is perfect!"

★ ★ ★

Conner jumped in with Stone and they followed the Mustang, inching up A1A in the summer holiday traffic. After a few blocks, McCabe pulled into an empty street space, and jumped out, darting across the asphalt between slow moving cars and into a hotel on the other side. Mathews also exited and made his way into another hotel on the ocean side of the street. Stone drove down another block before edging into a parking lot near the 13th Street intersection.

"Let's just kick back and see if they're able to find anything," Stone suggested, cutting the engine.

Ten minutes later they saw Mathews on the far side of the street going into another hotel before crossing 13th and heading up the red sidewalk. McCabe waved to them and shook his head a few minutes later as he passed and continued his search.

"Doesn't look promising," Conner observed.

Stone shook his head in agreement.

Conner leaned back in the cargo van's bucket seat and propped his arm up on the open window. He closed his eyes for a moment and began to think about the vehicle he was in. *Everything Stone owns is in here. It isn't a mess either, it's all organized and accessible in a way that makes sense. He spends all his time in really remote areas and he's got no backup, couldn't phone a friend if he wanted to. I wonder if I would feel free or trapped in that situation. He never complains, never blames anyone for how things turned out.*

Conner shifted slightly in the passenger seat and studied the side of Stone's lean, hard face. *So much self-assurance in his steady gray eyes. The ability to handle anything that comes his way.* He wondered what it took to project confidence like that. *Are some of us born with that ability? Or is it built up over time? I must look more sure of myself now than I did years ago. I certainly know more and can handle more.* But at the same time he remembered honestly believing he could take on the world when he was younger. Conner shook his head as he thought. *No one looks at a teenager and thinks they're solid like that though, even if the kid is feeling it. So it must be more than confidence. Something else must change along the way.*

What about Stone? Sure, it takes a certain kind of self-reliance to go live on your own in a van. Budget your savings out and trust yourself to not just sustain, but experience some kind of meaning or purpose in your life. Is he lacking something else though? Did he lose some other element that lets you be part of society? And why does he keeps getting hurt?

"Hey Stone," Conner swallowed hard. "Are you—are you alright man?"

"Something got you concerned?"

"Why do you keep getting all busted up? I mean your hand is broken and you got that jagged scar on your side."

"It happens," Stone replied.

"Well that's what I'm asking I guess, shit like that doesn't normally just happen. Not to most people anyway, at least not twice in two years. It seems like more than bad luck."

Conner exhaled hard. "I guess I just don't get how you keep getting in bad situations."

"That's because you live here," Stone pointed up with his casted hand, spinning his index finger around. "Where there's some kinda civilized pattern to most things. Rules, norms, it can be a little rough but there's a basic order. There's light switches and doors that lock. Most times when you close your eyes at night it doesn't even occur to you that you're safe because the feeling is so ordinary. Things mainly make sense. Out on the fringes—I mean the edge of society where the lost and the crazies and others who just can't get it together end up—out there, people need help all the time.

Conner ran his fingers through his hair and shifted his eyes ahead, out the windshield to the people passing on the street. *You can tell a lot just by the way people walk, how they carry themselves.* He watched as two short, tan blonde girls in matching outfits, perhaps sisters, made their way up the sidewalk, talking and laughing. *They got it easy,* Conner thought. *Born beautiful and with enough money to vacation in Miami.* A group of guys in pastel collared shirts and sandals strolled by. *Overconfident douchebags completely out of touch with real life, probably couldn't change their own oil if their lives depended on it.* A black man in business casual strode anxiously behind them, waiting for a chance to go around, as if he were late to an appointment. *In the hustle, trying to move up the ladder while missing the simple pleasures.* Conner chuckled to himself. *Or maybe, people keep everything away from the surface and I can't tell anything at all. Dozens of hidden dramas passing just in front of me. What did Stone say? You can't see anything if you look right at it?* He pondered it as he sat.

Stone... what put him in such a tailspin? All the deployments? No. Stretch? Maybe part of it. Shannon? I'd be a total mess of Joselyd ever left me. So lucky I found the right one and I don't have to worry about that. Conner shook his head. *It had to be Shannon.* He glanced at Stone in his peripheral as if he could discern the answer if he didn't peer directly at him. But Stone sat unflinching, staring ahead just as he had before. *McCabe said not to ask, and it's not my business. But maybe it's better to know. I could be a better friend.* He contemplated it. *But I leave tomorrow, and we clearly won't talk on the phone. Maybe it's just my own selfish desire to understand what happened. What had McCabe said? We learn about history to see what ordinary people do in extreme situations. Helps us prepare ourselves for what we might run into. Maybe this is like that.*

"Hey Stone," Conner said, turning slightly to look at him. "W-what happened man?"

"What do you mean?"

"I mean, what happened that made you leave and go live in a van?"

Stone continued to stare through the windshield as more people moved up the sidewalk.

"I mean, I'm sure it's sweet being out in nature hiking or biking all day," Conner felt a hint of guilt as his face flushed. "But was there another reason? Getting rid of your phone seems kind of extreme."

"I was tired of being around people for a while," Stone answered without turning to look at him.

Conner replied with a nervous nod which did nothing to alleviate the unsettling feeling of guilt now fully manifested in his gut. *Just let it alone, dumbass.* Outside, a group of college-aged kids made their way down the sidewalk in a slow bunch toward them. Several in the group wore Duke apparel and some of the girls had Greek letters on their tank tops. People had to step into the street to get around them but the kids didn't seem to care. They were joking around, kicking the backs of each other's heels as they walked, trying to trip each other up. *Rich parents.* Conner forced his mind to a new subject. *How else could they afford to go to college and vacation in Miami?*

"When I was maybe sixteen," Stone began, "I was staff at this Boy Scout camp. It was in the summer and I had a real great time. Typical really, hung out in the woods for two weeks, learned new things, taught younger kids stuff and made all kinds of friends."

Conner glanced at him side-eyed.

"Anyway, at the end there's this presentation and a campfire and people's parents were there, then everyone loaded up and went home. It was a real fun time, everyone was laughing and joking around because they had such a good week. I was walking back through the parking area afterward to get something, and it was a dark night, but I could see these two silhouettes. I could tell they were wrestling around. I thought they were playing. I rolled up on them kinda quick.

I wanted to see who they were, maybe join in or cheer someone on, I don't know.

"Well, it was this kid I knew, and I guess his dad, I can't be certain. But this middle aged guy was choking the hell out of him. The kid was saying 'Stop! Stop!' every time he could pull the man's hands back enough to get a breath, but the guy kept on. I just stood there and I didn't do shit. I didn't help, I didn't call for help. I didn't say anything at all, I just stood there.

"After about a minute the kid managed to do this maneuver where he threw both his fists up at once and broke the man's grip on his neck. The guy stumbled backward a bit, then he sorta turned and wandered off. I was just standing there, staring at my friend—I don't remember his name anymore—and when he caught his breath he looked at me and said, 'Hey, how ya doing?'

"I answered 'fine' 'cause I was just this dumbass kid who got caught by surprise and didn't know what to do. Then he said something else not important that I can't remember and I'm sure I responded with something just as insignificant. We walked off and camp was over and I never saw him again.

"I felt guilty forever after that. Guilty I didn't react. Guilty I didn't help my friend, guilty I wasn't the person I thought I was, 'cause I never in a hundred years thought I would have just stood there like that." Stone paused for a moment and took a drink from his water bottle without ever turning toward Conner. "Well that really stuck with me. It like, hung there in the back of my mind, like 'you're not who you think you are, you won't stand up when you need to.'

"Then a couple years later, right after I graduated, my high school friends and I went to the beach for senior week. We had to stay way up the road away from the action 'cause that's what we could pay for, and we'd ride the bus back and forth. At night it'd all be full of drunks, ya know? Anyway, there were these rowdy guys a few years older than us and they were being dicks, but I didn't pay much attention. At one of the bus stops this Asian guy got on. I mean, he was probably American, but with Asian descent. These assholes laid into him hard. 'Hey, go back to your country.' 'Need any American money while you're here?' Shit like that, and they wouldn't stop. The guy just sat there all quiet in the front seat and wouldn't turn around. I started thinking about that parking lot at Boy Scout camp for whatever reason, but I was still just sitting there. My buddy was beside me and he stood up all a sudden and yelled 'Let him alone!' I stood up too but I didn't say nothin'.

"I think it took 'em by surprise 'cause I was pretty scrawny back then and my friend wasn't much bigger. We were out-numbered by a lot, even if the Asian guy would have turned around and tried to help. One of those assholes stood up and pointed at us and started to say something, but before he could I shouted, 'Shut the fuck up! I'll knock your goddamn teeth down your throat and laugh while ya choke on 'em!' These guys started yelling back and I thought we were going to get pounded right there in the aisle of the drunk bus.

"Then outta nowhere, this random guy stood up and I'll never forget it. He was tall with that working-man strength look, a straight up mullet, and this dirty red NASCAR ball cap on. The dude sounded like a big southern redneck but he looked right at those fuckers and said 'Y'all ain't really American if you act that way.' Another guy took our side and started yelling at them too. After a minute the yelling stopped and we were all glaring at each other. It was like a Mexican standoff. At the next stop all those ass clowns got up and filed out. I don't think it was actually their stop because they didn't all get up at once. They were exchanging glances like they were trying to decide what each other were doing.

"That took a little of that persistent guilty feeling away. But I wasn't completely sure of myself. Maybe because my friend had been beside me and said something first. Or I thought maybe I just had a one off reaction. I don't know. But a year later, after basic and tech school, I took some leave and I was back home. I called around trying to see if any of my old friends were in town to hang out, and word must have got out because a couple days later this girl Brynn called my parents' house and asked for me.

"I was friends with her from high school. She was attractive and all, but I don't quite know how to describe her. I mean she was little, probably only five feet tall with light skin and these baby-blue eyes. When I looked at her I just wanted to protect her. It's hard to explain. She had this big scar on her forehead and we never found out how she got it. She'd try to cover it up with foundation but you could still see it. Her step dad had just booted her out of the house and changed the locks and she was staying at another girl's mom's house. He did it while she was at work and she just wanted some of her clothes and things because she had nothing, and was basically on her own. But Brynn was for-real scared he'd beat the shit out of her if she showed back up."

"Damn," Conner shook his head. "I was lucky never to have any tense family situations like that. Sounds like trouble. Why'd he kick her out?"

"Yeah, trouble for sure. I never asked though, and I could tell she was in a bad spot. He'd been after her as long as I could remember, and when she turned eighteen I guess he saw his chance. Keeping her clothes is just spiteful though. So I gave her a ride over and we parked down the street a little. She had garbage bags stuffed in the back pocket of her jean shorts. Her plan was to wait until it was just her little brother on the main floor and then knock on the door, slip in, grab all her stuff she could, and get outta there.

"We came up to the house and the garage was open but the interior door was locked. She crouched down and peeked through the front window, I stood off to the side. After a bit she rushed around through the garage and tapped on the door so slight that I couldn't hardly hear it. The door opened and this tiny little boy was standing there, he had shaggy hair and big blue eyes and could barely reach the door knob. When he saw Brynn his eyes welled up like he was about to cry. It was so fucking sad I can't describe it. She held her index finger up to her lips then hugged him and he didn't make a sound. She slipped her shoes off, I guess to be quiet and disappeared into the house.

"I was there near the garage entrance where no one could see me through the windows and I was trying my best to listen in case something happened inside. It seemed like a long while, but it was probably only a few minutes later when the door opened and she tossed two garbage bags out and disappeared again. I stuck them in the car and when I came back I could hear a commotion. The little boy was bawling and a man was screaming. I debated for a second on going inside but then the door burst open and Brynn was coming out with no shoes and another trash bag, this time half full. She made it partway through the garage and he was after her. He was this short wiry bearded guy with piercing blue eyes and big forearms. He got his fingers into the plastic and the trash bag ripped open, spilling bras and underwear out all over the concrete. Brynn looked terrified and tears were streaming down her face though she wasn't sobbing.

"He screamed some ignorant shit at her, and she yelled back 'I just had to get my things' and I stood to the side and watched with my arms crossed. He screamed some more—all irrational hurtful things full of F-bombs—as she slowly inched backward toward the garage door. When he lunged for her the second time, I moved quick and put myself in between them.

"That must have really thrown him off, because he jumped back. I'm not even sure he saw me before that. He was all 'Who the fuck are you? Get the fuck out of my house!' and I just stood there with my arms crossed. Then he screamed 'I'll fucking rip you apart!' and came at me. Now I don't know if it's because I'd been outta basic less than a year and I was used to getting yelled at, or if it's since he was substantially shorter than me, though clearly way stronger, or just cause the whole thing was so ridiculous, but I involuntarily tilted my head a little to one side and I could feel this smirk form on my face. We were staring each other dead in the eyes and when he was almost to me—I saw fear. He stopped himself before grabbing ahold of me and screamed again. Not even words, just screaming. He was so close I could smell his rancid-ass breath.

"He pointed at me and yelled 'I'll call the fucking police!' and then I knew I had him. Somehow he was scared of me, or at least unsure how things would go if he tried his luck. I said 'Sir, you take whatever action you feel is appropriate, I'll wait right here until they arrive.' That man didn't know what the fuck to do. He tried to shift around me and go after Brynn again but I stayed in his way with my eyes on him and just shook my head.

"We were there a few more minutes. He screamed and stomped and jumped up and down like a kid having a temper tantrum. I was standing there waiting to see what he'd do and eventually Brynn got brave enough to edge up behind me and start tugging on my shoulder until I uncrossed my arms. Then she grabbed my hand and pulled me toward the door and I walked backward without ever taking my eyes off him. I think that was the first time I ever held hands with a girl. The whole thing was weird because I was stepping on Brynn's bras and thongs and panties and stuff while I was walking backward locking eyes with her stepdad.

"I drove her back to my parents' house because I didn't know where else to go. We went inside and my family wasn't home. We were standing there in the kitchen and she came up and hugged me. Like a real intense hug. It was dark by then and the lights were on and I could see our reflection in the sliding glass door. She was hugging me so tight and on the glass was this beautiful girl with her arms wrapped around me. She was barefoot because we'd forgotten her shoes in all the excitement, and she had these super-fine muscular legs, and only those short jean shorts on and I could see all of us in the door. I was a full head taller than her so I looked a lot bigger, I guess because I was. It was like, I'd done something good and helped someone I cared about and here was this beautiful girl wrapped around me. It didn't seem real and I couldn't hardly believe it was me with her in the reflection."

Stone let out a long exhale. "I probably could have kissed her right then but honestly it didn't even occur to me. I don't know why. I wasn't amped up or anything, I was totally calm. A while later we sat on the couch and I put my arm around her and she cried for a long time because she'd left her little brother behind."

Conner shook his head, "That sounds rough. When I was a kid, if I was in trouble, my sister was always there for me. If anything crazy had ever happened and she had to leave me, it would have torn her apart on the inside, if she could have done it at all. I can't even imagine abandoning someone I care about."

"Yeah," Stone took in a long slow breath, his face unmoving. "Eventually I got scared my parents would come home, so I took her to her friend's mom's and dropped her off. We hung out a couple more times that week. Then my leave ended and I left. I called next time I was home, but by then another year had gone by. I heard she'd shacked up with some guy years older than us and moved. I hope she's alright now. I never saw her again either."

Conner glanced at his friend again but Stone just continued to stare ahead, perhaps over the heads of all the people on the street to the sky. Conner couldn't tell.

"After that, everything was ok. Air Force, deployments, missions, combat zones, sticking up for people when they need it. All the bad things that rolled up, I handled well enough. I never got that guilty, unsure feeling again. You guys helped a lot because I knew we all had each other's backs no matter what."

Conner kept watching him, debating a response. "Still do, Stone. Always."

Stone nodded as he stared out.

Conner sat in silence attempting to discern if somewhere in those stories lay the answer to his inquiry as to what led Stone to isolate himself and live out of his van. If the answer was there, Conner couldn't seem to identify it.

"When Shannon got pregnant, I felt this instant stress," Stone's voice remained perfectly steady and void of emotion.

"It hit me like a surge. I went to see her on my reconstitution time after we came back from Kandahar and that's when it happened. I found out after we'd all come back and I was already working insane hours again. I don't gotta tell you, you lived it too.

"It had always been a distance relationship so all the decisions were over the phone. She said she wasn't sure. I was scared as hell, but I said what you're supposed to 'I'll support you no matter what.' It didn't occur to me at that time that I might not be capable. Two days later I said, 'I'll get out of the military, so I can be around.' She said, 'don't make that decision for me.' I said, 'I'll make it for us.'

"It took me about a week to get my head straight. I thought, why the hell am I fighting this? I love this girl. I want to marry her, I want to have kids. So what if it's a couple years ahead of schedule? I hadn't PCS'd or retrained and I had enough years in that I was eligible to resign, I didn't have to wait for my enlistment to end. I dropped my papers and they processed much quicker than I thought. My terminal leave date was coming up fast.

"I thought when she found out, she'd decide to be a family. She went the other way though. Talking about grad school and her career. She'd never needed me. She was so progressive and independent. That's one of the reasons I was so into her, I knew she was just with me because she wanted to be, not because she needed taken care of.

"I thought about trying to do it on my own. Maybe if I brought that up she wouldn't go through with it. But I couldn't figure a way without the military. Staying in meant paychecks and insurance. I thought I could get a nicer place and try my best and maybe it would be ok. But as I pictured the way my life had been—never around, always in some other country on the other side of the world—I knew shit would be far from ok. How would it be for a kid to grow up depending on a guy like me? A fucking absentee. The kid would have the worst life ever. I thought maybe it could be different but I knew deep down it wouldn't. However things are, that's the way they are going to be. Anything but minute modifications and you're lying to yourself.

"On top of all that, a kid needs their mother, it's straight biological. There's some gaps I could never fill no matter how hard I tried." Stone took a deep breath, "That's just the way it is.

"I tried to keep my feelings hidden, you know, to be supportive. But I was so pressed it felt like a black hole was forming in the center of my chest. It felt like everything was crushing in on me. I knew McCabe and Mathews were leaving, and Lewis was getting out. I had all these weird feelings about Stretch because he died on the same leave that Shannon got pregnant. I know it doesn't work like this, but somewhere in my mind I had the thought, maybe the universe took something away and gave me something else. Or I just really wanted something good to happen. Anything good. A happy baby maybe.

"I was a wreck. I was afraid to tell anybody how I felt, especially Shannon. I was sure she'd take it as an attack against her ability to make decisions or women's rights or something. I thought just telling her how I felt might make her leave. The world is so fucked up. Guys don't have any rights at all. Society is all like, 'You have to *express* your *feelings*, *embrace* your *feelings*, *talk about* your *feelings*, stop pretending you're a tough guy with no *feelings*.' Then when I actually have a strong emotional response to something, something that I can't stop thinking about, something burning down deep inside me—and I actually get myself worked up enough to say something—I get attacked. Society's not ok with how I feel. My perspective isn't valid. People like us—no one fucking cares what we think. Doesn't matter if it's about the cargo compartment of your aircraft being full of young guys on stretchers with missing limbs, or your friend dying or your baby not being born.

"Shannon could sense all the emotions I was hiding. I know she could, she's sensitive like that. She tried hard. But it wasn't a good situation. I knew deep down it was my fault for getting her pregnant, my fault for not finding a way to express myself, my fault for not being in a good enough situation to try it on my own. My fault for being so stressed I couldn't function outside of work.

"After it happened I was so angry. Angrier than I was when Bush invaded Iraq and more upset than when my mother died. I tried to cover it all up when I talked to her, but it kept coming through. We communicated so poorly I never realized she thought I was mad because she was pregnant. She thought once she ended it things would go back to normal. After it was over, and I got worse instead of better, she broke down crying on the phone and told me. I still don't know how she could think that.

"My terminal leave started and by then I'd made her so upset she didn't even want me to come see her. I kept asking and one day she stopped answering the phone. That was it. Four years together, only girl I've ever loved and that's how it ended. I kept trying once a week anyway for months. At one point I was out of service for a few days and I convinced myself I'd have a message from her when I got connected again. When there was nothing at all, I got so upset that I broke my phone into pieces and never got another one. I decided I didn't want to be around people for a while and I put some stuff in storage, fitted the van out and left.

"Now that terrible guilty feeling is back and it's louder than ever. It's screaming inside my mind. I stood up every time it mattered in my adult life except for the one most critically important moment. My brain still can't even sort out the right solution, 'cause there's no way for me to tell now how she would have responded. But I do know everything I did was completely wrong."

Stone continued to stare, his sharp gray eyes unflinching as the world outside moved on without them.

"I guess it takes way less courage to infuriate your supervision sticking up for a friend, or chance getting your face beat in on some dirty bus floor or by someone's psychotic step dad, or volunteer to fly into the middle of a shooting war than it does to risk upsetting the person you care about the most."

Stone moved for the first time since they'd been talking. His hand came up to his forehead and his fingers combed straight back through his short-sandy colored hair. "I almost had everything," he whispered. "God, I love that girl, I think about her all the time."

A breeze blew through the open van windows as the un-ending stream of people persisted on the red sidewalk in front of them. Conner's eyes flashed from group to group, person to person, eventually settling on a young family across the street. A father about Stone's age, and a mother smiling as she held hands with her two little boys. *I wonder if people know it when they have everything?*

CHAPTER 25

Mathews appeared a few minutes later, crossing the street toward them. He went to Stone's window. "This ain't workin', we're wasting all our hang out time trying to find a place to stay. I got one of these mugs to call around for me again. There ain't shit unless we go back across the bridge and then to the total other side of the city. It'll take like an hour and all the stuff we want to do is here anyway. I say fuck it. Instead of blowing the cash to be somewhere we don't wanna be anyway, let's just stay out all night. If we end up stuck, we'll just hit up an all-night diner somewhere, and after that if we have to, we can head to the airport early, pass out in a chair at the gate for a couple hours before the flight."

"Is McCabe down?" Stone asked, his voice flat with no emotion.

Mathews nodded.

"Then sure," Stone agreed.

Mathews' eyes shifted to Conner.

"That's fine," Conner answered.

"Ok," Mathews began, but his eyes lingered, flashing between the two of them. "What happened? Something's different. You boys alright?"

"Nothing," Stone snapped, forcing a smile. "I just feel sorry for whoever has to sit next to you on the plane tomorrow."

"Yeah, whatever, I exude a very pleasant natural fragrance.

Come on, let's go find a spot on the beach for a bit. We can maybe even catch a nap. It's perfect actually, we can use the showers down there before we go out and then come back and change in your van."

Mathews turned away before spinning back around and pulling a long thin package from his back pocket. "I almost forgot, I bought you a present." He tossed Stone a plastic arm sheath with a rubber gasket on the open end. "It's for kids who break their arms but still wanna go swimming. I got the biggest one. I'm not sure I could handle watching you rip that duct tape off your skin a second time."

The guys made their way back down the crowded red sidewalk along A1A to the Mustang, where they grabbed water bottles, sandals and sunscreen. They pulled towels from the trunk—two of which Mathews had acquired from the condo their first night in South Beach—and stuffed them into their black backpacks, before heading toward the ocean. There were fewer people on the side street. Mathews walked ahead with Stone as Conner fell into step beside McCabe.

"I feel strange," Conner confessed, when the other two were far enough ahead that they couldn't hear. "Like I'm connected to you guys, but it doesn't feel the same. Something is... I don't know... off."

"Well, it makes sense, you've replaced us," McCabe answered as they continued up the sidewalk.

Conner's head yanked back in a reflex as he turned to look at his friend. "What do you mean I've replaced you? Nobody could ever replace you guys. All the shit we went through, all the times we backed each other up."

McCabe shook his head as he walked. "You didn't replace us as friends. That's not what I'm saying. We will always be friends if you ever call or come around. You've replaced us as your support network."

"My support network?"

"Yeah."

"What are you talking about?"

"You remember back in the day, whenever some fucked up shit would happen? Anything, when your ex-girlfriend bailed or when your dad got sick, or even when you just got pulled for weekend duty three times in a month, who would you talk to about it? Or just as importantly, who would you go hang out with, even if you didn't talk much at all?"

"Well," Conner began as they continued up the sidewalk next to each other, "sometimes I'd call my sister, but mainly it would be you or Stone or Lewis or Mathews."

"Exactly,' McCabe answered, "and when we'd get jammed up, we called you too. Who do you call or work things out with now?"

"Well it's different now man, you guys are all far away."

"Oh it's different for sure, but it don't matter. Was your sister close by before?"

"You know she wasn't."

"Exactly."

They strolled up the street in silence for a few dozen yards before Conner spoke again. "It's a two way street then, why'd you guys stop calling?"

"I can only speak for myself," McCabe replied, "but I'm pretty sure it's because you'd never answer the goddamn phone and it'd take you a week to call back."

"Well, I'm busy."

"Yep."

"What are you trying to say, it's bad that I have an amazing girlfriend I talk to and want to spend time with?"

"I said what I was trying to say. You have replaced your support network." McCabe took a deep breath. "I didn't say it was bad, I just said that's why hanging out with us feels different to you now."

Conner pondered it as they walked. "McCabe, none of you guys have seen each other."

"That's true, but Mathews calls me multiple times a month in the middle of the night, talking about all kinds of ridiculous stuff. And Stone is basically off the grid, but he sends me a big long email every couple of months. He won't say anything personal, but he tells me all the mountains and deserts he's hiked in." McCabe let out a long breath as he took the next few steps in silence, "I wish Lewis would get back in touch one day, but at this point I know he never will. I hope he's ok."

"What you're telling me, I don't know what to do with it."

"Look Conner, I'm glad that you are happy and have a girl-friend you're falling down in love with. I'm glad that if I call you once or twice, eventually you will get back in touch, even if it takes a week. I'm glad you're here hanging out. But you can't act different for years and then expect everything to feel the same. That's all."

Conner sighed, "I'm sorry, man."

"I'm not trying to make you feel bad," McCabe responded. "I'm just telling you because you asked. It's your life, you live it the way that makes you happy. I still love ya dude, or you wouldn't be here. I just wish you'd answer the phone more, that's all. I was having a real rough time for a while. Shit was hard, but I came out of it alright, and now I'm about to marry an incredible girl." He tilted his head up and to one side, glancing at Conner with a smirk. "I'm poised to live happily ever after."

They crossed through a narrow green stretch full of palm trees separating the asphalt from the sand. There were a lot of people on the beach, but ahead of them, Stone and Mathews had found a spot, and were already spreading out towels to lay on.

CHAPTER 26

"One of you mugs gonna hold our spot down while I jump in the water?"

McCabe nodded, pulling a book out of his black backpack.

"I'll go with ya," Stone offered, pulling his shirt off, but Mathews didn't wait. He raced toward the ocean in a dead sprint, flinging himself into the surf and diving under the first set of swells. He popped up fifteen yards further out with a woot and whipped his head around, shaking like a wet dog.

Stone chuckled before strolling across the sand after him—his cast covered in the plastic sheath with the rubber gasket sealing it against his arm.

It was hot, over ninety degrees, and likely much higher than that in the sun on the beach. It didn't bother Conner in the slightest, this heat was far more comfortable than wearing a uniform and working inside a sweltering aircraft that had been baking in the sun all day. Conner slathered himself with sunblock and glanced toward McCabe, but he lay there a few feet away with his book open and it seemed he didn't feel like talking. So Conner leaned back, enjoying the way the bright sunlight felt on his chest and closed his eyes. It wasn't long before he was asleep.

Conner awoke with a start a short time later hearing Mathews' booming voice. His eyes jerked open to see him standing over them and dripping with water.

"Come on, let's walk down the beach and check out some honeys!"

"I've got nice sunshine, a comfortable spot to sit and a good book to read, I'm fine here," McCabe answered.

"Come on, bitch! You're running out of time to ethically scope out ladies before you're bound by moral vows of monogamy for the rest of your life."

"I've been off the market for a year, dude," McCabe responded. "I'm happy with what I've got."

Stone walked in from the water, the hook shaped scar on his abs showing dully pink against his deeply tan skin. He crashed down on a towel and cocked one arm behind his head, gazing up at the sky. Mathews' eyes flicked to him, before settling on Conner.

"I guess it's you and me bro."

Conner willed himself to a sitting position, then he clasped Mathews' extended hand and was yanked upright.

"See you jokers later," he called as they strolled away.

Conner and Mathews moved side by side to the cooler, wet sand along the water, where it was easier to walk. "Let's try south," Mathews gestured to the right, "We'll get down to the end of this thing and see what it looks like."

Conner nodded, and they made their way in silence for several minutes. Scores of kids squealed loudly as they played keep away with a Nerf football in the surf. Spanish music pumped from a portable speaker by a group of middle aged Latino guys drinking from Solo cups. Elementary school aged children chased each other up and down the sand as the waves came in and out. They passed a group of black girls in American flag bikinis, then evenly spaced sets of uniform beach umbrellas and matching outdoor reclining chairs that you probably had to pay to sit in. The primary occupants seemed to be groups of fit white ladies in their thirties, wearing stylish swimsuits and holding expensive looking drinks as their oversized wedding bands glinted in the sunlight. They gossiped loudly while their young children played in the sand nearby.

"I'm glad you've still got some energy, Conner," Mathews began, "I can't believe those other guys just want to lounge around. I mean, we're on South Beach in Miami! This place is famous and we might never get to be here again."

"They're just taking it easy for a few. And don't give me too much credit, I was asleep ten minutes ago."

"I don't know if those boys get it. McCabe hangin' out reading a book. Don't they realize how fuckin' short life is? At least we're out here trying to take in the local fauna and seeing what's up, not staring at a book."

"Seems like mainly families out here."

"Yeah, you're right, but this was supposed to be the party spot."

"Maybe because it's a holiday?"

"Maybe. Or because of the Great Recession none of the young single people can afford to be out here. Most these ladies look like they're married to guys who make at least three times what we do combined."

Conner nodded.

"They look like the kinda housewives who drive Beamers to tennis lessons and hot yoga classes."

"Whoever they are, none of them have given us a second glance."

"Their loss!" Mathews answered.

"What's your deal anyway, how come you aren't dating anybody? No play over there in Japan?"

"Nahh, there's plenty. At least I think there is. A bunch of the guys I work with have married Japanese girls, and there's a few who've found American girls on base. Honestly bro, I just can't find anyone who understands me. I mean, not even a little bit. Like I say somethin' and they have no idea. I kept thinking, 'how are all these girls so completely out of touch with reality?' It took a long time before I realized that most people have just lived very different lives than I have. It's no wonder we can't relate to each other. Straight up, I think it's me that's the problem, not them."

"Don't say that, man. I think it's good you're not settling for someone who isn't right for you. Speaking of, I've been meaning to ask you. That grad school girl, what did she say when you told her that whole toxic masculinity theory wouldn't hold true in a combat zone, because people need to compartmentalize and keep focused and working instead of worrying about their feelings?"

"Ha! Still thinking about that, huh? You know what she said?" Mathews shook his head as they walked. "She said, 'If it weren't for toxic masculinity there would be no wars!' Holy hell, I was like yeah, great plan, humans have been engaged in violent conflict since the beginning of time, but we'll just hang out and hope Saddam Hussein and Osama bin Laden embrace a progressive ideology on their own and stop torturing people and throwing airliners into our sky scrapers. Not to mention Russia, they fucked that place up to begin with. Those bastards still invade a country for fun every ten or fifteen years. They hit Georgia last year and it barely made the American news. Even after September 11th, these people don't get it. They're all safe in their bubbles, most of them probably never even seen anything really bad happen. Which is great, I guess. It's just hard to find anyone who understands me, that's all."

"Yeah, I got super lucky," Conner admitted. "The girl I'm dating now is really amazing."

"Luck helps, but it's not just that. You're solid, Conner. You, Stone, McCabe, you all are. The guys I'm with now, I mean, they're pretty good guys, but it's not the same as working with our old crew. I don't know... it's just different. I miss you guys."

They'd reached a little stretch of beach that was mainly empty, Mathews stopped walking and stood there just beyond the reach of the rushing waves, shaking his head, "I work with a bunch of jokers now. They're clowns compared to the team we had. I hope I never have to go to war with those boys. I know it's a little different now because I'm a tech sergeant and have people working for me so they don't see me the same way, but I haven't made a single true friend over there."

"Really?" Conner stopped also, his eyebrows scrunched as he turned to look at his friend. "Man, that can't be true."

Mathews' eyes seemed far away. Behind him, a line of pelicans skimmed the crests of the waves, drafting off one another in perfect formation. *They always seem so sleek in the air and so awkward on the ground.*

"I did have a friend," Mathews began, "He wasn't flight line though, we didn't work together. I knew him 'cause he was my neighbor. Security forces guy."

"Well that still counts, man. All ya need is a couple good friends," Conner chuckled, "Though those security forces types like to party, they can get kinda wild."

Mathews' eyes focused back in on Conner. "Oh yeah, definitely! We both got there around the same time and neither of us knew jack about Japan. Bro! We went to Tokyo together and hung out in this HUGE park in the middle of the city, and went to see the palace. That shit is incredible. It feels like you're in the country, but you can look out and see all the skyscrapers at the same time. Then we went to a real Japanese steakhouse for dinner and hit the bars after that. We were doing our best to talk to all these Japanese girls, it was wild. You know I'm tall, and he was this big broad shouldered farm boy from Oklahoma. And most of those ladies over there are small, so we were TOWERING over these girls. It was so bizarre, every woman in the place had eyes on us. We had a BLAST.

"Anyway, when we tried to make our way back to base, we were all lit up and it was late. I was tryin' to study the map for their Metro system, and it was laid out in a way that made sense, except there's no words. It's just Japanese characters. Makes it super difficult to figure out 'cause I had to be like, 'change trains when I see this weird ass symbol, then again when I see this.' And that crap was hard for me to remember. If you're ever there though, the stop for the base looks like a milkshake and fries. Like this,   ." Mathews knelt and drew the symbol out in the wet sand. "My friend, he's basically comatose, just standing there like a big hulking farm-boy statue only with his head down and his shoulder slumped. I'd have to yell at him and push him off the train, then guide him to the next one and shove him on, but I got us through all the transfers.

"Finally we were on the last line and I relaxed a little, and I'm lookin' out the window at each stop for the shake and fries character. Like I'm in a drunken haze and I'm concentratin' hard. I knew we had a ways to go but I'm looking at each one anyway, I was afraid not to. Then one time I'm lookin' and I'm like, that's not it, and I glance over and my buddy just steps off the train onto the platform. I ran over but the doors closed and about that time he turned around and I was on the train and he was on the platform and both went wide eyed looking right at each other and then the train pulled off and he was still standing there."

"Aww man!" Conner laughed, "I can see your face in my mind."

"Bro, I didn't know what to do. I thought I could try and go back, but then he might be getting on a train coming to me, and I knew that mug would never remember the symbol for the Yokota stop."

"So what did ya do?"

"Shit bro, I just kept going and got off when I was supposed to. Then I waited forever on the other end. I was looking in every train that came in tryin' to spot his goofy drunk farm-boy ass so I could grab him and pull him off the car when it stopped, but I never saw him."

"What happened?"

"After a couple hours I gave up and walked back to base. I was sobering up by then and super tired and he wasn't anywhere to be seen. What else could I do?" Mathews shook his head. "I kept checking his place next door and it'd be empty. Eventually I had to go to work. Bro, that mug was gone for almost forty-eight hours! When he finally answered the door I was scared he'd be pissed at me for not going back for him but he just let out this deep hardy country-boy laugh and handed me a beer."

Mathews tilted his head back gazing up at the sky as he exhaled. "It was only a few months, but God we had such great times together!"

"Sounds like it," Conner grinned looking at Mathews, the shoreline behind him stretched up the seemingly infinite coast. "Where's he at now?"

Mathews exhaled again, still staring upward, "He caught a deployment pretty quick after he got stationed in Yokota. Anyway, he left and got killed in Iraq."

Conner's smile faded as he observed his friend's face. *Fuck.* He swallowed hard.

"I don't know what happened other than he was escorting a convoy and got really fucked up. They got him out. All the way to Kuwait, but he died in the hospital there.

"I just can't figure how they got that man out of the combat zone to an advanced first-world medical facility and then fucking lost him. I keep thinking some critical bit of medical supplies got delayed somewhere."

Mathews' eyes continued to study the sky, though there were no points to fix on. It was just a wide clear magnificent blue. "I know they happened more than half a decade apart and it doesn't make any sense, but somehow I feel like it's all linked to that life or death box in Djibouti. Like in my mind there's some kinda time warp. It's stupid, I don't know why my brain does that and I'm sure they have all the equipment and material they need in Kuwait. It's not like some backward-ass-third-world shit with a little military aid station like Djibouti must have, but ever since I found out he died, I think about that goddamn busted up Styrofoam cooler all the time."

Conner closed his eyes and tried to imagine the coastline. It wasn't endless after all, eventually it wrapped all the way up through Georgia, the Carolinas and Virginia to the Maryland and Delaware beaches that he knew. Beyond that it continued through New Jersey, New York and into New England, then up to the rocky coasts of Maine and eventually Canada until the ocean itself became a frozen ice pack. *All this warm water here is somehow at this very moment touching that frozen ocean there. What a strange and complex world we live in.*

"I tried to duplicate it after that," Mathews continued. "That first wild night we had out together. But it was never the same. The guys I tried to hang with were different and then after a while I gave up on that, tried just going it alone. Things got really dark, just bein' out there, having drinks by myself. It was no good, even when I did have some success with the local ladies. I just never had that wild happy feeling again. That's why I quit."

Mathews' big hand landed on Conner's shoulder, their eyes locking as his head angled down away from the sky. "I only drink now when I'm on leave with real friends and I know I'm gonna have a good time!"

Mathews produced a smile as his wiry mechanic's grip tightened up on Conner's shoulder. "Come on, let's keep goin'."

CHAPTER 27

At the southernmost tip they found a jetty, constructed from a crude pile of large black granite rocks, extending several hundred yards into the ocean. Right behind the jetty stood an extensive wooden pier, though it was marked 'closed to the public' and seemed to have been derelict for some time. Past the pier lay a shipping channel, with more land just beyond sporting a row of luxury condos ten stories high. They turned right into a park where a network of newly paved walking paths curved through palm trees and small rises covered in neatly mowed grass. Further along they paused by a playground to watch a group of giggling children taking turns running through a section of fountains. The kids would sprint out through the randomly gushing spouts of water, squealing with delight when one erupted nearby. If someone managed to make it through untouched, they'd hold back and wait for a burst of water to hit them before dashing to safety again.

When did we lose this ability? The one that allows you to have the simplest kind of fun. Somewhere deep in Conner's mind came the childhood memory of carefully examining a Lego castle in the store. Thinking one day when he had a job, he could buy as many blocks and knights as he wanted. Create a massive kingdom in his parents' basement. By the time he was bagging groceries for minimum wage though, it was far too late. His interest had faded along with the ability for that type of imaginative play. *But would it have really mattered? I had plenty of toys growing up. What these kids are feeling right now is something before all that, something that requires no possessions at all. Just the pure childhood joy of running through jumping streams of water with your new friends at the beach. How did I lose that?*

"This is nice," Mathews commented, his eyes flicking forward as they began moving again. Conner nodded in agreement as two college-aged girls passed them on inline skates.

They wound their way through couples holding hands, slowly strolling families, and a large group of Asian tourists frantically snapping pictures as they chattered away in their own language.

"Two years in Japan," Mathews acknowledged, shaking his head, "and I can barely differentiate between Mandarin, Korean and Japanese."

"I hear those tonal languages are tough."

"Bro, you've got no idea. I was trying to learn, but my brain's just not built that way I guess, because I still can't form basic sentences. Plus there's a lot of subtlety in their culture, the way they talk, their mannerisms. You gotta be so dialed in to have any idea what's going on over there."

"Yeah, I'd be lost too man. Thank god our society is pretty straight forward. People just tell you what they need, you don't have to try and figure too much out."

"If they know what they need," Mathews replied. "I feel like there are some pretty critical concepts that our language doesn't have words for, then people have trouble workin' things out in their minds because we think in English, ya know?"

They looped around onto a wide sidewalk lined with palm trees running parallel to the channel. "That must be the main port for the city," Mathews observed, pointing west across the water to another land mass. "I can see all the cranes they use to unload the container ships."

"What a job that must be," Conner answered.

"Oh! Here comes one right now!"

Conner turned back toward the ocean to see an enormous freighter entering the inlet. They watched as it grew larger. A hodgepodge of various colored containers were stacked twelve rows high on its deck. *Incredible, the things people are able to create.* He stared at it as it powered in. "They put our operation to shame. One of those ships would supply those little air fields we fly into in Afghanistan for years."

"Yeah," Mathews responded, "but they need all this infrastructure. We get the goods right up close to the action and all we need is a dirt strip a few thousand feet long to land on."

"Still seems like we're dramatically inefficient."

"Ha! Bro, I never said we were efficient! We just get it up close, that's all."

They watched the ship pass before continuing on. Mathews stopped when they reached the old wooden pier and stared out. "Too bad we don't have any fishing gear. We could walk way out on that jetty and cast into the current. Ahhh... That'd be great! I bet ya there's big ol' fish out there to catch."

As they stood there a cruise ship made its way toward the inlet. They watched it as it came in. It was massive, ten decks high with what looked like water slides perched atop it. "I wonder where they're going," Conner asked.

"Caribbean most likely, they probably just port in here for a few hours and let everybody off to go get drunk at the clubs and watch the fireworks."

Conner moved to a bench beside the walkway and sat as he watched the ship pass. The dark dilapidated wood planks of the condemned pier in the foreground contrasted the fresh, new appearance of the bright white cruise ship moving through the channel. *Seems odd the government hasn't repaired the pier. The pylons and framework are probably still good, even if the decking's shot. If not, they could at least recycle the materials, or at a minimum tear the thing down.* His mind flashed back to the old rail bridge adjacent to Veterans Key. He shook his head, trying to shift his thoughts toward something else.

Mathews parked himself on the far end of the bench. "It's amazing our country can produce incredible pleasure vehicles like this, while we're overseas flying around in aircraft as old as we are."

Conner turned to look at him, "You're starting to sound like ol' Brackish McCabe!"

"Ha! I'll never be that bitter." Mathews shook his head, "To be fair, he did have a pretty rough time after he was transferred. But, we were calling that mug 'Brackish' long before that."

"He kinda alluded to something like that. What happened?"

"Bro, it ain't nothin' you don't already know."

"Help me out a little."

"Shit bro, that joker took Stretch ending himself harder than anybody, well except maybe Lewis, I guess we'll never know how he's doin' with it all." Mathews let out a breath as he watched the cruise ship go by. "Think about it, you got a guy like McCabe who worries about everybody all the time, he kinda mothered all of us in the same way that Stone was everyone's big brother. He was talkin' to Stretch every night, trying to help that man cope, then it went down the worst way possible.

"After that, Lewis disappears and Stone goes off the grid. Understandably he was super upset about losing his father. You and I were the only ones left that he could talk to. I end up in Japan on a reverse time schedule and you quit answering the phone. A guy like that, who cares about everyone so much, to basically end up alone, he was destined to have a tough time. No way around it."

"Damn, I never thought of it like that."

"I talked to him as much as I could but it was only a few times a month. Hell, half the time I called I woke that mug up in the middle of his fucking night, and the other half I was all lit up. Not sure if it did him any good or if it was all just me trying to get myself through."

"He seems ok now, huh?"

"He's a lot better, I think anyway. He started running every time he gets real upset. Now he's met this girl he's marrying."

Conner turned to Mathews with his head cocked to one side. "He runs every morning."

"Yeah. Stresses out in his dreams, worrying about everybody, wondering if he should've said something different to Stretch, or turned him in to supervision or something."

"Holy shit," Conner's eyes went wide. "He really feels responsible? Like it was all on him?"

"Yeah, I try to tell him. Stop worryin' about everybody else. Focus on the good stuff. But maybe he doesn't get to choose what he dreams about," Mathews exhaled. "Hey, I think this girl he's marrying has been helpin' him get straightened out. Plus now the Air Force finally has gotten their deployment schedule squared away, so nobody should be on back to back rotations anymore. Just more time going by and creating some separation, it should all help. He'll be alright."

Conner turned back toward the channel where the cruise ship had passed, sunlight flashed on the tips of the aquamarine-blue ripples left in its wake. "Why you think Stretch did that shit to himself? You think it's cause he didn't have fun playing basketball? I mean for real, I'm not tryin' to be ignorant. He loved basketball. He was always so quiet, but when he talked, half the time it was about playing b-ball in high school. He even played college for a season before he enlisted I think."

Mathews turned and stared directly at Conner. "He did it because he quit, bro. It didn't have nothin' to do with basketball. It had everything to do with whatever was coming next. He was real fuckin' tired and real run down like we all were.

He just had a weak moment and quit. That's all. Don't try to read no more into it than that or you'll drive yourself crazy—end up dreamin' about it like McCabe every night."

Conner exhaled as his eyes drifted back to the shipping lane. It seemed like such a narrow strip that these mammoth vehicles had to navigate through, and strange that he could be sitting on the land while just a couple hundred yards in front of him the water was deep enough to support such massive vessels.

"Speakin' of Brackish McCabe, let's get back so we can hang out with those jokers a bit before we have to go track down dinner. My 'beer low' light has been on for a while."

Conner stretched out on a towel in the sand a few feet away from McCabe, who still seemed engrossed in his book. Stone was absent—perhaps he'd gone on his own walk—and Mathews was back out in the water cooling off.

Staring up at the clear blue sky through his shades Conner pondered how things could appear so differently after dark. *The night sky in fact, is still up there now, I just can't see it.* It was strange to think about. All those stars and distant galaxies being obscured by brighter light to such an extent they only seemed to exist in the night. *How many other things are out there all the time that I just can't see? Or comprehend? There's got to be something to it all.*

His mind shifted to the moon, how bright it could be without even creating its own light. *All the little things playing together to change the course of our lives. I probably wouldn't have even seen Stone out there on the beach a few nights ago without the moonlight. Or maybe if it had been that much darker he wouldn't have been there at all.*

Conner allowed his eyes to close, wondering why that image from the train of the moonlit German countryside covered in snow came to him so often before he fell asleep. *Maybe it's because it looked nice, and I felt safe and I was moving toward where I needed to be? Like I was tired and I'd just gotten to see all these new places and meet interesting people and just for a moment, everything was good.*

I guess you don't get to know which moments will stick with you while they're happening. I wonder if passing out on this beach in Miami with my best friends so close will come back to me years from now. Maybe not, maybe it's got something to do with the moonlight. As he lay there another memory surfaced. On leave after tech school before, September 11th, backpacking solo through the Smoky Mountains. The first day was ok, and then it had dumped rain for the next two. He'd slogged through it, but not nearly as far as he planned. Then on the afternoon of the fourth day the rain dropped down to a drizzle, and he made the decision to make up for lost time. He moved all afternoon through the trails, pausing only to eat. When evening came the sky was clear, the sun slowly slid beneath the horizon and when the moon rose it was so bright and full that the trails were lit.

Everything looked like some type of magical dream. I just kept going. I backpacked all night through the moon shadows. I remember it, twenty-four miles up and down in the hills. His breathing slowed as he began to drift. The peaceful rhythmic sounds of the ocean passing over him. *I planned it out—plotted the trails on topographical maps—carried all my gear on my back. Maybe one of the only times I really went out on my own. I set out to do something—to prove something to myself—and I did it. The weather slowed me down, but I made it all the way through on time because I drove myself hard. But it was only possible because of the moon.*

CHAPTER 28

"Much easier than the last time we tried to find this place," McCabe commented as he backed the Mustang in, parallel parking outside the brewery.

"Yeah," Mathews agreed, "Stone didn't even have a chance to pick a fight with any high schoolers outside 7-Eleven."

Conner glanced toward Stone to gauge his response, but he only smiled.

The brewery was half full when they walked in. The clientele seemed to be mainly in their twenties and early thirties. "Our girl better be working," Mathews hissed, "a thousand bars to check out in this town and we actually came back to this one."

"She can pour you another blueberry wheat!" McCabe gibed.

"Bro, you're just jealous 'cause she was into me!"

"*Yeah dude*," McCabe answered, "that's what it is."

"Shut up!" Mathews countered, and they both laughed.

They ordered a round of drinks at the bar, but it was a fast-moving girl with dark, curly hair who poured them. She didn't seem nearly as playful as the beach-blonde they'd hoped to find. There wasn't enough space for them all to sit at the bar so they grabbed their drinks and took up positions around a high-topped table by the wall on the far side of the room.

"Shit, it's gonna be hard to talk to her now," Mathews muttered as his light-blue eyes flicked around the room. "If she's even here."

"*If* she actually likes you, and *if* she's actually here, she'll find a way to make time," McCabe answered.

"Truth," Mathews nodded.

"Man, you guys better watch my back. Makes me nervous sitting where I can't see the door," Stone commented.

"Really?" Conner replied.

"Conner," Mathews began, "I don't know how you've managed to stay alive this long, bro."

Conner's eyes narrowed, "Whatever, I do just fine."

"I hear ya, Stone," Mathews continued. "That's why I grabbed this spot, it fucking stresses me out when I can't see what's going on. Don't worry though, I'll keep a vigil, you can take it easy, scope the scene and check out the ladies at the bar."

"Speaking of..." Stone answered, "It looks like you might be in luck."

The beach-blonde flashed a sassy smile as she made her way across the room to their high-top bar table. "Y'all need another round?"

"Please," McCabe answered, "double IPA."

"I'm good," Stone nodded.

"Sure, why don't you pick so these guys don't make fun of me," Conner suggested. "I promise I won't complain."

"You're not helping yourself out here, Conner," Mathews chuckled.

"What kinda man can't even order a beer for himself?" McCabe snickered, "That's worse than ordering a pilsner!"

I can't win. Conner shrugged, looking at the waitress.

"I'll take care of you, hon," she nodded before turning to Mathews.

"Lady, I need all kinds of stuff."

Her eyes narrowed, though there seemed to be a playful smirk hoping to find its way to the surface.

"I'm definitely ready for another hefeweizen for starters."

"That's not a problem," she replied, continuing to gaze at Mathews with suspicion. "What else you got?"

"I know you don't have a kitchen, but I've got to get some food up in this joint sometime real soon. I don't want to have to debate the merits of going hungry versus going thirsty."

"There's a food truck that just finished setting up out back, they've got badass Cubans and fried plantains."

"Excellent!"

"Why do I feel like there's more?"

"Because there is, but you're doing fine, you're doing just fine. I need to know your name."

She turned her head slightly, regarding him out of the corners of her eyes. "Why do you need to know my name?"

"Cause I'm going to ask you to come out with us later."

"Well you've certainly eliminated the element of surprise."

"Don't need it," Mathews continued. "So..."

"You need my name to ask me out?" She leaned toward him accentuating her low-cut top. "Does it really matter?" She waved a hand down over her body. "Isn't the rest of this just vagina confetti?"

Mathews' jaw dropped open. "Va—jay—jay what?"

"You know," she continued, raising her small hands up and wiggling her fingers as she brought them down in a rain-like motion. "Just the extra, frivolous bits that come with what you're really after."

"Of course it matters," Mathews shot back, feigning outrage. "What kinda person do you think I am?"

"You really want me to answer that?"

Mathews tilted his head as he shot her back a contrived glare.

"Sara"

"Bullshit."

"You think I'm lying about my name!"

"I don't think you're telling the whole truth."

"My name actually is Sara."

"Not with that country accent it's not. Where ya from?"

"A little town in Tennessee you've never heard of. Things got rough up there so I've slowly made my way south."

"Uh-huh," Mathews nodded with confidence. "And what did your mom call you in the little town in Tennessee that I've never heard of?"

The beach-blonde glared at him.

"I'm sorry, I meant what did your *mama* call you?"

"Sara!"

"Sara... what?"

Her face flushed a little as she stared at him. "Sara Anne."

Mathews grinned as he gazed back at her.

"But work people don't call me that, and neither do tourists, so if that's what you're going to call me then we have to be friends." The hint of her sly smile began to form. "And if we are friends, then there is no Sara, it's only Sara Anne."

"Ok great, so we have beer, we have food, we've got a spot picked out on South Beach to watch the fireworks and I just got the name of the prettiest bartender in Miami. Now all I need is for you, Sara Anne, to come out dancing with us after your shift ends. You can show us the best spots and I'll buy your drinks. It'll be great."

"No," she answered, tilting her head slyly to one side. "I don't sleep with tourists."

McCabe and Conner exploded in laughter. "You just crashed and burned, dude!" McCabe dropped a hand on Mathews' shoulder. "Let this nice girl alone so she can get our drinks!"

"Sleep with?" Mathews woofed, shrugging McCabe's hand off. "Who said anything about the sex? I offered to buy you some drinks if you came out and showed us the best spots to go dancing!"

"Are you saying you don't want to sleep with me?" Sara Anne leaned back, placing a hand on her hip.

"I'm not falling in that trap, kid," Mathews laughed. "I said nothing about the infamous yet intimate act of fornication. I just asked if you wanted to go out for some nice innocent dancing and maybe a fireworks show beforehand, that's all."

"Yes, I'm sure that's all you were hoping for. Just me taking you out for an innocent night of fun, getting a little tipsy, no doubt rubbing my beautiful body all over you in some sweaty tourist spot. I'm sure you'd never *dream* of trying to put the moves on me during any of that."

"Well," Mathews answered, "only if you wink at me or give me some kinda sign. Otherwise I'll be a perfect gentlemen. I promise."

"Sorry, sweetie, honestly there's no point in club dancing with someone I know I'm not gonna sleep with and, like I said, I don't sleep with tourists."

"Damn, she can see straight through you, dude," McCabe sneered.

Mathews turned and glared at them before facing back toward Sara Anne. "Who says I'm a tourist anyway?" he countered.

"You did a few days ago when you were first here! Wanted the local scoop on everything from gangs to beaches to nightclubs!"

"Well that was three days ago! I'm practically a local now!"

She tilted her head even further looking at him side-eyed.

"Alright, alright, but for real, you shouldn't consider me a tourist. We're on a business trip."

"*Really*," she enunciated skeptically. "A business trip?"

"Well sure, I'm an exec for Skippy peanut butter. We're down here trying to scout out new locations for peanut farms to help us better compete with Peter Pan."

"*Really*?" she asked again.

"Sure, we've got 'em beat on crunchy peanut butter without doubt, but people just love Peter Pan's smooth peanut butter more than Skippy, or Jif for that matter. We just can't compete. Ahh, I really shouldn't be telling you this, but we think expanding our peanut growing operation to southern Florida might change the texture just enough to give us a more competitive market edge."

"I see," she answered with a big, fun grin.

"Yes ma'am."

"Because your buddy there mentioned you were stationed in Japan last time you were here, and y'all look straight up military to me."

"Damn it, Conner!" Mathews turned and smacked his arm.

Conner chuckled, shaking his head.

"I'm sorry for the deception, we're on a secret mission and were told to disguise ourselves as peanut executives."

"You don't give up do you?!"

"Never," Mathews answered quick with a devious smile.

"You military boys are worse than tourists, you're like wrecking balls leaving wide swaths of destruction and heartbroken local girls behind in every town you pass through."

Mathews took a deep breath and glanced up for a moment before returning to her steel-blue eyes. "Yes, you nailed it, but I can assure you every girl I loved and left had an amazing time while she was with me!"

The bartender let out a genuine laugh as she brushed her sun-bleached hair out of her tan face and tucked it behind her ears. "You're cute. In fact, maybe I can even help you out. No promises though." She turned and retreated back toward the bar.

"You're relentless," Conner gibed.

McCabe shook his head, "Shameless, is more like it. What the hell is your plan, annoy her into fucking you?"

Mathews shook his head, "She's not annoyed, she loves it!"

"I wouldn't count on that dude," McCabe answered.

"Bro! She's a sexy-ass blonde bombshell of a bartender, in a party city like Miami. I guarantee she gets hit on all the time. But none of those amateurs can spit game like me!"

"You're awfully confident, dude."

"Just be glad you're getting married and you don't gotta do this shit no more." Mathews sighed. "You're done, Conner's locked himself down. It's just Stone and me, and I can't project that strong silent confidence like he does. Talkin' game is all I got."

"If you could call it that," McCabe replied.

"Bro, shut up and see what happens."

"One thing I know," Stone interjected. "Is that a girl will never do anything to *help you out*. She may do something that inadvertently benefits you, but it's never about *you*. A girl might set you up with her friend for instance, but if so, her whole point would be to help her friend out. They're not worried about us. At least that's how they operate in my experience."

Mathews shook his head frantically. "Look, there's no way to know. Anyway, you boys alright with the food truck? I know it's our last night and all, but I'm hungry now."

"Saturday night, Fourth of July, if we go anyplace nice we'll probably be waiting for hours," McCabe answered.

"Cuban sandwiches sound good to me, I'll go put us all in for one," Stone offered, standing.

"I'll go pay for them," Mathews announced.

"You stay here in case she actually decides to *help you out*," Stone grinned, making air quotes with his fingers before turning and heading toward the door.

Conner jumped up. "I got it, man. Just hang out, you paid for mine the other day in Key West."

"I appreciate you Conner, but if I can't buy my buddies a couple sandwiches, what's the point?" Stone called without breaking his stride.

"I wasn't saying that."

Stone flashed a quick smile back over his shoulder without stopping.

Conner slowly slumped back onto his seat. He watched Stone walk away, his Hawaiian shirt and new khaki pants weren't nearly as bright and fresh as they had been a few days before. Something else was different though. He didn't seem as heavy as he had before. That last grin, it seemed genuine. *Did something change?* Conner closed his eyes for a moment and scratched his head. "You guys feel like Stone is coming back to life just a little bit?"

Mathews nodded. "Something's different. I fucked up and tried to buy his dinner again but it didn't even slow him down tonight. It's like he got a little spark back or something. I don't know what it is, but something seems better just in the last couple hours."

"When you two were having your romantic walk on the beach together," McCabe began, "he started telling me a story about getting in trouble with his high school friends. Some stupid shit about getting busted by the cops for riding around on top a car in the school parking lot. But the point is he started laughing halfway through. First time I've heard him laugh for real this whole trip."

"You think he just needed some time hanging out with real friends, like instead of being on his own out in his van? Or getting his side slashed open trying to," Mathews held his fingers up making air quotes, "help someone?"

McCabe shrugged. "Honestly, I don't know."

"Hell, maybe it even helped him just sleeping indoors in a bed, getting hot showers every day and eating good food."

"It certainly didn't hurt."

"Bro, maybe he just straight up decided. Mind over matter, he just chose to stop focusing on whatever it was that was dragging him down and have fun."

McCabe shrugged again. "You know, I'm not even sure we should try to figure it out. I'm just glad he seems to be having a good time for a change. Actually, speaking of a good time..." His eyes flicked toward the bar.

The bartender approached with another girl in tow, carrying a tray with their drinks. She was fit and taller than Sara Anne, with Asian features, a bright smile and toned skin. "Hey, this is Kira. She's going to help me out with your table 'cause I'm getting pretty busy up front."

"Here you go!" Kira beamed, placing their drinks in front of them.

"Her father was in the military," Sara Anne continued, "So maybe she can actually keep up with you guys." Leaning back beyond Kira's view she nodded to one side throwing her hands up in a wide eyed shrug.

"Really?" Mathews eyes sparked with interest. "Where was he stationed?"

Kira angled her head to the side and pulled her dark hair back with one hand, as she gestured to her face with the other. "Ummm, Japan obviously!"

The table let out a collective chuckle.

"I'll be right back with a round of waters for you guys also." Everyone's eyes followed her as she skipped away in her Chuck Taylors, denim skirt and black tank top.

"Listen, be nice to her," Sara Anne insisted in a hushed tone. "She's just working here for the summer so she's basically a tourist, too. Don't come after her with all that bullshit you were throwing at me. Cut the swagger in half and just talk to her ok? Her shift ends in an hour and earlier she was looking for someone to go to the fireworks with."

Mathews turned his head slightly but his eyes stayed locked on Kira.

"If it all works out maybe I'll even meet up with y'all for a bit later."

Instead of leaving when her shift ended, Kira pulled a stool up to the guys' table. She smiled broadly as Mathews recounted his experience getting caught by the American MPs in Uzbekistan while buying a backpack full of black market Russian vodka.

"That was before we had enough sense to dye the stuff green and hide it in Scope bottles," he continued. "A hell of a lot better than finding myself on the wrong side of that fifty caliber machine gun they had mounted on top their Humvee. That thing scared the shit out of me, I couldn't get my hands up high enough! I was legit reaching for the sky!"

"I can picture you," Kira laughed. "I bet you looked ridiculous!"

"That's not even the crazy part," McCabe cut in. "Somehow he brought the vodka back to us."

"What?! *How?!*" she belted out.

"Bro, that MP kept yellin' 'what's your unit?' and I was telling him, and he was like 'bullshit! I never heard of that unit being deployed here.' I kept saying 'I know! I'm telling you I'm supposed to be on that C-130 on the ramp. I'm not deployed here! It's leaving in twenty minutes.' Well he wouldn't believe me, so we went back and forth, and back and forth. Finally the flight crew cranked up the engines and we could hear it. They're louder than hell. I was like 'Bro, I gotta go!' I'm sure my eyes were bigger than saucers.

"He stared at me for a minute, then turned and looked at his guys, then back to me. I could see his face change. I'll never forget it, he said 'You're fucking serious?' and I was nodding so fast I must have looked like a crazy person. That man said 'That plane only landed ninety minutes ago, how'd you get in this much trouble this quick?'

"I was still reaching up as high as I could, and one of his guys was still on the Humvee with the fifty cal pointed at me and I started shaking my head. I was like 'I don't know bro, it's some kinda fucked up talent I got.' When that man started laughin' it was one of the most intense feelings of relief I ever had in my life. I mean, I've seen negative pregnancy tests and not felt that relieved. The time the pilots T-handled the number two engine over Pakistan and I watched the fire go out through the porthole window, I wasn't that relieved."

Mathews sat there on the bar stool shaking his head. "He said 'go, and if you don't get on that airplane I'm putting you in zip cuffs.' I said 'Don't worry sergeant, I'm getting on that 130 and I ain't never coming back to this place.'"

"Oh my goodness!" Kira let out. "Your lives are so crazy! I remember my dad and his buddies telling stories like that when I was a kid!"

"Yeah, and McCabe and the boys here got drunk for free out of it," Mathews concluded.

"Did you ever go back?"

"Fuck no, a couple months later they found a bunch of buried Russian nuclear material on that base. It was irradiating all the guys who were working there and no one knew it until people started getting sick. It still took them a couple years after that to close the place down."

"Typical military bullshit," McCabe mumbled.

"Ahh come on Brackish, let's not start this again. Even if you are right sometimes."

"Why do you keep calling him Brackish?" Kira asked.

"HA!" Mathews turned to McCabe, "Can I tell her?"

McCabe shrugged and took another swig of his beer, "Why not?"

"I'll remember this shit as long as I live! We got an eight hour pass in Doha on our first real deployment. After we came back on base, ol' McCabe here wouldn't stop bitching about the locals having an ice skating rink in their mall, and cooled swimming pools at their hotels, while we working in a hundred and twenty degree temps and couldn't get anything to drink but hot bottled water. The master sergeant was like 'how long you been in, McCabe? Two years? How are you so fresh and so salty at the same time? You're Brackish.' And we've been calling him that shit ever since."

She tilted her head and gazed side-eyed at McCabe, "I mean... it kinda fits."

The table exploded in laughter, a grin even forced its way across Stone's face.

"Yeah, yeah," McCabe responded.

"Yo, I like this girl," Stone confessed, reaching out to bump fists with Kira. "You should be an honorary member at our next bachelor party."

"Oh you wouldn't regret it," she promised, "I'm great fun. Who's getting married next?"

"We're not sure," Stone answered, "We're gonna draw straws later."

Everyone laughed again. Conner's eyes found Stone and recognized something in his friend he hadn't seen since he left two years ago. He couldn't quite identify it, but he was sure something had changed.

"We might need you for real," McCabe agreed. "A couple days ago we had a sunscreen impasse you *really* could have helped out with. We barely made it out without second degree burns."

"Sunscreen impasse?" Kira asked.

"Ignore him," Mathews cut in. "Let's worry about the next bachelor party after we pick ladies out and propose to them. We've got more immediate issues to deal with right now."

Kira glanced at him. Her eyes narrowed.

"Are you tryin' to come to the fireworks with us? They're supposed to be kick-ass down on South Beach."

"I don't know..." she sighed, "It's Saturday night and I worked a long shift. I was thinking about going home and watching Netflix by myself."

Conner, Stone and McCabe's eyes all locked onto her, then together slowly tracked her gaze to Mathews, whose face visibly drooped as his shoulders slumped.

Kira let out a suppressed giggle, her dark eyes bright with amusement. Mathews' sky-blue eyes flicked toward her and she threw her head back with a boisterous laugh.

"Ughh," Mathews let out gazing up at the ceiling.

"Did you guys see his face?" she pointed, giggling. "I got you so good."

"What can I say, you nailed it!"

Kira reached out touching Mathews' shoulder. "Seeing the fireworks would be lovely."

"Honestly, I'm pumped," McCabe confessed. "I know maybe it's a little childish or something. But I haven't gone to see the fireworks in a really long time, I always seem to be stuck at work or out of the country on the Fourth. I think this is going to be great."

"Don't feel silly about it," Kira offered. "Lots of adults go, it's not just for kids. I'm excited to see them too. I've never seen them at the beach and I bet they'll be pretty by the water. You guys are fun, I'm glad we get to go together."

"I mean, when I was a kid," McCabe continued, "my dad used to take me. I remember it being really fun. For real. I know you guys tease me about being bitter all the time, and there's probably something to that. But seriously, I remember watching the fireworks in the park with my dad as being one of the best things ever. I really do. All the booms and bright colors. It was great. I don't think I've thought about it until now, but I haven't seen the fireworks since my dad died. Too busy I guess. Always at work, or maybe I just didn't want to go by myself. I'm not trying to be all sentimental or anything but it seems kinda special that we all get to see them together."

Though she smiled, Kira's eyes carried a soft sadness as she reached out, her hand settling on McCabe's bicep, her thumb gently skimming the surface of his dark Celtic bands. "There's so many difficult things in life. But really there's so many good things, too. It's wonderful that you've all kept in touch so well and stayed so close! That takes so much effort. It really shows you're not just friends of convenience, ya know? Loyalty like that is hard to find. I think losing touch with all his buddies is my dad's biggest regret. He still talks about them every time I see him."

Conner swallowed hard, his face tinting red as he watched her across the table.

"It really is special when you find your people. I didn't fit in anywhere. Growing up overseas I never felt like I was a real American kid and I definitely wasn't Japanese." Her smile seemed to grow warmer as the sadness faded from her dark eyes. "I remember the day in middle school that I met my best friend. She is hāfu like me and we just clicked. It was like we completely understood each other the first time we met. We did everything together. She was like my sister. I never knew what that was like before. You guys have that too! I can just tell seeing you all together."

Conner's attention flicked to each of his friends.

Stone reclined back with crossed arms, his storm-gray eyes steady as he watched Kira.

McCabe stared down at the table, sucking in a deep breath.

Mathews' center of gravity had shifted forward as if being pulled by an invisible force. His eyes seemed lost as he gazed at Kira, and he nodded as she spoke.

"Her dad got transferred to Germany in the ninth grade though, and we promised we'd keep in touch forever, but I never saw her again."

Her eyes darted around the table. "I'm sorry, I didn't mean to get so serious or make this about me!" She exhaled hard, "Seriously though, I'm glad I get to watch the fireworks with you all. I didn't want to go by myself."

Conversations from other tables reverberated off the wall beside them, people laughed and ordered more drinks, the knocks of beer glasses being set up on the stainless steel bar sounded through the hum of air conditioning ducts high above them.

"I'm glad I'm here with you guys, too," Conner offered. "One day when we all have families we should get together and watch them as a group. Make a whole weekend out of it. Maybe we could rent a beach house together, or even make it a tradition."

"That sounds really nice, actually," Stone agreed as his eyes drifted down to the table.

Mathews reached around Kira with a lanky arm and clasped McCabe's shoulder. "Hey, you know I'm in, and seriously man, I'm excited too. I haven't seen any fireworks since I left the States."

Everyone's eyes seemed to have drifted down to the table, dull chatter from around the room filling the void in their conversation. Mathews exhaled hard before glancing back up toward Kira. "Hey, you wanna go outside for a cigarette?"

"Ew! No way! I hate smoking!"

"Yeah me too," Mathews answered, holding what remained of his cigarette pack up and crushing it in his fist before chuckling as he tossed it over his shoulder.

Kira's mouth dropped open as she stared at him, "Did you just quit smoking?"

"It certainly appears that way," Mathews smirked.

McCabe shook his head. "Holy shit, you're too much." He stood up and swallowed the remaining bit of beer in his pint glass. "I'm going to step outside and call my fiancée."

Stone and Conner shared a knowing look before heading to the food truck in back. Instead of returning, they hung around the bar eating their second set of Cuban sandwiches. McCabe eventually joined them and ordered another round of drinks.

Nearly an hour had passed before Mathews stepped up to the bar next to Conner and held two fingers up to the bartender.

"I thought you were done with Asian-A-cups," Conner taunted when Mathews turned toward him.

"Bro!" Mathews' eyes went wide before glancing over his shoulder to the table where Kira was sitting. "Keep your damn voice down!"

"Calm down, she can't hear us."

"Besides, it ain't like that."

"*Sure*," Conner answered.

"Have you really talked to her? This girl is great. She's smart, knows about all kinds of stuff. She's in grad school up in Gainesville, and just down here for the summer banking up some cash."

"Did you ask her about toxic masculinity?"

"Fuck no! Don't be stupid I'm not trying to wreck things," Mathews stared at Conner intently, as if pondering something. "She might actually understand though. I feel like this girl knows what's up."

"You seem to have a decent track record with grad-school girls."

"Cut me some slack bro, I like her for real. Ohh! I didn't tell you! Her dad was in the Air Force, and get this! That joker was stationed at Yokota and he was a flying crew chief on a herc, just like us! That's where he met her mom. She totally gets it. I can't believe it."

"No shit?"

"This might be the first girl I've ever met as an adult, who's had any concept of what my life has been like. I always try to put those conversations off, but eventually, that shit always comes up and I hate it, because no one ever gets me."

Conner nodded and tilted his beer back. Somewhere inside he wondered how Joselyd understood him so well. *One in a million I guess.*

"This is incredible! I can't remember the last time I've felt this way."

"Easy man, you've only known her a couple hours and we're leaving tomorrow."

"I don't know bro, maybe I'll extend my leave, come back here after I see my parents."

"Seriously?"

"Why the hell not? What else am I doing?" Mathews' sky-blue eyes lit up, "I didn't even tell you the best part! At the end of the summer she's going to stay with her grandparents for a month! Twenty minutes from my apartment, bro! What are the odds of that shit?!"

Sara Anne placed two pint glasses down in front of him. With effort she leaned her short body across the stainless steel bar, her steel-blue eyes locked on Mathews, "You treatin' that girl right?"

"I promise."

"You better," she insisted, pointing, before hopping back down with a grin and returning to the beer taps.

"Well honestly, I like her man, she's got a real good personality. You've got her coming to see the fireworks with us, that's a great start."

"I can't even express to you how good I feel right now, but I gotta go, I'm not letting this girl sit, somebody's gonna scoop her up!" Mathews grabbed the two pint glasses and stepped away before spinning back around and leaning in close to Conner's ear. "But for real, you need to calibrate your inspection equipment, anything more than a mouthful is at least a B-cup."

CHAPTER 29

"Shotty," McCabe called, tossing the Mustang keys to Stone as they stepped out onto the street.

"Ahh come on, Brackish!" Mathews threw his lanky arms out to his sides. "How's that gonna work? We got a lady present. Don't make her cram in the back seat with us!"

McCabe shrugged and smiled. "I'm sure you'll figure something out."

"Shit man, there's hardly enough space for two of us back there."

"So it makes even less sense to put the smallest person we got in the front seat."

"It's no big deal, guys! I'll fit!"

"*See?*" McCabe said, before turning to Stone. "Don't hit anything dude, you're not on the rental agreement."

"Shouldn't be a problem," Stone replied.

Conner climbed into the back seat, then Kira wiggled her way onto the middle hump, where there was no seat. When Mathews attempted to get in, it was clear it wasn't going to work at all.

"We're about to get close, Conner," Kira giggled before flopping her upper body into his lap. She held her denim skirt closed with one hand as she lifted her legs, pointing her Chuck Taylors toward the sky.

"Oof," Conner's face flushed as he instinctively cradled the girl's head with his left arm. His right hand having nowhere to go except across her abdomen. "You alright?" he asked, looking down into her eyes, their faces so close it felt like they were about to kiss.

"Better than alright!" she chirped.

Climbing in, Mathews pulled the front seat back, locking it in place for McCabe. "Ahh man," he groaned, tapping Kira to let her know she was clear to lower her legs into his lap. "How come I didn't get the fun half?"

"What's wrong?" Kira giggled. "You don't like my ankles?"

"I can't complain," Mathews answered. "You do have some mighty fine ankles."

"Watch your heads," Stone called back. "I'm going to put the top up so we don't draw so much attention."

When the convertible roof snapped into place, the engine started with a roar and Stone pulled the Mustang out onto the road. Kira's hair felt thick and coarser than Conner had expected. As she lay across him, he could feel each breath she took, and the way her stomach muscles tightened every time she laughed at one of Mathews' jokes. He couldn't remember the last time he had a girl in his lap that wasn't Joselyd. It triggered some strange excitement that he hadn't anticipated. Even still, he missed his girlfriend.

He was actively avoiding looking down into Kira's face, because anytime he did he got that feeling like they were about to lock lips. *It's a muscle memory thing. When Joselyd's this close, you kiss her. It's just a mental association. Your brain and reflexes are mixed in with some alcohol and it's messing with you right now. That's all. Nothing else to it. Excited to see Joselyd tomorrow.*

Even as he thought, his eyes involuntarily shifted to the girl in his lap. Kira met his gaze and beamed up at him. As the Mustang cruised across the causeway, he remembered how exotic and strangely good it felt his first night in Miami, the brunette in the dance club grinding up against him. *What is happening?* An urgent need to talk to his girlfriend manifested in Conner's mind. At the minimum to pull his phone out and look at her picture. But neither would be possible in the back seat of this packed car even if he had decided to.

One massive cruise ship after another rolled by through the window, all ported in across the narrow shipping lane to his right. A new series of thoughts filled his mind. *Why are we flying into war zones on aircraft built before we were born when we live in a country that has the resources to produce massive luxury liners like these?* The concept had been festering ever since Mathews had put the idea into his head that afternoon, and now it seemed to be taking hold. Combining with what McCabe had said earlier about Americans never thinking of the wars. The conflicts having no recognizable impact on their daily lives.

Do most people really only focus on what's right in front of them? Out of sight, out of mind, they say. Civilians don't see war. They haven't flown across the desert in a cargo plane filled with nineteen year olds in litters with their legs blown off and their faces covered in bandages. They don't know what it smells like. Or how strange it all looks—cast in green night vision lighting—the body bags just cargo strapped to the floor, not yet placed in American flag draped coffins.

Conner shook his head. *I'm not any better. Four of my best friends left and I didn't talk to them for years. One beautiful girlfriend completely filled the void. Now she's at home and even though I'll see her tomorrow, I'm completely distracted. My mind stuck on some booty-grinding club girl I'll never even see again, and this grad student in my lap that I only met a few hours ago. It doesn't make any sense.*

Out of sight, out of mind. Just like Lewis, wherever he is now. Like McCabe out at March Air Force Base when I didn't know his dad died and I never made time to call him back. Like Stone out west on his own in some national forest, living in his van. Just like all those veterans in the Keys no one bothered to pick up when the hurricane was coming. Just left there, impaled by flying building materials, or their heads bashed in by coconuts hurled by the storm at one hundred and eighty miles per hour, or just drowned in the twenty foot storm surge when they couldn't hold onto the rail bridge any longer.

Conner closed his eyes and tilted his head back. Against him, Kira's chest slowly expanded and contracted as the Mustang rumbled forward.

Stone pulled into a parking garage and the group loaded up two tactical backpacks with beach towels and water bottles before walking the last few blocks toward the ocean. They made their way between two tall luxury hotels to a large patio crowded with people on outdoor furniture. Just beyond, a row of palm trees separated them from a much larger group sprawled out on the beach with blankets. They shifted through the crowd together—Mathews leading the way with Kira in tow clinging to his hand—eventually finding a decent spot to sit down on the outer edge of the sprawling mass of spectators.

"Nice," Mathews grinned. "Just in time to get settled before the show starts."

"Yeah," Stone replied. "This should be good."

"There's a lot of money here," McCabe observed. "It oughta be amazing."

"It has to be!" Mathews agreed. "Look how close they're setting up. We are gonna have a great view."

In front of them children laughed and squealed as they tossed glowing light rings back and forth. Conner let his eyes shift out to the dark ocean where foamy caps riding the crest of the waves were illuminated by the nearly full moon which was already high in the sky. *The same moon,* Conner thought, *the same moon that lit the mountain trails up for me the time I hiked all night in the Smoky Mountains, and the German countryside the winter evening I took the train back from Berlin. The same moon that was in Qatar, when I was lucky enough to work night shift and dodge some of the heat, and Iraq when I sat outside the tent because I couldn't sleep. The same moon that terrified the navigator on my first flight into Afghanistan in 2002, when there were no clouds for cover and he was convinced the entire country-side was going to open up on us the moment we descended within small arms range for landing. The same moon that controlled the tides and is over Joselyd right now, and Lewis, wherever he is, and shining on Stretch's gravestone.* Conner shook his head. *All the good, all the bad... it's all connected somehow. Anytime I'm away from Joselyd I can't seem to filter the bad out and leave it behind.*

Conner continued to ponder as he stared out over the dark water. Stars slowly began to appear in the darkest corners of the night sky, farthest from the moon and lights of the city. He was ripped from his train of thought by the triumphant beginning of the national anthem, booming over speakers from somewhere behind him. Conner jerked upright to the position of attention, before relaxing slightly and placing his hand over his heart.

Frances Scott Key entered Conner's mind as the music played. How just seeing the American flag had inspired him to write a song that persisted for nearly two-hundred years. *Why haven't I ever been moved enough to write a song? Maybe it's just not who I am, I don't have that kind of mind? Or perhaps it's because I've never been captured by the enemy—thank God—and had to witness an American position being shelled all night by a superior force, only to realize the US fortification had remained intact when the sun rose in the morning. I suppose that would inspire anybody.*

He was pulled from his thoughts again, this time by a group of teenaged coeds talking loudly and laughing as they passed behind them searching for a place to spread out.

"Hey, are you Russian or Chinese or something?" McCabe barked, glaring backward at them.

Conner felt his chest tighten.

"Easy Brackish," Mathews murmured, as Stone reached out and placed a hand on McCabe's bicep.

The perplexed looking group stopped, as if frozen. One boy squinted at McCabe with his head tilted slightly to the side, while the girl beside him stared back with her mouth gaping open. Still another girl turned to her friends and asked, "Was that racist?"

"No, I'm not racist!" McCabe groaned. "This is your national anthem playing. Situational awareness people. Look around."

To Conner's surprise, the teenagers' eyes did begin to flick across the crowd. One at a time and then the rest all at once, the high schoolers straightened up and placed their hands on their hearts. Stone released his grip on his friend's arm as McCabe shook his head letting out a long breath, before facing forward again.

Way smoother than I thought that would turn out. Conner inhaled deeply and felt himself relax.

When the song ended, people started to settle back onto their blankets as conversations began all around them. Conner glanced up the beach to see the technicians huddled near the launching point for the fireworks. *It won't be long now.*

Mathews leaned toward them, "Hey, we're going to go look at the water."

"Have fun," Stone responded with a little smirk.

With that Mathews scurried off, Kira giggled as she held his hand, allowing herself to be pulled along behind him. A few minutes later the first rocket went up. It burst in a bright circle of red clusters radiating outward from the center. Then another, this time blue. After a few more radiant booms, the show was in full display. An oscillating dispenser fired a fantail pattern of rockets which detonated midway up the sky. Then larger fireworks went off above them producing a brilliant pre-sentation of colorful patterns accompanied by pound-you-in-the-chest-explosions.

Damn! Mathews was right, these things are right on top of us! Turning, Conner scanned the edge of the dark ocean for his friend. He missed him at first, but then in a flash of light his eyes caught Mathew's tall silhouette and what had to be Kira in front of him. Mathews was facing away from him, toward the water, where reflections of the colorful fireworks danced across the incoming swells. He seemed to be leaning forward, then in the hodgepodge of lights it was clear they were kiss-ing. A moment later they tumbled down into the sand together and were difficult to see. Conner chuckled, *Good for them*, and turned to take in the show in front of him.

Smiling, Conner remembered watching the fireworks as a little kid, and his father telling him 'you have to say Oooo or Ahhhh, after each one.' *I was lucky growing up with parents who made an effort to take me to things.* Scanning the crowd in front of him, his eyes settled on a few little kids excitedly pointing up at the sky together. *Probably brothers.* He grinned watching them. *One day...* Conner thought, envisioning Joselyd. *What great lives we are going to have together.* But then his thoughts drifted to Stone, who sat beside him. *Would seeing all these happy kids throw him off?*

Conner turned toward his friend quick, but when he saw him, Stone was leaning over with his arms around McCabe—practically cradling his head. He was talking but the words were hidden by the succession of chest-rattling booms. In the irregular series of flashes he could make out McCabe's face. His lower lip quivering, his dark eyes filled with terror. His mouth was open as he sucked in deep sporadic breaths. The explosions seemed to grow louder and even closer together until they were on top of each other in one long unending roar joined by the distant wail of car alarms. The show persisted for what felt like an incredibly long time with no indications of a finale. The sharp pops and loud bangs reported again and again, then echoed off the surrounding buildings to sound for a second time.

McCabe stuffed his fingers in his ears and slumped forward, sweat pouring off his face and tears in his eyes. Conner stared at him, with a helpless paralyzed feeling he'd experienced before, watching streams of tracers arc their way toward his aircraft through the window, while having no available course of action to improve the situation. Just standing there hanging on, being completely reliant on the pilots to maneuver away from the multitude of lethal threats streaking up to meet them.

Stone stood, pulling McCabe up with him and ushering him away from the crowd. Conner rose in an instant to follow, but Stone grabbed the back of his neck, yanking him in close and yelling, "Either stay with the bags or bring them with you," before continuing to pull McCabe away. Conner hustled to gather their things then turned, racing to catch up with his friends. Their silhouettes in front of him—one with an arm around the other—trudging through the sand, their backs lit by the explosions in the sky. Sharp shadows stretched across the beach in front of them from a wide array of angles, each lasting only an instant before being replaced by a new dark line from another burst of light.

"What about Mathews?" Conner called when he was close.

"We'll find him later," Stone answered as he continued to drag McCabe away.

In the flashes of colorful light with the endless sequence of overlapping booms behind them, Stone hauled McCabe two hundred yards up the beach before depositing him in the sand and crashing down next to him.

"It's alright, buddy," Stone assured him.

McCabe sat slumped forward with his chest heaving. Conner stood back, a tactical styled backpack over each shoulder, watching his friends, unsure how to help.

"Nothing to be ashamed of man, it's a normal reaction. All that noise, so close like that—feeling the percussion of it—it just took you back to those rocket attacks in Kandahar, that's all. It makes total sense, it's hot, we're in the sand, you're with some of the same people, and it's just after dark when they used to hit us the most."

McCabe sucked in deep, shaking his head rapidly.

"You're alright man, I promise," Stone continued, patting his friend on the quad as they sat next to each other.

McCabe exhaled long and slow. "I just..." he began.

"You ain't gotta talk man, if you don't want to. You don't have to explain anything to me."

"The goddamn terrorists," McCabe attempted again. "We kicked their asses so bad."

"Yeah, sure we did," Stone responded. "We spent years turning wrenches on C-130's delivering death-dealing army grunts and gear to the war zone so they could whoop some ass."

"Naw, dude," McCabe began again, sweat pouring off his face. "The fucking terrorists, we beat 'em down so bad they can't fight us anymore. Not head on. Not even big, planned out September-11th-type shit." McCabe paused and took another deep breath as he reached up to wipe the tears from his eyes. The heaving in his chest had slowed. "They've changed tactics, it's all over Pakistan and Iraq and Turkey. All soft targets now. Civilian shit. Crowds, a lot of times people on vacation because their guard is down and they're drinking and unfamiliar with the area. They're wiping people out. It's coming here next, here and Europe for sure. Complex, low tech Mumbai-style attacks."

McCabe propped his elbows on his knees and let his head fall into his hands. "Just a half dozen assholes with homemade explosives and semi-automatic rifles killed a hundred and seventy people last year in Mumbai. I just started thinking if these bastards started the attack during the fireworks, nobody would fucking know. Nobody would fucking hear it.

"Dude, I got so worried about you boys, and then there were kids everywhere and I didn't want nothin' bad to happen to them, then I started thinking my fiancée's probably at the fireworks too and I didn't want nothin' to happen to her. Fuck! I'M A FUCKING MESS!"

"No, you're not," Stone answered, "I promise."

McCabe's forehead rested on his palms and he wouldn't look up.

"You ever have something like this before?"

McCabe shook his head, his voice quivering, "Something, but never like this."

"It's a lot of stress man, military life, and world affairs being what they are and then a marriage coming up on top of it all. You wouldn't be human if you didn't have some kinda reaction."

The roaring explosions in the distance ended in a massive finale followed by cheers from those watching on the beach and the reverberating echo of half a dozen car alarms. Conner dropped the packs and moved in, sitting on McCabe's open side.

The three of them sat there in silence, the dark water ahead of them rhythmically rushing in and out, their shoulders touching slightly as they stared together at the little flashes of moonlight reflecting off the crashing ocean waves.

CHAPTER 30

The distant car alarms had all timed out as the crowd of Fourth of July spectators down the beach to their right slowly dissipated. The bright moonlight drowned the city lights to such an extent Conner felt as if he were on some natural expanse of coast, and not just outside one of America's largest cities. *I'd love to be camping on some empty stretch of beach with the guys right now. Have a nice little fire and no people anywhere nearby to worry about.*

He thought of mentioning it. *Maybe we could all get together again and do something like that. Maybe even camp on the Tortugas like the people we saw earlier today.* But he decided against it. *I can tell them later,* he thought, not wanting to break the silence, beyond the natural sounds of the ocean.

In complete honesty, I'd rather sit here with my friends than disappear into some loud sweaty dance joint anyway. I hope there's something nice and calming about this for McCabe and Stone too, not just me. Conner continued to watch the sea and decided whatever happened he would not be the first to speak.

"I can't do this right now," McCabe eventually mumbled.

"No one's asking you to do anything, brother," Stone responded without shifting his eyes toward him.

"I..." McCabe began again, "I can't be social right now."

"You are being social," Stone answered. "Social don't gotta mean talking."

"I... uhh, I'm going to go for a run." McCabe continued. "Then I'll be good. I'll be good to go for the rest of the night. I promise."

"You don't owe me nothin', man," Stone replied. "But you can run all night if you need to, I'll be here when you get back."

"Naw dude, just half an hour, forty minutes maybe." McCabe pulled himself up. "Then we will go have fun, I promise. Can you take my stuff?" He emptied the pockets of his khaki pants, holding the contents out to Stone before kicking off his shoes and unbuttoning his flannel patterned collared shirt.

McCabe wiped what must have been tears from his eyes. "I'll meet you boys on the beach here in just a little bit. Ok?"

"No problem," Stone nodded.

McCabe turned and jogged barefoot toward the ocean, when his shadow reached the wet sand it angled north along the shore line and broke into an open run.

Conner searched Stone's face for some type of guidance. But Stone stood there like a moonlit statue, revealing only the slightest hint of a frown. He said nothing as his eyes tracked McCabe's dark shape growing ever more distant up the beach to their left. Conner turned away and felt an overwhelming urge to talk to Joselyd.

He pulled his phone out of his pocket and stood in the moonlight staring at her picture. *She told me like fifty times not to call.* He continued staring, studying her dark intelligent eyes. Only a small sliver of color remained within the contours of his battery indicator. *If I'm going to call, I need to do it now.* Turning away from Stone, he took a deep breath and hit the dial button. For some reason he couldn't explain, his heart rate accelerated as he listened to the phone ring. Then just before the voicemail answered it buzzed against his ear with a text message.

You ok?

Yeah. Just wanted to say goodnight before my battery died. Go have fun with your friends and I'll see you tomorrow!

Conner squinted down at the phone before hitting the call button again.

"Hello?" Joselyd answered.

"Hey, I just wanted to talk to you for a minute."

"*Listen*, go have fun and I'll be there tomorrow to pick you up."

"Hey, what's wrong? I miss you. I just wanted to see how your weekend was and see if you saw the fireworks and to say goodnight."

"I can't be your everything," her voice hung there in the humid air. "Ok?"

Conner stood in silence with the phone pressed to his ear. "I don't know what you mean," his voice broke. "I love you. You are everything to me."

"I know, and I love you too, and I want to be with you, but there has to be more for you than just me. Go spend time with your friends and enjoy your last night. You can tell me all about everything tomorrow, ok?"

Conner swallowed hard.

"I love you ok? I can't wait to see you, but right now go hang out with your friends!"

Conner's free hand came up to his forehead, his jaw clenched tight as he began to pace.

"I-" he began, closing his eyes and visualizing her beautiful face.

"Everything is fine," she insisted. "We are fine. But you need more than just me. It's not healthy. You have to have your own life beyond me and going to work."

"Ok," Conner managed and stopped pacing.

"I want to be with someone who is independent," she sighed. "It's wonderful that you're so attentive and you care about me so deeply, but you hang on my every move. It's too much."

Conner gulped as his throat seemed to swell.

"We can talk about it tomorrow. Have a good night, ok?"

Conner took a breath and worked hard to steady his voice, "Sure."

"Alright, g'night."

"Good night," Conner answered as the line went dead.

Conner exhaled hard as he turned back toward the ocean, his eyes landing on Stone.

"Everything alright?" his friend asked.

"Probably," Conner replied, drawing in a deep breath. "I don't fucking know. Maybe not." He brought his hand up and ran his fingers through his short hair. "She's never acted this way before."

"Come on, let's go find Mathews. If anybody can lighten things up, it's that guy. He ought to be done kissing by now." Stone chuckled, "If not, he'll have a serious case of chapped lips in the morning."

They cut diagonally across the beach—angling toward the water as they moved south—each wearing a backpack, McCabe's shoes dangling from Conner's fingers. Conner searched for Mathews' tall lanky silhouette as they moved, but before he could lay eyes on him a dark moon shadow called out to them.

"Hey! Where you jokers been? We been lookin' all over for you boys! It's party time!"

The much smaller shadow of Kira materialized next to him as they closed the distance between them.

"I told you, right? One hell of a show. You want the best fireworks? You gotta go to the party place with the most money!"

"I never doubted you," Conner answered, "but the real question is, did you see any of it?"

"Ha!" Mathews let out. "You don't worry about what we saw!"

Beside him Kira's eyes went wide then tracked up and to the left as a broad smile crossed her face. She may have been blushing, but it was difficult to tell in the blue-gray light of the moon. "We definitely *heard* it all," she finally answered with a little laugh.

"Where were you guys?"

"We just walked up the beach a bit," Stone replied.

Mathews' eyebrows drew together as he diverted his attention to Conner, then glanced down at the shoes he was holding. "Where's McCabe?"

Conner swallowed hard, but remained silent.

"He went for a run," Stone answered.

Mathews took a deep breath, sucking in his lower lip and biting it then exhaling through his teeth.

"Running now?" Kira asked.

"Yeah," Mathews responded. "Sometimes he does that."

Kira squinted up at him but didn't ask another question.

Mathews turned back to Stone. "You think that mug's coming back?"

Stone shrugged, "He almost has to. He took nothing with him."

Mathews nodded rapidly and drew in another deep breath. "Well, let's have some fun while we hang out." He threw his arm around Kira, "We were about to go streaking up the beach to howl at the moon."

"What!?" she gasped, pushing his arm off her shoulder. "WE WERE NOT!"

"Really? I thought that's just what people did. A Saturday night, holiday, on the ocean with damn near a full moon?"

"Oh my gosh, you're ridiculous," she allowed Mathews' lanky arm to pull her back in before wrapping herself around him again.

"Well I know we can't now, the ratio is shot."

"Ratio?" Kira asked, her eyes narrowing as she stared up at him.

"Well sure, there's got to be at least one girl for every two guys or it would just be weird."

"You're weird!" Kira laughed.

Mathews shrugged.

"Oh oh oh!" Kira glanced inland and waved. "Heeeeey!" she called.

The guys all turned together to see a short female figure approach in the moonlight. *You gotta be kidding me,* Conner thought. *Mathews has more play than he knows what to do with.*

"Hey boys!" Sara Anne called out.

"Never thought I'd see you again!" Mathews shouted and stepped forward, throwing one arm up for a hug.

"Don't get too attached," the bleach-blonde chuckled as she accepted his embrace. "I'm just hanging here for half an hour or so, then I'm out."

"I see," Mathews continued. "So you left work, drove twenty minutes across the causeway, found a place to park, then almost certainly had to walk a few blocks, all just to hang out for half an hour? That makes perfect sense."

She dropped one hand to her cocked hip and tilted her head as she stared back at him with a little smirk.

"Of course not, you came out to live it up and have an all-night blast!

"If you must know," she began again, "I actually got hit with a heavy bout of guilt when I started to drive home and texted Kira to see where y'all were. I'm not sure pimping her out to you like I did was the most moral decision I've ever made. I really just came by to make sure she's doing alright. Honestly, I was afraid I might have to rescue her and drive her home, but I can tell by the goofy glow she's got and her radiant grin that she's having the time of her life with you military boys."

"Woot! Woot!" Kira squealed, raising her palms up and down in the air.

"Well," Mathews offered. "Since you're here and everything is just fine, you might as well have a good time."

"Hey, what happened to your other friend?"

Mathews eyed Stone before responding, "He'll be back soon."

"Haha, where did he go?"

"For a run."

"A run?"

"Yeah."

"Wasn't he all dressed up to go out?"

"Well yeah, but he's a big exercise guy. I think he got worried about how many calories he drank at your brewery."

"Bluh," she let out, shaking her head. "I'll never understand boys as long as I live!"

"Ha! Yeah, *we're* the complex ones! You've lost your mind."

"Yeah, that's what they say, but you'd be surprised at the nonsensical stuff I've had to deal with."

"Sounds like you're hanging out with the wrong kinda guys," Conner cut in.

Her eyes flicked to him, then to Stone and back to Mathews, "I'm definitely hanging out with the wrong kinda guys!" she laughed.

"Come on," Mathews continued, "we're about to go swimming."

"Swimming?!" Kira yelped. "It's dark out there!"

"What are you afraid something's gonna eat you?"

"YES!" Kira yelled.

"Don't be ridiculous. We'll be fine!"

"But we don't have swimsuits, our clothes will be soaked."

"Simple, don't wear clothes!"

"What? You can't be serious."

"Yeah, it's dark, it'll be a non-issue. We can wrap up in towels and rinse off at the outdoor shower up there when we're done. Then we just dry off and get dressed and we're good."

"You're killing me!" Sara Anne cackled. "Everything about you is such a bad idea, yet you're so much fun."

"No way! People will see me rinsing off up there."

"No they won't! I'll hold a towel up so they can't watch. Your friend can block the other side. You'll be good."

"Well then you'll see me."

"Turn around, Conner," Mathews unzipped the backpack Conner was wearing and pulled out a beach towel. "I'll close my eyes like this if you ask me too." Mathews' eyes winked shut, as he held the towel up in front of her. "See? I can't see shit, you could be naked right now and I'd never know."

"I'll look though!" Sara Anne laughed. "I'm going to get a big ol' eyeful of those sexy half-Japanese curves you got going on."

Kira shot her a look in the dark.

"So, we doing this?"

"No! You'll all see me naked on the beach."

Mathews turned toward her, "What's wrong, you don't look good naked?"

"Yes," she pulled back. "I mean, no. I don't know!" She leaned in and smacked his shoulder.

"Don't even worry about it, we'll do a screamin' towel-drop streak in. That's the only way to guarantee I won't accidentally see Conner naked anyway."

"Hey!" Conner took a power stance puffing his chest out. "You'd be lucky just to catch a glimpse!"

"Towel-drop streak in?" Kira giggled. "What are you talking about?"

"That's when we're wrapped up in towels with nothing underneath. Then we go running down the beach together screaming, and we drop our towels right before we hit the water. It'll be great."

"I don't want to get my hair wet," Kira crossed her arms and stared at him. "It'll get all salty and frizzy."

Mathews' eyes found Sara Anne. His boyish expression fell somewhere between an ask for permission and a plea for help.

The bartender responded with her sly smile and gave him a little nod. He winked at her as if she were a co-conspirator and pulled off his shirt.

"Come on Kira, live a little," Sara Anne demanded, slipping off her sandals and stripping down to her bra.

Kira glared at her.

"What are you afraid of? Strangers seeing you topless?" she cupped her breasts with the palms of her hands. "I'm pretty sure half of Jacksonville saw these girls my freshman year of college in '02, when the Stone Temple Pilots were on tour. Ha! It's no wonder I didn't make it through my sophomore year. Anyway, no point in being shy now, though I haven't done anything like that in a while."

Mathews had already wrapped a towel around his waist and dropped his cargo shorts in the sand.

"Wait," Sara Anne continued. "One condition before I get wild."

The eyes of the entire group found her face at once.

"This guy's got to come with us," she said pointing at Stone. "If anybody needs to get a little crazy, it's you. Ever since you walked into the brewery a few days ago you've looked like you have the weight of the world on your shoulders. I don't know what you've got going on, but if I'm gonna play, we're all gonna play."

Everyone's eyes tracked from Sara Anne to Stone, who produced a genuine grin.

"What do ya say, buddy?" she asked, her blonde hair falling down over her full breasts in the pale light.

"Who am I to stand between the moonlight and your tantalizing sun-kissed skin?" Stone answered, and dropped the backpack he was wearing into the sand.

Two minutes later they were all side by side in a line chanting, "One! Two! Three!" Then surging forward together toward the ocean. Conner stutter stepped over a dip in the sand falling a second behind. Still, he dropped his towel when the others did, his eyes fixating on the bright white flash of skin revealed beyond Sara Anne's bikini line before cold foamy splashes of ocean water leapt toward him, forcing his eyes shut. A few more strides and he plunged under the first breaker. The brisk rush stunned his system and he popped up sucking in a full gasp of air.

"It's cold!" Kira shrieked.

"You'll be used to it in no time!" Mathews laughed, letting his legs go slack and bobbing over the incoming swells.

Further out, Sara Anne let out a cheer, then held her nose and dove down. She came up in what had to be an underwater handstand—her tan legs protruding from the ocean and toes pointing to the sky—for a few moments before tilting over and smacking the water with a splash. Stone surfaced near her, throwing his wet head from side to side before tilting back toward the moon with an unmistakable smile. There was something in his slate-gray eyes that reminded Conner of how he had always been before. *Perhaps he really did just need some time with friends to get back to normal? Or with girls maybe?* Before he had a chance to ponder it, Kira side stroked past him on her way to Mathews.

Conner followed her, filling some unarticulated desire to remain close to his friends in the opaque water. Mathews winked at him as he approached. Then maneuvered himself behind Kira, took a deep breath and slowly slipped beneath the surface.

"Hey wait," Kira gasped, a frantic expression of confusion filling her eyes. "Wait, what's happening? What are you doing?!" she bounced up and down as if she were hopping on one foot beneath the water. Then yelped in protest as her body was abruptly thrust upward, riding on Mathews' shoulders, as she straddled the back of his neck. She scrambled to cover her breasts causing her to wobble awkwardly backward, off balance. Releasing her chest she flung herself forward wrapping her arms around Mathews' forehead. When they had steadied, Kira straightened out, arching her back while simultaneously jerking a forearm up in an attempt to cover herself again.

Mathews had one of his big mechanic's hands on her calf while the other ran across his face, attempting to brush away the ocean water so he could open his eyes. "This girl's not gonna chicken fight herself!" he called. "One of you mugs better lift up Sara Anne unless you want another dude on your shoulders!"

Conner glanced at Sara Anne. "No offense Stone, but I'm not ever trying to have that much contact with another naked guy."

"Valid," Stone answered. "You go first, if Sara is down."

Sara Anne raised an eyebrow as she stared back at Conner, but it was only a moment before that sly smile crossed her face again. "Sara Anne," she corrected, pushing off the sand and gliding toward Conner.

Conner squatted, leaving only his head above the water. "Mount up, lady!"

Her small hands briefly touched his shoulders before being replaced by her muscular legs. She clasped tight to his head and let out a joyful, nervous squeak as he rose up. Together they moved away from the beach and descended into shoulder deep water.

Conner started toward Mathews—hands riding on Sara Anne's knees to stabilize her as he approached. His gaze flicked between Mathews eyes, and Kira's naked body above him—brown except for a swath across her chest where her swimsuit top must normally have been. Everyone must have been hyper aware of where the others were looking because Kira caught him immediately, her dark eyes shining in the moonlight as she let out a little giggle and gave up on attempting to hide herself.

"We've come a long way since that dip in the Persian Gulf," Mathews chuckled as they closed in on one another.

"That was a fun day," Conner responded, "But this is on a whole 'nother level!"

The girls' hands locked together above them and Conner struggled to keep his balance as Sara Anne's smooth muscular thighs tightened around the back of his neck. She tucked the tops of her feet behind his lats for leverage as her weight shifted back and forth on his shoulders.

Squealing and grunting, the girls worked hard to throw each other off balance as the waves broke around them.

"They definitely have the height advantage," Sara Anne called as she slid heavily to one side, prompting Conner to grip her knees even tighter.

"We've got a lower center of gravity! Go low and knock her off balance!" Conner responded, his eyes ever darting about, attempting to catch a glimpse of Kira's jiggling breasts between the girls' constant splashing and the incoming waves.

"They're getting the high ground!" Sara Anne hollered, her tight abs flexing as they slid across the back of Conner's head to the side of his face while she desperately worked to remain upright.

"I'm losing you!" Conner shouted, side stepping further out—into deeper waves—in a last ditch effort to keep the naked beach-blonde on his shoulders from being yanked into the dark water.

Feeling a swell rise behind him, Conner attempted to push off the bottom. When it wasn't enough, he sucked in a breath as his eyes shut tight. "Whoa!" he yelled, something brushing past his leg as his head broke the surface again. His eyes flashed open in time to see Mathews go under as Kira twisted in the air and smacked the water sideways, one hand still clinging to Sara Anne, jerking her off Conner's shoulders as she fell. Sara Anne landed beside him with a splash.

Wiping his face, with his heart pounding and his knees pulled up close to his chest, Conner stared down into the dark water—attempting to see what had touched him—but it was useless. Turning to glance behind him to ensure he wasn't about to get hit by another big wave, his mind snapped to that swirling cloud of sand on Big Pine Key, while his eerie imagination prepared him to see a dorsal fin, knifing its way toward him in the moonlight. His eyes flicked about skimming across the surface, but there was nothing there. Just a dark, seemingly infinite ocean with flickers of moonlight on its ever moving surface as red and green channel markers glowed in the distance.

Turning back, he reached for Sara Anne, who burst straight up—waist high above the surface—with a splash, before sinking back down to her neck and treading water. Her loud boisterous laugh radiated out as she grabbed his hand. He pulled her in, bouncing off the sandy bottom toward the shore. An uneasy feeling stirred in his mind that he couldn't shake. *Where the hell are the others?*

The black ocean that had been so enjoyable just moments before suddenly appeared malevolent. His mind circled around the entire mystical world he'd witnessed through his snorkel mask a few days earlier. It all lay just beneath the surface, in this water that was connected to every bit of ocean on the planet. *No barriers between me and every sea monster that exists. No barrier between them and my friends.* His eyes darted back and forth, scanning the contours of the waves, and then the hidden gaps between the swells.

Sara Anne clung to his side as he made his way forward—her touch a slightly reassuring reminder that he wasn't out there alone. In the breaks between the swells he could reach the bottom again now, which should have helped, though his heart rate continued to accelerate. Sara Anne laughed again behind him. "We really got sucked out there for a minute!"

Kira called out between a set of crashing waves. His head jerked toward her as he exhaled in a sigh of relief. Twenty yards away she momentarily hoisted herself far enough out of the water to be seen and waved. "Hey," she called again in a playful tone. "You didn't win—it was that crazy wave that got us!"

Conner moved toward her with Sara Anne in tow. They'd only made it halfway when Kira SHRIEKED—disappearing beneath the water with a splash.

"Hey!" Conner yelled. His eyes went wide as a chill radiated down his spine. "Hey!" he called again, pushing Sara Anne's hands off his shoulders and kicking forward towards the spot Kira had vanished.

When he arrived he had no idea what to do next. He reached out as far as he could, jerking his arms and legs through the water, hoping to touch her, but felt nothing. His heart pounded as he swung his limbs around again, more desperately. Turning back, he stared at Sara Anne as if for help, though he wasn't sure what she could do. They shared a frightful wide-eyed expression in the pale light that seemed to intensify as the realization set in.

Conner looked away, frantically extending his arms again hoping to feel her body. In front of him the water exploded in a spastic splash. Stone burst through the surface with Kira cradled in his arms. His dark wet skin shining in the moonlight, Kira's slightly lighter tone glowing against him. Both of them gasping for air.

"I hate you," she yelled between deep breaths, smacking Stone's shoulder with an open palm. "I hate you, I hate you, I hate you!" She tilted her head back in his arms, her wet hair fanning out in the dark water. "You almost scared me to death!"

Sara Anne howled with laughter. "Conner, did you see her face?! Oh, that was amazing! That might have been the best thing I've seen in a week. Girl, you had a look of sheer terror!"

Kira exhaled hard. "Oh my God, I'm glad it was you!" She wrapped her arms around Stone. "I thought I was dead!"

"That was tough," Stone grinned. "I was creeping up on you forever! Every time you glanced back I had to slip beneath the surface."

Conner let out a long hard breath. "You scared the shit outta me, too."

"Hey, at least you went and tried to save her!" Sara Anne called. "I was just treading water hoping you could do something. Maybe you military boys really are regular American heroes!" She laughed again. "Oh Kira, your face was priceless!"

"I'm sure it was." She let out a long sigh, arching her back so that her head shifted backward out of Stone's arms and into the sea as her breasts poked through the water's surface.

Conner's eyes lingered for a moment, before snapping back to the ocean around him in a near panic. "Where the hell is Mathews?"

"Relax," Stone answered before extending a knife hand south. "He got pulled way down. I've been watching him trying to get back to us for the last few minutes."

Tracking Stone's extended fingers just beyond the long line of breakers rushing into the shore Conner did see a dark shape making its way toward them. Relief flooded his mind. When Mathews eventually reached them, he leaned back in the water, allowing his chest to float while his lower half remained submerged.

"Yo, I swear something in that wave took my legs out," Mathews exhaled hard. "Then it was like the water sped up or something and all of a sudden I was way the hell away from you guys."

"Right!" Conner snapped, "I swear something brushed passed my leg in that wave, right before you went down. I didn't wanna say anything. I don't know why, but that's why I got so freaked when I didn't see you guys come up after."

"Stop trying to scare us!" Kira chirped, her head still floating outside of Stone's arms.

"I'm not lying," Mathews responded. "I promise you."

"I believe you," Conner answered.

"Whatever," Sara Anne scoffed, rolling onto her back and floating—the length of her body exposed. Arms spread out overhead, hair darker now with the water, eyes shut and mouth closed, chest gently rising and falling with each breath, skin dreamlike in the ethereal light, her flat stomach a deep tan—broken by the bright white stripe where her bikini bottoms must normally ride, compact muscular legs like those of a gymnast were drawn together, her toes pointing in line with her body as she rhythmically flowed over the incoming swells.

Somewhere deep within Conner's mind he knew it was the moon controlling the water, raising and lowering the stunning girl in front of him. *So serene. So incredibly beautiful.* In that instant she was complete—the swirl of dark hues surrounding her, perfectly contrasting her moonlit skin—her body held by the ocean in an equilibrium generally only seen in works of art, or sunsets when colorful clouds stretched across the horizon just right, bringing balance to the sky.

And then it was over. "Rematch bitches!" Sara Anne called, flipping back upright. She slapped the water, sending a splash in Mathews' direction.

"I've created a monster," Mathews replied without moving. "You jokers go ahead, I'm exhausted.

"I'm riding on Stone this time," Sara Anne announced, reaching out to pull Kira away.

"What!?" Conner called after her. "I thought we were a team?"

"Nahh, I'm a player! I plan to get all I can get."

Conner shook his head. "But I like having your legs wrapped around me."

A mischievous smirk crossed Sara Anne face. "Most guys do!" She flicked her tongue out as she winked at him, bouncing backward toward Stone.

Conner's eyes went wide as he stared back.

"Whatever, now you'll get to have this sexy Asian booty on your shoulders!" she responded, smacking Kira's ass.

"Hey!" Kira squawked. The two exchanged a momentary

glance that may have conveyed volumes of in-depth feminine knowledge—forever inaccessible to the likes of man—or perhaps communicated nothing more than a passing whim. Either way, the two girls simultaneously let out a brief burst of laughter as they glided past one another.

Together the group moved toward the beach until the water was only midway up Conner's abdomen. Kira climbed onto his shoulders as Sara Anne hopped on top of Stone in front of them.

"This moment right here," Stone confided with a grin as the two pairs faced off, "All of it, the way air feels, the way the water moves, how everything seems all half mystical under the nearly full moon and dim-lit stars, being in the company of these lovely ladies, and hanging out with the most amazing friends I could ever have—I'm alright with the celestial light carrying all of this out into the universe. I hope it goes on forever, perpetuating out there for all of eternity."

CHAPTER 31

McCabe was sitting in the sand beside their backpacks when they returned from the sea, his clothes damp with sweat that still poured from his forehead in the humid air. He tossed Conner a towel, and then when he was close enough, handed him a can of beer.

"Don't open that yet!" Mathews called from behind, pausing to catch the towel McCabe flung in his direction. "It's too late for sipping beers, we gotta step it up a little."

"What did you have in mind?" McCabe asked, pulling another can from the backpack and extending it toward him.

"You got the car keys?"

"I'm sure they're here somewhere."

Mathews took the beer and leaned in close enough that the girls behind him couldn't hear. "Bro, you alright?"

McCabe nodded, "I am, I promise you. I feel great. Honestly I feel even better now, knowing you boys were having fun and I didn't drag anybody down."

"Ahh, come on Brackish, you do get a little negative here and there, but you'll always be a net gain. We all balance each other out, bro. That's why we make such a badass team." Mathews leaned in again with a smirk. "Though Sara Anne might have been a little disappointed she didn't get to see that scrawny white Irish ass you've got. She asked about you."

McCabe shook his head. "I'm sure she survived without

me. I can't believe you got her to come out… and then take her clothes off. Those Japanese girls must have taught you something. You've got more game than I gave you credit for."

Trudging through the sand toward them Sara Anne paused for a moment, her eyes finding McCabe in the moonlight. "Hey! How come this guy gets a free show?"

"Ahh, let him look," Mathews responded. "He's about to be locked down for life."

"Where the hell were you? You should've been the first one in the water for naked time! Being the one who's about to give up their freedom. Isn't that the point of a bachelor party? Get all the crazy out now so your wife doesn't have to put up with it?"

"You right, you right," McCabe answered. "I went for a run. Tried to get the crazy out that way."

Sara Anne tilted her head glancing at McCabe side-eyed as she dropped one hand to her bare hip. *"Strange flakes!"*

"I won't argue with you," McCabe chuckled, and tossed her a beer.

After digging through the backpacks and discarded clothing, Mathews had come up with a set of keys. He cradled his can of beer in one hand, while using a key to bore out a hole the size of a half dollar in it with the other. He held it out to Sara Anne when he finished.

"Oh no, I've gotta drive home. I'm not shotgunning beers with y'all."

"Not yet, ya don't," Mathews persisted. "Come on."

"Nope."

"Girl, you're standing *naked* on the beach, the time to embrace your inhibitions has passed."

She cocked her hip out even farther and stared at him out of the corners of her eyes. "Well that's a good point, actually."

Mathews continued piercing cans, passing them to Conner and McCabe as Kira came inching up the beach backward, glancing over her shoulder while holding one hand behind her in an attempt to cover her butt crack. After she'd wrapped herself with a towel, Mathews handed her the beer and the group formed a little circle together. Only Stone stood alone on the outside.

"Here's to new beginnings," Mathews proposed, his eyes locked on Kira, "and old friends. Congratulations McCabe!"

Each wrapping their lips around the beer cans' punctures, they tilted their heads back together, cracking the tabs open and rapidly swallowing as their mouths flooded with the carbonated liquid. Mathews dropped his empty can to the ground first, holding his arms up victoriously into the air. "Boom!"

Sara Anne pointed at him and coughed. "I almost had you!"

"I'm getting too old for this shit," McCabe managed, spitting before crushing his can and dropping it into the center with the others.

Conner tossed his down too, flashing a smile and jerked his thumb toward Kira as his eyes flicked around the circle.

"It's up my nose," she gagged, then attempted to bring the can back to her lips for another drink, but instead ended up spitting a mouthful of beer into the sand.

"Come on, Kira!" Sara Anne laughed. "I thought you college girls could take it!"

"Don't you work at a brewery?" Mathews gibed. "Shouldn't you be good at chugging beer by now?"

Kira attempted to speak but let out a belch instead, prompting a burst of laughter from her little ring of friends. "One more and we hit the showers!" Mathews cheered.

McCabe groaned, but took the beer he was handed and the whole scene—minus Kira— played out again. When they'd recovered, they gathered up their empties and clothing, Sara Anne rolled her eyes before reluctantly covering herself with a towel as the group moved away from the ocean.

Kira nudged Mathews. "No looking when I take a shower ok? Just like you promised me earlier?"

"Sure," Mathews answered.

"No, you have to promise me!" Kira insisted.

"What's the big deal? We were just naked together in the ocean for like an hour."

"I know, but that's different. It'd be super weird if you were just standing there watching me rinse off."

"Alright, I promise," Mathews answered.

"I'm serious! You look and I'll never kiss you again." She tilted her head, her dark eyes following his pupils. "I won't even give you my number or anything."

"I said I promise!"

"For real?" she asked, raising her eyebrows.

"I swear!" Mathews yelled. "I ain't gonna look! What else can I tell you?"

Pulsating Latin beats slowly replaced the sound of crashing waves as they reached the rinse station. Only a beach volleyball court and a few palm trees separated them from groups of drunken vacationers making their way up and down the sidewalk that ran along Ocean Drive. McCabe maneuvered in close to Sara Anne as she shook out the towel she would hold up as a curtain for Kira. Bringing a cupped hand to his mouth he whispered something into her ear that brought out her crafty smile, she nodded as her eyes shifted toward him.

A few minutes later Sara Anne was perpendicular to Mathews, shielding Kira from the world. Mathews stood with his head turned away, eyes shut tight and lanky arms outstretched to hold a towel in the proper position. Kira's head was still visible, and she eyed him suspiciously for a moment before shifting around and then tossing her towel to Conner. The water came on and she tilted her head back letting it rinse through her thick dark hair.

"It's cold," she squeaked, "but it actually feels good."

That sly smile crossed Sara Anne's face again. "Oh my, Kira you should be a model."

"I don't know about all that," Kira giggled.

"No, I'm telling you, the way the water's rolling over your skin... it's just exquisite." Sara Anne let out a seductive little moan. "It's like it's holding you, outlining every curve on your perfect body. Oh baby, you're so incredibly beautiful!"

"Ok, now you're just being weird!" Kira snapped, her arms working, likely running across her body trying to remove the salt and sand.

Beside her Mathews' head seemed to involuntarily twitch.

Sara Anne let out a suggestive sigh, "Oooooh," glancing at Mathews out of the corners of her eyes. "I can't hardly take it."

Mathews jerked again. His arms and shoulders seemed to spasm as he turned his head even further away from Kira, his eyes squeezed together tight. Sara Anne continued, letting out a long sensual hum that somehow made the back of Conner's scalp tingle.

Kira's gaze darted between the faces of her new friends over the towel. First to Sara Anne, whose eyes were now shut as her low provocative tone elevated to a subdued orgasmic squeal. Then to Mathews, whose face was scrunched tight. When Kira's stare landed on Conner he only offered a wide-eyed shrug.

"What the fuck is going on out there?" Mathews asked without turning his head.

The pattering of the water on the concrete around Kira changed as her face disappeared behind the towel, probably attempting to expedite the cleaning process. McCabe seized the opportunity, slinking forward without making a sound, and positioned himself behind Mathews. Sara Anne turned her face toward the sky, bit her lower lip and engaged in a series of intensifying moans, releasing her bountiful sexual energy into the humid air around them.

In one quick motion, McCabe ripped Mathews' towel off howling with laughter as he sprinted toward the beach. Kira screamed as Mathews instinctively yanked the towel he was curtaining her with back to cover himself. His face turned bright red in the glow of the yellow street lamps as they stared at each other wide-eyed. A round of cheers came from a group of girls on the sidewalk across the volleyball courts as Kira leaned forward, hands jerking around attempting to hide herself. A series of hoots and drunken shouts followed as she caught the attention of a few guys nearby. Mathews thrust the towel toward Kira before looking down at his exposed manhood and pulling it back again.

Sara Anne cackled hysterically, leaning forward and fanning herself with one hand instead of holding up the towel she had been using to cover her friend. She was too overcome with amusement to make a run for it, or offer any resistance when Kira grabbed the towel from her.

"I hate you guys!" she squealed as the eruption of laughter continued around her.

Kira had retreated to a bench in a darker corner of the sandy park between Ocean Drive and the dunes that delineated the beach. One of her feet anxiously tapping with a nervous energy as she watched the little group she'd separated herself from. Sara Ann continued to break into bouts of uncontrollable cackles as she rinsed off and got dressed with the others. Each time she began, McCabe lost it, and the two howled in joy together. Sometimes, after they'd gotten a hold of themselves, Sara Anne would let out a little copulatory squeal, and they'd burst into laughter again.

"Oh, you're just hilarious," Kira cried out from the bench, one Chuck Taylor still bouncing rapidly as she shook her head.

Sara Anne and McCabe heaved into another series of uncontrollable giggles in response.

"Come on, Kira," Mathews suggested. "It's over. We're gonna go out and have fun now."

Kira threw her head dramatically from side to side.

Sara Anne's frayed denim short shorts and compact tan muscular legs caught the moonlight as she moved toward Kira. "Ahh, don't be like that! I'm sorry," she began before immediately slipping into a bubbly round of giggles. "Oh," she exhaled, "one day I hope you see how funny that was."

"Yeah sure, you seem real sorry!" Kira squawked.

Sara Anne shook her head, "What's your deal? You've been strutting around with your tits out all night!"

"Yeah, in the dark in the ocean with you guys! Not for all these drunk strangers who just saw me naked!" Her dark eyes swelled with emotion. "Friends are supposed to protect each other!"

The entire group made its way toward her. Mathews sat down next to her as the others stood around. "Where do you want to go?" McCabe inquired. "You pick, we'll go anyplace you want."

"What time is it?" she asked.

McCabe pulled his cell phone from his pocket. "Quarter 'til midnight."

Kira twisted toward Mathews. "What time is your flight?"

"Ten, gotta be there at eight. Plenty of time for fun!"

Kira's eyes snapped to McCabe, "I want to go home."

"Oh come on, don't do me like that!" Mathews pleaded.

"If you don't want to sleep in the back of a van with your buddies, you'll come with me," she spouted out in a flat tone.

Mathews' mouth dropped open as his eyes went wide.

"Oh baby!" Sara Anne squealed.

Mathews blinked.

"I think she's serious," Conner added.

Mathews blinked again.

"Yeah, that's no joke," Stone confirmed.

Mathews managed to close his mouth and swallowed hard. "I guess we're going for a ride."

Stone backed the Mustang out of the parking space in the garage so they could open the doors all the way and figure out how to get everybody in.

"I'm riding in the front," Kira announced.

"Ahh come on," McCabe responded. "You and Sara Anne are the smallest ones. It'll be way easier with you in back."

"No, you've already had your fun with me."

"It's boy girl, boy girl, we gotta alternate like in middle school," Mathews interjected, nudging his thumbs toward McCabe and Conner. "That way I ain't gotta get too close to these mugs."

"No," Kira said again. "I'm done with the shenanigans tonight. You can all cram in the back and play with Sara Anne."

Sara Anne lifted her eyebrows and nodded, "I'm ok with that," she boasted before laughing again.

"Window!" Mathews and McCabe shouted simultaneously.

"Ugh," Conner groaned.

Mathews unzipped his backpack and tossed McCabe a beer. "We're going to need more alcohol to get through this."

"Ahh, just what I wanted… warm beer," McCabe said, cracking the can open.

"Gotta use it up, we're all flying out tomorrow," Mathews insisted, passing one to Conner and another to Sara Anne.

"Suck 'em down before you get in the car fellas," Stone suggested. "Saturday night, Fourth of July, after midnight, there's probably cops all over South Beach right now."

The four who'd been relegated to the backseat chugged their beers, and through a substantial amount of effort, somehow managed to maneuver into position. With Mathews on his left, and McCabe to his right, Conner managed to ride the hump between the two backseats. He angled forward slightly, the vehicle not wide enough to span the width of all of their shoulders side by side. Sara Anne somehow made it into his lap, extending her legs in front of her between the two bucket seats.

This may be the first time I've ever had a beautiful girl pressed up close against me and didn't like it. If he'd thought the back-seats were uncomfortable before, he'd been seriously lacking in perspective—Conner could barely move.

Shifting heavily off balance Conner toppled into Mathews as the Mustang rounded the last bend out of the parking garage. With his hands on her hips, he attempted to stabilize Sara Anne, but she tumbled along with him. They managed to right themselves in time for the next curve, where Mathews threw his weight into Conner's shoulder, dumping them both onto McCabe. McCabe groaned before twisting a thumb into Conner's ribcage making him cry out as he flailed around.

"Quit it, y'all," Sara Anne called out as she bobbled in Conner's lap before bouncing forward and getting wedged between his knees and the center console.

Before Conner could wrangle away from McCabe, Mathews moved in from the other side, grabbed his pec and yelled "titty twister!" as he clamped down.

"Yaawww! YOU MOTHERFUCKER!" Conner shouted, throwing an elbow with all his force, knocking Mathews' grip loose.

Cackling with a wicked smile Mathews came back at him undeterred.

"Get the hell off me!" Conner yelled, his hands clenched tight over his pectoral muscles. But Mathews persisted, his strong fingers attempting to work their way under to give him another twist. "Get off me, you jackass!" Conner threw his weight to the right only to face a similar assault from McCabe on the other side. When Conner's tight grip and tense muscles proved to be a challenge, his friends only laughed louder and started working together. McCabe attempted to rip Conner's hands free while Mathews tried to move in and squeeze. Conner twisted violently from side to side, throwing his shoulders in an attempt to break McCabe's iron grip.

"Y'all quit squirmin'!" Sara Anne protested. "Your bony knees are not what I want jamming into my pelvis!"

"Yeah, quit squirming Conner!" Mathews howled.

"It'd be a hell of a lot easier if you held still!" McCabe joined in.

"My God, when did you get so strong Conner?" Mathews continued.

"Damn it Kira, how far away do you live?" Conner yelled as he thrashed and twisted again, prompting more groans from Sara Anne.

"It's another twenty minutes," she chirped, turning her gaze into the tight confines of the back seat. "See, that's why I'm riding in the front."

"Yeah, this sounded way more fun than it is!" Sara Anne admitted.

"Yo! How do I have this hot-ass blonde girl in my lap and the only thing you guys want is me!" Conner let out as McCabe worked to peel his fingers back one at a time.

"She'd like it too much," Mathews answered. "You're way more fun!"

"No one likes titty twisters!" Sara Anne laughed. "You'd have to at least work me up to it, start with a little ass smacking and hair pulling!"

Mathews released Conner with one hand. "No one likes wet willies either!" then promptly licked his little finger and stuck it in Conner's ear.

"Ahh! Gross! You sick fuck! What, are we in middle school?"

The whole back seat exploded in laughter. McCabe became so overwhelmed he let go, giving Conner enough leeway to shove Mathews off. Conner sucked in a deep breath and attempted to rub his ear on the shoulder of his shirt.

"Thank the lord!" Sara Anne let out, attempting to shift her short body away from the floor board and back into Conner's lap.

When they finally reached Kira's apartment, Mathews, Conner, McCabe and Sara Anne worked to untangle themselves and climb around the tilted seats and out of the car. Mathews made his rounds, smacking hands with each of his friends before wrapping them up in powerful bear hugs.

"I can't believe it's over already. I'm gonna miss you boys! If you get the chance you gotta take some leave and space-A out to see me. I'll make sure you have a blast, we'll tear Japan up!"

McCabe gripped Mathews hand tight and didn't seem to want to let go. "Thanks for crossing the Pacific just to see me."

"Are you kidding? I had to make sure you ended your single life right! None of these jokers were up to the challenge without me!"

"Well you did good brother, I had a fucking blast," McCabe smiled.

"I loved meeting you all!" Kira beamed. "Come back and visit!"

"I'll see you tomorrow, honey," Sara Anne responded before pointing to Mathews with a serious look. "Be good to her!"

"I promise." Mathews grinned, threw his tactical backpack on, shouldered his duffle bag, then took Kira's hand as he turned away. After two steps he glanced back toward Stone. "Get a phone bro, I miss talkin' to you."

Stone nodded in response, "I'll be sure to send ya my number if it ever happens."

"Hey wait!" McCabe called. "Take the rest of this beer. You're the only one who can drink this much."

Mathews' eyes angled toward Kira before he shook his head. "Nahh bro, I think I'm good." They held hands as they turned and walked up the steps to her apartment together.

CHAPTER 32

The Mustang was silent when they departed. Stone kept his eyes on the road with one hand propped up on top the steering wheel, while McCabe hunched forward beside him, covering his face—his index fingers making little circles against his temples.

Conner glanced at Sara Anne to find her steel-blue eyes tracking his own in the shadows of the back seat. He squinted at her. She responded with a warm grin before slowly extending an open hand toward him. His heart rate accelerated as his hand inched toward hers. When the tips of their fingers touched it felt like electricity traveled up his arm. They lingered there—just barely contacting one another as the Mustang cruised down the highway. Conner's gaze found her face again and she closed her eyes as she took his hand, interlacing his fingers with her own. Her hand felt small and soft in his hardened mechanic's grip.

She leaned toward him, her free hand caressing the inside of his forearm, her beach-blonde hair spilling down onto his bicep. Conner's heart pounded in his chest. Frantic thoughts raced through his head. Closing his eyes he focused on taking deep, slow breaths. Colorful bursts of fireworks splashed across his mind, followed by flashes of Joselyd smiling at him from the airport security line, then her smile was gone and she said, *'I can't be your everything.' What does that even mean? 'I want to be with someone who's independent.'* Sara Anne's thumb worked back and forth against his skin as they held hands. *Independent.* The thought rattled through his brain. *Isn't the whole point of a relationship to be a team?*

His jaw tensed as a wave of anxiety overtook the excitement Sara Anne was fostering. *Could she be done with me?* At first it seemed impossible, moving on to live happily ever after with Joselyd was just the way it was going to be. But as he tried to tamp down the thought, it only seemed to take a tighter hold. *It's gotta work, I love Joselyd.* Her beaming face flooded his mind again. *I can't go back to being alone. That gap of time after these guys left and before I met Joselyd was horrible.* The idea spiraled through his head, as his fingertips subconsciously began to massage the back of Sara Anne's hand.

Stone backed the Mustang in next to Sara Anne's bright yellow Volkswagen Beetle, in a parking lot on Washington Ave a few blocks from the beach. McCabe pulled himself out of the car, wobbling upright and then leaned back with his arms out in a broad yawning stretch. "I gotta rally," he mumbled. "Last night out and it's go time."

"Your party, McCabe," Stone responded. "I'm following you."

McCabe's eyes flicked from Stone to Conner before landing on Sara Anne. "Where should we go?"

"I'm out for real this time," she answered. "I'm not on vacation like you military boys."

"Anything I can do to change your mind?" McCabe asked.

She shook her head.

"Well then come here," McCabe extended his arms again, this time bending down so Sara Anne could hug him. "Thanks for helping make my last hurrah so kickass."

"Congratulations!" Sara Anne replied, standing on her toes to reach her arms around his shoulders. When McCabe released her she shifted to Stone.

"Hey kid," Stone said, wrapping his tan compact arms around her, his cast settling in the small of her back. "We'll always have naked chicken fights in the Miami moonlight."

A broad smile slipped across Sara Anne's face. "I'm glad you finally cut loose enough to enjoy yourself a little."

"That was legit fun, I'm glad you showed me I wasn't too far gone for it."

When Stone let her go she moved to Conner. Pausing for a moment she glanced back, making eye contact with the other two and shooing them away with quick flicks of her small hand. McCabe chuckled as he and Stone turned and made their way across the street.

Conner stared at her, her eyes seemed to shine, as she moved toward him.

She reached out and her little hand rubbed the side of his bicep—her eyes never flinching as she slowly closed the distance between them. At the last moment she stood on her toes to reach him as her eyes slid shut. Her lips felt warm and inviting and it was only a moment before Conner was kissing her back. He grabbed her waist, pulling her against his body before releasing her with one hand to run his fingers through her still damp beach-blonde hair. The way she moved felt magic—her tongue dancing with his own—a nervous excitement building in his mind as she released him. Her magnificent blue eyes opening again as she lowered herself off her toes.

"Come with me," she beckoned, her hands moving down his forearms until their fingers were again interlaced.

Conner swallowed hard.

"I promise I'll make sure you make your flight tomorrow."

"You serious?"

Her eye's remained locked on to him as she nodded.

"I thought you didn't sleep with tourists?"

A sly smile crossed her face as she gave him a playful shrug.

Conner's eyes went to the sky as a whirl of images streamed through his brain. Joselyd's broad smile and fun mischievous eyes as she waved goodbye. The first time he'd seen Sara Anne, barely hiding her amusement as Mathews worked to make her laugh. How happy Mathews seemed as he and Kira walked up the steps to her apartment hand in hand, then Sara Anne as she floated on the ocean, perfect breasts, tight abs, and short tan muscular legs all glistening in the moonlight. Conner swallowed hard again.

"I know you want to," she continued. "The first time y'all came into the brewery you were checking me out every time I turned around. Now's your chance."

Conner's eyes darted back down to meet hers. "You could tell?"

"Well sure, I could feel it. You and Mathews both were. Mc-Cabe would sneak a peek every now and again, but no more than any other married guy I've ever met."

"Nothing from Stone?"

"I've never met anyone like him before. There's something going on down deep within that man. Even on the beach he talked to me like we were pondering the mysteries of the universe together. My tits were out bouncing in the moonlight and he's always making eye contact, then actually listening to what I had to say. I'm glad he finally had some fun, but anyway, you're stalling!"

Conner glanced up again, releasing a long exhale, before his eyes drifted back down to her. "I have a girlfriend."

She reached out and rubbed the side of his arm. "Honey I'm blonde, but I'm not stupid."

Conner stared at her.

Her little hand closed on his forearm. "I know you have a girlfriend. It's really obvious."

"Then why you asking me?"

This time Sara Anne looked away, she drew in a deep breath and let it out slow. "Look, I'm real fun, but I've pretty much made a mess of my life. I guess I thought it'd be nice to spend the night with a good guy for once." She let out another breath. "Even if he is flying home to his girlfriend in the morning. Hell, maybe knowing you're leaving even makes it feel safer for some reason. I don't know, I'm a wreck."

Conner inhaled and held it, still fixated on her eyes.

"I promise I won't show up and mess your life up or nothin'."

Conner attempted to speak but couldn't seem to form any words.

Sara Anne's mouth twitched into a little frown. "It's ok. I should have known. You're *too* good of a guy. It was selfish of me to ask." She pulled a slip of paper out of a shallow pocket in her cut off denims. "Let me at least give you my number, you never know." She fumbled with her car keys before opening the door of the dented yellow Beetle and retrieved a pen. Scribbling it down she slid the little paper into Conner's back pocket.

"Maybe one day," she murmured, wrapping her arms around his waist and placing her head against his chest. "One day."

CHAPTER 33

It was past one a.m. when the three of them strolled down the red sidewalk of A1A. Conner and McCabe didn't have to be at the airport for another eight hours, and the little group had no clear plan for what to do in the meantime. There were only occasional cars passing on the street now, and the majority of the pedestrian traffic must have been a block over on Ocean Drive. Ahead, a short man with a dark complexion slowed his pace, making eye contact as he continued toward them. The baggy black hoodie he wore seemed out of place in the warm humid air.

"I got yo weed, cuz," he said as they neared.

"No!" McCabe barked.

"Good price."

"No!" McCabe let out as they passed. "Can't you tell we're military?"

The man turned, walking beside McCabe as they continued down the street. "It's nitro weed, cuz. No show on they drug test."

McCabe spun toward him, throwing his arms wide as he shouted. "What?! Do you think I'm fucking stupid?! What if you spit that bullshit to some young airman who's just drunk enough he believes you? You'd rather destroy somebody's career for a few dollars than go to work like a normal fucking person?!?"

"Easy, Brackish! Easy man!" Stone asserted, throwing his

casted hand on McCabe's shoulders and shoving himself between the two.

Conner lunged forward, intent on ensuring Stone didn't catch a knife in the back, but then just stood there, unsure how to assist further.

"Shit cuz, yo don't know!" the short man spewed out, stepping forward, his words laced with the smell of grain alcohol. "Yo don't know me!"

"Bullshit I don't know!" McCabe roared over Stone's shoulder flexing hard against his friend. "I joined the fuckin' Air Force to better myself! To get outta my town! You want to be a piece of shit, that's fine! But don't drag nobody else down with you!"

"Yo don't know me!" the man screamed.

McCabe opened his mouth as if to shout again, but Stone shoved him back far enough to lock eyes with him—holding an index finger in front of his face—somehow completely deflating his taller, stronger friend. McCabe exhaled hard, his tense muscles going slack as he turned away.

Stone spun around and through clenched teeth, hissed, "Keep on walking or I'll break my other hand on your face."

The short man held his hands up and backed away before turning to continue up the red sidewalk.

"You alright?" Stone asked.

McCabe nodded.

Stone's eyes flicked to Conner.

"I'm good," Conner offered.

They stood there together, taking a few breaths. A lowered Jeep Grand Cherokee cruised by with rap music blaring, followed shortly afterward by a Dodge Charger, whose driver felt the need to mash on the gas—squealing wheels—just as he passed them. Stone nodded forward, his eyes flicking to McCabe and the three of them continued south together. It was another block before McCabe apologized.

"Don't worry about it, man," Stone answered. "Didn't even get my heart rate up."

"You're good," Conner confirmed.

They traversed halfway down the next block, still with no destination, before McCabe spoke again. "Fucking Mathews," he laughed. "I don't believe that shit. I can't even be mad at the dude for ditching us."

"Hell no, you gotta let him take those shots when he can get them," Stone answered. "Plus she's a really nice girl. Who knows, maybe they'll work it out to actually see each other again when she visits Japan."

"Incredible, the man lives on an island full of Japanese girls and he's going to fly a Japanese American in."

"Fuck that," Stone replied. "I don't believe in that shit."

"What?" Conner asked.

"Our country is too damn divided already, I don't believe in putting anything in front of American. Asian American, African American, Mexican American, European American whatever. The flag stands for every one of us. We're all on the same damn team, and our country has enough conflict already.

We're all just Americans."

Conner pondered it as they walked. "I think it's just people trying to maintain a little bit of their heritage."

"Maybe, or maybe it's some element trying to make us tribal, divide us from within. The vast majority of people don't think about things they don't have language for. That's a proven fact."

"I think it's more complicated than that," Conner responded.

"Sure it is, it's extremely complex, but the fact of the matter is, there's a lot that society bakes into us without us realizing. I'm actively trying to eliminate some of it from my mind. Make sure I'm seeing other people and the world in the most effective way I can." Stone took a breath, as they waited at the intersection of Ninth Street for a car to pass.

"You're out in left field, dude," McCabe cut in.

"Nahh man, you gotta think about it," Stone continued as they crossed the street. "It goes both ways. There's all kinds of things that don't occur to us just because we can't easily define them. And some of those things would be really helpful in navigating our way through life. It's why it is so hard to describe a feeling or emotion or event that doesn't fall within the framework of our preexisting words. Some people believe it's the purpose behind art, makes you feel something you otherwise can't—because there's not a word for it. Maybe music too. Maybe even literature, although it seems odd—using an entire book full of words to describe some particular feeling that we don't normally consider because there is no verbiage for it."

Something Stone said seemed to connect in Conner's thoughts. *Not having a word for something... was this the ultimate out of sight, out of mind. Like you can't hold the idea in your head because there is no way to say it.* His eyes narrowed and he turned toward his friend as if seeing him in some new light for the first time. He seemed different than he had a few days before. His fresh face now sporting a three-day beard, the stylish Hawaiian shirt was missing some vibrant quality it had contained before. The bright white cast around his left hand now seemed dingy and had begun yellowing—perhaps from the ocean water. A small steak sauce stain tainted the front of his khaki pants. But something else was different too, something was back in his ash-gray eyes that had been missing when he first arrived. Something he couldn't identify. *Is it something I don't have words for?* He laughed in his mind.

His train of thought was broken when Stone grabbed his arm. "Something's not right."

"What's going on?" Conner asked, his eyes scanning the street.

"That black SUV behind us with the tinted windows," Stone tilted his head back toward it. "That thing is creeping on us." His eyes flicked about. The street was lined with buildings that were either connected or had tall white iron gates filling the spaces between them, leaving no obvious escape route.

"Are you sure," Conner began but was cut off.

"He's right," McCabe answered. "That thing ain't acting normal."

Conner glanced back, the vehicle slowly idled toward them, its occupants hidden behind darkly tinted glass. Then as he watched, the SUV surged forward, jerking across the center line and angling straight toward them. Stone shoved Conner forward before diving to the red concrete. A male figure appeared in the sun roof as the vehicle swerved, turning parallel to them at the last moment. The tinted windows retracted and something burning and hissing came flying at them from the sun roof.

Conner threw himself to the concrete and attempted to roll away as a loud series of cracks and snaps sounded around him, making his ears ring. Covering his head, Conner glanced toward the SUV, recognizing the assailants hanging out of the sun roof and windows as fair-haired teenagers. Wisps of gray smoke hovering near their hands as they cackled with laughter. Stone was upright again—bright white streaks ripping past him as he sprinted toward their attackers. Conner shielded his eyes with his forearm as the lights screeched over his head, or snapped off the concrete beside him. A new round of pops and bangs accompanied the flashes which appeared even through his closed eyes.

"HEY!" Stone boomed, smacking the side of the vehicle. "No bottle rockets, ya jackasses! You'll put somebody's eye out!"

Fear streaked across the chubby driver's pasty face as Stone lunged through his window. The kid slammed on the gas in a panic, unprepared for Stone's lighting-quick response. Stone kept pace alongside the SUV for a moment before tumbling forward—legs working fast—keeping him vertical long enough to protect his face as he slid on the asphalt. The car accelerated away, wheels squealing as it hung the next left and disappeared out of view.

"You'll put somebody's eye out!" Conner chuckled, awash in the post-adrenaline-rush glow of survival. Jumping up, he pointed at Stone who had already sprung to his feet. "That moment you realize you sound like your parents! What a bunch of future frat-boy douche bags! Even riding around in their rich ass parents' car!"

"I almost had their damn keys," Stone lamented, glancing at the palm of his good hand before attempting to brush the asphalt grit from it on his pants, leaving little smears of blood on his thigh. "I would have if it wasn't for this damn cast, I couldn't get a tight enough grip on the steering wheel to hold myself in. I couldn't get the shifter in park."

Conner laughed again, "What were you going to do if you got 'em?"

"Throw them on top that fucking balcony," Stone pointed to the condominiums beside them. "Then they'd have had to come out and act like men. Be accountable for their actions instead of running away."

"Ha ha!" Conner grinned, still lit with the simple elation of living. "No time like the present for a good life lesson!" His eyes locked on Stone and his smile faded as he registered the concern on his friend's face. Hesitantly he turned, following the steel-gray gaze around to McCabe who lay crumpled on the sidewalk in a shaking heap.

Stone moved forward and knelt beside McCabe—fabric from the now torn pocket of his deep-blue Hawaiian shirt hung down as he placed a steady hand on his friend's trembling shoulder. Conner watched as a helpless feeling manifested somewhere deep in his gut.

He blinked as his chest tightened and could feel the sweat running down his face and back, pouring into his oily flight suit. The distinct smell of blood occasionally wafted through the hot mechanical air and stench of jet exhaust as the load master hydraulically raised the aft ramp so the aircraft could taxi. The normally open hardscape of metal surfaces comprising the C-130's cargo bay now transformed into a kind of primitive medical ward—cramped with racks of men, five rows high. An aero med in a flight suit administered something into the arm of a shaking teenaged soldier strapped down to one of the lower litters. The kid's eyes were shut tight and his hair was dark like McCabe's. Conner's hands clenched into fists. He stood motionless as if confined by the heavy air surrounding him in the packed cargo compartment. Someone was calling his name over the roar of the aircraft. It seemed far away as he stared on at the dark-haired soldier with a face full of pain attempting to curl into a ball—his body flexing against the straps holding him to the litter. *Pain, not fear, maybe too much pain to feel fear.*

"Conner!"

He sucked in a deep breath and when his eyes focused, Stone was in front of him again—twisting to gaze back with a hand on

McCabe who lay tucked into the fetal position. The Celtic bands pulled taut across McCabe's bulging biceps, his twitching arms working to ratchet themselves ever tighter into his chest.

"You ok?"

Conner nodded, willing his quivering fists to loosen.

"Could you go get the car?"

Nodding again, he managed to catch the keys when they were tossed to him. Turning, Conner shook his head, wondering if the kid made it, and if so where he was now and if he'd ever be able to enjoy the beach under his own power. *He couldn't have been in the military long. He looked way younger than me, and I'd only been in about four years at that point.*

With quick strides he made his way north again along the red sidewalk, his mind adrift. Picturing McCabe curled up on the concrete shaking, and that trembling kid in the back of the 130. *Why him? There had to be more than forty patients in the cargo compartment that day, all young, all hurting.* Joselyd filled his thoughts and he wanted so badly to talk to her. But his phone was dead, and it was late, surely she was already asleep. *She told me not to call anyway.* His mind continued to spin. *Is it like Mathews said? One day Afghanistan and Iraq will be nice places like Germany and Japan are now. Good countries, full of regular people, not homicidal extremists. Are these things just the unavoidable costs of making that happen? Unavoidable, at least when you're operating under a massive bureaucracy— like the US government—that's unwilling to compromise the comfort of its citizens at home.*

At first glimpse, the gray Mustang hit Conner with an un-expected twinge of emotion. His face forced a frown as he took it in. *Was this really the car we were in half an hour ago? Sara Anne holding my hand in the back seat? Mathews and McCabe gig-gling like school girls as they attacked me from all angles just a twenty minute ride before that?* Conner shook his head and tried to will the frown away. He couldn't think of it. *Stop fucking around and get back to the guys.*

Starting the Mustang and hearing the engine rev made Conner feel like he was in a movie. Pulling out of the park-ing lot and onto the street, it occurred to him that he'd never driven a sports car before. De-icing vehicles and aircraft tugs, big man-lifts and all kinds of trucks, but nothing in the civil-ian world beyond the little Toyota Corolla he owned. He had a sudden urge to go screaming down the open road. He imag-ined Joselyd riding shotgun with a big grin on her face as they tried to see how high the speedometer could go.

Maybe one day, he thought as his mind shot back to his friends.

When he pulled up, McCabe was in a sitting position, his elbows on his knees and his head in his hands. Stone sat near-by with his back against the gate of the multi-level condo with an Easter egg-blue stucco exterior. They made eye contact, but Stone's face revealed no further information. Conner left the car idling and climbed out.

Stone rose, his deep-blue Hawaiian shirt no longer ap-pearing new, a front button was missing and its pocket ripped open. Stains and narrow smears of blood along with a dark burn mark tainted his khaki pants, while a snag visible in one knee made them look worn.

"Come on, brother," Stone offered, standing in front of McCabe and reaching down to give him a hand. McCabe squeezed his eyes shut tight, but allowed himself to be pulled upright.

Conner climbed in the back seat after they'd walked McCabe to the passenger side door. "Where are we going?"

"Back to my van, until we figure something out. That way we can drop the cot if somebody needs to lay down and you won't have to stay all jammed up in the back of this thing."

When Stone pulled into the parking lot, it gave them the same view of Ocean Drive they'd had earlier that afternoon. Something about seeing it this way felt odd as Conner gazed out at the empty lamp-lit street that had been drenched in sunlight and so full of people not even twelve hours before.

Stone tilted the seat forward to let Conner out, but when they attempted to move McCabe he wouldn't budge.

"I'm sorry guys, I just really need to be by myself," McCabe mumbled without making eye contact with either one of them.

"Well, I can appreciate that," Stone answered. "But we're just a little worried about ya."

"I'm fine, I promise. Just take your van and go have fun. I'll take this to the airport tomorrow and go home and see my fiancée. Things will be alright after that."

Stone glanced at Conner, before turning back to stare at McCabe hard.

"Please," McCabe pleaded, managing to meet his gaze and hold it. "Please go. I can't be around people right now. I love you boys, but just being close to you is stressing me the fuck out."

Stone closed McCabe's door and gestured toward the back of the car.

"What the hell we gonna do?" Conner asked. "We can't leave him here."

"Yeah, no way. At this moment, I don't trust him to get himself to the airport tomorrow either."

The two friends looked at each other.

Conner scratched his head. "We could take him to the airport now?"

"Well, we can't leave him here. I think he needs some more time before he'll be willing to talk to the check in people and go through security and all. He's getting better, half an hour ago he was in a ball on the concrete. Now he's talking. He just needs a little more time and he'll be alright."

"The cell phone lot! Then we can come back and check on him later and if I need to I can get the car turned in and get him to the right gate when you drop me off for my flight."

"Yeah, alright. Maybe he'll even be alright by the time we get there."

Conner followed Stone's van in the Mustang, back across the causeway where most of the cruise ships had departed, and onto the interstate toward the airport.

"We got you in the cell phone lot, brother. Your bag is right there in the shotgun seat. All you gotta do is pull out over there, and follow the overhead signs for the rental car return. You can go there whenever you want and hang out at the gate, and if you pass out, Conner has an alarm set on your cell phone for two and a half hours before takeoff. Nothing to it man."

McCabe met his eyes and attempted to force a smile, but he couldn't pull it off.

"You sure you're good?" Stone persisted.

McCabe nodded rapidly, staring at his friend with eyes full of tears. He tried to speak but his words couldn't seem to form.

"I'll sit here all night if you need me to, brother. We ain't even gotta talk. You ain't even gotta look at me if you don't want, I can hang out over there in the van and let you be. You can just come over or tap the horn if you need something.

McCabe shook his head, and with tears streaming down his face, opened his arms and the two men held each other in a tight embrace. "I'm sorry," McCabe managed. "I hope you guys had a good time. I fucking love you guys. I-" McCabe choked up again and released his friend. For a moment it seemed he was about to sob.

He sucked in a ragged breath and tried again. "Dude, I thought..." McCabe swallowed hard, "I thought it was a fuckin' drive by. I don't know why, firecrackers ain't nowhere near as loud as automatic fire. But I thought they'd shot you guys up. I thought it was my fault for yelling at that asshole weed dealer. I kept thinking about Stretch and Lewis and I thought you were gone like them. I don't know what the fuck is wrong with me."

"Nothing's wrong with you man," Stone began. "Whatever

you're experiencing, it's normal for a solid guy like you who feels the need to protect everyone."

"I feel like all my insulation is gone and every thought I have is cutting into me. Please guys, just go. I gotta be by myself."

"No problem, you change your mind just hit Conner's cell phone. We'll be right back. I promise."

McCabe nodded, but he didn't look away. "I think I can't be worrying about you guys anymore. I mean, I care about everybody, but I think I can't worry about how you guys are. It's crushing me. I get so stressed something bad is going to happen to someone, that I couldn't even do anything to stop it if it did. I think I need to just focus on myself and my fiancée."

Stone smiled, "That's all you gotta do man. We're all ok. We got each other through. You ain't gotta worry about us anymore. You just live your life now and if anybody needs you they'll let you know."

McCabe swallowed hard and wiped his eyes. Reaching out he bumped fists with Stone, then slowly pivoted to Conner and did the same.

"I'll find some way to call you in a few days man," Stone assured him. "Maybe I'll buy one of those burner phones, or see if they still make calling cards."

"Yeah right," McCabe laughed, wiping his cheekbone with the heel of his hand. "Take care of yourselves. I'm going to get myself together and I'll be here if you ever need anything."

"I know you will, brother," Stone nodded. "I've always known it. We've got you, too."

Conner tossed his backpack and duffle bag into the van, and returned to his friends. They formed a little circle and threw their arms around each other's shoulders—the tops of their heads gently touched in the center for a moment before they broke apart.

CHAPTER 34

Conner scratched his head as he read the overhead highway signs identifying different parts of Miami International. "Where the hell do we go now?"

"I don't know," Stone answered. "Pull in somewhere and pass out maybe, it's late. Or we could try and find a spot by the bay. A park or something."

"It doesn't feel right leaving him there."

"No," Stone agreed. "But all amped up like he was, he'd never sleep or anything if we were nearby. He'd just be all agitated, afraid something bad was gonna happen to us or upset that we weren't out having fun, even though it's the middle of the damn night by now."

Conner's mind went to Sara Anne, wondering if she got home alright. Then immediately to Joselyd, '*I can't be your everything...*' and hoped she'd feel different tomorrow. *Life, what a mess.*

"We can roll back in the morning, before his flight and make sure he got himself into the terminal."

Conner nodded. "Hey, actually, we need to stop off somewhere. I need a cell phone charger in case he does call for some reason."

"I doubt he will, but we can hit an all-night gas station and grab one. I need to fill this thing up anyway or I'm not going to get too far."

"Yeah... I have to have it anyway or Joselyd will have a hard time picking me up at the airport."

"Pretty name."

Conner chuckled, "Well she's a pretty girl. You should come up and meet her."

Stone stared straight ahead at the empty interstate.

"You could stay as long as you wanted. She gets super caught up in her job sometimes. If she's got a project going, I just end up cooking dinner by myself and hanging out. It'd be good to have you around, we could have some fun."

Conner glanced at Stone, but his expression never changed. Thinking about it all was starting to weigh on him. Lewis out there somewhere, McCabe having some kind of breakdown on the sidewalk, Mathews going back to a base full of guys he never connected with, and Stone... he'd be driving out west on his own, to nowhere. Just a couple of days ago he had thought they could all get together once a year, maybe rent a beach house for a week. Now he wondered if he would ever see any of them again.

"You guys would really like each other. She's great. We could really have a good time if you came to visit."

Stone's expression seemed to soften. "Yeah?"

"Yeah man, it'd be great."

"She wouldn't be all annoyed that some old guy was hanging around soaking up your guys' personal time?"

"Not at all man, she'd love to meet you. I told her all about you already. All the crazy deployments we were on and shit we went through. You should totally come."

"Alright," Stone nodded. "You call her in the morning. Pick a date out. I'm going to go hiking in the Everglades for a few days, then I'll start making my way up."

"Really?!"

"Well hell yeah, I'm already on the East Coast," Stone chuckled. "You're only like thirteen hundred miles away."

"Ahh man, this is going to be awesome! I'll take some more leave when you get in, I've got plenty."

"Yeah, I gotta meet this girl, see if she's as great as you say." Stone turned toward Conner and grinned. "But I already know she is. I'm real happy for you man."

★ ★ ★

Stone pumped gas into his panel van as Conner placed two Gatorades and a new cell charger on the counter in the convenience store. The middle aged clerk at the register seemed completely distracted. Instead of turning to Conner, he focused his attention on a group of overhead security monitors.

Conner stood there patiently for a moment, debating. *Indian? Light skin though, maybe Pakistani? Definitely an immigrant and without doubt South Asian.* The rest he couldn't be sure of. "Hey, I'm ready to check out when you get a minute," he said when the man never turned.

The clerk held up an index finger. Conner leaned forward over the counter and peered upward at the security footage in an attempt to discover what had the man so concerned.

"Not good," he said with a heavy accent. "I get robbed three weeks ago. Now new security system, now I see them behind store."

Conner saw the group of five on the black and white screen, all teens or early twenties. They stood in a small circle, a muscular white man in a sleeveless undershirt with a dark bandana seemed to be talking, his hands moving as he gestured to the others. *Are there weapons hidden in those baggy jeans he's wearing?*

"I don't know they the same guys," the clerk stroked his chin as he stared up. "Maybe?"

"W-what are you going to do?" Conner stammered, his eyes flashing to the second monitor showing Stone's van in front of the store as it backed away from the pump into a nearby parking space.

"What they are going to do?" the clerk countered. "No reason for behind store. It is gang."

Gangs normally aren't multiracial... Conner thought looking at the combination of light and dark skinned individuals on the monochrome screen. *No point in arguing. How the hell would I know anyway? TV?*

A dark SUV pulled up to a gas pump in front of the store on an adjacent monitor, Conner's gaze flicked to see it through the storefront windows surrounding the commercial glass entrance. The driver's side door flung open and for a moment techno dance music flooded out. Then the key was switched off and a beautiful Hispanic girl in heels, with tan, muscular legs, a short skirt and oversized hoop earrings stepped out and fumbled with her wallet for a credit card. Loud female voices and laughter came from the vehicle where several other ladies bantered from the passenger seats.

Conner felt his pulse accelerate and turned leaving the items on the counter as he headed for the door. "Are you ok?" he called over his shoulder. "I gotta go tell my buddy something's up."

"There the gun!" the clerk shouted pointing at the screen. "I press button, police come now."

Conner closed the last few yards in an instant, he hit the panic bar with both hands to throw the thick glass door open but instead slammed into the unmoving exit. He shoved again, but nothing happened. Conner glanced up, below the exit sign a run of armored cable entered a silver box on the door frame. His eyes snapped back to the gas pumps, where the five men strode in a huddle toward the girl outside the SUV.

"Hey!" Conner yelled at the clerk. "Open this goddamn door!"

The clerk glanced at him blankly. A land line rang at the counter and he reached for it.

"Yes!

"Yes!

"They here, they is gun.

"Yes! Police now!"

A feminine shriek came from outside and Conner wheeled around to see that a tall, skinny, white kid had produced the firearm in view of the woman pumping gas. Abandoning the nozzle sticking in her fuel tank, she made a dash for her driver's door, but a short Latino kid with dark curly hair lunged toward her, grabbing her bicep. She yanked free but spilled forward, off balance in her heels, and skidded chest first across the asphalt, tearing open her sequined top and skinning her knees. Wallet, credit cards, cell phone, and car keys scattered ahead of her as one heel skipped off to the side.

Jesus! This shit is really going down. "Open this fucking door!" Conner shouted without looking away.

"All door locked! Police come now!" the clerk called back.

The four unarmed aggressors surged forward. A young black kid in a Miami Dolphins jersey hopped from point to point snatching the Hispanic lady's items off the ground. "Get outta the car!" came the bass filled shout of a thick, muscular, dark-skinned man in a flat brimmed cap. "Get outta the car!" he screamed again, but the occupants stared back motionless, as if paralyzed. The curly haired Latino teenager jerked on the rear door handle but it didn't open. A collective, ear-piercing shriek rang out as the compact bandana-wearing white man in his twenties bounded forward, kicking the downed girl in the stomach with a dirty sneaker. With a shout he demanded car keys, before kicking her again. The fifth man held back, awkwardly gripping what looked to be a black nine millimeter pistol with scuffed paint revealing hints of shining gunmetal on its hard edges. His finger hovering on the trigger, though he wasn't pointing the weapon at anyone.

Conner's adrenaline surged as he glanced toward the panel van and realized the driver's door was open. His eyes scanned the storefront settling on Stone—who walked almost casually, creeping up behind the skinny, white pistol-brandishing man. Conner stared wide-eyed at his friend, recognizing a long thick steel lug wrench dangling from his uncasted hand and a can of bear spray protruding from his back pocket. His first instinct was to hit the glass, get Stone's attention and wave him away. But he restrained himself, if that skinny pistol-wielding thug turned, he'd see Stone, and all hell would break loose.

Aside from the young black kid who was now pulling cash from the wallet and stuffing it in his pocket, the men were focused on the petrified girls in the SUV. They shouted disjointed demands at the occupants to exit the vehicle, but none did. The thick dark-skinned man reached through the open driver's door, unlocking the rear door, and the assailants grabbed the closest girl by her ankles, attempting to yank her out. She kicked frantically as the ladies clung together with such an intense primal strength that they all remained inside.

They're not robbing the store, it's a fucking carjacking! For the love of God get out and let them have that SUV before-

Conner took a deep breath—his heart pounding in his chest as Stone accelerated to a trot. He covered the last couple yards in an instant, clutching the tire iron in the best two handed baseball bat grip he could manage with his casted left hand. With a single fluid swing, Stone smashed the tall man in back of the head. The impact made a sickly thunk and the pistol dropped from his hand clattering across the asphalt. Conner flinched expecting it to go off, though the sharp crack never came. The skinny white man hung there as if suspended by invisible lines, then his knees buckled and his limp body crumpled forward hitting the ground all at once in a heap.

On the pavement, the pretty Hispanic girl sobbed as the handgun skidded to a stop beside her. The shorter tough-looking white guy in the bandana went for it, but Stone was quick and angled for the man instead of the weapon. As the compact twentysomething rose up attempting to point the firearm, Stone's lug wrench came down. The man glanced up at the last moment as if to take aim, and jerked his head to one side, saving his skull from shattering and instead taking the blow to the top of his collar bone. He shrieked as his shoulder slumped at an unnatural angle. His arm drooped and as he attempted to raise the pistol again, Stone clubbed his wrist with the bent piece of steel.

The pistol accelerated down, took an improbable bounce off the asphalt over the bleeding, sobbing woman in the sequin top and slid to a stop in front of the young black teenager. He stared up wide-eyed as his mouth dropped open. His jumbled hands pressing a wallet, cell phone, car keys and an assortment of credit cards tight against his Dolphins jersey. The kid edged backward as the items slowly tumbled from his grip. Then he turned, dropping what remained, and sprinted away without glancing back.

Stone bounded forward, twisting to face the remaining aggressors while positioning himself between them and the firearm, but he wasn't quite fast enough. The thick black man was already in a head-down charge toward him. Stone managed to throw a wild elbow at just the right moment, catching the man in the eye, but his inertia was too great. He crashed into Stone and they hit the pavement together in a jumble of knees and elbows. The bright red can of bear mace was flung from Stone's pocket making a metallic scraping sound as it bounced across the pavement and into the street, twenty yards away.

"My fucking arm's broke!" the bandana-wearing man in the wife beater bellowed as he rocked from side to side on the concrete. "Beat the life outta that fucking asshole!" he gasped, gripping his swelling forearm as his eyes settled on his companion a few yards away. "Oh God, I think he killed my brother!"

Conner threw himself back and began kicking the panic bar with all his force, but the entire door frame seemed to shake as a singular unit. Letting out a primal roar he slammed his body into the structure again and again, but the powerful electromagnet refused to yield. Steadying himself, his eyes locked on Stone once more through the glass. The Latino teen had picked up the pistol and seemed to be cocking it. Conner's eyes went wide as he screamed.

Stone had lost the tire iron, but managed to push his muscular opponent off long enough to kick him in the chest. The man gasped as if the wind were knocked out of him. Stone rolled wildly into what looked like the starting position for a sprinter in blocks. There were two bright flashes beneath the gas station's fluorescent overhang as he launched from the ground toward the pistol-wielding youth. Bullets skipped off the pavement and clinked into the grill of the Stone's van as he slammed into the short curly haired teenager, knocking him backward. They were on the ground, the pistol jammed against Stone's side, though during the struggle Stone had managed to slide a finger from his casted hand inside the guard behind the trigger—squeezing the uncomfortable sliver of metal as hard as he could preventing the weapon from going off. With his right hand Stone gripped his adversary's wrist, attempting to break the firearm free.

Stone remained on top as the shooter flopped against the ground, but the teenager had an unrestricted hand, and alternated between grabbing for Stone's throat and knocking him in the side of the face. Despite taking the hits, Stone—amidst a storm of violent curses—peeled the kid's fingers back, one at a time until he wrenched the gun free. Bounding off the pavement, Stone's eyes flicked toward the dark-skinned man who'd now regained his breath and was again charging him headfirst. Stone raised the pistol but it was in his broken left hand and he'd gripped it by the barrel. It didn't even provide a deterrent since the man sprinting at him had his head down and probably couldn't see.

Stone attempted to run for it, but realized too late the teenager on the ground had ahold of his ankle. As he tumbled forward at the bigger man charging toward him, Stone twisted and, in a last ditch effort, lobbed the weapon underhanded at the convenience store roof where it landed with a clatter.

The dark-skinned man plowed into Stone, folding him backward onto the teenager who only partially broke his fall. The back of Stone's head smacked off the asphalt. A series of fists and elbows followed as Stone receded into a purely defensive position. He thrashed from side to side in silence clutching the back of his head while extending his elbows in an attempt to cover his face. Blood splattered from his nose making dark impressions on his deep blue Hawaiian shirt, oil from the ground stained the now ripped khaki pants that had been new just three days before. He let out a yelp as he was kicked in the ribs and attempted in vain to roll away.

"Kill that mother fucker!" the brawny white man in the bandana screamed from the ground as he rocked himself up into a sitting position.

Conner punched the glass door as hard as he could, succeeding only in ripping his knuckles open. He forced himself to suck in air realizing he hadn't taken a breath in some time. *Think, you stupid motherfucker, think!* He pulled his phone from his pocket as if to call the police, but already knew it was dead. Eyeing the armored cable leading to the electronic door lock he flicked his knife from his pocket and reached for it. Stretching to maneuver the blade onto the metallically clad wiring, Conner positioned himself to use his body weight to slice through. His eyes darted outside as he leaned forward and yanked back hard.

The female driver of the SUV was bleeding, makeup smeared across her face, shirt open with bright red scrape marks on her sternum. Her breasts bounced from side to side in a lacy black bra as she scrambled toward her vehicle on her hands and knees—a key ring looped around one finger. In front of her Stone rolled back and forth as the thick man and short curly haired teenager shouted and kicked him from either side. They alternated between his head and his ribs, sometimes attempting to stomp on his chest. Just beyond the glass door—between the fight and Conner—the muscular white man was standing again, he staggered forward one shoulder drooping, one arm hanging limp, and made a long, concentrated effort to pick up the lug wrench. Once he had a grip on it, he straightened out, wincing in pain and spewing curses as he hobbled toward the attack on Stone.

Sirens sounded in the distance before being momentarily obscured by a blast of techno music as the SUV started and quickly accelerated out of the parking lot. Dark blood splattered across the black asphalt in the haze of fluorescent lighting as Stone groaned. Conner's hands shook, he yanked his knife into the cable with all the force he had, but instead of slicing through the casing into the wire, a metal clamp broke free somewhere above him and more cable came down with bits of broken ceiling tile. "FUCK!" Conner screamed, watching the stocky man holding the tire iron inch closer to his friend.

Outside they pulled Stone upright, and he hung there helpless in the arms of his attackers as blood poured from his tan face. The muscular white man teed up on Stone with the lug wrench in his good hand. As he swung, Stone sputtered to life, kicking the thick man on the outside of his knee, making him release his grip and scream as he fell off to one side. The steel bar missed Stone completely, though heavily off balance, he dropped to the ground anyway. His uncasted hand managed to yank the knife from his pocket and flick it open in front of him, but before he could attempt another move he was being pummeled by a barrage of kicks and stomps. The sound of the approaching sirens grew ever louder as the strong man in the bandana stepped forward raising the tire iron over his head and hurled it down on Stone. Stone managed to shield his battered face at the last moment, wielding his casted arm to deflect the blow. The hollow crack was immediately followed by a primal, animal-like shriek louder than Conner thought humanly possible. Conner's hair raised as his heart pumped rapidly in his chest. Tears poured from Conner's eyes as he saw it happen again, Stone blocking with his good arm, as his casted left hand lay limp beside him. Then the man raised the bar for a third time, bringing it down with intense force. A dull thud filled the air.

"NO!" Conner shouted and stared wide-eyed through the storefront glass, again forgetting to breathe. *They fucking killed him!*

Sirens blared now, headlights shining on the small group surrounding Stone, then jerking to the sky and landing on them again as a police cruiser jumped the curb and stopped diagonally in the parking area. The cop barked instructions over the PA, but instead of showing their hands and dropping to their knees as ordered the three scattered in different directions. The officer rolled out of his car chasing the curly haired Latino kid, while calling for assistance on his shoulder mounted radio.

Three more cop cars arrived almost simultaneously. The thick, dark-skinned man had disappeared, but his stocky white companion had only been able to lope away at a slow pace and the newly arrived officers quickly knocked him to the ground.

Stone's fucking dead! He's fucking dead! They fucking killed him! Conner's mind raced as tears streamed down his face. *Get a fucking grip, you're in the military for Christ's sake. Concentrate!* Conner stared, studying the thin metal sheathing on the now slack cable in his shaking hands. He worked his knife into the spiral seam.

Through the glass, more flashing lights appeared as an ambulance opened up beside the tall man Stone had initially thumped with the tire iron. Medical technicians hovered over him performing checks as a backboard was unloaded.

"Fuck that asshole! Help my friend!" Conner kicked the glass hard enough to make the EMT flinch and pointed in Stone's direction.

Conner braced himself, anticipating a jolt of electricity that never came as he sliced through the now exposed wire. The door flung open as he raged into the parking area. "You gotta help my friend!" Conner screamed again, pointing toward Stone.

"Whoa!" an officer shouted, one hand in a stop gesture, the other un-holstering his sidearm. "Drop the knife and back up!"

Conner glared at him, his eyes shifted back to the EMT as he released the blade lock, snapped the knife shut, and clipped it to his pocket.

The officer shouted more demands which Conner ignored.

"Another ambulance is coming," the technician answered.

"You gotta help him now," Conner pleaded. "Please, they beat the hell out of him."

"This guy has a chance if I work quick," the EMT answered, this time making eye contact. "Your buddy is real messed up and the chopper isn't available."

"Please!" Conner's voice broke.

The officer barked more orders, but Conner didn't hear them. He drifted toward Stone, terrified of what he would see when he got close. His mind filled with surreal images he'd forgotten he'd even witnessed. His C-130 cargo bay washed in green night vision lighting, floor-loaded with dozens of body bags on the way to Kuwait from Iraq. The Styrofoam cooler with LIFE OR DEATH penned on the side—filled with dry ice and bags of blood—as it was handed off to Mathews with engines running. Lewis shaking his hand with an upset face the last time he'd seen him, saying "I gotta get out Conner, I can't do this anymore." Stretch with hydraulic stains on his desert camouflage uniform, pounding fists with Stone and looking at him with a smile. Conner frowned as Stretch faded away. The memory of Joselyd's beautiful face beaming at him as he glanced back from the airport security line four days earlier hit him in a flash. *God, please don't let her ever have to see anything like this.*

Vaguely, he became aware of a female officer on his left side shouting more orders, but he was almost there. Stone lay on his side facing away from him in a dark, viscous puddle. A chunk of his scalp laid open, his skin and hair scrunched unnaturally together revealing thick, coagulated blood where they should have been. His right hand lay behind his back, the small and ring fingers jutting out at a sickly angle perpendicular to the way they should have been. A mixture of bright and dulling red splotches sharply contrasted the white cast on his left hand in the fluorescent lighting.

Conner was just one yard away when he saw it. It was faint and he stopped his slow approach, steadied himself and focused on Stone's side to be sure. There it was again. A rise, ever so slight. Conner's heart swelled. *He's fucking breathing! Get your shit together, no one is helping him. You need to. Now! Compartmentalize your feelings and get to work. Get his spine straight, make sure you don't block the airway. Look for hemorrhages. Move! Slow, steady.*

Conner knelt, placing one knee on either side of his friend's head. Dark crimson blood penetrated his jeans as he gazed down, studying Stone's face—the entire right side already bruised and swollen. Blood continued to spill from his nose, though slowly now, through heavy clots. His cheek bone was clearly fractured, his jaw was messed up and some of his teeth may have been broken. "You hang on, brother," Conner whispered. "Just hang on."

Conner's eyes methodically moved over Stone as his voice raised to a conversational volume. "Don't worry buddy,

I know I'm not a medic but you're way less complicated than the aircraft we worked on together," Conner allowed himself a little grin. His fingers slowly working their way down the back of Stone's neck, then feeling each of his vertebrae. "Your neck's alright man, and your back ain't broke. Internal bleeding in the abdomen, you got knocked in the head bad, and your face is all beat up, but I know you. You've been through harder stuff than this.

"I'm not leaving you man, I just got to go grab a backboard from the ambulance. I'm going to place it right here next to you and then roll you onto it. Keep you secure until they get ya to the hospital."

Conner rose and stepped carefully around his friend. Two strides later he was blindsided by a uniform doing a bear-hug tackle and smacked the ground hard. A fist came in and clobbered his cheekbone, surges of pain shot through his face.

"FUCK!" Conner screamed, glancing up in time to see the fist coming at him again. He threw his head forward and tucked his chin in causing the cops knuckles to impact the top of his skull instead of his face.

"You bastard," the officer shrieked, shaking his hand frantically before drawing back again and smashing Conner in the eye with his elbow.

"What the hell's wrong with you?" Conner's vision blurred as the sharp gushes of pain were joined by a dull throbbing ache. "Stop hitting me and help my friend!"

Behind him, another set of hands clenched his wrist,

twisting and wrestling around until something cool and metallic clicked into place. First one hand, then the other. Conner flexed but the restraints were limiting his movement.

The two officers propped him up on the curb against the gas pump and began to pepper him with questions. Conner didn't respond, instead shouting, "Stone, hang on buddy! It's going to take a couple extra minutes!" The first ambulance rolled out, sirens blaring, but Conner's eyes remained locked on his friend. *Was his chest still rising... yes. Looks less than before though, slower interval.* "Hang on brother, help is coming!" One of the officers had donned surgeon's gloves and slowly removed the contents from Conner's pockets. Inspecting each item before dropping it in a pile on the pavement. A second ambulance was finally on scene, and the EMT hustled to work.

A tall, barrel-chested police officer with coal-black skin and stripes on his sleeves strode from the convenience store toward the small cluster of medical personnel surrounding Stone.

Conner watched, waiting intently for the next small rise in Stone's chest. "Just a little longer, Stone! Keep fighting!"

The sergeant paused and turned toward Conner. His eyes narrowed for a moment honing in on his busted knuckles and then the blood stains on his knees before scanning his now swelling face. The man's gaze drifted to Conner's wallet, pocket knife and the remnants of the shattered cell phone lying beside him, before focusing on his airman's coin and slowly moving to meet his eyes.

The sergeant's expression seemed to soften, "Are you the one who was trapped inside when it all happened?"

"I couldn't help him. I tried to get to him but I didn't think fast enough and I didn't get out in time."

"I watched the security footage, your friend put up a hell of a fight. He could have just walked away."

Conner nodded. "He doesn't want nothin' bad to happen to anybody. I wanted to help him, he needed my help. I couldn't get there."

The sergeant's gaze shifted to the officer next to Conner. "Let him go."

"Sir, we got him on brandishing a deadly weapon, destruction of property, failure to obey and resisting arrest."

"Let," the sergeant clearly and deliberately enunciated, "him," as his dark eyes sharpened under the gas station's fluorescent lighting, "go."

"I'm the arresting officer!" the man gulped. "How to proceed is up to me."

The sergeant's dark eyes were piercing. Without shifting his gaze, he pointed up to the tinted globe of a camera, mounted on the underside of the canopy above the fuel pumps. "Do you really want me to go inside and review the footage? Ensure you have just cause?"

The officer swallowed hard.

"Uncuff him before I have to come over there and do it," the sergeant shook his head as if in disgust before walking away.

Conner flexed his freed wrists and slowly moved toward

his friend. His head was wrapped in gauze now and his neck was braced. "Stone, never give up!" Conner yelled, making the EMTs glance in his direction. An officer held a hand up warning him not to get any closer.

What do I do? What do I do? I need help! Conner exhaled hard. *Get your shit together.* Spinning around he snatched the pieces of his shattered iPhone off the ground, somewhere deep inside knowing he didn't have a single number memorized—a consequence of living in the age of mobile devices. *Even if I find a way to call, it'll be impossible to talk to Joselyd.* Conner's eyes went back to Stone, as the EMTs continued to work.

Fuck! Fuck! Fuck! I need help! There's no way I'll ever remember how to get back to Mathews at Kira's apartment. The guys were attacking me half the way there and I didn't pay any attention at all. Conner exhaled hard. *Maybe McCabe is still in the cell phone lot?* But he was shaking his head even before the thought was fully formed. *I can't dump this on him! He's wrecked as it is!*

Sara Anne! Sara Anne... she gave me her number! Conner's hand fidgeted with nervous energy, his fingers finding their way into his back pockets and coming out with the small slip of paper that contained her digits. *Shit! I can't call her! I'm not strong enough, I'll destroy my life! What could she really do anyway? What can anybody do right now?*

Ok, simple. I just get Stone's keys, and follow the ambulance with his van. Then I know where he is and I make a decision from there. No problem, one step at a time. He exhaled and turned toward the van, immediately registering the sweet smell of antifreeze. His eyes traced the trail of coolant and oil slowly rolling toward him from beneath the vehicle, before settling on a glaring hole in the grill.

Conner brought his hands up to cover his eyes. But when he made contact a surge of pain spiked through the left side of his face. *Fuck!* He sucked in a deep breath and spun back around, stomping the asphalt. *Get control of yourself! Think!*

There's nothing to think about, I just make these guys let me in the back of the ambulance and ride to the hospital with him. But what fuckin' good will I be sitting in a waiting room with no way to communicate?

I could get back to the airport, make my flight, Joselyd will be there to pick me up. We go buy a phone, call my supervisor so I'm not AWOL and get on the first flight back down here together to be with Stone. His chest tightened. *But I can't fucking leave him here now! Oh God, that'd be horrible!*

Conner leaned back, his eyes settling on the moon as he exhaled out into space. *The same moon that has been here with me every place in the world I've ever traveled, the same moon that will still be here no matter what happens now, or tomorrow or twenty years from now. It's been there an eternity before I ever existed at all, and it'll still be here forever after I'm gone. Its powerful forces dictating so many things in our lives that we never stop to think about. The movements of the ocean, and in the absence of electric lighting, even the timing that we can create new life. Its reflection allowing us to see in the night during certain times, while abandoning us in darkness during others.*

So colossal we can see it from thousands of miles away. Its mass... giving it the gravity to affect the world. But what's strange is—in theory—it's all relative and my own weight is actually having an impact on the moon as well. Slight though it may be, my own little force is projecting out into the world and beyond.

It's on me now, I have to weigh it out, and make the best decision I can, there's no Air Force regulations or supervision to tell me what to do next, no friends to follow, no girlfriend to call for help. There's Stone—barely breathing and I can't get close to him—about to be transported to an unknown hospital in a city full of strangers. There's a flight leaving in six hours for Joselyd, and I have one phone number that I shouldn't call.

He ran his fingers through his short hair and focused back on his friend. The man he had looked up to through all their deployments. The man who had held them all together and kept them pressing forward when things got tough. *That's all gone now. I was real lucky to have people to depend on for so long. I relied on them too much though, it held me back. But that's over now, too—today and every day after this—I make the decisions that are on me, I deal with the things I need to deal with.*

Conner's eyes fixed on Stone as he floated toward him. Moving slowly at first, brushing past an EMT who had paused in his work, and then launching into a mad rush as two police officers sprang at him. A whoosh of air swept through his hair as he ducked the first cop, though the second caught Conner by the shoulders. Her shoes grinding against the pavement as she slid backward, battling to hold him in place. Then her arms buckled and Conner's chest smacked into her ballistic vest as he continued to drive toward Stone. Scrambling to regain his positioning, the male officer threw his weight into the fray. He held strong for a moment before being forced to take a half-step back and brace himself, suspending Conner's progress. Straining as his muscles quivered, Conner peered over the officers' shoulders, studying his friend's battered face. "Never stop fighting, Stone! Never give up!"

A jolt of energy surged through Conner when Stone's eyes flicked open. His dilated pupils nearly filled his hazy gray irises, which twitched rapidly as his focus seemed to settle on Conner. "Never," Stone murmured, wincing as he took in a ragged breath. "I'll never give up." The EMTs moved him onto a stretcher and strapped him down. Stone stayed locked on Conner until they lifted him, then his eyes drifted toward the dark sky. Perhaps tracing some invisible wave of light out into the cosmos. His broken face formed a grin as they rolled him away.

www.ingramcontent.com/pod-product-compliance
Lightning Source LLC
Chambersburg PA
CBHW031111160726
47991CB00004B/1328